The Last Queen of India

Michelle Moran's experiences at archaeological sites around the world first inspired her to write historical fiction. She is the author of *Nefertiti* and its standalone sequel *The Heretic Queen*, as well as *Cleopatra's Daughter* and *The Second Empress*. She lives in Texas.

MICHELLE MORAN

Quercus

First published as Rebel Queen in 2015 in the United States by Touchstone.

First published in Great Britain in 2015 by

Quercus Publishing Ltd
Carmelite House
50 Victoria Embankment
London EC4Y 0DZ

An Hachette UK company

A CIP catalogue record for this book is available from the British Library

TPB ISBN 978 1 78206 561 6
EBOOK ISBN 978 1 78206 560 9

10 9 8 7 6 5 4 3 2 1

Printed and bound in Great Britain by Clays Ltd, St Ives plc

For my husband, Amit Kushwaha. And for our son, Liam.

Author's Note

In order to make nineteenth-century India more accessible to twenty-first-century readers, I have made several changes to the historical record. For one, I have used the word *India* throughout the book, although the country of India as we know it today only came into existence in 1947. The term *Hindu* is also anachronistic, with the "ism" added by Westerners in the erroneous belief that Hinduism was a religion. It is more than a religion; it is a way of life. The term *Hindu* comes from the word *Sindhu*. It is the name of a river and is secular in meaning; even an atheist can be Hindu.

I have made other changes as well. In keeping with their modern-day spellings, several city names have been changed, so that Kashi has become Varanasi, and Cawnpore has become Kanpur.

Lastly, some of the titles used to address people in positions of power have either been shortened or eliminated. Raja Gangadhar Rao, for instance, has become simply Raja Gangadhar, and Rani Lakshmibai has been shortened to Rani Lakshmi.

Every Englishman is born with a certain miraculous power that makes him master of the world. When he wants a thing, he never tells himself that he wants it. He waits patiently until there comes into his mind, no one knows how, a burning conviction that it is his moral and religious duty to conquer those who have got the thing he wants.

—GEORGE BERNARD SHAW, 1897

Prologue

1919

Seventy-five years' worth of diaries are spread across my bed, nearly covering the blanket Raashi sewed for me last winter. Their spines all open, the books look like old moths, just too worn out and tired to fly away. At eighty-five, I find it difficult to read my own handwriting. But I have read these words so many times that they are imprinted on my mind; they are the patterns on a butterfly's black-and-orange wings.

I take an envelope from my desk and bring it to my bed. Most of my writing now is done here. I address the envelope carefully to "Miss Pennywell," and I am proud of the fact that I've remembered to call her *Miss* and not *Mrs*. It was this kind of detail that saved my life when her countrymen came, looking to turn my home into a little England—only with the added benefit of exotic women and chai. But if what Miss Pennywell believes is correct, and the English will read this old woman's story, perhaps that will change.

You see, when I was a child I lived in the small kingdom of Jhansi, under the rule of Maharaja Gangadhar and his queen, Rani Lakshmi. Now, I live in a vast country called India, with borders that stretch from Burma to Kashmir. Instead of a maharaja, we are ruled by a foreign emperor, the grandson of Queen Victoria, King George V. And where carved stupas once pierced the sky, enclosing our sacred images of the Hindu prince Siddhartha (who eventually became Buddha), we have tall English crosses perched on church steeples. Yes, I am old, and no one can expect to reach my age without witnessing great change. But I have also lived through a terrible war between India and England, and have watched for almost a century as our ancient traditions have slowly been erased.

There is an old Hindi saying that my father once taught me. *Bandar kya jaane adrak ka swad.* It means, "What does a monkey know about the taste of ginger?" And I expect that this is true for the English. They know nothing about the people they came to rule. So why should we expect them to preserve our temples and respect our gods? At best, they view them as foreign decorations. At worst, reminders of the "heathen barbarism" that runs rampant in a country that gave the world chess and the number zero.

I look down at the address, which Miss Pennywell gave to me two months ago. I was standing with Raashi at the railway station in Bombay when a woman rushed up, the sound of her sharp heels clacking against the stone. In a country of red saris and saffron dupattas, she was dressed in a gray shirt and a matching gray hat. Her black skirt made its way only to her calves. She was English.

"I'm terribly sorry to disturb you, Mrs. Rathod. It *is* Mrs. Rathod, isn't it?"

I hesitated for a moment. But the British government no longer cares about hunting down rebels, so I told her the truth. "Yes."

She held out her hand, and I knew from my schooling in English manners that I was supposed to shake it. "Emma Pennywell," she said.

I assumed she was another reporter, wanting to ask me what

had happened to the rani's wealth after she was killed. Instead she said, "Sixty-five years ago my grandfather escorted you to London. His name was Wilkes. He'd like to speak with you again."

It took several moments for me to comprehend what she was saying. When I did, I shook my head. "I'm sorry. That was a different life." I took Raashi's arm and we started walking toward the train. "I was from a different India then."

"Which is why I've come." When she saw I wasn't interested, she began to speak faster. "My grandfather is a publisher and he's interested in memoirs set in the colonies. He wants to tell your story. I know you have a train—"

I stopped walking to explain to her there were things in my past I never wished to revisit, but she didn't even have the decency to look shocked.

"We've all done things we'd rather keep in the dark. It's only by shedding light on them that our demons can disappear."

Miss Pennywell was no more than twenty-two. What did she know about darkness and demons? "Miss Pennywell, I just don't see the purpose of such a book."

"Don't you regret how the British have changed your country?"

"Some of it has been for the good," I said, hoping to end our conversation. "This train station, for instance. Without the British, it could not have been built."

"But think of all the temples that have been destroyed."

I kept my expression neutral. I didn't want her to know how often I thought of this.

"Please, just consider it," she said, then pressed a calling card into my hand. "What if your story convinces the British that Indian traditions are important? What if the King of England himself were to read it and decide that your rani was right? That she wasn't a Rebel Queen, as they've been calling her in England, but a true queen, willing to take up a sword to defend her people against empire builders. Just as *you* did, Mrs. Rathod."

Now she was baiting me. I knew it. But I took her card, and after two months of persistent letters, she has finally changed my mind.

Raashi thinks I am brave to write about my past. But my guess is that she really means foolish. After all, memoirs are not open doors into another person's house. They are more like broken windows, with the owner trying to explain away all of the damage. And I'm not blinded to the truth. I am writing this as much for myself as I am for India.

The sweet scents of garam masala and coriander fill the house, and I know that Raashi is cooking. I should probably begin before this cool morning thaws into a scorching afternoon when nothing but sleeping can be done. But I continue to look at my friends, their worn leather covers as creased and familiar as the backs of my hands. When this memoir is finished, I will not save my diaries. I will take them to the Ganges during Vasant Navratri, when everyone is floating their old calendars down the water, and I will let the goddess of the river determine if the things I did were right; if what happened to my sister, and to India's bravest queen, should still weigh so heavily on an old woman's heart.

Chapter One

1840

Imagine I took you down a long dirt road to the edge of a field, and we entered a farmer's house built from mud brick and thatch. Now imagine I told you, "This is where I stood with the Rani of Jhansi during our escape from the British. And that corner, there, is where we changed into peasant's clothes so she could reach the Fortress of Kalpi." I suppose you would look from me, in my respectable sari and fine gold jewels, to the dirt floor of that one-room home and laugh. Only my eyes would remain serious, and slowly, the realization would dawn on you that all of the stories you heard must be true. The Rani of Jhansi—or Queen Lakshmi, as the British persisted in calling her—really did elude the powerful British army by dressing like a common farmer's wife.

I'm not sure why this is so surprising to people. Didn't Odysseus manage it when he disguised himself as a beggar? And the Duke of Vienna in *Measure for Measure*? Perhaps people's surprise then is that I was the one who suggested she do it, taking inspiration from characters who'd only lived on the page. After all, I was not born to read such texts. In fact, I was not born to read at all.

It was Father who insisted on my education. If it had been left to Grandmother, I would never have seen anything beyond the walls of my house. For, as I'm sure you know, women throughout India are nearly all in purdah.

When I was seven years old, I asked Father how this concept of secluding women came to be, and he guided me to a cool place in the shade. Our garden was large enough for a peepal tree, and it wasn't until I was much older that I learned that not every house in Barwa Sagar was so spacious. But we were Kshatriyas, meaning our ancestors had been related to kings, just as their ancestors had been related to kings, and so on, I suppose, since the beginning of time. People have often asked me what these different castes mean, and I explain it like this: Imagine a beehive, which has workers, and breeders, and finally, a queen. Well, our castes are very much the same thing. There are Brahmins, whose job it is to be priests. There are Kshatriyas, who are the warriors and kings. There are the Vaishyas, who are merchants, farmers, and traders. And then there are the Shudras, who serve and clean. Just the same as a worker bee is born a worker bee and will die a worker bee, a person can never change their caste.

But that evening, as the setting sun burnished the clouds above us, turning the sky into a wide orange sea, Father explained purdah to me. He patted his knee, and when I climbed onto his lap, I could see the knotty muscles of his arms. They bulged beneath his skin like rocks. I held out my hand, and he used his finger to trace his words onto the flat of my palm.

"Do you remember the story of the first Mughal leader in India?" he wrote.

I took his hand and drew the words, "He was Muslim, and we are Hindu."

"Yes. He was the one who brought purdah to our land."

"So it's Emperor Bahadur Shah's fault that I can't leave our house?"

Father's arm tensed, and I knew at once that what I wrote must be wrong. "Purdah is no one's fault," he traced swiftly. "It's to keep women safe."

"From what?"

"Men, who might otherwise harm them."

I sat very still. Did he mean that for the rest of my life, I would never know what lay beyond the walls of our garden? That I would never be able to climb the coconut trees? I felt a deep agitation growing inside of me.

"Well," Father went on, "what's troubling you now?"

Of course, Father didn't use words like "well." That was my addition; the way I imagined he would have spoken if he hadn't lost his hearing while fighting alongside the British against the Burmese. Although you may wonder what the British were doing in India, and why any of us were fighting against the Burmese at all. It began in 1600, when English sailors first arrived in my country. If you've ever heard the story of the camel's nose and how, on a cold winter's night, the camel begged its master to allow it to place its nose inside the master's tent, then you will quickly understand the British East India Company.

In the beginning, it was nothing more than a trading company buying up all of our rich spices and silks and shipping them to England, where a fortune could be made. But as the Company grew more successful, it needed to protect its profitable warehouses with several hundred armed guards. Then it needed several thousand armed soldiers. And one day, the rulers of India woke up to discover that the British East India Company had a powerful army. They were exactly like the camel, who promised at first it would just be its nose, then its legs, then its back, until finally it was the camel living inside the tent while the master shivered in the cold outside.

Soon, when one of our rulers needed military aid, they didn't turn to other maharajas like themselves; instead they asked the British East India Company. And the more favors they asked, the more powerful the Company grew. Then, in 1824, a group of maharajas in northern India decided they'd had enough. They had been watching the Burmese take over their neighbors' kingdoms year after year, and they knew that, just like with that cunning camel, it would only end once the Burmese were seated on their thrones as well. I can't tell you why these same maharajas didn't see that this story might apply to the British, too. You would think the safest thing would have been to turn to each other for help. But none of those powerful men wanted to be indebted to another maharaja. So instead, they indebted themselves to an outsider. They enlisted the help of the British East India Company, which was more than happy to wage war on Burma for their own, mostly economic, reasons.

Father fought in this war. Because of his caste, he was made a commanding officer and the Company paid him one hundred rupees a month for his post. I was only a few months old when he left for Burma, and there was every reason to believe that a glorious future lay ahead of Nihal Bhosale. He sent my sixteen-year-old mother letters from the front telling her that even though British customs were difficult to understand, fighting alongside these foreigners had its advantages. He was learning to speak English, and another officer had introduced him to a writer—a brilliant, unequaled writer—by the name of William Shakespeare.

"According to the colonel, if I wish to understand the British, I must first understand this Shakespeare." Father took this advice to heart. He read everything Shakespeare wrote, from *Othello* to *The Merchant of Venice*, and when the war took his hearing two years later, it was Shakespeare who kept him company in his hospital bed.

Many years after this, I asked Father which of Shakespeare's plays had comforted him the most while he was coming to terms with a world in which he'd never know the sound of his child's voice or hear his wife sing ragas to Lord Shiva again. By that time, I had become a soldier myself in the rani's Durga Dal—an elite group of the queen's most trusted female guards. And by then, I, too, had read all of Shakespeare's works.

Father thought for a moment, then told me what I had already guessed. "*Henry V*. Because there has never been a clearer, more persuasive argument for why we go to war."

But war wasn't what concerned me on that evening Father explained purdah to me. I was too young to understand about politics. All I knew was that I couldn't play outside like the boys who drank juice from hairy coconut husks and staged mock battles with broken shoots of bamboo. I looked up at Father, with his bald head gleaming like a polished bowl in the sun, and wrote:

"Will I always be in purdah, even when I'm grown?"

"If you wish to be a respectable woman with a husband and children—as I hope you shall be—then, yes."

But just as a crow will build its nest in a tree, only to have the sparrow come and tear it apart, the life Father had planned for me was ripped away by a little bird.

Chapter Two

1843

My sibling's birth came at the height of the summer's monsoon. Hot rain lashed our village, pooling in the fields and flooding the streets so that even the farmers' children—long used to these conditions—were breaking off taro leaves and using them for umbrellas. I watched as the boys folded the giant leaves around their heads, and I thought of how fun it must be to use a leaf like a living shield. All of Barwa Sagar was under siege, and as I looked out the window, I imagined that each raindrop was a tiny soldier marching from the sky to our fields.

"What are you doing?" Grandmother said when she saw me at the window.

I was supposed to be in the kitchen, watching the fire.

"The water is still heating up, Dadi-ji. I was just—"

She slapped my face. "Don't you know what's happening in there?"

"Yes. Maa-ji is giving birth." I bit my lip to keep it from trembling. *Ji* is a term of respect, and we add it to the name of any person who is older.

"Let me tell you something about childbirth, *beti*, which you may not learn from the books my son reads with you."

Grandmother could never grasp why Father would waste his time teaching a daughter. Some things have changed for the better under British rule: for example, they have forbidden the killing of infant girls. At that time, however, the practice was common, which tells you how girls like me were valued. Even today, on the birth of a son there will be music, and dancing, and sweets will be distributed among the poor. But on the birth of a daughter, silence as thick and heavy as a blanket will descend on the house, since there is no reason to speak, let alone celebrate. After all, who wants to honor the birth of a child you will have to feed, and clothe, and educate, only to watch all that money and hard work disappear once she is married off?

Now, this isn't to say that daughters are never loved. But for a father, the birth of a daughter means saving money from the moment she takes her first breath, since she will need a dowry within nine or ten years' time. For a mother, the birth of a daughter means growing to love a little girl you are likely never to see again once her husband takes her away to his village.

But I suspect Grandmother suggested opium when I was born—a favorite trick for getting rid of daughters. And when neighbors ask what's become of the infant they heard crying the night before, the reply is always that the wolves have taken her. When I was young, wolves took so many girls in Barwa Sagar that many of the beasts must have died from overeating.

So when Grandmother said, "Let me tell you something about childbirth, *beti*," you can be certain it wasn't because she wanted to enlighten me. It was her way of making sure I knew how much trouble Mother had gone through to have me: a useless girl. As the light of the window framed my grandmother's high cheekbones and long, thin neck, I was reminded of a bird I'd seen on the lake behind Barwa Sagar's fort. Father called it a swan, and said that what made it special was its ability to move through the water without getting wet. And this, it seemed to me, was exactly what Grandmother did in life. She floated through the house but nothing touched her; not my tears, and not Mother's cries from the back of the house.

"Bringing a child into this world is the most dangerous journey a woman will take," she began. "Your mother is in there with the midwife, but it could just as easily be the priest. When I gave birth, I labored for two days. Do you know that means?"

It wasn't a question; it was a cue for me to shake my head, which I did.

"It means I didn't eat or drink for two days. They shut the doors and closed the windows and I suffered like an animal until I thought even Goddess Shashti had abandoned me."

I knew this must be true, because I had seen the midwife arrive and heard her instruct Grandmother to be sure that neither fresh air nor light was allowed into Mother's room. I thought of Mother trapped inside and tears clouded my vision.

"Are you listening?" Grandmother's voice rose.

"Yes, Dadi-ji. But the water—"

She followed my gaze to the pot. "So why are you standing there? Bring it!"

I took the boiling pot from the heated bricks and followed Grandmother down the hall. Our lime-washed walls and mud-brick floors might not have been beautiful, but we had more than two rooms, and we always had enough food to eat.

Grandmother knocked sharply on the door, and when the midwife appeared, I caught a glimpse of Mother: she was covered in sweat, as if the heavy rain outside had fallen over her body, but left everything else in the room dry.

"The water," the midwife said.

I held up the pot, hoping she would say something about Mother's condition, but the old woman simply took the hot water and shut the door. Perhaps it's mean to call her old, since she was the same age as Grandmother. But truthfully, there couldn't have been a greater difference between them than if you were comparing a cat with a lion. The midwife's face was round and soft, with deep creases around her mouth and eyes; Grandmother's was tight and full of angles. My aunt once said I had inherited these angles. Then she added, "It's a compliment, Sita! Don't make such a grimace. The sharpness of Dadi-ji's face is what makes her so beautiful, even at sixty-three. You have the same striking features."

We stood for a moment, listening to the cries on the other side of the door, then Grandmother said, "Go and tell your father to fetch your aunt."

Father's workshop was my favorite room in our house. It had four windows facing onto the busy streets and the ceilings were as tall as our peepal tree. As soon as I approached, I could hear the sabjiwalla outside, pushing his cart past our neighbor's fields despite the rain, and calling out the names of the vegetables he was selling: onions, tomatoes, cucumber, okra. If Mother was well, she would have been bargaining with him through the window, concealed behind the lattice in order to keep purdah.

Inside, Father sat with his back to the door. Wood shavings covered the floor around him, making me think of orange peels, and the room was filled with the woodsy scent of teak. When Father was carving the image of a god, the air would be thick with incense; he would light a stick of sandalwood on our altar, then lay a long jute mat across the floor as a place to work. But on the days when a villager placed an order for a weapon, the room smelled only of woods and earth.

I approached him slowly, since Father didn't like to be surprised. I suppose it's the same with others who've lost their hearing.

"Pita-ji," I said when I was standing before him.

He searched my face for some sign of distress, then his shoulders relaxed. He put aside the bow he was carving to offer me his palm.

"Grandmother says to fetch Esha-Masi," I traced above the calluses of his hand.

"Now?"

I nodded.

He stood, and the wood shavings fluttered from his dhoti like small brown moths. I've heard the English call these dhotis kilts, and I suppose they are similar. But unlike a kilt, a dhoti is white and worn without a shirt. Father left to change into pants and the long cotton shirt we call a kurta. When he returned, I was still staring at the half-finished bow he was making.

"Bartha," he said aloud, letting me know the bow was for our neighbor, Partha. Father could speak when he was in a great hurry, but now that he was deaf, he had lost the ability to tell the difference between letters like *p* and *b*.

I still understood. I looked at the bow—which Father might have been making for me if I had been a boy—and tears filled my eyes.

"Afraid?" Father wrote.

"What if it's another girl?" I traced.

"Then I will consider myself twice as blessed."

It took twenty minutes to reach my aunt's house at the other end of Barwa Sagar—where she lived with her husband and two young sons—and then return to ours. I watched through the latticed window as the rain now fell slantways through the streets. In our neighbor's field, even the buffalo looked sorry for themselves; they had taken shelter under the trees, and their tails hung between their legs like wet rope.

When Aunt arrived, the bearers lowered her palanquin in our private courtyard, then opened its curtains. As soon as she stepped outside, she shielded herself from the eyes of the bearers by wrapping her dupatta—or scarf—around her head. Father escorted her to our door.

"Where is Dadi-ji?" Aunt asked when I greeted them. It occurred to me how similar she was to Mother: her tiny bones, her small lips. No one who saw them in a room together would fail to pick them out as sisters.

"The midwife needed Grandmother's help," I said. "She told me to stand here and wait for you."

"Nothing bad has happened?" she whispered. But she needn't have bothered; Father couldn't hear her. People often forgot this.

"No."

She hurried down the hall. After two knocks, a door opened and closed.

With so many people inside our house at one time, it should have been cheerful. Instead, I could feel anxiety building inside of me the same way you can feel the slow coming of a fever. Father must have felt the same way, because he went quietly back into his workshop, though I suspected he wasn't interested in his work.

I remained in the hall and watched as our maid, Avani, poured mustard oil into each of our brass lamps. Then she lit them in the small stone niches along the wall. It may sound strange that a family as modest as ours should have had a maid, but this wasn't uncommon back then, and still isn't today. Unless a person belongs to the very lowest caste, they will likely employ someone to help with cooking and cleaning. The wealthier the family, the more maids they will have. In our case, we could only afford one.

Like most girls, our maid Avani had been married as soon as she turned ten, still young enough to be molded by her mother-in-law. Her husband, who was fifteen years older, was a kind man who allowed her to remain with her family until she came of an age to bear children. But three years later, when she went to live in her father-in-law's house, her husband suddenly took ill and died. Now in India, despite British rule, there is still a terrible practice called sati. I suppose I could explain to you where this came from, and how our goddess Sati built her own funeral pyre and then walked into the flames for her husband, Lord Shiva, only to be reincarnated as his second wife, Parvati, but it wouldn't help to explain this practice, since it has less to do with the goddess Sati and more to do with unwanted women. And so, every day, in every city in India, a woman can be found ascending the steps of her husband's funeral pyre. Refusing to commit sati by burning in your husband's flames brings dishonor to your family. But even worse than this, it brings great disrespect to your father-in-law's house.

That Avani's father-in-law—and her own father—were both against sati was highly unusual, especially at that time. Of course, it was understood that she could never marry again, and that all of the joys belonging to wives would never be hers, but at least she was alive.

Which is not to say that she had escaped a cruel fate entirely.

Many years later, I learned from Father that of all the families in Barwa Sagar, none were willing to employ Avani except ours. It was the only act of charity I'd ever heard of Grandmother performing—perhaps because she, too, had been saved from the flames when she was widowed. And for an unwanted woman whose family refuses to take her back into their home, where is there to go? Where can she work if no house will employ her?

At the time, I was unaware of these things. I simply knew that I liked watching Avani work—the way her dark braid swayed from side to side when she was lighting the lamps, and how her skin took on a deep amber glow in the flickering lights. She was feminine in a way I imagined I'd never be, with an older person's knowledge that seemed unattainable to me as a child.

"Do you think it will be much longer?" I asked.

She lowered the jar of mustard oil she was carrying. Her face took on a thoughtful expression. "I don't know. I've never had any children of my own."

I should have nodded silently and gone back to my room, but I was nine, and I could be incredibly thoughtless. "Why not? Dadi-ji told me that every woman wants children."

Her lips turned down. "Because my husband had the misfortune of dying six years ago."

I knew she wore the white sari of a widow, the same as Grandmother, but it had honestly never occurred to me that in order to have children, a woman needed a husband.

Avani must have recognized my embarrassment, because she crossed the hall and took my hand in hers. "Don't worry." In the golden light of the lamps, she looked to me like Lakshmi—the goddess of beauty. "It will all be over soon."

But Mother's cries went on for two days. By the second night, Aunt was called home by her husband; he felt she'd been with us for long enough.

"Sita," she said to me from the doorstep before she left, her voice low, like the rain clouds behind her. "You must take good care of your mother. Do whatever the midwife says. Without questions."

"Can't you stay, Esha-Masi, just for one more night?"

"I'm sorry, Sita." Her eyes teared. She didn't want to go. "If I can, I will come next week."

Father walked alongside her palanquin. He would do so to the other end of Barwa Sagar. I watched them leave, and when they were out of sight, I could feel Grandmother standing behind me the way you feel the presence of a threatening animal. She grabbed my shoulder.

"Go into your mother's room and don't come out until she's had the child."

If she had asked me to do anything else—anything at all—I would have gladly done it. But the idea of going into that dark closed space made my chest constrict as if someone were sitting on it. "But what if something happens, Dadi-ji? Aren't you coming?"

Her face looked as if it were carved from teak. I told this once to Father, and instead of reprimanding me, he laughed. Then I told him how Mother's face looked to be cedar, since that wood is soft and easier to carve. He, however, was cypress. At this Father looked puzzled, since he knew I had never seen a cypress tree. I reminded him of Shakespeare's *The Taming of the Shrew* and told him, "Gremio says he stores his most precious belongings in cypress chests. Well, you're my most precious belonging."

Father looked quite surprised—as if what I'd said was a very original thing.

The day after this conversation took place, I found a book on my bed. It must have cost a small fortune, for the leather cover was painted with an image of Saraswati, our goddess of the arts, and the pages were all very carefully trimmed. They were also empty.

"Of course they're empty, Sita." His eyes creased at the sides. He was trying not to laugh. "They're for you."

I didn't understand.

"To write your thoughts. In England, they call it a diary," he traced over the flat of my palm. "You're a very clever girl."

I would have been less shocked if he had gifted me an elephant and told me he expected me to become its trainer.

"Perhaps no one will ever read what you write except for your children," Father went on, "but you are a *kalakaar*, Sita."

In Hindi, this means artist. It was the greatest compliment he ever paid me.

I thought of these words as I walked down the hall to Mother's chamber. But what good was a *kalakaar*? I had no real skill, like the midwife or like Father. I knocked on the door and I could already smell the stench of sweat.

"Where is your grandmother?" the midwife asked as soon as she opened the door.

"She told me not to leave this room until the child is born."

The lines deepened between the midwife's brows, but she didn't say anything. I shut the door and approached Mother's charpai, a wooden bed whose woven top is made from rope. She reached for my hand, but when I gave it to her, she had no strength left to squeeze my fingers.

"Sita," she said softly. Her pretty face was creased in pain and a single white blanket clung to her damp skin. "The baby doesn't want to come. Where is your grandmother?"

The midwife glanced at me, which I took to mean that I should be silent and let her answer.

"She has gone to the temple," she said. "Concentrate on your pushing."

Mother's braid trailed out over her pillow; it looked like a long black snake curling over the bed to strangle her. I stood at her bedside and did as the midwife instructed. When she needed hot water, I fetched it. When she wanted help rubbing primrose oil onto Mother's stomach, I did that, too. But when Mother's breathing grew more labored and the midwife turned to me and said, "Go and get your grandmother," I hesitated.

"*Now!*" she said forcefully. "This child won't come without a doctor."

I turned and rushed to the puja room, where we kept our altar and statues of the gods. I thought I would find Grandmother praying there. Instead, she was sitting in the kitchen, eating chapatis.

"Dadi-ji, the midwife has asked that you come."

She lowered the chapati onto the table. "What did I tell you?"

"That I should only come to you when the child is born. But Dadi-ji, the midwife says the baby can't come into the world without a doctor."

Grandmother's eyes widened, and suddenly, she jumped up. She washed her hands in a bowl of lemon water, then went down the hall and opened the door. Inside, she covered her nose with the edge of her sari. The smell was overwhelming.

"Dadi-ji," the midwife addressed Grandmother respectfully. "Your daughter-in-law is in desperate need of a doctor. There's nothing more I can do."

Mother's eyes were closed. The only sound in the room was her heavy breathing.

"We will not have a man delivering this child," Grandmother said.

"Your daughter-in-law will *die* without a doctor, and the child will die with her. I would fetch him now, before it's too late."

But Grandmother was as still and immovable as a tree. "My son would never compromise the dignity of this house by allowing another man to touch his wife."

"Dadi-ji!" I felt myself becoming hysterical. "You're wrong. I know Pita-ji would want—"

"Out!"

"*Please!* Pita-ji will come home and you'll see—"

"Do not make me fetch the stick!"

But I can tell you, at that moment, I didn't care. What did a beating matter if Mother died? I turned to the midwife, but her head was lowered in the shame of having to witness such a scene. I ran from the room and—for the first time in my life—out the front door and into the street. I had no idea which roads Father might have taken to bring my aunt home to her husband and family at the other end of Barwa Sagar, but I ran as if the demon Ravana were chasing me. It was only when I reached a fork in the road that I realized what a terrible idea this was. First of all, Father had warned me that it wasn't uncommon for children roaming the streets to go missing. And secondly, I probably don't need to tell you what awful things can befall a girl in the middle of the night.

I stopped where I was and looked around me. The full moon cast a silvery light over our neighbor's fields. I watched the tall stalks of rice sway in the breeze. Even if I screamed, our neighbor's house was so far away that no one would hear me. What had I been thinking, leaving the house like this? My heart began beating so loudly that when the sound of someone's sandals against the gravel grew near, I wondered if it was coming from inside my head. I was frozen in terror.

"Sita!"

"Pita-ji!" I ran to him. In my excitement, I started to speak, then I took his hand and started to write. "Dadi-ji is refusing to get a doctor. Mama-ji is dying!"

Chapter Three

The shouting went on for some time before a doctor was sent for. Of course, it was Grandmother who was doing the shouting, and the horrible words she used against Mother made me thankful for once that Father was deaf.

I went into my room while Grandmother was still raging and lay on the bed. The rain had started up again, and if I listened to it falling against the windows, I could block out the sound of her voice.

"Sita?" Avani appeared at my door. It was late and she should have been at home, but she had chosen to stay with us these past three nights. "I thought you might like some milk," she said.

I sat on my bed and swallowed the terrible pain in my throat. "Is she going to die?"

Avani crossed the room and sat down next to me. "I don't know." She passed me the milk, but I couldn't bring myself to drink it.

"What do *you* think?" I watched her face carefully and saw her lower lip tremble.

"That there are some storms that can be weathered," she said, "and others that simply wash everything away. Only the gods know which one this will be."

"So what do we do?"

"Build the strongest ship we can. Your father has sent for the best doctor in Barwa Sagar."

But the strongest ship sailed too late.

Several hours later, Avani woke me in order to tell me a child had been born.

"A girl," she said. "Beautiful and healthy. Your father has already sent for a milk nurse. But Sita—" She didn't say anything else. She didn't have to. It was there in her eyes, just the same as if I was reading it from a book.

I ran from the room to Mother's chamber. Father was lying on her bed, his arms wrapped tenderly around her body.

"Maa-ji!" I cried.

"Get her out of here," Grandmother said. But even though he couldn't hear her, Father held up his hand to keep me from leaving.

If you have ever witnessed something unspeakably painful, then you know what I mean when I say that everything stopped: the rain falling in buckets outside, the cries of my newborn sister in the midwife's arms. Mother was lying motionless on her bed, and the sheet that twisted around her was stained with blood. I looked at her face: how could it be possible that someone so beautiful could be gone from this world?

"Maa-ji?" I whispered, and fresh tears pooled in Father's eyes.

"Sita, your mother is dead," the doctor said. "She's not going to wake."

I reached out and caressed Mother's cheek, but the skin was cold and I drew back my hand.

"Until the milk nurse comes tomorrow," the midwife said, "I will take care of Anuja."

This was the name Mother had chosen, in case it was a girl.

The midwife came to me and put her hand on my shoulder. "This is the way of all things," she said. "Birth and death. Samsara. Change is the only constant in this world."

I looked down at Mother, who looked so lonely there, even with Father's arms around her. How would life in our house go on without her? Who would teach my little sister her favorite hymns, or how to dress her hair in jasmine blossoms? "But why does it have to change for the worse?"

The midwife blinked back her own tears. "I don't know. But these will be difficult days for your family."

The midwife was right: the days that followed were terrible and traumatic.

Yet when I think back to this time, I remember very little. Perhaps this is the mind's way of protecting us from events that are so devastating we would otherwise lose all reason. The same way a lizard, if its body is threatened, will drop its tail, providing a distraction to the predator in order to escape with its life. And grief, for anyone who has ever experienced it, is exactly like a predator. It steals first your happiness, and then—if you allow it—everything else.

There are some things I do recall, however, and my hatred for Grandmother is one of them. It's interesting to think that in all of Shakespeare's plays, there are almost no grandmothers. If I could have taken up a pen and written her out of my life, I would have done it. I was certain that if a doctor had been called while Father had been escorting my aunt to her home, Mother would have survived. Grandmother had chosen death, and for this I was determined never to speak with her again if I could help it.

Over the days immediately following my mother's death, neighbors came to visit, and Grandmother made a show of taking them to Mother's body. She walked each woman slowly through the house, dabbing her tears with the edge of her white sari, and every time she reached the chamber where Mother was laid out on an open palanquin, she drew in the same long staggered breath. She would have made a very fine actress.

I visited Mother only once in the three days her body lay in our house. It was when the priest arrived to make my newborn sister's Janam Kundli, or natal chart. A person's natal chart determines nearly everything in their life. What that person will do as a career, what kind of luck they will have in business, even who they will marry. This last is the most important, because if a prospective couple's Janam Kundlis don't agree, the match will not go forward, no matter how eager the couple or their parents are to proceed.

When Avani came into my chamber to help me dress for the priest's arrival, she sat at the edge of my bed and watched me read *King Lear*.

"Do you understand all of those words?"

I nodded, since I believed that I did. Before Father and I read any play together, he explained it to me, writing out the summary so that even if I did not understand every word in English, I would know what was happening and what to expect.

"The king was betrayed by two of his children in this story. His own family," I said, and I knew that Avani was clever enough to understand the point I was trying to make.

"I know you are very angry," she said, and before I could form a reply, she added, "but you should understand something about your grandmother's life."

Then Avani told me something my own mother had kept secret from me.

"Your grandmother came from a very wealthy family. She had more servants than she could count, and half a dozen women to help her dress. She was also very beautiful. They say that men would try to sneak into her garden just to steal a glimpse of her face."

This, I believed. Even though meanness had hardened her eyes into sharp pieces of onyx, Grandmother was a stunning woman.

"When she married your grandfather, her family gave him the highest dowry ever paid in Barwa Sagar. Everyone expected it to be a successful marriage. And why not? They were young and wealthy with beauty and good health. Then your grandmother fell pregnant and gave birth to a girl. Over the next five years there were two more girls."

"But Father has no sisters."

She nodded quietly, letting the implication of this sink in. "I suspect the wolves took them," she said finally.

The answer was so terrible that I was silent for several moments. I couldn't imagine looking into the perfect face of a child, then tainting its milk with opium. It seemed too cruel, even for Grandmother. "Does Father know this?"

"Yes."

"So he was her fourth child?"

"No. After giving birth to her third child, your grandmother's sister died in childbirth with a boy. By then, your grandfather despaired of ever having an heir, so when your grandmother suggested they adopt her nephew, he agreed. Her sister's husband preferred drink to work. So the adoption benefitted everyone."

I fell silent again, trying to absorb this. Grandmother wasn't my grandmother, but my great-aunt. My *real* grandmother was dead! I fantasized about all the things my real grandmother must have been: beautiful and sweet and patient and kind. *This* was why Dadi-ji didn't love me.

"It was two months after the adoption," Avani continued, "that your grandfather took sick and died. Your grandmother went from the most envied woman in Barwa Sagar to one of the most pitied."

"But she didn't have to commit sati," I pointed out. "Her father took her back."

Avani folded her hands in her lap. Her eyes looked very tired. "It's a hard life, Sita, with no friends, or money, or anyone to love you." She was speaking of her own experience.

"But *I* love you." I wrapped my arms around her as tightly as I could. She smelled like jasmine blossoms, the same as Mother, and I felt an overwhelming need to go on hugging her. Still I pulled away. If Grandmother saw us, there would be trouble. Avani was a maid.

She wiped away her tears with the back of her hand. "I pray to Durga that you will never understand what it's like to go from great wealth to poverty, Sita. It was very devastating for your grandmother."

"Buddha was a Hindu prince," I said. "A Kshatriya, like us, and he found freedom in casting off his position and embracing poverty."

"Because he chose it. And—more important—he was a man. A man can change his life anytime he wishes. A woman can only change her appearance." Avani stood and handed me a white sari. Now she and I would look the same. Except I would only wear white for thirteen days. Avani was forbidden color for the rest of her life.

I wrapped the white sari around my body, and Avani made sure it fell in neat folds to my feet. Outside, the sun had already risen, and a flock of birds were making noise in the rice paddies. It was terrible to realize that life was simply carrying on while Mother lay on her funerary litter. It made me think of the scene in *King Lear* when the king discovers his beloved daughter's body. He asks the gods how it's possible that a dog, a horse, even a lowly rat can have life, *and thou no breath at all.* It felt like a betrayal to Mother that the birds outside should still be singing. Shouldn't Lord Brahma silence them in sympathy?

I stood at the window and looked out over the rice paddies. The priest was coming not just to write my sister's Janam Kundli, but also to bless my mother's spirit, which was already on its way to Svarga, where souls go before their next reincarnation. I tried to imagine her there, as a spirit, but since her body was still lying in the next room, I found it difficult.

Eventually, Grandmother came to the door and demanded to know why Avani hadn't brought me to our puja room, where we made our daily prayers. "The priest is already here," she said.

"Sita's feeling upset," Avani explained.

"We're all upset," Grandmother replied. "And we'll be more upset if this baby girl ends up manglik."

Avani and I both gasped.

Manglik is the worst thing a person can be. If a priest determines that you are manglik, it means you are cursed. There are all sorts of repercussions for people whose natal charts read this way, and marriage becomes extremely difficult. Most mangliks marry other mangliks, so that the bad luck can be canceled out.

But even Grandmother could not control the stars. It was up to the priest to read them.

I followed Grandmother to the puja room, where the priest would pray for guidance in reading my sister's Janam Kundli. I sat down cross-legged with Avani on fresh jute mats. Father must have bought them that morning. I looked across the room at him. He was sitting near the priest in front of our mandir, the wooden temple that housed the images of our gods. I tried to catch his gaze, but even though he was looking at me, he was somewhere else. Next to him, the priest was speaking with our new milk nurse about my sister and how she had come into the world. It was the first time I had seen the baby properly. She was a pretty baby, and I could see at once her resemblance to Mother. She had the same small nose, thick black hair, and a pair of dimples on either side of her cheeks. The midwife had wrapped her in a swath of yellow cloth. I felt a heaviness in my chest because I wanted Mother to be the one cradling her.

"Beautiful, isn't she?" Avani said. "Coloring like your grandmother, but darker eyes."

"I think she looks like Mother," I said, to be defiant.

The priest took his place in the center of the room and we waited in silence while he prepared the puja. A puja is a prayer, the same as you might make in any church. To perform the ceremony you need incense, flowers, ghee, and a round bowl for making a small fire. If you want it to be elaborate, you can add painted oil lamps and large brass bells. With the exception of the priest and the fire, this puja for my sister's Janam Kundli was not so different from what my family did every morning, when—after our bath—we entered our puja room to stand before images of our gods. I've learned over the years that Catholics and Hindus have similar rituals: Catholics light a candle before statues of their saints and repeat a mantra they call Hail Mary; Hindus light a stick of incense and repeat mantras to the gods.

A puja can be long and intense, or it can be quite simple and short. That afternoon it was long, and since eating is prohibited until the ceremony is finished, it seemed to go on forever. After the priest finally stopped chanting, he turned to me. "Have you seen your mother's body?" he asked.

I shook my head.

"The child should see her mother before the body is taken away," he announced. "When is the cremation?"

Since Father couldn't respond, it was Grandmother who told him.

"Tomorrow. My son will go today to make the necessary arrangements."

We followed Grandmother into the spare room. Mother was laid out in a new yellow sari, her litter illuminated by a ring of oil lamps. Women from the village had scattered marigolds at her feet, and when the priest kneeled above her, he added roses. Then he spread sandalwood paste across her forehead and intoned another mantra. I glanced up at Father, but his eyes were focused on some distant point, like a sailor who's seen the ocean for so long that he's lost all hope of spotting land.

The priest handed me an orange carnation. It was my turn to lay a flower on Mother. I approached the litter as slowly as I could. She looked cold and lonely. In life, I had rarely seen Mother sleeping. She had always been in motion; if her feet weren't moving, then her arms were moving—as well as her lips, since she loved to sing. I laid the flower in her hands, then stood there and waited for her to move. It was childish, but I believed that if I concentrated hard enough, Brahma would take pity on me and bring Mother back to life. But no such thing happened, and I wondered yet again what I had done to so offend the gods that they would take my mother away.

We moved into the front room to eat rice and lentils, then the priest finished interpreting my sister's Janam Kundli, which was favorable.

"Tell me," he said as he was about to leave. It was only Grandmother and me at the door. "What arrangements has your son made for this girl?" He looked down at me, and I immediately looked away, so he wouldn't think I was shameless.

"Now that there's two of them, there's no money for a dowry fortune," Grandmother said, "if that's what you mean."

"She's already eight, is that right?"

"Nine," Grandmother corrected.

"And very pretty. But if there's no money for a dowry—"

"We are dedicating her to the temple," Grandmother said. "She will become a devadasi."

At the time, I had no idea what a devadasi was, except that it meant "god's servant." Now, of course, I can understand the horror on the priest's face when she said this, since a devadasi is really no different from a prostitute. Many years later, I came across an English translation of a poem written in the fifteenth century about devadasis, "sacred servants of god":

I'm not like the others. You may enter my house.
But only if you have the money
To step across the threshold of my main door, it'll cost you a hundred in gold. For two hundred you can see my bedroom, my bed of silk, and climb into it.
But only if you have the money
To sit by my side and to put your hand boldly into my sari: that will cost ten thousand. And seventy thousand will get you a touch of my full round breasts.
But only if you have the money
Three crores to bring your mouth close to mine, touch my lips and kiss.
To hug me tight, to touch my place of love, and get to total union, listen well, you must bathe me in a shower of gold.
But only if you have the money

The priest stared at her for a moment, and his mouth opened and shut, as if he had lost the words he'd meant to say. "Does her father know this?"

"Not yet. But it's the sensible thing to do with two girls and no heir."

The priest looked at her in a way that would be of great comfort later on when I was able to think back on these events with a clearer mind. I wasn't the only one who recognized Grandmother's cruelty.

Late that afternoon, Father found me in the garden, twisting the wildflowers into a crown the way Mother had taught me. He sat on the grass and waited for me to offer him my hand, but I had nothing to say. Finally, he took my hand in his.

"Someday," he wrote on the flat on my palm, "when Dadi-ji and I are both gone, you will be the only one who is be able to tell Anuja what her mother was like."

Tears obscured my vision, but I could sense that this wasn't the time to cry.

"Do you still have empty pages in the diary I gave you?"

I nodded.

"Perhaps you can list all of the wonderful things you remember about your mother. Before you forget."

I was still writing that list when he left with our neighbor, Shivaji, to arrange for Mother's cremation. I watched from my bedroom window as they crossed the rice paddies together; anyone who saw them would have thought they were still soldiers. It was something in the way that they walked; tall, muscular men with shoulders like oxen. Aunt said there was nothing bigger in Barwa Sagar than Shivaji. I didn't know if this was true, but I could certainly believe it of his wide mustache, which he waxed and curled at both ends. With his long dark hair, Shivaji reminded me of a character in *The Book of One Thousand and One Nights.*

"Get dressed," Grandmother said from the door, although I hadn't heard her approach. "We're leaving."

Before Mother's death, the excitement of leaving our house would have prompted me to ask where we were going, but now I simply rose and put on my sandals. There was no question of whether or not to change into a colorful sari.

I met Grandmother at the door; a palanquin had been arranged and she waited for me to climb inside it, then followed behind me and yanked the curtain shut. I have never enjoyed dark, enclosed spaces, but there was no other way of traveling. Women were to be neither seen nor heard, and so we lived like shadows outside of our homes.

If I had been riding with anyone else, I would have peeked out from behind the curtain to see what was happening as we moved along the streets. Instead, I sat huddled against the wooden boards, wondering where we were going.

"Sit straight, and don't speak when we arrive."

When I didn't reply, Grandmother became irritated.

"You may think my son loves you, but don't confuse love with duty."

I thought she should take her own advice, since I felt certain that Father couldn't possibly love anyone as cruel as Grandmother, but I continued to keep my silence, which irritated Dadi-ji even more.

"I hope you're listening to me, *beti*, because what I'm about to say I'm not going to repeat. There is nothing special or different about you. You're going to live, and cry, and suffer the same way that every woman suffers. And where we're going," she warned, "the mind won't be very useful."

She didn't say anything more, and I didn't try to puzzle out what she meant. I was too young to have understood anyway, even if she had explained it to me.

When I heard the deep bellowing of conch shells, I knew where we were. There is nothing else like the sound of a temple; the trumpeting shells, the trickling fountain water, the ringing bells.

"The Temple of Annapurna," one of the palanquin bearers shouted, and we were lowered to the ground. When I stepped outside, I saw that we were in a high-walled courtyard with a dozen other women who were paying their bearers for transportation. Grandmother paid our men from a purse she carried tucked into the waist of her white sari; then we left our sandals on the smooth marble floor and climbed fifteen steps to Annapurna's temple.

I had never been to this temple before, so everything looked foreign and new. Not just the elaborate bronze lamps that illuminated our way to the top, even though it was daylight, but the giant metal pots housing sacred tulsi plants and the colored cages housing jewel-toned parrots. Someone had spent a great deal of money ensuring the temple was well maintained. The marble steps were clean, and fresh incense burned from costly hanging censers where the image of the goddess Annapurna resided.

Since there are three hundred and thirty million gods in our religion, it shouldn't really come as a surprise that I had never heard of Annapurna. Of course, when people hear this number, they think that Hindus go around making up gods at whim. But in the Hindu religion, there is really only one god—Lord Brahma—and all of the other gods and goddesses are merely aspects of Brahma himself. Take Durga, for instance, who is the warrior goddess of female power. She represents Brahma's ability to meet any challenge. Or Shiva, the Destroyer, who illustrates Brahma's power to take as well as give. On a day-to-day basis, only a few gods really feature in our lives, and they're the ones we pray to every morning for guidance: Durga, Rama, Lakshmi, Krishna, Buddha, Saraswati, Ganesh. Few Hindus know the names of more than a dozen or so aspects of Brahma.

When we reached the top, I bowed, as everyone else was doing, then took a few moments to stare into the golden face of Annapurna, crowned with yellow and orange carnations.

"We're not here for prayer," Grandmother said. "Remember what I told you. Keep silent."

I looked to my left and saw a skinny priest walking toward us. He was dressed in a very peculiar fashion, with red and white beads around his neck and thick clusters of them on his wrists and feet. But it was the unusual crown of neem leaves in his hair that caught my attention. I found myself staring at them even when I should have been looking away. He pressed his hands together in a respectful gesture of namaste, and I realized how young he was. No more than twenty or twenty-five.

"You returned," he said. He sounded surprised, though not as surprised as I was. I had no idea when Grandmother might have visited this temple before. But the days after Mother's death had passed by in a haze; it was entirely possible that she had left the house without my noticing.

"And this must be the girl," he said. There was something uncomfortable about the way his smile remained in place while his eyes looked me up and down. "She's thin."

"Yes, but she's only nine."

He nodded thoughtfully, then circled around me and stopped when we were once again face-to-face. "She's very pretty. With a face like hers, you'd think she'd find a good husband. Why is her father agreeing to this?"

"It doesn't matter why. How much is the goddess willing to pay?"

He raised his eyebrows. "That all depends. Is she a virgin?"

"Of course. She was raised in my house."

A group of women passed us and bowed very low to the priest, giggling as they went by. Their glass bangles made music on their arms, and they were dressed in the most exquisite saris I had ever seen—silk trimmed with elaborate beadwork of silver and gold. The fabrics rippled as they moved, and I longed to reach out and brush my fingertips against them.

"Three thousand rupees," the priest said after the women passed.

"You do realize she's not some Dalit. This child is a Kshatriya."

"If she was a Dalit, we would not be having this discussion. This temple serves the richest men in Barwa Sagar."

"And a girl like this will have them coming all the way from Jhansi. You think I don't know what kind of men pay for a girl who speaks English as well as Hindi? Her customers will be rich British soldiers."

I couldn't imagine why I would ever have customers. Perhaps the temple wanted me as a translator. Grandmother said that this was a place where my mind wouldn't be very useful, and what could be more boring than translating letters for soldiers?

"Five thousand, and that's it."

"Fifteen thousand."

The man's smile vanished. "You forget we're in Barwa Sagar. Not Jhansi."

"And you forget that I can easily dedicate her to the Temple of Durga down the street."

They stared at each other, but what the priest didn't know was that Grandmother could be as immovable as stone. Finally, the priest let out his breath and said, "Thirteen. But that's the highest we've ever paid for a devadasi."

It was one of the few times I ever saw Grandmother's smile reach her eyes. She grabbed my hand and started walking.

"Where are you going?" The priest's voice rose. "I thought we had a deal?"

"The child lost her mother and the funeral is tomorrow. I'll return with her next week."

"But—"

Grandmother turned around. "I know you're very eager, and I assure you—you produce the money, and I'll produce the girl. But she's not coming until next week."

The priest stared down at me, and if I live to be a hundred years, I will never forget his look. If you have ever had the opportunity to visit a zoo, then perhaps you've also seen the lions being fed: that fierce, untamable flash of their eyes. Well, this is the look the priest had as we left. No man, either before or since, has ever dared to stare at me in that way, and all the way home I tried to make sense of it.

When the palanquin stopped in the courtyard before our house, Grandmother pushed her cheek next to mine so that when she spoke, I could feel her breath on my ear. "We didn't go *anywhere* today. We'll surprise your father with the good news next week."

But Father came home that evening looking so worn that keeping my silence made me feel like a traitor. I don't know how Grandmother convinced the milk nurse and Avani to keep quiet about our trip, but she had her ways. After all, their employment—and really, their lives—were in her hands. Only a very foolish woman would jeopardize her own well-being to tattle about a trip to a temple. For me, it was much harder. I couldn't stop thinking about the skinny priest in his neem-leaf crown, circling me like a cat. What did he expect from me? And why had those women been giggling when they went by?

These questions kept me awake all that night into the morning.

There are only a few times in an Indian woman's life when she's allowed to break purdah, and funerals are one of them. That evening, our family and friends gathered on the banks of the river Sindh. A black scar in the sand marked the place where other funeral pyres had been built, and we watched as the men piled new wood on this spot. I've heard some women say that if they break purdah, they feel dread and shame. But even though I was attending my own mother's funeral and my body was raw with grief, I also felt an overwhelming sense of freedom. I watched the geese make formations in the sky, their bodies silhouetted against the purple dusk, and I wondered: is this what it is like to be a man? I stood at the edge of the river while a soft wind pulled at my braid. Then I closed my eyes, trying to imagine having this kind of freedom every day.

But when the funeral pyre was complete, I felt as cold and insignificant as the grains of sand beneath my feet. I cried as the priest arranged Mother's body, feet to the south, so her spirit would know to walk in the direction of the dead. As the fire began to burn, I thought: would Grandmother have taken me to the temple if Mother had been alive? Somehow I knew the answer was no.

Father put his arm around my shoulders. I knew he was looking down at me, but I was too distraught to look into his eyes and risk seeing my own misery mirrored there, so I kept my chin to the ground. The rising flames felt hot on my face, drying my tears even as they fell. Father held out his palm, but I had nothing to write. There were too many images passing through my mind: the man in the neem-leaf crown, the women in their saris, the temple with its soft piles of red kunkuma, a powder made from dried turmeric for devotees to smear across their foreheads as a sign of devotion. I tried forcing my thoughts back to Mother and two images came; one of her in the garden picking tulsi—called holy basil by some—for our altar, and one of the little tortoiseshell brushes she used to line her eyes with kohl in the mornings. Then the images of the temple came back to me, and I felt an overwhelming sense of dread.

When Father's hand remained outstretched, I took it quickly and wrote, "Please don't send me to work in the temple."

"What temple?"

"Where Dadi-ji took me yesterday. I don't want to work for soldiers. Please, Pita-ji. I want to stay with you."

Father looked across the burning pyre at Grandmother, and when her eyes met mine, I knew she realized what I had done.

It didn't matter that our neighbors had gathered in our courtyard or that half of Barwa Sagar was outside. There was never a bigger fight in our house. The walls seemed to shake with Father's bellowing and Grandmother's shrieking, both sounds incoherent with rage. I hid in my room, and Aunt came to sit with me.

"Did she really take you to the temple, Sita?" she asked.

"Yes. The priest said he'd pay thirteen thousand rupees. Do you know what that means?"

Aunt nodded, her eyes closed, but she didn't explain. We listened to the fighting until suddenly, my door swung open, and Father pointed to my diary. I fetched it from its shelf and gave it to him, unsure whether I was supposed to write in it, or if he was.

A moment later Grandmother appeared, and Father took a pen

from my desk. On an empty page in the diary he wrote, "Every person here bears witness to the fact that if something should ever happen to me, neither of my daughters shall ever"—and he underlined the word *ever*—"become devadasis. There is no money for a dowry fortune large enough to find them both suitable husbands. So tomorrow, I begin training with Sita for a position in the Durga Dal."

Since Grandmother couldn't read or write, she looked to Aunt for a translation. When she heard what he had written, she sucked in her breath.

"The Durga Dal is the most elite group of women in this kingdom! No woman in Barwa Sagar has ever become a Durgavasi," she said.

My father's nostrils flared. He might not have heard her words, but he understood her meaning.

Only ten women are chosen for this role. "You want Sita to become one of the women who not only guard the rani but *entertain* her?" She took the pen from Father's hand and handed it to Aunt. "Ask him what will happen if she fails. Ask him!"

Aunt wrote the question in her small, neat handwriting.

"She will not fail," Father wrote back. "She has me and she has our neighbor, Shivaji. We will train her."

As soon as Aunt relayed this message, the color rose on Grandmother's cheeks.

"They haven't held a trial for a new member in three years. You don't have the time for this!" She instructed Aunt to write. "What about a new wife? A woman who can raise your baby and give this family an heir?"

Father replied, "Until Sita becomes a member of the Durga Dal, I will never consider remarrying. Ever."

He put down the pen. The decision was final.

From this moment, Grandmother began to pretend that I didn't exist. And since she could only communicate through crude signs to Father, our house became extremely silent. I'd like to tell you that this was ideal, that it gave me more freedom, but as anyone who's ever lived inside a house of eggshells knows, nothing is more fragile.

In the mornings when Avani came to help me dress, there was no more laughter. Grandmother had told her I was a shameless child, and whether or not Avani believed this, we no longer shared happy moments together. But I watched her with Anuja, and the tenderness she showed my baby sister made me understand that if I had been younger, more pliable, less shameless, things might have been different. Eventually, I grew so accustomed to the silence in our house that I became like a frozen stream—hard and impenetrable on the outside, but secretly bursting with life within.

Chapter Four

1846

Father honestly believed I would be accepted into the rani's Durga Dal and become a member of the elite Royal Guard. True to his word, he enlisted our neighbor Shivaji to help prepare me for the day when one of the rani's Durgavasi retired. It could happen in a month or in five years—we didn't know—but whenever it occurred, I had to be ready, for the rani always had ten women protecting her, and as soon as one retired a trial would immediately be held to find her replacement.

Although Shivaji had three sons at home, he came to our house for several hours each day to train me. I was the only child in our village rising before dawn to begin lessons in poetry, Sanskrit, English, Hindi, and all of the martial skills the Durga Dal required: swordsmanship, shooting, fighting, archery. Before we began my mind was filled with the swashbuckling tales I had read with Father: *The Three Musketeers* and ballads about Robin Hood. I wore a new pair of nagra slippers for my first day of training: they were plain leather with simple red and gold lotus designs, but I thought they were the most exotic things I'd ever seen.

"You see these thick leather soles?" my father wrote, turning the shoes over when he presented them to me. "These will keep you from slipping."

"Can I wear these every day?" I couldn't believe my luck.

"Yes. Especially when it's raining."

"And what about those?" I pointed to a green angarkha he'd brought in with the shoes; a cotton, knee-length shirt that was fitted at the waist.

"Yes. And these churidars," he said, holding up a pair of green pants. I had never worn pants before. They were tight at the ankles and waist, but loose and airy in the legs for quick movement. With a white piece of cloth, or muretha, tied around my head to keep the sweat from dripping into my eyes, I felt powerful.

But the truth of it was far different: nothing is less glamorous than being woken from your bed in the predawn chill to set up a target and shoot arrows at it not once, but a hundred, even two hundred times, until all of your shots hit their mark. In the summers, the heat in my village was suffocating. In the winters, when the wind blew like a river of cold air, I could feel it in my bones, no matter how many layers I would dress myself in. When you're standing in an open courtyard with a frozen scimitar in your hands, fighting against a man who is more than three times your size, there is very little that feels like something out of *The Three Musketeers*. It is hard, grueling work.

But I learned how to fight using only a stick. And how to sever a man's head with a single stroke of my sword. And in case I was ever rendered weaponless, I learned how to defend myself with punches, kicks, choke holds, and shoulder grabs. Day after day I practiced these moves until they came as effortlessly to me as walking or running.

And over several years, I metamorphosed from Sita the child

into someone else. At first, the changes were subtle. Muscles appeared in my arms and legs that had never been defined before. My hands, which had once been full and soft, grew strong and callused. Then, the physical changes became more obvious. My waist grew narrower, my cheeks more hollow. The roundness of childhood was gone. In its place was a tall, lean girl who could carry heavy rocks from one end of the courtyard to another, morning after morning, and still not feel fatigued. She was a girl who could swing a metal sword, carry a man's burden of wheat on her back, and lift multiple buckets of water with both arms. Sita the *child* could do none of these things. She'd been an average girl with average strength. Now, I was probably the strongest woman in Barwa Sagar.

On the first morning I bled, I told Avani, who let Grandmother know I had become a woman. It felt more frightening to me than anything I had learned with Shivaji in the courtyard, and Grandmother's rage didn't help. I could hear her in the kitchen, shouting at Avani, "Well, it's all over now. There's not a man in Barwa Sagar we could trick into taking her."

I was in too much pain to see Shivaji that day. Instead, I stood in front of my small basket of playthings and ran my hands over each one in turn. When I was a little girl, my father had given me two cloth dolls, a wooden horse, and a small block carved into the shape of a bear. I took out the doll with long black hair and held her in my lap. I could remember how I used to give the doll a voice and walk her around my room, but doing this now seemed silly. I was twelve years old.

I sat at my desk and thought about other girls my age. The ones who had become women, like me, were preparing to leave their homes, overseeing the packing of their bridal chests and saying farewell to their families. In this way, I was much luckier than they were. I would never have to bid Father good-bye, knowing that the next time I would see him would likely be on his funeral pyre. I could stay in his home, watch Anuja grow, sleep in my own bed, and eat Avani's mushy lentils until I undertook the rani's trial, which might not be called for many years yet. But then, if I succeeded in becoming a member of the Durga Dal, I would also never marry. And I would certainly never have children. I would belong to the rani from that moment on.

"What are you doing?" Anuja asked, joining me in my room. She was three and always filled with questions, like a lidded pot holding back too much steam.

"Thinking."

Anuja climbed onto my lap. "Can I think with you?"

She not only had Mother's delicate face, but her tenderness, too. She always wanted to know why Grandmother yelled at her or why the baby bird outside our window had died. There is special providence in the fall of a sparrow, Hamlet says. But there was no explaining that to her. "Yes."

She was quiet for a moment. Then curiosity got the better of her. "Why aren't you practicing with Shivaji?"

"Because he gave me the day off," I improvised. "He said, 'Go and find Anuja and tell her that today Sita is going to teach her how to hold a sword.'"

"No swords." My sister shook her curly head. "I want to play with Mooli." This was her toy cat, since real cats weren't allowed in our house.

"But we played with Mooli yesterday."

She snuggled her head against my chest. "Then will you read me a story?"

I closed my eyes and imagined having a conversation with someone who understood how hard it was to train so relentlessly and wait for a day you weren't even sure you wanted to arrive. Certainly there were hundreds of women preparing for the next trial in Jhansi, the city where Maharaja Gangadhar Rao and his rani resided. But in my village, I was unique.

So when Anuja laid her soft head against my chest, I wished, more than anything else in the world, that she was old enough to understand what my training was like. I rubbed my calf, which was sore from the previous day's training. "A story . . ." I tried to think of one. "How about the tale of *The Peacock and the Turtle*?"

She nodded and I began.

It might have been true that nearly every family in Barwa Sagar had heard Father and Grandmother's fight after Mother's funeral, and it was certainly true that everyone in my house knew Father's feelings about either of his daughters ever becoming devadasis, but so long as Grandmother was alive, there was a very good chance that if something happened to my father, we would end up in a temple anyway. You might wonder how this could be, but if my father died, who would actually step forward to welcome two extra girls into their home? Aunt had children of her own; her husband wasn't going to work harder to feed and clothe my sister and I for as long as we lived, since that was what would be required. I was too old to be marriageable, and since no trial had been announced I was not even earning money for Anuja's dowry fortune as a member of the Durga Dal. Who in Barwa Sagar would take on a heavy burden like us?

You will understand why, then, when Father became sick that winter, Shivaji insisted I stop studying subjects like Hindi and Sanskrit—both of which I was proficient in anyway—and study horseback riding instead.

"Every member of the Durga Dal knows how to ride," Shivaji

wrote in father's small red book. "I know you're afraid to see her on a horse, but we'll find a gelding before we give her a stallion. It's her only weakness."

My father was wrapped in three layers of heavy clothing, resting beside our charcoal brazier. The doctor had said it was a sickness of the lungs and not to expect any improvements for several weeks. But he had instructed Father to take in hot vapor with eucalyptus oil three times a day—Ayurvedic medicine.

If you don't know about Ayurveda, it is the oldest medicine in the world. It is based on several *Vedas*—what we call certain texts composed in ancient Sanskrit—written more than two thousand years ago, and it details everything a doctor should know, from eye and nose surgeries to the delivery of a child who isn't positioned right in the womb. A hundred years ago, British physicians came all the way from England to watch our doctors perform surgeries on patients. They took what they learned with them across the seas and spread their new knowledge throughout Europe. Some people find it unbelievable that the *Vedas* can still be relied on more than two thousand years later. But really, why is it so surprising? Sanskrit was the language Pingala used two thousand years ago to write about poetic meter; a treatise that mathematicians later realized was really about binary numbers.

Even with Ayurvedic medicine, however, Father hadn't left his room for two days. I'd brought him half a dozen books, but anyone who has ever been sick can tell you that reading for pleasure and reading to pass the time are two very different things.

Father's pen hesitated beneath Shivaji's words. Finally, he wrote, "Where will we get a gentle horse?"

"Give me permission to work with Sita every morning and I'll find one."

"When is there time? We study languages in the mornings."

"And how will that help her," Shivaji wrote, "if the rani announces a trial next year? Sita may pretend she's seventeen, but her skills won't lie. Nihal, she must learn to ride."

Father stared out the window onto Shivaji's land, which bordered our own; a thin layer of frost had settled over his fields, giving them the appearance of a wide glass lake. Now that the rice had been harvested, there was little for Shivaji to do. It was the best time to teach me to ride. "Fine. We will no longer study Hindi or Sanskrit," Father wrote.

Shivaji twisted the ends of his mustache in thought. "I don't see the point of English poetry either."

My heart beat swiftly. No one could have been more grateful to their teacher than I was to Shivaji, but I knew his limitations. If you have ever looked at a tree blowing in the wind and thought that it resembled a woman's long hair, or seen a cloud passing by that reminded you of a turtle, then you were someone with too many flights of fancy for Shivaji. I stared at Father and silently begged him not to stop our morning readings. In a day filled with swordsmanship, archery, and shooting, it was the only time when my mind felt free, like a hawk liberated from its tethers.

"The point of English poetry," Father wrote, "is to make Sita a better soldier."

Shivaji raised his eyebrows until they practically disappeared in his long mass of hair.

"What are Sita's best subjects?" Father went on.

"Archery and swordsmanship," Shivaji wrote.

"Because both of these things require rhythm. Shooting four arrows, one after the other, into a bull's-eye requires not just accuracy, but timing. It's no different from reading Shakespeare's sonnets."

I had never thought of archery this way. But the act of reaching back into my quiver, drawing an arrow, knocking it, then letting it loose—there was a cadence to it when it was done right. It was poetry in action, the way Shakespeare intended his words to be. "Arise, fair sun, and kill the envious moon." Iambic pentameter, echoing the natural rhythm of the human heart—and the rhythm of practicing weaponry with Shivaji in the courtyard.

Shivaji looked at me for confirmation, and I was surprised to hear myself saying, "It's true."

He blew the air from his cheeks. "Tomorrow, then. I'll find the horse, you find the time."

After Shivaji left, my father pointed to the chess set balanced on the wooden chair across the room. He had carved it from mango wood and teak years ago, before I was born. We usually played in the evenings, but we hadn't played since he'd first become sick.

"Are you sure?" I wrote on his palm. "Perhaps you should rest."

He laughed. "And give up the chance to win?" My father hadn't won in several months. The student had outgrown the teacher. "I know you wouldn't let a sick man lose."

I grinned. "I think I would."

But out of three games, my father won two.

"Either your mind is distracted," he wrote, "or you really do feel sorry for me."

Maybe it was a little of both.

"You're nervous about the riding," he guessed.

I shrugged.

"You shouldn't be." He held up one of the chess pieces and wrote, "Every skill you master is like another chess piece, designed to bring you closer to the king. You can do this."

"I hope so."

"You've mastered chess. You'll master this as well. If you don't let this get in the way." He reached out and tapped my head.

When Shivaji came back later that afternoon to tell Father of his plan to borrow a horse from the local overseer of wedding baraats, I was certain the animal would arrive bedecked with flowers and draped in satin. After all, its sole purpose in life was to carry a bridegroom through the streets to his bride, and any of the horses I'd ever seen wore gem-studded saddles and silver bells. So when Shivaji arrived in our courtyard the next morning and the horse was bare, I'm embarrassed to say that the first thought that came to my mind was that it was naked. My second thought: the beast was enormous.

To say I was scared is like saying a mouse has slight reservations about the cat that prowls around its hole. I had never seen a horse up close, and had certainly never touched one.

But Shivaji motioned me forward. "Sita, this is Raju. Raju, meet Sita."

I could hear nothing except the blood rushing in my ears. I was too paralyzed to reach out and pat the horse's muzzle, as Shivaji was doing. I prayed that it wouldn't take a bite out of me.

"It's a horse," Shivaji said, "not a wild bear. Come."

He took my hand and guided it to the horse's long face. Father had given me strict instructions not to disobey Shivaji, no matter how frightened I might be. "Animals can smell fear," he'd warned earlier, before lying back on his pillows and closing his eyes. I didn't want to disappoint him, especially in his weakened state, so I stroked the white hair along the horse's nose. "He likes it," I said to Shivaji, surprised.

"You see? It's nothing to be afraid of. Every bridegroom in India has ridden one of these. Even Anuja is interested in it."

I turned and there indeed was Anuja, eager to see what sort of beast had taken up residence in our courtyard. She had obviously escaped Avani's watch, because her hair was unbraided and still hanging in wild curls. And instead of wearing juti to protect her feet, she was standing barefoot on the hard-packed earth.

"It's a horse," Shivaji said to my sister. "Would you like to come and see?"

Her eyes went big, and I was thankful for any distraction that prolonged my having to mount the thing.

Shivaji picked her up and carried her toward Raju, who sniffed her and gave a giant sneeze.

"He likes you!" Shivaji said. "Horses only sneeze on little girls they like."

Anuja laughed. She reached and patted his muzzle. "His fur tickles."

"It's called hair. And I think he's saying he'd like you to climb on his back."

He slid Anuja into the saddle, holding her there while she giggled. It made me feel ashamed that I had been terrified of the prospect of doing the same thing only a few moments earlier. Then a sudden shriek made us all turn.

"Do you have any idea what the neighbors will say if she breaks her neck like this? What sort of family allows a girl on a horse?" Grandmother's voice was shrill. She hurried into the courtyard without any juti on herself.

Shivaji gathered Anuja into his arms and set her down.

"Get into that house!" Grandmother screamed. Anuja ran back inside, then Grandmother turned her gaze on me. "There will be no dinner for *either* of you tonight."

"It was my fault," Shivaji said.

"It is *her* fault!" Grandmother pointed at me. "The one who plans to ride around Jhansi like an uncovered whore, with her hair streaming behind her and a sword in her belt!" Other women might have stomped back across the courtyard. But Grandmother glided away like a ghost, with just as much care or tenderness for the living.

I approached the horse slowly. Shivaji said the horse was wearing an English saddle, and I shouldn't be scared, but no creature had ever looked so frightening to me. I found it difficult to concentrate. I glanced across the courtyard and saw Avani, who had come out to wash our linens in a bucket on the steps.

"Your mind is wandering."

"I'm sorry."

He folded his arms across his chest. Then his voice grew very low, although the only person who could have possibly heard us was our maid. "Tell me, Sita. Who will support this family when your father is too old to work?"

"Me."

"And you alone. You *must* become a member of the Durga Dal. Your father saved my life twice in Burma and I owe him this."

My father had never told me this story. I wanted to question Shivaji further, but his look was firm.

It took three attempts before I successfully mounted Raju. But I did it, and I felt immense gratitude when the lesson was done and he hadn't thrown me from his back.

That evening, after Father was served hot tahari in his room, my sister and I were instructed to leave the kitchen. Anuja stared at the pot of rice and potatoes, inhaling the warm scents of garlic and peas. "But I'm hungry."

Grandmother's smile was as thin and sharp as the curve of my scimitar. "You should have thought about that before following your sister onto that dirty animal today."

Anuja didn't understand. "But why?" My little Anu's voice sounded so small.

I nudged her in the direction of my room. "We'll read," I said with a cheerfulness I didn't feel. "Food for the mind instead of the stomach." When we got inside, I took *The Brothers Grimm* from my shelf; a treasure Father had given me for my tenth birthday, telling me it had come all the way from Jhansi.

"*Cinderella* or *Snow White*?" I asked.

"Rapunzel!"

I read the story, hoping my sister would fall asleep and forget about her hunger, but just as her eyes began to close and her lashes brushed against her cheeks, Grandmother swung open the door. She was carrying a tray with a lidded bowl.

"Tahari!" my sister said, and ran to Dadi-ji, throwing her arms around her legs.

"Get off!"

My sister immediately backed away. It wasn't tahari. The bowl was too small.

"Stand."

We did as we were told. Then Grandmother lifted the cover and began to spoon salt from the bowl onto the floor.

"Kneel." When neither of us moved, she threatened, "Lift up your kurtas and kneel or I will fetch the stick!"

I lifted my kurta first, showing Anu how to obey, and pressed my knees into the salt. But when Anu followed, it hurt her soft skin and she stood up again.

"Kneel down!" Grandmother grabbed her arm and forced her into position. If Father hadn't been deaf, he would have heard her screams from Shivaji's fields. "You will stay this way until I return."

Tears made thick trails down Anu's cheeks, and her cries became hysterical.

"Dadi-ji!" I exclaimed. "She can't breathe—"

"Enough! You will be quiet," she threatened Anu, "or I will bind your mouth shut."

I glanced at Anu and made my eyes wide, in case she didn't believe her.

Grandmother came for us an hour later. By then, Anu had wept herself dry. But I could never tell Father. If I did, Grandmother would simply wait until I was accepted into the rani's Durga Dal, then punish Anu by doing this again—or something even worse. I carried my sister to the charpai in her room and poured her a glass of water.

"Why does Dadi-ji hate me?"

"She doesn't hate you," I whispered. "She's had a very difficult life, that's made her very angry and mean." I pulled back the covers and waited for Anu to wiggle inside. "Do you remember the kitten who wandered into our courtyard last month?"

"The one with the broken leg?"

"Yes. And what happened when you tried to touch her leg?"

"She bit me!"

"Like Dadi-ji. Pain can make us miserable creatures."

"But what hurts Dadi-ji?"

Nothing, I thought. She has a son who loves her, kind neighbors, and enough to eat. "Her pain is not outside, like the cat's. It's in here." I touched Anu's heart. "When things hurt inside, there's no healing them sometimes."

"So she'll always be mean?"

I hesitated, wondering if I should lie. But what was the point? "Yes."

Chapter Five

1850

When a woman celebrates her sixteenth birthday in Barwa Sagar, it's nearly always with a special dinner she shares with her husband and children. Her father-in-law's house is decorated with flowers, and her husband might buy her a small gift—perhaps a new comb or a very special sari. Since I had no father-in-law's house to decorate with roses, I celebrated my sixteenth year by giving a present instead of receiving one.

Anu waited on my bed while I fetched a small package wrapped in cloth, and when I took it from the basket where I'd hidden it several weeks before, her dark eyes went big. She was a seven-year-old miniature of our mother, I realized. "For you," I said, holding out the package.

She felt the edges of the gift. "A diary?" she guessed. I had taught her to read and write when she turned six. "Like yours?"

"Open it."

She unwrapped the cloth and took out a book. "It *is* a diary!"

I shook my head. "Look inside."

My sister's eyes grew red and weepy as soon as she did. The pages were filled with every memory I had of our mother. Good ones, bad ones, the times when we sat together in a quiet place and she sang ragas to Lord Shiva. "Thank you, Sita. Thank you!" Anu hugged me as tightly as she could. "But why? It's *your* birthday today."

"Because I know you would make Maa-ji very proud. And I want you to know her."

"When you pass the trial," Anu said suddenly, "will you come back here to visit me?"

"Of course. We'll never be apart for long." If a trial is ever called, I thought.

"Is that a promise?" She looked up at me with our mother's eyes.

"Yes. And now it's time for puja."

I led her into our puja room and I let her ring the bell, so the gods would know we were there. Then we knelt before the images of Durga and Ganesh and I recited the Durga mantra. We touched the gods' feet with our right hands, then touched our foreheads with the same fingers. Finally, I lit two sticks of incense and prayed that the day would go smoothly for us, and as always, that a trial would be called for soon.

A few days later, while I was practicing archery with my father, the gods answered my prayer. Shivaji arrived in our courtyard with the unbelievable news. "The rani has retired one of her Durgavasi," he said. "There's going to be a trial in twelve months."

"I'll be seventeen. I won't even have to lie!"

Shivaji was about to reply when I heard Anu cry, "Sita!" She came running over to join us. "There's a bird on the ground and his wing is broken!" We walked over to where she pointed and saw a small bulbul with dark feathers and bright red cheeks nursing a broken wing by keeping it close to its tiny body. Anu reached down and scooped the bird into her hands. "Can it be fixed? Does anyone know how to help him?"

Warring emotions crossed Shivaji's face—the desire to begin our lesson, and the desire to help. "My youngest son might be able to mend it. He has a gift for healing. Sometimes he visits the animal hospital to be of service."

While Shivaji returned with his son, I fetched my dupatta and drew it over my head, covering my hair with the light scarf women wear around their necks.

"You remember Ishan?" Shivaji said as an introduction.

The boy next to him smiled shyly. I'd heard he'd recently celebrated his fourteenth birthday, but he was slight for his age, the youngest and smallest of his brothers. He bent to touch Father's foot with his right hand, then immediately touched his third eye and heart. This is a typical greeting in India, especially if a younger person has not seen an elder in some time.

"Ishan?" Grandmother said from the door. She hurried out into the courtyard and Anu instinctually stepped closer to me. "Just look at him!" Grandmother said, as if she was seeing a wondrous animal for the first time. "Exactly like his father. Tall and handsome."

In reality, he was none of these, but to watch Grandmother you might actually believe it. Grandmother was like an opal. You could never be sure which colors were really there, and which were just tricks of the light.

"The gods have always blessed you, Shivaji. *Three* sons, and not a single daughter."

"Perhaps that's why I feel so attached to your grandchildren," he said. "They are the little girls I never had."

I never felt more grateful to our neighbor than I did in that moment.

But even with Father standing beside her, Grandmother didn't bother to hide her disgust. "I keep reminding Nihal that sons make up a house's worth. He must remarry, or he'll be fated to rot here with only daughters as heirs. Aren't I right?"

Our neighbor looked deeply uncomfortable. He tugged at his mustache, and his son looked at the ground. Finally, he said, "It's not for me to say what another man should do. Ishan, why don't you go take a look at the bird?"

My sister was still cradling the little bulbul in her hands, pressing him against her chest for warmth. Reluctantly, she offered the creature to Shivaji's son, who took him to a small table below our kitchen window.

Anu stood next to him while he worked. He asked her to hold the bird steady while he wrapped a strip of linen around its body, immobilizing the bird's broken wing. The two of them worked quietly together. I glanced at Shivaji and saw that he wore a thoughtful expression on his face.

That evening, I went to our puja room. I prayed before the statue of Durga, the goddess of female power and the slayer of demons. I asked for help not just in passing the trial, but also in saving the kind of fortune that would find my sister a respectable husband.

"Someone tender," I prayed, "who will take care of her when Father has passed and I am away."

I touched my forehead to the jute mats, then lit a second stick of incense and watched the smoke curl around the goddess's body. Long before I was born, Father had taken great care to carve each of her ten arms wielding a different weapon; soon, I would be using most of those weapons in a trial that would determine not just my fate, but Anu's.

A sniffling sound echoed from down the hall. When I rose to investigate, I found Anu on her bed, weeping.

"Why are you crying?" I asked.

She buried her face into her pillow.

"Anu?"

She turned and faced the wall. I sat on her bed and waited for her to speak.

"Nobody wants me," she said at last.

"Who told you that?"

"You did. You're going away."

"Anu . . . I'm going away to try to give you a better life. Don't you want to marry and have children?"

"I want to be with *you*."

"But if I pass this trial, I'll be living in the city as a soldier. I will never marry. I will never have children. Don't you want more for yourself?"

"You're going to leave me here with Dadi-ji."

"And Pita-ji. Remember that."

"He's always busy."

"Yes, but never too busy to read to you."

She smiled a little. Then the fear came back into her face and she whispered, "Please don't leave me here with her."

"Anu, I'm not leaving forever. This will always be my home."

And you should know that these were not empty words. I really did believe what I was saying.

Chapter Six

1851

Once, when I was five or six, one of the maharaja's envoys passed through Barwa Sagar on his way to a much bigger city. When he crossed through our village, everyone came out to see his incredible procession. He arrived in a caravan of carts drawn by satin-draped camels and bullocks, and behind him swayed a long line of pony-traps whose riders were shielded from the midday sun by large silver umbrellas. The women of our village stood huddled together behind the latticed screens of our largest temple, watching in awe as the men in their heavily jeweled saddles rode by. Even Mother, who was not impressed by luxuries or gold, had wide eyes that day. "This is something you will never see again," she told me.

Now I wondered what she would think if she knew that in a few days, an even larger procession from the city of Jhansi would arrive in Barwa Sagar for the sole purpose of deciding whether I had the skills to become the tenth member of the queen's Durga Dal.

It should have been incredibly intimidating to know that

whether I passed or failed, the entire village—and probably the surrounding villages as well—would learn about it as soon as it happened. But I was too busy practicing to feel nervous. If I failed, then there was little I could do. But if I passed, I would leave the next morning with the queen's Dewan, or chief minister, for my new home in Jhansi Palace.

For the next two days, whenever I wasn't training with Shivaji I was readying my weapons—polishing my father's dagger to a sheen, restringing my bow. Of all the women who were vying for this position, I wouldn't have the fanciest weaponry, but I knew I would have the skills. If my nerves didn't get the best of me, I wasn't going to fail that part of the trial.

At one point, as Grandmother watched me shoot arrows into a target Shivaji had set up beneath our tree, I heard her remark to Avani, "So she can shoot an arrow. Who's taught her to be entertaining and charming?"

I knew I shouldn't pay attention to anything Grandmother said. She wanted me to fail; was actively trying to make me doubt myself. Still, the next morning, as the orange blush of dawn crept over the courtyard, I asked Shivaji if Grandmother was right, if I needed to be charming.

"Yes. The queen's women are not just chosen for their skills," he said, sitting crossed-legged under our peepal tree with Father. "Durgavasis are also chosen for their ability to keep the queen company and entertain her. That means they have to be beautiful and clever as well."

I had trained for the last eight years. I could outshoot Shivaji with a bow and arrow. But no one had ever said anything about being beautiful or clever. "And how am I supposed to do that?"

"There's nothing you have to do, Sita. You are all of those things already."

I glanced at Father, who seemed to understand what Shivaji was saying, because he smiled.

"I think we should work on being charming today," I said.

Shivaji laughed. "Charming is something a woman learns when she realizes how beautiful she is. Not enough people have told you how beautiful you are, Sita."

I touched my hair self-consciously.

"Not just here." Shivaji indicated my face. "Here." He placed his hand on his heart. "You are charming because you are educated and you are honest. Those may be refreshing traits in the palace. Instead, let's work today on what you will say when the Dewan arrives."

So for the next three days, Father and Shivaji spent our usual training time preparing me for the Dewan's interview. We rehearsed answers to the questions the Dewan might ask, even surprising ones, such as, "What is your favorite food?"

On the last day, Shivaji said, "There are hundreds of girls across this kingdom who've also been preparing for years for the Dewan's visit. For nearly every job in the palace, bribes are expected."

I'd heard this, and my heart sank at the idea.

"But no one has ever bribed their way into the queen's Durga Dal. The final choice rests with the Dewan; when he believes he's found the right girl, the search is called off."

I was silent. What if they found the right girl today before I had a chance to prove myself?

"When it's time for the interview," Shivaji continued, "the Dewan will try to trick you. He will ask you about imaginary situations involving the rani, and in every case, there is only one right answer: the rani herself. If he asks who the ultimate authority is in the palace, for you it is Rani Lakshmi. If he wants to know to whom you owe your allegiance, it is Rani Lakshmi. The Durga Dal are her personal guards, not the maharaja's. They are there to protect and entertain her, no one else."

Father took up his pen and wrote in his book, "A list of your skills was sent to the Dewan three months ago. He may choose to challenge any one of them."

"Which skills were listed?" I wrote back.

"Only what you do flawlessly. Archery, swordsmanship, shooting, riding, lathi, malkhamba."

Lathi, if you don't know, is a type of exercise performed with a stick. Malkhamba is a form of gymnastics.

"And all of your intellectual skills," Father continued. "Your talent at chess, and your ability to speak Hindi, Marathi, and most important, English."

I didn't need to ask why English was most important. It was the only skill that might separate me from the hundreds of other girls hoping for this chance, since anyone could call the Dewan to their home for a trial. In 1803, the Raja of Jhansi signed a friendship treaty with the British East India Company. Thirteen years later, another treaty was signed in which the British agreed to allow the current ruler to carry his line forward without their interference. In just a few years, the treaty had turned from one of mutual protection to one in which Jhansi had to seek British approval for the right to its own throne. The camel's nose was not just in the tent. The entire camel had entered. By the time our raja, Gangadhar Rao, took the throne, it was only because the British had chosen him. Now English was spoken at court as often as Hindi.

But Shivaji warned, "The Dewan will be able to speak English. If there's a word you're unsure of, don't use it to impress him." He took Father's red book and added, "If she passes tomorrow, she will need new clothes. At least two angarkhas for travel and another for court. Plus slippers."

We didn't have the money for new clothes, let alone another pair of slippers.

"Can't I wear what I have?" I asked.

Shivaji was firm. "Not in Jhansi."

"If she passes," Father wrote, "I will get whatever is needed by afternoon."

But I couldn't think that far ahead. My thoughts were with the Dewan, who even now was traveling east to see me.

The following morning, Anu trailed behind me while I took my bath. She kneeled with me in the puja room, praying as I did for the strength to impress the Dewan. Then she sat beside me while Avani lined my eyes with black kohl and rouged my lips. But when I reached out to take her hand as Avani braided my hair, she withdrew hers. I understood why she was upset.

"Do you remember when we read the *Bhagavad Gita* together?" I said.

She didn't reply.

"How Lord Krishna convinced Arjuna to fight a war against his own brothers even though his heart wasn't in it? Why did he fight that battle?"

Anu remained silent while Avani slipped green bangles onto my wrists. She wasn't going to answer, so I did it for her.

"Because it was the right thing to do. The death of his brothers would save thousands of innocent lives in the future. Sometimes, Anu, we have to take actions that make us sad because it's the right thing to do for the future."

She watched while Avani fetched Mother's gold earrings and thin gold necklace from the locked chest. When Avani was about to put them on me, my sister said suddenly, "Can I do it?"

Avani stepped aside. I felt Anu's small hands at the back of my neck and fought the urge to cry. I was doing this for her as well, I reminded myself. I'd watched for several weeks while she had nursed the tiny bulbul back to health; her tears of joy when it finally flew away. Sometimes birds are injured and they die. But then they are reborn into healthy bodies. That is samsara. But Anu was too gentle and tender to rationalize these things. Loss, pain, separation . . . these were things I needed to protect her from.

"Look in the mirror," Anu said wonderingly. "You're a princess."

She was right. I didn't recognize the girl with her long neck ringed in gold and her full lips bright against her pale face. This was someone who belonged to a wealthy family, with a good marriage and at least two children and a long life of family duties ahead. None of that had happened for me, and standing there in front of Mother's mirror, I was determined to make it happen for Anu.

Everyone assembled in our courtyard—Father, the priest, Shivaji and his three sons, plus countless neighbors pretending to be there for Father's sake but truly there for a glimpse of the Dewan. Even Aunt had traveled across Barwa Sagar with her husband and children to witness my trial. Our house had not had so many visitors since the day of Mother's funeral.

The women in our neighborhood gathered in the kitchen, where Avani and Grandmother had prepared trays of food. There were terra-cotta bowls filled with sweet milk, fresh slices of fruit, fried milk balls dripping with syrup, and sherbet garnished with rose petals. But I wasn't hungry. I sat alone in my room and waited for the sound of the procession. I was not to exit the house until the Dewan's arrival; it would be the first time our neighbors had ever witnessed a woman in Barwa Sagar breaking purdah.

"There is no shame in it," Shivaji said. "In Jhansi, none of the women are in purdah," he reminded me. "They ride as freely through the streets as men."

"Is that the same for every great city?"

"No. Only Jhansi. But there, no one thinks twice about it."

He made it sound simple, but when Father came and wrote on my palm that the Dewan's procession had been seen entering our village, my heart began to beat wildly in my chest.

"There's nothing to fear," he added. "Pass or fail." He reached into his kurta and placed a long leather necklace in my hand. At the center dangled a single charm—a peacock carved from bamboo. "Today, you must be all-seeing," he wrote, "like a peacock with a hundred eyes. But you must also be like bamboo. When a storm comes, bamboo bends. It doesn't break."

Music began to echo through the courtyard. The Dewan's procession had arrived. The people in the courtyard immediately stopped talking, and Anu's small feet slapped down the hall to fetch me.

Father's hand closed over mine. "*Shubhkamnaye*, little peacock," he mouthed. Good luck.

I fastened the necklace and tucked the charm beneath my angarkha. Then Anu burst into the room and said breathlessly, "Sita, he's here! The queen's Dewan is here! It's time!"

I hurried to the door, where Grandmother stood with a silver plate. In India, new guests are welcomed by passing this plate in a circular direction close to their head. Different houses will put different items on it, but there will always be a lit aarti—or lamp—and a small dish of vermillion with which to make a red tilak, or mark, on the welcomed guest's forehead.

For all of my brave talk with Anu, I couldn't have been more nervous stepping out into my own courtyard than a stranger would be taking his first step in a foreign land. The Dewan was waiting just before our wooden gate, surrounded by two dozen well-dressed men in double-breasted Western-style coats; a servant holding a small tasseled umbrella was shielding him from the early morning sun. The servant himself was thin, but the Dewan was even thinner, and so tall that, with his giant head, I thought that he looked like an enormous stalk of corn.

Father took his place at my left and Shivaji stood to my right. "Calmly," Shivaji whispered as we approached.

I held the aarti plate as steady as I could before the Dewan, then moved it in a circular direction. When it was time to push my thumb into the small cup of vermillion and use it to create a mark on his forehead, my hand was shaking. Breathe, I told myself. I would have to perform the same short ceremony for every man there.

When I was done welcoming each of the men, the Dewan crossed our courtyard and took a seat on the wide yellow cushion a servant had arranged beneath our tree. All of his men immediately positioned themselves to his left, while the villagers of Barwa Sagar sat on the ground to the right. I was left with Father and Shivaji in the middle. All three of us bowed before him. I could feel the villagers watching me, the first woman in Barwa Sagar to have broken purdah in the history of who-knew-when.

"Sita Bhosale," the Dewan began, and his voice was surprisingly deep. I thought it would be high and thin, like a reed. "You are the daughter of Nihal, who is the son of Adinath, a member of the Kshatriya. Is that right?"

"Yes."

"And you are seventeen?"

"I turned seventeen last month."

The Dewan snapped his fingers and a servant beside him brought him a pipe, which the young man hurriedly lit. The

Dewan inhaled deeply, then exhaled, never taking his eyes off me. "You look like one of Nihâl Chand's paintings," he said. He sat forward on his cushion, and the smoke from his pipe curled around his face. "Have you seen them?"

I knew my cheeks must be flushed. "Yes, Dewan-ji."

Who hadn't seen copies of Nihâl Chand's work, one of India's greatest painters? When he lived, the Maharaja Savant Singh gave the artist a sketch of his favorite singer, the beautiful Bani Thani. Nihâl Chand took the king's simple drawing and created a series of paintings that represented the ideal woman: pale cheeks, sensuous lips, a high forehead, thin brows, and wide lotus-blossom eyes. He used her face for all of his images of our goddess Radha, much as some European masters used prostitutes for the faces of their Madonnas. To be compared to Nihâl Chand's Bani Thani . . . Well, it was as much a compliment as an insult.

"Shall we see if your skills are as impressive as your beauty?"

He had his servants produce each of the weapons I'd been training with for eight years: matchlock muskets, knives, bows, swords, rifles, pistols, axes, and daggers. Targets were set up around the courtyard, and I was asked to pick my favorite weapon first. I knew immediately—the Dewan's teak bow. It was inlaid with ebony and polished to a very high sheen. I'd only seen a bow this beautiful once before, when my father had gotten a commission from a very wealthy merchant who wanted an impressive dowry gift for his daughter. But even though I knew I'd be choosing the bow, I hesitated in front of each weapon: I wanted to give the Dewan the impression that I was exceptional with all of them and was simply having a hard time making up my mind. Finally, I picked up the bow. I slung the leather quiver over my shoulder, then stood in front of the small, white target across the courtyard and knocked my first arrow. Father always made me practice with different bows, so I had no difficulty adjusting to the Dewan's weapon.

I could feel the eyes of all those present watching me shoot one, two, then three arrows squarely into the target. And I heard the women behind me cheer when the final arrow pierced my very first shot, shattering the wooden shaft. I will admit to feeling some smugness then. I desperately wanted to see the Dewan's face. Instead, I turned, and with my eyes modestly pointed to the ground, laid the weapon before him.

"The pistol," he said. It was impossible to tell from his voice whether he was pleased or simply bored.

I was tested on each of the remaining weapons in rapid succession. I performed well and I'm sure every person in that courtyard was watching me with at least some degree of fascination since they had only known me as Sita the girl, not Sita the warrior. Then it was time for the interview. I am ready for this, I thought as I took my place between Father and Shivaji before the Dewan. Ask me anything.

But the Dewan was silent. When I risked a glimpse at his face, his expression was inscrutable. Was that good or bad? And why were his men quiet, shifting from foot to foot in the heat without saying a word?

"Tell me," the Dewan said at last. "Are these the men who trained you for the role of a guard in Her Highness's Durga Dal?"

"Yes, Dewan-ji. Pita-ji, and our neighbor, the honorable Shivaji."

"Repeat that in English."

I did as I was told, and the Dewan seemed satisfied.

"Would you die for the rani?" he asked suddenly.

"Yes."

"Your preferred weapon is the bow and arrow, is that right?"

"It is."

"To whom would you owe your allegiance in Jhansi Palace if you were brought there tomorrow?"

My heart soared. Shivaji had prepared for this. I answered, "The rani."

The Dewan picked up his pipe and inhaled. When he exhaled, he snapped his fingers and three of his servants stepped forward. Two of them had eyes made up with kohl and were wearing women's dupattas over their hair. The Dewan's men laughed, but no one from our village smiled. I knew they were wondering: is this what men do in Jhansi; dress like women with bells on their ankles and bangles on their wrists?

"One day," the Dewan said, and I realized that he was narrating a story, "you find yourself in a room with the Rani of Jhansi."

One of the men dressed in a woman's dupatta stepped into the empty space between the Dewan and myself. Again, the men around him snickered.

"Also in the room is the maharaja's mother."

The second man dressed as a woman joined his friend and gave a little bow.

"I am there as well."

The final man, wearing a loose yellow turban like the Dewan, stepped into the center and pretended to look official.

"Suddenly, an intruder enters the palace!"

A servant I hadn't noticed, dressed entirely in black, jumped into the center of the group and all three servants pretended to be shocked.

"There is only one pistol in the room with which to defend ourselves," the Dewan said. "To whom do you give it?"

A murmur spread throughout the courtyard, and the Dewan's men exchanged knowing looks. They had heard this question before. The obvious answer, of course, was the rani. But then what about the maharaja's mother? Didn't she outrank everyone in the room? Or the Dewan himself? Surely, he would think he deserved the glory of defending the royal family.

It was almost noon and the sun was high. Sweat began to trickle down my back. I glanced at the villagers around me, who sipped mango juice from our terra-cotta cups, completely indifferent about whether or not I passed the trial. I was the day's entertainment. Next to me, Shivaji cleared his throat. He was nervous, and suddenly I realized why. He had given me the wrong advice.

"No one gets the pistol," I said, and there was a murmur of surprise throughout the courtyard.

The Dewan sat forward on his cushion. "Why not?"

"Because I would keep it."

From the corners of my eyes, I could see the villagers shaking their heads. But the Dewan's men were completely silent.

"You wouldn't give it to the rani?" he asked.

"No."

He put down his pipe, and now there was real interest in his eyes. "Explain."

"What would she need with a pistol when she has me to protect her? Isn't that what I'm in her chamber to do?"

The Dewan sat back on his cushion and smiled. "Sita Bhosale from Barwa Sagar," he said, "be prepared to journey with me to Jhansi by sunrise."

Before dawn the next morning we performed a small puja in our home, and Father presented me with four new angarkhas and two pairs of nagra slippers. Aunt placed each item in the carved wooden chest I'd be taking with me, and suddenly I felt the overwhelming urge to cry. What if it was years before I returned to Barwa Sagar? Or if the rani didn't allow her Durgavasi to visit their families at all? No one could tell me what Jhansi would be like. It was an entire day's journey from our village, and even Father, who had traveled all the way to Burma in his youth, had never been to the raja's palace.

I rose before our image of Durga, and each face around our puja room told a different story. Aunt and her husband were smiling and hopeful, Father was proud yet sad, Grandmother was critical, my sister was devastated.

Father crossed the room and took my hand. For a while, he simply held it in his. Then finally, he opened my palm and wrote, "You will be deeply, deeply missed. But I am proud, Sita." He placed my hand on his heart, then reached out and touched the peacock pendant he had carved for me and mouthed, "Like bamboo. Bend but don't break."

The Dewan's servant knocked on our door, and we heard him announce that a horse was waiting. Just as Grandmother had predicted, I would be riding for Jhansi on a horse with a sword in my belt. Purdah would never apply to me again.

Anu cried, "Don't go! Please, don't go!" She wrapped herself around my waist as my wooden chest was carried out to be loaded onto the back of an oxcart.

I glanced at Grandmother, who was smiling strangely. Then she laughed. "You didn't think she was going to stay here with you forever? Sita has one loyalty," she told her. "To herself."

"Anu, don't listen to her," I told her. "I'll be back before you even realize it."

"When?"

"I don't know. But I promise."

We walked out into the courtyard, and the Dewan's men watched as I mounted a dapple-gray horse with an English saddle. Peacocks scattered around us as the horse snorted and stomped in response.

"Just one more day!" Anu pleaded.

The Dewan's men smiled, no doubt thinking about their own daughters, but I'm sure I saw the Dewan's lips thin in disapproval.

I untied my favorite blue muretha from my forehead and held it out to her. "Keep this for me until I return," I said.

She reached up for my gift and clung to it tightly. Then she nodded, and it was Father's turn for farewell.

By the time we rode out, the lump in my throat had grown so large I could hardly swallow.

Even though it felt like a great betrayal to my grief, I would be lying if I said I wasn't excited to see the world beyond my tiny village. Men lined the roads to see our glittering procession go by, and from behind the wooden screens of temples and houses, I could feel the eyes of Barwa Sagar's women watching as we passed. Riding next to the Dewan, I felt like a bird at the head of a great flock. I knew there were those who believed I was a *veshya*—a common prostitute—for riding out uncovered and breaking purdah, but no one made anything but sounds of approval as we went by: I was someone of importance now.

As we left the village with its buildings of burnt brick and stone behind, the landscape began to change. An expanse of cornfields filled the horizon, and waves of golden heads bobbed in the early morning breeze. The men joked with one another as we rode, but no one spoke to me. Slender fingers of sunlight were beginning to move across the horizon, and as they did, boys began appearing in the fields, the strings of bells on the necks of their cattle making high, prayerful sounds. People were preparing for another long day of work, but as they caught sight of our procession, they stopped what they were doing to watch us pass. Boys jogged alongside us, offering us juice from mud cups. "It's a girl!" some of them cried when they saw me, and then there was a great deal of giggling.

I'm sure that for the Dewan and his men, none of these things seemed particularly interesting. But I had only left the confines of my courtyard very few times in my life, and for me everything was exhilarating: the variety of flowers that grew alongside the roads, the spice markets, the temples . . . No woman in my family had seen these things for hundreds of years.

By noon the ride became hot. The dirt roads shimmered in the heat, and I regretted giving Anu my muretha. The Dewan shifted uncomfortably in his saddle. Then, without warning, he shouted, "Lunch!" and the entire procession came to a stop. The men tethered their horses beneath the shade of several banyan trees, and half a dozen servants became incredibly busy producing cushions, teakettles, cups, bowls, and jars filled with rice, vegetables, and sweets. I was given a red cushion next to the Dewan, and a servant handed me a handsome brass bowl for my lentils and fried okra. We also ate gajar halwa, and I immediately thought of my sister, since carrots and almonds were two of her favorite foods.

When the meal was finished, the Dewan's men began breaking off sticks from a nearby neem tree. Then they lay back on the grass, their heads propped up against their silk cushions, and began to brush their teeth. In Barwa Sagar, we used such sticks once in the morning and once at night. So one thing, at least, would be the same in Jhansi.

"Chess?" the Dewan asked. "According to your father's letter, you play."

A handsome chessboard was produced from a carved wooden case. We waited quietly while the pieces were arranged, and I could honestly hear my heart beating in my ears. Chess was invented in eastern India more than one thousand years ago, but few have truly ever mastered it. What would the Dewan do if I lost? Could he still change his mind about me?

I can recall the dryness in my mouth as I moved the white pieces across the board, and how difficult it suddenly felt to breathe. It was the first game of chess I had ever played with someone other than Shivaji or Father. We played for a while until the Dewan—who held his chin throughout the game as though he was trying to keep it above water—suddenly snapped his head down when he realized that I had checkmated him.

"She beat me," he said, as though witnessing a miracle. Then he repeated it, as if saying the words again made the fact less unbelievable. "She beat me. She's a master!"

You should know this wasn't actually the case; that a great number of his men probably lost to him on purpose, giving him a much greater sense of his own abilities than he actually had. But everyone around us nodded eagerly, and I felt I could finally breathe again.

As soon as we remounted and were back on the hot, dusty road, I wondered if the Dewan would tell the other women in the Durga Dal of my "mastery." It would make them want to test me. This was not how I wanted to begin my life in the palace, and my mood sank. Then, in the distance, the city of Jhansi rose like a white and gold mountain from the banks of the Pahuj River. It was unlike anything I had ever seen: the entire city was spread out like a vast white blanket beneath the sun. My sour mood disappeared and every worry I had slipped from my mind like sand from a sieve.

The Dewan noticed my reaction. "It's a magnificent sight, even for those of us who have seen it many times."

As we rode closer, I saw buildings that towered four and five stories high. I was mesmerized. Beyond the city of Jhansi itself, the whitewashed facade of Raja Gangadhar's fortress rose like a white heron from the hills.

Our horses passed through the city gates, and if you can picture an anthill, with thousands of ants scurrying back and forth, well, that's what the city looked like to me. People were everywhere. Not the kind you see in a village, walking barefoot in dhoti and carrying sticks. These were people in the finest cottons and silks, wearing heavy gold earrings and belts of precious stones. And everywhere I looked, there were *women*. They strolled by themselves or in groups, and no one paid any more attention to them than if they were leaves blown about by the wind.

"Make way for the Dewan!" a man began to shout as we pressed forward. We were sharing the road with pigs, goats, and cows that wandered aimlessly—just as they do in India today. Still, the streets were immaculate. The Dewan said they were swept clean by a team of men three times a day and once at night.

Hundreds of stone urns lined the road, bursting with red and yellow flowers. And there were so many trees! Some bore fruit, but most were Palash trees, spangled with red and orange blossoms and bright as a monsoon sunset. Shakespeare would have had a difficult time describing the streets of Jhansi as they existed in my youth, they were that beautiful. Shops of every kind also lined the narrow streets. One caught my eye with a blue and gold sign above the window that read, BOOKS: HINDI, MARATHI, ENGLISH. I was a blade of grass next to a soaring peepal tree. There was almost too much to see.

Monkeys jumped from rooftop to rooftop, following our long procession, hoping for a handout. Women followed our horses as well, offering up baskets of silk from Murshidabad, conch bangles from Goa, bright cloth from Dhaka. "One rupee!" the bangle woman cried. I shook my head, staring in astonishment. What would Grandmother say if she could see this?

We passed through the city and continued on to the raja's fortress on the hillside. When we came upon it, I saw it was protected by high granite walls that were pierced by ten gates, each large enough—according to the Dewan—for an elephant to pass through. We approached one of their enormous gates and guards dressed in the red and gold colors of the city of Jhansi immediately stepped aside to let us pass. We rode down a cobbled avenue in single file, then the Dewan held up his hand and the procession came to a halt. We had stopped in front of a grand building that the Dewan announced was the rani's Panch Mahal. This palace would be my new home. It was a building of light and air; the high, arched windows and sweeping balconies were visions out of fairy tales.

A woman a full head taller than me stepped out from the doorway holding a silver tray in her hand. Her hair was pulled back from her face in a tight braid, and she was wearing the most extraordinary red angarkha I had ever seen—a combination of gold thread and light silk that looked extremely comfortable even in the terrible heat.

The Dewan dismounted and indicated that I should do the same. He said, "This is the girl. Sita Bhosale of Barwa Sagar."

The tall woman stepped forward and bowed at the waist. Then she performed a welcome ceremony, circling her tray with its oil lamp over my head. She dipped her thumb into the little bowl of sandalwood paste, making a tilak on my forehead. Then she took several moments to look at me. She had small wrinkles around her eyes and strands of silver hair in her thick braid. I could see that the muscles of her arms were sleek, like a cat's, and her eyes were the golden shade of a cat's as well.

She put down her tray and turned to the Dewan, who was

holding his yellow turban in his hands. "Thank you, Dewan, for discovering our newest member. The rani is eager to meet her, but first, I should think this girl is quite tired from her ride."

"Please give Her Highness my highest regards," the Dewan said, bowing.

The Dewan wished me luck. Then he and his men took their leave and the woman with the cat's eyes introduced herself. She was Sundari, the leader of Her Highness's Durga Dal. She said I was not to call any of my fellow members "Didi," as you would call a respectable woman back home; I was to use their real names. The sole exception was the rani, who was to be referred to only as Her Highness, although her husband called her Lakshmi, and her best childhood friends—Tatya Tope and Nana Saheb—called her Manu. "Tatya Tope is the son of an important nobleman," Sundari said. "And now he's Saheb's most trusted general." Saheb's father, of course, was Peshwa Baji Rao, whose throne had been taken by the British years earlier.

"We bow whenever we greet the rani in the morning, and again at night when we leave her in her chambers. She is in her fourth month of pregnancy and sleeps for most of the afternoon, but in the mornings and evenings, we are all expected to entertain her. You should know that she doesn't tolerate foolishness. She's twenty-three and a practical woman. Her father raised her as a son, and her favorite escape from tediousness is chess."

I felt the color drain from my face.

Sundari continued. "You must be very clever if the Dewan felt strongly enough to bring you from a village. There is only one other village girl here: her name is Jhalkari. She has made a positive impression on the rani. I hope we can expect the same from you. The rani won't hesitate to dismiss anyone from her service if she feels they are wanting."

"I will not be a disappointment," I said.

Sundari stepped into the cool entryway of the palace and I followed. A pair of guards bowed first to her and then to me. No man had ever bowed to me before. With every step I took, I was entering not just a new world, but also a new life. She slipped her feet out of her embroidered juṭi and I did the same. Then two servants appeared to place our shoes into a long cupboard. If I live to be a hundred years, I doubt I will ever forget the first time I felt plush carpeting beneath my feet. Not even the wealthiest man in our village had carpets in his home.

We passed several doorways draped with long, airy curtains that stirred slightly in the breeze. Beyond them, I could see the faint outlines of men, some of them talking, others arguing. I've heard people describe Svarga, the equivalent of heaven, as a place of unparalleled beauty. Well, the Panch Mahal in its glory, with its jasmine-scented chambers and its high, arched windows overlooking the raja's flowering gardens, is what I believe Svarga to look like.

When we finally reached the farthest end of the hall, I saw a flight of stairs.

"The raja lives on the second floor," Sundari explained, "and his Durbar Hall, where guests and officials are met, is on the fourth. The rani visits the Durbar Hall once a day, always after her nap. She is sleeping right now, so this is a good time for you to become familiar with the palace."

Sundari stopped in front of a wide door hung with gauzy curtains. Here, in the fresh light of the nearby window, the silver strands in her hair appeared white, as if someone had taken chalk and traced thin lines over her scalp. "You are the tenth member of Her Highness's Durga Dal," she said before we entered, "which means there are eight other women here who are extremely competitive and hope to take my position. The servants who wait on us were all once members, and are now retired. I suggest you treat them accordingly, because some day that will be your fate. No one is guaranteed a long career as a guard, so be careful what you tell the women in this room. The Dewan said you have a sister?"

"Yes."

"Does she hope to become a member as well?"

"No. Whatever I earn here will be used for her dowry fortune. She is almost nine, and my family wants her to marry."

Sundari's eyebrows rose like a pair of startled birds. "That's not much time to save a dowry fortune." She pushed aside the curtains and we entered the largest chamber I had ever been inside. The ceiling was carved and painted in gold, while the walls gleamed like polished eggshells, and were just as smooth. A fountain splashed musically in the center, while a dozen yellow cushions were arranged around its base, nearly all of them occupied by women dressed in the most elegant angarkhas I had ever seen. Instead of the simple knee-length tunic that I was wearing, these were full-skirted ones sewn from silk and elaborately tied at the waist. And whereas I smelled of horses and dirt, these women smelled of jasmine blossoms and roses. They stood as soon as they saw us, and I counted seven. Sundari must have been counting, too, because her face took on a very stern expression and she said, "Where is Kahini?"

"In the garden," the shortest girl said. She had the round, bright face of a pearl and wore a beautiful angarkha of deep purple and gold.

"Please bring her here to the queen's room, Moti."

The girl left the room, and I wondered if Moti was really her name or just a nickname someone had given her, since in Hindi, it means pearl.

The other women gathered around me.

"This is Sita Bhosale from Barwa Sagar," Sundari said, "and I expect she will be treated the same as those of you from this city."

"Are you truly from a village?" one of the women asked.

Someone else said, "We heard you speak English."

The comments were coming so quickly that I didn't have time to answer a single one before Moti returned with the woman from the garden, and a kind of hush fell over the group.

Kahini was stunning. To this day, I have never seen such an exquisite face. Her features were so precise and sharp they might have been carved from alabaster. She was dressed in a blue silk angarkha and close-fitting churidars. Both pieces were trimmed in silver and delicately painted with images of open lotus blossoms. Her hair was divided into four dark braids that were twisted together, her ankles and wrists were ornamented with small, silver bells, and around her neck was a delicate turquoise and silver necklace.

"So you are the new guardswoman," she said, and her voice was devoid of either welcome or criticism, like an empty pot waiting to be filled.

"This is Sita Bhosale of Barwa Sagar," Sundari repeated. "One of you must show Sita to the Durgavas, and then to the maidan. Who wishes to do this?"

"I will," Kahini said.

There was a pregnant silence, as if no one had expected her to offer.

Sundari hesitated. "Fine."

The other women immediately backed away, and I wondered if Kahini held some sort of special status in the Durga Dal.

"Come," she said with a smile.

The women parted before us, and I followed Kahini across the queen's room into a long hall painted with images of birds. The artist had taken care to render each bird in its common habitat. There were peacocks strutting across marble courtyards and egrets feeding near shallow lakes. "We'll go to the Durgavas first," Kahini said. Then she stopped beneath a painting of a heron. "You do know what the Durgavas is?"

I shook my head, and felt my cheeks flush.

"No one has told you how the guardswomen live?"

I'm sure if the roots of my hair could have turned red, they would have, too. "We get very little information about Jhansi in my village."

"Of course," Kahini said pityingly. "Which village did Sundari say you were from?"

"Barwa Sagar."

"That's north?"

"South."

Her smile was so brief that I might have imagined it. "Well, the Durgavas is nothing more glamorous than a room with ten beds. Our servants sleep outside this room on the floor."

"The former members of the Durga Dal," I said, repeating what Sundari had told me.

"Yes. Although the members of the Durga Dal who become leaders are given estates of their own with handsome pensions."

"So Sundari-ji will be given an estate when she retires?"

"As will the woman who takes her place." Kahini stopped outside of a curtained doorway and regarded me. "We are all aiming for the same thing."

"And how does the rani choose the leader?"

Kahini allowed herself a full smile, and a row of perfectly white teeth flashed against her red lips. "Humility." She pushed back the curtains and stepped inside.

Ten beds, with fluffy mattresses and massive wooden frames, lined the frescoed walls of the Durgavas. I followed Kahini across the room, and when she stopped in front of the last bed near the wall, I immediately reached out to touch it. It was something fit for a maharaja.

"Certainly you've seen a bed before," Kahini said.

"No. I sleep on a charpai at home."

"Well then, you're going to be quite surprised when you see the Durbar Hall. Though I doubt you'll see it today. The rani hasn't gone at all this week; she spends most of her afternoons praying to Durga to keep her from the sick bowl. Which is too bad, because soon she'll be as fat as a sow and unable to walk anywhere."

I covered my mouth with my hand. I had never heard anyone talk about a pregnant woman this way, much less the Rani of Jhansi.

"Oh, you don't have to pretend to be shocked. It's the truth, and I tell it to the rani herself."

"She doesn't get angry?"

"Perhaps. But she values my honesty."

"And humility," I offered.

"Yes." She sat on the bed, and I tried to look as elegant as she did while doing something as simple as taking a seat. "Honesty is an extremely important quality to the rani. Pay attention to what she wears," she said. Then she lowered her voice, as if what she was about to say was a secret. "Most days, her only jewelry is a plain pearl necklace and pearl carrings."

"What must she think of your jewelry, then?"

Kahini sat back to get a better look at me. "Only the rani shows her humility in her dress. *We* are expected to show it in our actions. If you noticed, the women in the rani's room were all dressed in silk saris." She glanced at my traveling chest, made from old wood and tarnished silver buckles. "You packed a few yourself, certainly?"

I owned nothing made from silk. Just two new kurtas and the best juti my father could afford. "No."

"Oh." Then with forced cheer, she added, "I'm sure the other guards will let you borrow a few things until you purchase better clothes."

A knot formed in my stomach as I thought of how much silk would cost. "But how is silk evidence of humility?"

"It isn't. But we can't go around the palace looking like we belong in a village market, can we? The rani is allowed to look humble because she is the rani. We are merely her servants." There was an edge in her voice as she said this. Then she stood and said, "And now I will show you the maidan."

I followed her out the door into an open courtyard. A multitude of flowers poured like brightly colored waterfalls from the urns, and a fountain splashed musically beneath the sun. But I didn't allow myself to be distracted. I was focused, like a point of intense light, on whatever Kahini was about to tell me. We turned down a narrow lane, and the people who passed us pressed their palms together in a respectful gesture of namaste. Most of them Kahini ignored.

"Tomorrow," she said as we walked, "you'll be asked to watch us practice. It would be a great mistake to look too confident when you're asked to join us. Remember—in all things, humility."

"How does a person look humble while practicing archery?"

"By not immediately accepting the offer to join us. And when Sundari-ji insists, telling her you are too unskilled to accompany us."

I was thankful that Kahini had offered to accompany me on this tour; I doubted the other women would have taken the time to give such advice. "Will the raja be there as well?"

"Gangadhar-ji?" she said, using his real name. "No. He'll be at his theater." Then we stopped when we reached a large grassy field, at which point Kahini announced, "The maidan."

It was a wide, open space bordered on one side by a flagstone courtyard and on the other by barracks that housed, I'd learn later, the raja's soldiers. This was where I would prove my fitness as a member of the Durga Dal, change my destiny, and change Anuja's life for the better.

"Seen enough?" Kahini asked. "It's about to rain."

I looked up. The blue sky was indeed vanishing behind a blanket of clouds. It seemed impossible that just a few hours ago I'd been standing in Father's courtyard. And yet my journey still wasn't over: I had to meet the rani.

I followed Kahini on the short walk between the maidan and the Panch Mahal. When we reached the courtyard and Kahini paused to straighten her dupatta, I stared at the stones beneath our feet. They were the soft color of sanded teak. In my village there was no floor so exquisite; not even in our temple to Shiva.

As soon as we returned to the queen's room, Sundari announced that the rani was too ill to be escorted to the Durbar Hall that day. Kahini gave me a pointed look, then retired to one of the cushions around the fountain. After Sundari left the room, I was on my own. Still standing, I watched as four of the women played pachisi. Two more were playing a game of chess. A pretty girl of nineteen or twenty with an oval face and a fair complexion motioned for me to sit next to her in the corner. "It was all new to me when I arrived here as well," she said.

"You aren't from Jhansi?"

"Kahini didn't tell you?" She looked surprised. "I thought that would be the first thing she'd reveal. I'm a Dalit from a village even smaller than yours. My name's Jhalkari."

You may remember how I told you that people are divided into four groups by birth: Brahmins, Kshatriyas, Vaishyas, and Shudras. Well, at the very bottom of those castes—so low they're never even mentioned—are the Dalits, or Untouchables. A Dalit is born to perform jobs that are spiritually unclean: anything from washing toilets to preparing the dead. You might go your entire life without ever speaking to someone from this caste. So to be sitting on the same cushion as one—even to be speaking to one—well, no one in Barwa Sagar would have believed it. I found myself holding my breath, in case the air she breathed was being tainted.

I know this must sound as ridiculous to you as it does to me now. But understand that this is how it has been for thousands of years, from the time the *Purusha suktas* were written and the concept of castes were laid out. All sorts of superstitions revolve around Dalits: they can turn your milk sour with a look, to touch one is the same as touching filth, and to speak to them is an act that might displease the gods. A person doesn't become a Dalit: they are born one as a punishment for a great misdeed they have committed in a previous life. It is all a part of samsara—the karmic wheel that never stops.

You have heard, no doubt, of the famous Lao Tzu, who lived fifteen hundred years ago in our neighboring kingdom of China. He said: "Watch your thoughts; they become words. Watch your words; they become actions. Watch your actions; they become habit. Watch your habits; they become character. Watch your character; it becomes your destiny." Because most Hindus believe this is true, you can see why they also think that Dalits deserve their desperate situations. Their past actions have shaped their characters, which now shape their current destinies.

Of course, some people believe this is nonsense. The Rani of Jhansi was one of them. When I came to know her, I learned that she thought dividing society into differing castes was the same as dividing a tree into different parts and pretending that the leaf is better than the trunk. How can the leaf exist without the trunk, or the other way around? "Certainly, there is karma," I once heard her say, "and Lao Tzu was right. But our punishments for bad acts in previous lives are created internally, not externally. We punish ourselves with bad choices."

At the time I was sitting with Jhalkari, however, I had never heard of Lao Tzu, much less talked of spiritual matters with the rani. I was simply stunned that no one else in the queen's room seemed appalled that Jhalkari and I were sharing the same cushion.

"I'm the first Dalit you've ever spoken to," Jhalkari said.

"Yes," I said truthfully. "But I did very little speaking to anyone, so that's not so unusual."

Nothing bad was happening. We were talking, just as you would talk to anyone else.

"Some of the women here," she said loudly, "aren't comfortable being close to me, even though I could be the rani's sister, we look so similar. I bathe in the same water, I eat the same food, I sleep in a similar bed. But because I was born of Dalit parents, I must somehow be tainted."

I'm ashamed to admit that I didn't know then whether or not this was true, so I kept my silence. Jhalkari could see how uncomfortable she was making me, so she changed the subject.

"While the rani is sleeping, we are free to relax," she told me. "Listen to music."

I could hear someone playing the veena outside, but I felt too tense to enjoy the sound.

Soon, Sundari reappeared with a woman dressed in a green Chanderi sari that fell in thick folds across her waist. Aside from a simple pearl necklace and a small diamond ring, she wore no other jewels. But I knew she was our queen because she bore such a striking resemblance to Jhalkari. Their features were nearly identical, from their perfectly oval faces to their bow-shaped lips, and long, straight noses. It was astonishing: a Dalit and a queen looked enough alike to be sisters.

I rose immediately, and the others did the same. When the rani approached us, I followed Jhalkari's example by pressing my hands together in a respectful gesture of namaste.

"Sita Bhosale of Barwa Sagar," she said. "Look at me. Never be afraid to look your rani in the face. I'm not a goddess."

I did as I was instructed, then waited for her to say something.

"Sundari was right. She's an excellent reader of faces, and she told me that yours was very guarded. You don't give up your secrets easily, do you?"

Once again, she waited for me to say something. I kept my silence.

The rani chuckled. "Has anyone introduced you to the other women?"

"Your Highness. I have met Sundari, Kahini, and Jhalkari."

The rani clapped her hands and the women I hadn't named fell into a half circle around us. "This is Moti."

The woman who had collected Kahini earlier nodded.

"This is Heera." With the thick, beautiful braids.

"This is Priyala." I tried to think of some detail to remember her by, but nothing came to mind. Perhaps that she was thin?

"Kashi." She had a sweet and innocent smile.

"Mandar." Who looked like a man.

"And Rajasi." With the face of a horse.

I folded my hands once more in namaste. "It is an honor to be here."

Rajasi gave Kahini a meaningful look, and I wondered if I had already made some mistake.

"We are going to the Mahalakshmi Temple now to feed the poor," the rani said. "Find something more suitable to wear when we go tomorrow; I'm sure one of these women will let you borrow something if you have nothing in silk."

Several women nodded. One of them was Jhalkari.

"Yes, Your Highness."

"I suppose you are tired from your journey today, Sita?"

"Only a little."

"Then join us."

I wasn't asked to bring any of the weapons I saw the other women carrying beneath the belts of their angarkhas. But there was a dagger tucked into a thin sheath beneath my tunic. I would be able to do my duty if someone was foolish enough to attack our pregnant rani along the way.

Sundari and Kahini walked ahead of the queen, while Heera and Priyala walked on each side of her. I took a place at her back. Servants had appeared to shield us from the rain falling in thick gray sheets outside. But even with their umbrellas, the hems of my pants became mud-soaked the moment we filed out the door. As I looked to see what other women were doing, Moti fell into step beside me.

"Wait until we get to the temple," she said. "The rani's cooks prepare the best imerti for the poor. You'll never have tasted anything like them."

"What are imerti?"

Moti's big eyes grew even bigger. "You've never had imerti?" She turned to Jhalkari, who was walking next to her. Neither of them seemed to notice how wet the legs of their pants had become. "You ate imerti in your village, didn't you?"

Any time someone was uneducated about something, they obviously turned to Jhalkari for help. Because if Jhalkari had done it—an ignorant Dalit girl from an ignorant village—well then, everyone must have.

"Outside of Jhansi, women are in purdah." Jhalkari's voice sounded thin. "There aren't many occasions to eat imerti when your world is confined to the walls of your house."

Moti slowed her pace to match mine. "So you never went outside?" she asked me.

"A few times. But only in a palanquin."

"Then this must be absolutely overwhelming."

"Which part?" Jhalkari answered for me. "The torrential rain or the beautiful sites?" As Jhalkari said this, we crossed in front of the elephants' stables. The mahouts were sweeping out the stalls and piling dung into giant heaps, which they would probably burn once the rain was finished. I tried not to laugh, but Jhalkari met my gaze, and I couldn't help it.

"Sita understood what I meant," Moti said. "Didn't you?"

"Yes. I had a very small life, but I was able to make it much bigger with books."

If you have ever met someone who rarely reads, then you will understand the blank look Moti gave me. For nonreaders, life is simply what they touch and see, not what they feel when they open the pages of a play and are transported to the Forest of Arden or Illyria. Where the world is full of a thousand colors for those who love books, I suspect it is simply black and gray to everyone else. A tree is a tree to them; it is never a magical doorway to another world populated with beings that don't exist here.

We crossed an avenue filled with shops selling coffee and tea, and a pair of English women passed by us. Their umbrellas were prettier than any I'd ever seen, and their skin was as thin and pale as moonlight.

"Foreigners," Moti said when she saw the direction of my gaze.

I wanted to stare after them, but suddenly—several steps from a stall selling holy necklaces made from mango beads—we were at the Temple of Mahalakshmi. It stood on the shore of a Mahalakshmi Lake, surrounded by peepal trees that provided a nearly perfect cover from the rain. The servants lowered their umbrellas, and we left our wet juti on the marble steps.

"Mahalakshmi is the royal family's deity," Jhalkari said as we entered. "No other goddess is as revered by the rani. Not even Durga."

Inside, the temple walls glowed like burning embers. They were made from amber and teak, and every time an oil lamp was lit the entire room gleamed. I tried not to stare at the other patrons, but most of them were so poor they couldn't afford proper kurtas or dhoti. And their smell in the hot, sticky rain was overwhelming.

We spent nearly an hour standing behind a long wooden table, helping to oversee the distribution of food. I was astonished to see how familiar the rani was with the people of Jhansi: you would have thought she had known them all of her life, although she had become their queen only nine years before. They bowed to her and made respectful gestures of namaste, but they also looked into her eyes and made jokes. One of them had the audacity to say that in another few months, the rani would be as round as the imerti she was serving. I held my breath when the old man said this. Who knew what happened to people who dared to be overly familiar with a queen—prison? Execution? A fine?

But the rani tossed back her head and laughed. She thought it was funny.

"You shouldn't encourage them," Kahini said after the man had passed.

"Why not?" the rani said. "It's true." At this, she looked down at her stomach and patted it fondly. "I've waited nine long years for this. Looking like an imerti will be a blessing."

I turned for an explanation to Sundari, who was standing next to me with a giant ladle and helping to serve *daal*, but her expression didn't change.

"Is Gangadhar-ji also so intimate with his subjects?" I asked.

Sundari glanced at the rani, then lowered her serving ladle. "Who told you to use the raja's name?"

"No one." My heart beat baster. "I heard Kahini—"

"She is the raja's cousin. What she is allowed to call him is her business. For everyone else, he is His Highness. The raja."

I looked over at the rani, but she was talking to someone new and hadn't heard me. "Of course." I was so humiliated that I forgot what it was I had been asking. "I'm sorry."

"Be careful. The rani does not abide anyone who is overconfident."

So it was exactly as Kahini said.

"Let me explain something to you," she added. "Every day, the rani wakes at six to start her morning prayers and then watches us while we are on the maidan. Before her pregnancy, she would practice with us as well. After we return, she bathes, and then we all attend puja. Afterward, we read, she has a nap, then we accompany her to the Durbar Hall and she eventually makes her way here. When we return to the Panch Mahal, we have the evening meal and some entertainment. Then we sleep and the next day begins again at six. The rani is a firm believer in routine. It's never altered." Then she said, "The rani is very predictable. The raja, however, is not. Only Kahini is allowed to call him by his name, and that is because they grew up in the same house."

I lowered my head, and I couldn't have felt worse if I had just offended the rani herself. I spent the rest of our time in the temple in silence.

When we were finished, we retrieved our juti on the marble steps. The evening rain had gone, and as we walked, the puddles were bathed in the glow of oil lamps hanging from the eaves of every building. The walk to the temple had been downhill; we now had to walk uphill, but without the rain, it was a much more pleasant task. I suppose everyone was lost in her own thoughts, because no one spoke.

When we reached the Panch Mahal, I stood in the courtyard for a moment and looked out beyond the gates and over the city. In the light of the setting sun, the houses were bathed in pools of gold and purple shadow. Somewhere below I knew there was a sign that read, BOOKS: HINDI, MARATHI, ENGLISH. Books never led to trouble the way interacting with people did, and you couldn't be overly familiar with them. I wished I could afford something from that shop.

"Are you coming inside?" Jhalkari asked.

I followed the other women back into the queen's room. Bowls of soup had been laid out at a low wooden table. I took a place on an empty cushion next to Jhalkari while servants brought in trays of steaming rice, curries made with green chilies and coriander, and vegetables cooked in heavy sauces. I wanted to savor it all, especially the fruit, which came last. But the meal was cut short since the rani wasn't hungry. Afterward—because of what Sundari had said—I anticipated that the rani would ask one of us to read aloud, or perhaps call for court musicians. Instead, she announced that she had a meeting to attend.

"At this hour?" Kahini said.

"Nana Saheb has come with Tatya Tope and Azimullah Khan. They're only staying for the night. We have news to discuss."

Kahini made a dismissive noise in her throat, which seemed tremendously disrespectful to me. "Important news? Did Saheb's favorite tailor die?"

The rani gave Kahini a very sharp look. "I'll remind you Saheb is the son of the Peshwa."

"Who lost his crown to the British before he could teach his son anything of use."

"That's enough." But the rani didn't really seem angry.

"I'll bet he is wearing more gold than you are," Kahini predicted.

"Are we to accompany you?" Sundari asked.

"No. I'll make my own way to the Durbar Hall," the rani said.

Kahini's face remained neutral until the rani left. Then she rose from her cushion and exclaimed, "What kind of news would suddenly demand a private meeting?"

"The rani is free to do as she wishes," Sundari said.

"And we are her Durgavasi! We're here to protect her."

"From what?" Mandar arranged her masculine features into a scowl. "Her closest childhood friends?"

But Kahini would not leave it alone. "If I was the rani, I would not remain friends with men as ignorant as Azimullah Khan and Tatya Tope."

"Why would you say that?" Sundari demanded.

"I grew up at court. I recognize dangerous men when I see them."

But two hours later, the rani returned looking completely at peace. Nothing dangerous had happened. She was simply tired and ready for bed, so we followed her down the hall, past the Durgavas where my own bed awaited me, to an enormous chamber. The richly paneled walls were painted in blues and whites, but it was the furniture you noticed first. In the flickering light of the hanging lamps, I could see that everything—from the four-poster bed to the elegant dresser and its matching nightstands—had been made from silver. A breeze passed through the room from the gardens outside, and suddenly the room smelled like vetiver. I would discover later that servants took the long kusha grass blinds and soaked them in water so that whenever the wind blew, an aromatic breeze flowed through the chamber.

We stood in a half circle around the rani's bed, and my feet sank nearly ankle-deep into the soft white carpets spread across the room. Sundari drew the silver curtains closed around the bed while the rani changed into her sleeping garment. Then the curtains were opened again and the queen bid us good night. I followed the other women out the door; only Sundari stayed behind. As captain, her job was to sleep on a bed at the entrance of the rani's chamber, while three male guards stayed posted beyond the door.

Inside the Durgavas, I went to the bed that Kahini had shown me earlier in the day and where the chest that my father had given to me was waiting.

"You're my new neighbor," Jhalkari said.

She had the bed next to mine, and while the other women undressed, changing into long, simple kurtas for the night, she sat cross-legged and watched me take out Father's murti: he had packed two mango-wood images for me, wrapping each one tenderly in several layers of cloth. Seeing them made my heart ache for home. It was the first night I had ever spent away from him—from all of them. I looked down at Father's carvings. One was of the warrior goddess Durga riding her tiger. The other was Ganesh, the Remover of Obstacles. I placed the murti on a low wooden table next to my bed, and put Father's chest on the ground below it.

"Tomorrow, after practice," Jhalkari said, "you can borrow one of my silk angarkhas."

"That's very generous of you." I sat on my bed and faced her. "Thank you."

Jhalkari shrugged, and I was struck once again by how similar she looked to the rani. "Someone lent one to me when I came."

"One of the women here?"

"No. She's gone." Jhalkari leaned forward, and her voice grew very low. "She was with one of the soldiers, and the rani doesn't tolerate immorality."

I glanced over her shoulder to see who might be listening, and realized that one of the beds was empty. "Someone is missing."

"Kahini. Didn't you notice?" Jhalkari uncrossed her legs and began to undress. "She left after we ate. She goes to the raja's theater." Jhalkari finished, then lay down on her bed and turned toward me. "She leaves every night."

"And what does the rani think of that?"

"Are you asking if he's taken her as a concubine?"

My cheeks warmed at Jhalkari's bluntness. But I guess that's what I was saying. "Yes."

Jhalkari glanced at Moti, who had risen from her bed to blow out the oil lamps. Jhalkari waited until Moti was across the room before she whispered, "The rani depends on Kahini to keep the raja happy. She is very close to Kahini, because Kahini helps her keep the raja entertained. And entertainment is everything in Jhansi. You'll see."

I wondered what she meant by entertained. I put on one of my kurtas from home and lay down on the mattress. It appeared to have been stuffed with feathers, and nothing had ever felt softer. I watched the remaining lamp make shifting patterns on the ceiling, and thought of how much life was like that light, illuminating one thing at one moment, then casting it into darkness and illuminating something else. A few days ago my greatest concern had been passing the trial and providing for Anuja. Now, I was in a new bed listening to new voices and building new concerns. What if I failed to impress the rani with my skills? Or if the raja took a disliking to me? What if new angarkhas were so expensive that it was impossible to save a dowry fortune for Anuja? I couldn't waste any time: she was growing up fast and no man is interested in taking an old bride.

I should have been exhausted, but my mind was like a spinning top, going around and around in the same circle. So I took out my diary and recorded my impressions of the day. When I was finished, I closed my eyes. I could hear the rhythmic breathing of the other women, but even when I tried to concentrate on that sound, I couldn't find sleep. At some point the door of the Durgavas creaked open and the slim, elegant shadow of Kahini appeared. I listened to the soft tinkling of her silver anklets as she made her way through the darkness to the bed across from mine on the other side of the room. Obviously, the rani had great trust in Kahini if she was allowed to come in so late after entertaining the raja each night.

She slipped her juti under her bed and blew out the last lamp. Then the room was silent, and I was the only one left awake.

Chapter Seven

The next day as I dressed, I watched as the other women retrieved heavy brown packs from beneath their beds. Next to me, Jhalkari made a silent inspection of hers. All of the women possessed identical weapons—leather quivers filled with arrows, polished yew-wood bows, bejeweled swords, silver-handled pistols, and expensive two-handed daggers we call kattari.

I hadn't been given any of these things yet, and I watched with envy as each of the women strapped first their pistols, and then their daggers, to the belts of their angarkhas. The swords, quivers, and bows they carried in the brown packs over their shoulders. No one said anything to me; each Durgavasi prepared for the day in contemplative silence.

After a breakfast of melons and tea, I followed the women outside and then down the hill to the maidan. When we reached the field where Kahini had taken me on a tour the previous day, Sundari instructed me to follow her into a long, thin building nearby. It smelled of dried summer grass and earth. Sundari didn't say a word until we reached a stall at the very end. Then she pointed to a handsome stallion so black he might have been dipped entirely in ink. Only a bright white diamond between his eyes made him distinguishable from the early morning darkness around him. I was told that his name was Sher, which means lion in Hindi.

"And why did they name you that?" I whispered to him, because there was nothing about him that looked like a lion. "It can't be your coat. And it certainly isn't your mane." I reached over the low door to stroke his muzzle. I thought he might shy away from me, but he didn't move. "Maybe it's your brave personality. Is that why?"

I turned and saw that Sundari was there, arms crossed, waiting for me to finish. "You'll be expected to ride six days a week. Sunday is a day of rest," she said. She started to walk. I withdrew my hand and followed her out of the stables. "This is a Christian tradition," she continued, her voice brittle, like dried leaves passing over stones. "The British soldiers insist that no work be done on Sundays."

"There are British soldiers living here?" I asked, glancing at the nearby barracks.

"Not inside the fortress; the British officers live in a cantonment two miles from here. But their decisions are definitely spreading to the Panch Mahal."

I thought of the two foreign women I'd seen on our way to Mahalakshmi Temple and concluded that they'd been officers' wives.

"We train all other mornings," Sundari said, changing the subject. "Shooting, malkhamba, and archery on Mondays, Wednesdays, and Fridays. Swordsmanship and lathi on the remaining days. Today, you will join us for archery. Take a seat next to the rani and watch until then."

On the maidan, the dew felt cool against my toes. Tomorrow, I would remember to wear closed slippers. A short distance away, an open yellow tent had been erected with four large cushions underneath. One cushion was occupied by the rani; two were taken by old men whose eyes were set so deep in their wrinkled faces it was impossible to tell if they were awake or asleep. Sundari led me to the empty cushion, and all three looked up as I approached, but I wasn't introduced. I took my seat quietly, then Sundari left for the field.

"Remember what Prince Arjun was taught by Lord Krishna," one of the old men was saying. His white hair fell in thick waves around his ears. I imagined he'd been very handsome when he was young. "There's a reason for war now if it saves lives in the future."

"I understand all of this, Shri Bakshi. But I'm not convinced that war is inevitable," the rani said.

"Look at their behaviors in other kingdoms," the second man suggested. He was younger than Shri Bakshi, but with less hair and finer teeth. "In which kingdom have they landed where they didn't eventually seek to gain control?"

"Shri Lakshman, I understand all of this," the rani repeated. "But war—"

"Is sometimes the prudent move," Shri Lakshman finished for her.

The rani sighed. She turned her attention to the women on the maidan, and over the next hour, I studied the other Durgavasi's skills. They were adept at archery, but none of them hit the center of the target every time. The bows the women were using were made from yew, which I knew to be extraordinary. One of the wealthiest men in our village once purchased this wood from an Englishman in the British-controlled city of Bombay and chose Father to make a bow with it. My father asked me to test the finished weapon. I was fourteen, and knew that I was using something truly superior. I watched as Rajasi missed her target entirely, and I glanced to my left to see the rani's reaction. She simply raised her eyebrows.

The early morning mist began to roll back to reveal the farthest corners of the maidan. Temple bells sounded from the city below, then the raja's soldiers started pouring out of their barracks like bees from a flooded hive, dressed in the crisp red and gold uniforms that Kahini had said were given to them by the British, who oversaw the raja's army. Some stopped to watch the women practicing. I thought the rani would order them away, but she allowed them to remain. Some of the men stood for fifteen or twenty minutes, taking long, slow drags on cigarettes. Then Sundari ordered more archery targets to be set, and I felt a familiar ache in my hands.

"Sita, come and join us," Sundari said.

The rani and her advisers both turned to me, and I knew what was expected. I immediately rose and pressed my hands together in namaste. "I am deeply honored by your request," I said. "However, I see now that I am not worthy of being in the presence of such skilled women."

Sundari glanced at the rani. "Sita, I am asking you to show the rani your skills," Sundari said. "In fact, I am asking you to show us all. If you would please follow me, I will give you my bow."

But I was determined to do as Kahini said. The other women had moved to the edge of the maidan, and to be sure they all heard, I said loudly, "I was brazen to believe that I could be part of such an elite group. But with your permission, I will endeavor to watch and learn, and when the captain feels I am ready, I will be honored to take a place on the field."

There was a moment of silence. Then the rani spoke.

"The captain feels you are ready now."

"It is a great honor, Your Highness, but I am not ready."

I had done exactly as Kahini had instructed, but like a changing wind, I could sense a shift in the mood on the maidan. Soon the rani was standing.

"Fetch the Dewan who brought this girl here."

Sundari's face reflected deep disappointment, and I could see Jhalkari, standing beside her, shaking her head. It was only then that I realized what Kahini had done.

I willed myself not to cry. But I can tell you that those moments, waiting there under the tent for the Dewan to appear, were the longest of my life. I searched for Kahini on the field, and this time, I saw malice in her perfect face. Yet when our eyes met, she showed no recognition of her role in this.

The Dewan arrived, looking as if someone had woken him from his sleep. When he realized that I was the cause of his early morning disturbance, his brows furrowed. He bowed at the waist before the rani and made the gesture of namaste. Then she took him aside and they conversed for several minutes in quiet tones. During that time, I tried to keep my eyes on the ground, but every so often I would sneak a glance at Sundari, who was now watching me with a curious expression.

After what seemed like an eternity, the rani and the Dewan approached.

"The Dewan swears that this girl is everything he promised," the rani said to Sundari. But it was clear from her tone that she no longer believed him. "He also maintains that she is the best archer he has ever seen. Better than Kahini."

At this, Sundari looked in my direction. "Without excuse."

I bowed as low I could. "Of course. I will take the field at once."

Sundari lent me her bow and quiver. As we walked together toward the maidan, she said in a voice that only I could hear, "The rani says you have three shots. I say you have one. Because nothing will replace this first impression now."

She brought me to the red line in the grass where the other women had been standing. Then she stepped back and I was the only one on the field. Soldiers were gathering to watch, and I became conscious of the fact that I was once again the morning's entertainment.

The yew bow was extremely powerful. Like the others, it was strung with horsehair. A strong arm was necessary to draw it, and I tested it several times before reaching back into the leather quiver and knocking the first arrow. Then something extraordinary happened. Instead of thinking about the target, or the growing number of onlookers, or even the rani, I heard a line from *Richard II* as if Father was reading it to me: *The very beadsmen learn to bend their bows. Of double-fatal yew against thy state.* I have been doing this since I was a child, I thought. There was nothing to fear.

I released the arrow.

It pierced the air and struck the red center of the target with a heavy thud. The second arrow splintered the first, and the third arrow shattered that one. I lowered the bow and turned to see the rani's reaction. She was pleased. Next to her, the Dewan looked relieved. But Kahini turned to make a comment to the horse-faced girl called Rajasi who I knew had repeatedly missed the target entirely during practice.

Sundari approached me. I returned her bow and quiver. "Sundari-ji, I would like to explain—"

"Don't. You are obviously capable," she said, shouldering the bow.

"But Kahini-ji—" I wanted to defend myself.

"You are part of the palace now," she said, stopping me. "I'm sure Kahini said many things on your short tour yesterday. But if you are incapable of telling an enemy from a friend, then it's best to be alone."

I felt like the most ignorant person in Jhansi. What was the matter with me? Living with my grandmother should have taught me that it was important to be wary of everyone.

Sundari strode ahead, and I was left to walk across the maidan behind her. When I reached the other Durgavasi, it was Kahini who spoke.

"Well done," she said, although I could tell she really meant, *Such a shame you didn't fail.* "The rani was about to send you back to your village. I don't suppose you would have had such an audience there." She was looking over my shoulder as she said this, at the throng of soldiers who had watched my three shots.

"And I hear that in these villages," Rajasi added, "the women are all in purdah."

"Yes. And purdah makes relationships with other women extremely important," I said. "There is no room for snakes when all you have is grass to live in."

Rajasi knew she had been insulted. "What is that supposed to mean?"

"You're clever enough to figure it out," Jhalkari said, joining us as we began the walk back to the palace. She fell into step beside me. "Kahini told you to do it, didn't she?"

I didn't say anything. I couldn't tell an enemy from a friend.

"Everyone was surprised when she volunteered yesterday," Jhalkari said. "She must feel threatened by you."

I felt a pang of worry. All of my dreams for Anuja's future depended on my being in the Durga Dal.

"Sundari almost denied her permission when she asked," Jhalkari said, smiling. "You must have seen her hesitate?"

I had, and I should have been quick enough to understand why.

"Please don't judge the rest of us by Kahini," she said. "Kahini and Rajasi are the only snakes in the grass here."

"Then why doesn't Sundari-ji dismiss them?"

Jhalkari's smile thinned as we reached the courtyard. "They're popular with the raja."

"I thought we belonged to the queen."

"And everything that belongs to the queen belongs to him." After a moment she added, "And what belongs to him belongs to the British."

In Barwa Sagar, we took our baths from a bucket. Here, an entire room was dedicated to washing. Thick beams of sunlight pushed their way through billowing curtains, illuminating a smooth marble chamber with long cedar benches and a single, sunken tub of truly enormous proportions.

This was where we went after our practice, so that we could prepare for the afternoon's Durbar Hall. I found it impossible not to look around in amazement.

Following the other women, I swiftly undressed and took a long cotton robe from a polished bronze hook on the wall. I tied it around my waist. Then I sat on a wooden bench next to Jhalkari and did as she did, beginning by neatly folding my clothes and tucking them into a hollow space in the wall. I glanced at the servants waiting with thick bathing towels and sandalwood platters of richly scented soaps.

"How nice," Kahini said with exaggerated politeness. "Two village girls helping each other. It was only two years ago that you had your first bath, wasn't it, Jhalkari?"

As Kahini said this, the rani passed behind her.

"I hope you're not being insulting, Kahini."

"Not at all. I'm just remembering the day Jhalkari joined us."

The rani walked toward the marble tub, and one by one, we all slipped out of our robes and joined her in the scented water. I had never felt such luxury. "Tonight," the rani said to me, "I would like you to read something to us in English."

I bowed my head. "It would be my pleasure, Your Highness."

If you can imagine a fish taken from a tiny bowl and released into a giant pond, then you know how I felt that first time, bathing with the women of the Durga Dal.

I watched as a servant tenderly washed the rani's hair while another scrubbed her skin. It was almost impossible to tell that the rani was with child. Her body was still slender; only her full breasts gave any indication that she might soon give the kingdom of Jhansi a boy, its long-awaited heir. The raja's first wife had failed to give him a child. When she died, he took years before he chose our rani. And since then, nine years had passed. Which obviously meant that the problem was with him. I looked nervously at the other girls in the tub, hoping none of them could read my disloyal thoughts.

But they were all occupied with talking or bathing. Only Sundari was silent, quietly looking across the chamber at the three servants who were carefully arranging silver boxes, spacing them out on a long marble table. As they opened each box, I could see the expensive contents inside: English lace, ruby hairpins, gold anklets with emerald charms.

It seemed impossible that only a day ago I was squatting in my courtyard with an old bucket and a rag. But what seemed even more impossible was that I had never questioned that bathing could be any other way. What else would I discover in Jhansi that would make life in Barwa Sagar seem small?

As soon as the other women began to climb out of the water, I stepped out of the bath, too, and let a servant help me back into my robe as the others did. We left the queen and returned in a group to the Durgavas; the sound of our bare feet slapping against the marble made me think of small whips being cracked. Someone was going to have the job of cleaning up all the water we left behind.

When we reached our room, Jhalkari went straight to her wooden chest to pull something out. "I don't have the right coloring for this shade of green," she said, handing me an angarkha made of rich, jade silk and stitched in gold. She waited while I tried it on.

"It's lovelier than anything I've ever owned," I admitted. The feel of the silk against my skin was as wonderful as the hot bathwater we'd just been in.

"Keep it," Jhalkari said. "Pay me when you can."

"But I might never—"

"Whenever you can," she repeated. "I don't wear it."

A growing sense of uneasiness settled over me. I had fallen for Kahini's trick, and she had almost cost me my place in the Durga Dal.

Jhalkari read my thoughts. "Don't worry. I'm not Kahini. You don't know that now, but you will. Although you'd also be smart to take Sundari-ji's advice about friends and enemies."

"How did you hear—"

"I didn't. She gave the same advice to me. She had other things to say as well." She hesitated, debating whether or not to tell me. "She also said that everyone is surprised the first time they see the raja, so prepare to conceal your emotions when you enter the Durbar Hall."

We walked up to the fourth floor of the palace and passed through a pair of heavy gold curtains into a sandalwood-and-camphor scented chamber. A giant throne rose from a platform in the middle of the room like a bejeweled mountain of gold. Before it, red silk cushions were arranged like a fan, above it was a canopy of rich velvet cloth.

"The throne once belonged to Sheo Rao Bhao," Jhalkari whispered to me. "The raja's father."

Rugs as thick as a sheep's fleece were spread across the floor, dyed red and gold and woven into stunning patterns. In a windowless niche, a pair of female musicians played the sitar and the veena. There was so much to see, and hear, and smell. But I couldn't take my eyes from the man on the throne himself. Raja Gangadhar had long hair that flowed past his shoulders and curled around heavy gold chains that he wore on his chest. Jewels shimmered from his thin hands, his slender wrists, his ears, his turban—even his waist. And he was dressed in the most elaborate kurta I had ever seen.

Jhalkari nudged me forward; I hadn't even realized I'd stopped walking.

A handsome young *chauri* bearer stood at the Gangadhar's side, holding the ceremonial silver-handled whisk that represents a raja's right to rule. The *chauri* bearer's dress was slightly less ostentatious, and the pair looked like colorful birds on a perch. A heavily latticed ivory partition was set up next to the raja. Behind this sat a small throne and a dozen silk cushions.

I asked Jhalkari, "Why must the rani be in purdah here?"

"For show. The raja thinks it makes the durbar seem more mysterious." She emphasized the word *mysterious*—as if the screen was some flight of fancy.

The rani took her place on the throne, but she didn't seem inconvenienced. Then as soon as we were seated, she leaned close to the lattice to look out at the people who were assembling before the stage. I say stage, because this is really what it was. A cast of characters streamed through the door: soldiers, advisers, who knew who else—and the most elaborately dressed men sat in front of the platform just below the raja. I recognized the Dewan, and later, I would become familiar with the others—advisers Lakshman Rao and Lalu Bakshi, the general Jawahar Singh.

Then the public was allowed into the hall, and soon there was a crowd.

The young *chauri* bearer bowed reverently before the royal couple. Then, with a wild flourish he announced, "His Royal Highness, the humble and honorable Maharaja Gangadhar Rao of Jhansi."

Gangadhar rose and bowed before his throne, thanking the gods, and in particular Mahalakshmi, for placing him there. Then he faced the room and solemnly placed his hand over his heart. "People of Jhansi, we are here for you. What can we do?"

A great number of voices rose in response, and the raja chose one of the youngest men in the crowd to go first.

"In the field behind my house, the British have slaughtered two cows and are using their skins to make shoes."

There were murmurs of horror. Certainly, we Hindus wear leather, but only from cows that have met natural deaths.

"Where is your house?" the rani asked from behind her latticed screen.

"To the north of Mahalakshmi Temple, near the shrine to Ganesh."

"We will meet with British officials tomorrow," the rani promised. "There will be no more slaughter in Jhansi."

"Who else?" asked the raja, strutting like a peacock up and down the stage. "You." He chose another young man from the front.

And for every petitioner the raja chose after that, it was the rani who answered and made the ruling. Interesting things happened during that first durbar—decisions about the digging of a new well, and whether the raja would buy his twenty-third elephant (the rani said no)—but the image of the bejeweled raja strutting before his silk and velvet throne is the memory that stands out to me the most. At the conclusion of the durbar, several advisers gathered around the rani to ask her advice about daily matters, but no one asked the raja for an opinion. Meanwhile, the raja chatted merrily with his young *chauri* bearer, making him laugh.

"Your first durbar," Jhalkari said as we left the hall for our next destination: again feeding the poor at the Mahalakshmi Temple. Her tone suggested she expected me to pass judgment on it, but I had learned my lesson. All I said was, "Yes."

"Not what you imagined, was it?" She filled the silence.

I looked at her and felt that she was being genuine. But I held my counsel.

"Last year, a British general mistook the raja for a woman," she whispered. "And can you imagine the rani's shock when she came here to marry him?"

I shook my head. I could not.

That evening, the queen's room was brightly illuminated with hanging lamps. The other Durgavasi had taken up spots on cushions around the fountain. Paper and pens had been provided on small tables and they were all engaged in writing letters. Sundari led me to a fine silk cushion next to the rani, where I sat cross-legged and arranged my hands in my lap. As she had requested earlier in the bath, I was going to read for her in English.

"Your Highness," said Sundari. "I will fetch the Master of the Letters."

The man she escorted inside was as short and thin as a river reed, and with just as many knots in his body. His face revealed he could not have been older than forty, but the way his bones poked out, you would have thought he was a knobbly old man of sixty-five. He pressed his hands together in namaste, and then made the deepest bow before the rani I had seen so far.

"The day's letters, Your Highness. Along with the two you requested from Major Ellis."

"Thank you, Gopal."

"And would Your Highness like me to read them?" he asked with a look of such eager expectation that telling him no would almost seem cruel.

"Today, my newest guardswoman, Sita, will be reading them."

Gopal looked as if I had stolen the food from his bowl. "You can read and write in English?"

"Yes."

He looked down at the rani. "Perhaps Her Highness wishes me to stay, in case anything should be misinterpreted."

The rani smiled. "That's a fine idea," she said, although I felt certain she only said this to be kind. "Sundari, bring in another cushion."

A seat was arranged to her left, and Gopal handed me the letters with the same enthusiasm he might have shown if handing over the keys to his house. I unfolded Major Ellis's missive and read, "From Major Ellis." When I translated this into Marathi, the rani shook her head.

"English only. I am learning."

I continued reading in English. The letter was about Indian soldiers who were serving with the British army stationed in Jhansi. They had joined the British because the pay was regular and good. The British called them sepoys. The letter said that there was growing discontent among these men. British officers had ordered all sepoys to erase the red caste marks from their foreheads, shave their beards, and remove their gold earrings. The sepoys had accepted this, but now, even more British regulations were causing outrage.

Instead of allowing the sepoys to wear turbans, the men had been issued leather caps. And if that wasn't insulting enough, the cartridges being used in their new Enfield rifles were smeared with the fat of both pigs and cows. Now, perhaps these things are not so shocking in England. But here in India, we Hindus do not butcher our sacred cows to make hats or cartridges out of them. And if you are a Muslim, as some of the sepoys were, then the idea of handling any part of a pig is more than just insulting; it is an act against the Sacred Law of Islam. What made it even worse was that in order to load these fat-smeared cartridges, the sepoys—Hindu and Muslim alike—had to bite them open with their teeth. So what Major Ellis wanted to know was this: could the rani calm these irrational sepoys down?

"It is only a little fat," he wrote, "and nothing to be terribly alarmed about."

It seemed interesting to me that Major Ellis had addressed his request to the rani, and not to the raja. But when I handed the letter back to Gopal, he did not seem surprised by this.

"So was her English acceptable?" the rani asked.

The Master of the Letters arranged his features into a somewhat less sour look. "Your new guardswoman's ability to read English is beyond any doubt," he said.

"Shall we write a response?"

I had never seen a man move so quickly. Before the rani could specify which one of us should write the letter, Gopal had already taken a pen and paper from his bag.

The rani caught my eye, and I understood at once that she knew Gopal was foolish, but was willing to humor him anyway.

"Shall I begin with the regular greeting?" Gopal said.

"No. Only one line will do this time. He thinks our traditions are irrational, so I want you to write: 'It is only a little mutiny, Major Ellis, and nothing to be terribly alarmed about.'"

Gopal laughed loudly. "Oh, that's very clever, Your Highness. A little mutiny!"

"There is talk of mutiny?" Sundari cut through his laughter. She didn't speak English and hadn't understood the letter. But she knew enough to guess. "The sepoys are angry about the cartridges."

"Yes. And it's up to the British to right what they have done. The sepoys aren't my soldiers."

"But they're stationed in Jhansi," Sundari said. "If they mutiny, the blame will belong to you. Not only because they're here, but because they're Indian."

Even I could see the sense in Sundari's words.

"And remember, seven Englishmen were recently killed when Indian men poisoned some of their slaughtered cow meat. Be careful, Your Highness. We do not want to see the loss of more lives."

The rani nodded. "Gopal, add two more lines."

We all waited to hear what she would say next.

"'But if you truly wish to avoid mutiny,'" she dictated, "'then listen to the sepoys—those men you count as fellow soldiers. Their traditions are older than yours by many thousands of years and deserve your respect.'"

In the Durgavas that evening, Jhalkari turned to me and whispered, "The rani is going to value you very highly for your English, but the other women will grow resentful. Always remember this is a job, not a family. That's what my father told me before I left, and he was right."

"Did he train you?"

"Yes. Before he died." She didn't say anything more. Then, long after I thought she had fallen asleep, she added, "My husband says the same thing."

I sat upright in my bed. "You're married?"

"To one of the sepoys being forced to wear leather and taste cow."

I was stunned. "But how can you be in the Durga Dal? My father said—"

"There's no law against being married while part of the rani's guards if there are no children. My husband was wounded many years ago and cannot have children. No other family would take him for a son-in-law. I'm better than nothing, so he married me."

I couldn't tell whether or not she was joking. But I thought about Jhalkari's husband for quite some time before I fell asleep.

Chapter Eight

There was only one mirror in the Durgavas. I waited until the other women left for the maidan before I hurried over to see what I looked like, and I couldn't stop staring at the weapons on my belt. Although Sundari had presented them to me, it was as if they belonged to someone else. I was lost in this vision when I heard a familiar voice over my shoulder.

"Well, there's our little *ganwaar*!" Kahini and her ugly friend Rajasi appeared at the door, and every muscle inside of me tensed. *Ganwaar*, if you don't know, is an insulting term for someone who comes from a village. It is worse than calling someone foolish or naive. "Just look at her, Rajasi. Staring like an owl at all her fancy weapons."

I have learned since then that in Western culture, the owl is considered a symbol of wisdom. But if you have ever seen an owl, you will understand why this is so hard to believe. It has giant eyes and wears the most shocked expression of any bird, as if it's constantly surprised by everything it sees. I very much doubt that I looked like an owl, but this was Kahini's attempt at insulting me.

"Do you plan to stand here all morning," Kahini said, "or will you be joining us outside with the rani?"

I hurried past them as quickly as I could, but when I reached the doorway where Rajasi was standing, she stuck out her foot a little and I tripped. I would have been able to catch myself if I hadn't been carrying Sundari's bag. But as it happened, I made my entrance into the courtyard by falling almost flat on my face and, in the process, tearing the pants Father had ordered for me before I left Barwa Sagar.

Tears filled my eyes, and a rage burned inside of me with an intensity of feeling I didn't know I was capable of. Moti, who was standing nearby, picked up my bag and offered me her hand. I took it and brushed off the dirt from my angarkha. Then Moti turned to Rajasi and said, "You're lucky the rani wasn't watching you." Although now, of course, everyone was staring.

"As if the rani cares what happens to some little *ganwaar*. Isn't that right, Kahini?"

Kahini ignored her. "If Sita doesn't want to be the center of attention," she said to Moti, "then perhaps she shouldn't call it to herself."

Moti took my arm and led me toward the group. "Are you hurt?"

"No."

"I don't know why they're treating you this way. But two years ago, on the maidan, Kahini injured one of the new recruits so badly that the girl had to be returned to her father."

"That isn't going to happen to me."

Moti glanced up at the determination in my words. "Be careful."

When we reached the maidan, I saw a crowd of men had already gathered there. Moti explained that the ones with white murethas tied around their foreheads were part of the queen's guard.

"But *we're* the queen's guard," I said, and then I realized how foolish I sounded. I had seen men lining the halls outside the Durgavas. And the same uniformed men stood guard in the courtyard while we joined the rani in the bath.

But there was no contempt in Moti's voice when she replied. "As soon as His Highness heard that the rani was carrying his heir, he ordered his best men to guard her chambers. That one is the captain." She pointed to a man who wore the same open white vest and loose churidars that the other guards did, but I thought he looked too young to be a captain.

"Arjun was one of the most skilled men in His Highness's army," Moti said. "That's why the raja has him guarding the rani."

The other women had now gathered on the field, cutting the air repeatedly with their swords. A low platform had been set up, and Moti explained that for practice, two Durgavasi would be chosen to do battle until one of them made contact with the other's body five times. The loser would be replaced; the victor would keep fighting until she lost.

"The rani insists that we use wooden swords when we practice," Moti said. "So there isn't much chance that Kahi—that anyone can do injury to you here."

We walked toward the stage.

"Good news," Kahini said as we approached, and in such a way that I knew it wouldn't be good news for me at all. "Sundari-ji would like you to take the stage first."

I looked to Sundari to confirm this, and she handed me a wooden sword. Immediately, I knew what she was doing: she was arranging it so that I could lose quickly and not face Kahini on the stage.

"Good luck," Kahini whispered as I passed.

"Heera," Sundari said loudly, "please follow Sita onto the platform."

When I reached the top, I could see the entire maidan laid out before me. More soldiers had now gathered to watch, and I noticed the rani was under her tent, speaking with the man Moti had called Arjun. As Heera ascended the steps, the rani and Arjun both turned to watch us.

I had no idea how Heera liked to fight, but I can tell you a secret about sword fighting. Whatever you think you know about it, you are probably wrong. All sorts of foolish myths exist, most of them learned by reading books and watching plays. For example: the goddess Chandika attacks Karalasur with a simple sword; she thrusts once and the demon is slain. Or Edgar battles Oswald in *King Lear* armed with a wooden staff, and the audience believes that he kills Oswald, who is fighting with a rapier. But in reality, sword combat is about being in constant motion, grappling and using your weight as leverage.

Within the hour, I had defeated seven of the Durgavasi, including Rajasi and Jhalkari. Then Mandar ascended the platform. She was the largest woman in the Durga Dal.

"There's quite a crowd watching," Mandar said.

She was trying to distract me, so I didn't turn to look.

Suddenly she lunged. I blocked her thrust. It was impossible to leverage my weight against her, for she was heavier and built like a well, round on all sides and completely solid. But I was lighter and quicker, and that counted far more. I wore Mandar out in the end.

Finally, Kahini ascended the stage—my last competitor. I was tired. My hair was dripping with sweat. In my ripped churidars, I'm sure I was a sight to behold.

As soon as Kahini reached the top of the platform I made my first lunge. She immediately crumpled to the floor and grabbed her ankle. "It's twisted!" she shrieked. "I've twisted it!" And the look on her face was one of pure agony.

Now, you can believe what you like, but I seriously question whether Kahini was in any pain at all. Still, she remained prone until Sundari arrived to help her to her feet. Then she hobbled down the stairs, moaning dramatically as she went. At the last step, Rajasi hurried to her side, and Kahini shifted from Sundari's shoulder to Rajasi's.

Sundari looked at the pair of them. "What a shame your accident happened just as you were about to fight Sita, Kahini."

Kahini scowled as they led her away.

In any case, I was glad not to have to face Kahini that day, who was quickly positioning herself as my competitor.

After my performance on the maidan, the Durgavasi seemed to split in two: those who felt threatened by the skills that my father and Shivaji had taught me, and those who were impressed. It didn't surprise me that Kahini and Rajasi wanted nothing to do with me. But when we went to the baths and I reached for my towel, I was surprised when Mandar stood in my way.

"Excuse me," I said.

Mandar didn't move.

"Will you please—"

The rani sighed. "Step aside, Mandar."

I reached for my towel and began to feel as though everything I had worked toward was becoming both a blessing and a curse. What had been the point of all those years of hard work if they only brought loneliness and resentment?

I left the baths early, and while the other women took their time changing into their clothes, I sat in the courtyard opposite a fountain, watching the peacocks flit from tree to tree. The rani paid the Durgavasi weekly, and in two days, I would be able to buy a new angarkha with my wages. I would find whatever silk was cheapest and make something from that. Whatever was left over, I would send to Anu.

I was thinking about my sister, mentally writing the letter that I wanted to pen her that evening, when I caught a slight movement at the edge of the courtyard. Someone was sitting on a bench on the other side of the fountain, turning the pages of a small red book. Just as I noticed him, he looked up.

"Ah, the new recruit everyone's talking about," he said. I recognized him as the young captain of the guards. He closed his book and made his way over.

I looked down, since I was sure I was blushing. "And why is that?"

"Are you searching for compliments?"

"I was searching for something to say," I said, and I'm sure I sounded defensive. "You didn't introduce yourself."

He gave a bow. "I'm Arjun, and the men are talking because you're beautiful."

"I'm Sita, and I would much rather they talk about me because I'm skilled."

He grinned. "May I sit?" He indicated a respectable distance away, so I nodded. "I saw what happened," he said, "and I'm willing to bet the only injury Kahini received today was to her pride."

"So she has a reputation."

"I wouldn't say it too loudly, but yes." Arjun looked over my shoulder to the entrance of the queen's rooms, and when it was clear that we were alone, he said, "Be careful with her. She has the ear of the raja. You don't know me, but I'm giving you honest advice."

"My father has already given me advice: the only words free of suspicious motives will be the ones I find in books."

Arjun realized that I was including him among my father's suspects, but he continued, "Your father was the one who taught you to read?"

"Yes," I said quietly. I was afraid if I answered too loudly, he might hear the heartache in my voice. "He loved to read with me in English. Mostly we read Shakespeare."

"There's a great deal to read in our languages. Hindi, Urdu, Marathi," he said. "Have you read Rumi?"

"The Persian poet?" Of course, I'd heard of him. But Father had been more interested in teaching me the Western classics, so I wasn't familiar with him. "No."

"Well, he's the Shakespeare of the East."

"Arjun-ji!" Kahini emerged from the queen's room. You would have thought she was trying to sing his name, as if seeing us together was the very best thing that could happen for her. "I had no idea you were interested in talking to *ganwaars*. If I'd known that," she said as she approached, "I'd have asked Gangadhar's servant to pay you a visit."

At that, I rose from the bench and bowed formally to Arjun. "It was kind of you to introduce yourself, but I have duties inside." Then I smiled at Kahini. "I'm glad to see your ankle has healed so swiftly."

That evening, the rani was too sick to join us in reading or writing. I was a little disappointed, and entirely for selfish reasons. I had been hoping that she might ask me to read for her again.

Instead, I seated myself next to Jhalkari and wrote two letters, one to Father, the other to Anu. I wrote the letter to Father first, since that was far easier. For Anu, I wanted to be careful not to seem too pleased with myself.

Certainly, it's beautiful here. But I have trouble enjoying the sights and sounds without you. When I passed by the elephants' stables for the first time, and saw the hardworking mahouts tending to these giant, gentle beasts, I immediately thought of you; how much you would enjoy watching them interact with one another, the sound of their trumpeting clear for miles around. I miss you so much, Anu. But every week I am earning money, and soon—very soon—there will be a dowry fortune for you. Then our dreams of seeing you as a wife and a mother will come to pass.

I reread what I had written, then sealed the two letters with the rani's wax. Anu would be so excited to receive a letter from the Palace of Jhansi. But then I noticed that Jhalkari had kept hers unsealed and asked why.

She glanced at Gopal, who had entered and seated himself next to Kahini. "I pay a private courtier to deliver my letters. Consider doing that yourself. The Master of the Letters is in charge of correspondence, and any letter entering or leaving the palace is read by him."

I didn't have anything to hide. Still, if Jhalkari didn't trust Gopal, perhaps I shouldn't either. "How much is a private courtier?"

"Three *annas*," Jhalkari said.

It was the price of a cheap bangle. But I was saving for Anu's dowry fortune, and I needed to buy at least two angarkhas soon. Plus, I'm ashamed to admit that the thought of the bookshop in town, with its blue and gold sign, crossed my mind as well. Even if Gopal did read my letters, what information would he gain?

"Perhaps another time," I decided.

Jhalkari frowned but didn't say anything.

Then I took my letters and placed them in Gopal's open cloth bag. "So you'll deliver these?" I asked him.

"*Personally?*" He peered down his nose at me. "No. But I will see that they get to their destination."

"Is he always so grumpy?" I asked Jhalkari when we went back to the Durgavas.

She sat on my bed. "He thinks he was a raja in his past life." She laughed. "Sort of like Kahini."

"Maybe that's my grandmother's problem," I joked.

"You don't get along?"

I didn't intend for it to, but my voice grew quiet and cautious, as if Grandmother were in the room with me. "No! I think she suggested opium when I was born."

Jhalkari nodded. "Mine too. She didn't want a girl. My father didn't mind though."

I smiled. "Mine neither."

"And your father had two girls. Is your sister like you?"

"Not at all. She's sweet and pretty and well behaved. She'll make a good wife someday. That's why I'm here."

"That's really kind of you."

"It's not entirely selfless. It was this or a temple."

Jhalkari nodded. "It was this or a temple for nearly everyone here."

Chapter Nine

During my third week as a Durgavasi, in the beginning of July, Sundari woke us early to say that we wouldn't be practicing on the maidan. Apparently the rani was presiding over a ladies' durbar that afternoon.

Immediately, the other women were on their feet, sorting through their baskets of clothing and passing around one another's jewelry. I sat on the edge of my bed. I only had one angarkha—the one Jhalkari had given me the first day I'd arrived. I couldn't afford anything else. Not yet. Not if I wanted to save for Anu.

"You can't wear the same angarkha you've been wearing for the past two weeks," Jhalkari said, sitting down next to me. In the early morning light, her resemblance to the rani was uncanny. "This is a durbar. It only happens once a year. I'll go with you to the shops right now, and you can buy something."

"But there will be no time to fit it."

Jhalkari curled her lip, and I realized she was imitating Kahini. "I don't know what you people do in the village, but here in the city, we buy things that have already been sewn."

I laughed, despite the fact that across the room, Kahini could hear us both.

We stopped at the treasury, where the rupees we were paid each week were kept, and I withdrew an amount that Jhalkari assured me was sufficient to buy a silk angarkha and a simple necklace. Then we walked together through the heavy monsoon rain and headed to the shops at the base of the fortress.

Jhansi was one of the most prosperous kingdoms in India. It was green and lush, filled with sheltering mango trees, orange trees, and rolling gardens. It had been created to be the emerald of northern India, a green and gold jewel rising from the sands of the Pahuj River. As I'd seen on my arrival, all five of the turreted gates leading to the city were indeed large enough for an elephant to pass through. I wondered what my family would think to see me walking through these gates with a pistol strapped to my hip and my friend Jhalkari for an escort. What great power and freedom the women of Jhansi enjoyed. We were allowed to shop without male relatives or husbands and spend money as we liked.

It took three shops before we found angarkhas Jhalkari believed were acceptable for a ladies' durbar.

"What about this one?" I held up an outfit tailored from purple Benares silk. It was exquisite. The top was trimmed in silver and the pants were stitched with pink and silver leaves.

"How much?" Jhalkari asked the shopkeeper.

"For the rani's Durgavasi?" The man made a great show of twisting the end of his mustache, reminding me of Shivaji back home. "Ten rupees."

It sounded like a fair price, but Jhalkari laughed. "Does she look like the captain? She's the latest recruit. We'll pay five."

"Do I look like a beggar? Because that is what I'll become if I sell my best pieces for five rupees. Eight."

"Five." Jhalkari was firm. "There are dozens of shops in Jhansi, my friend."

"And how many of them carry pieces like this? With her coloring, she would be a queen in this purple. You won't find it anywhere else."

Jhalkari arched her brows. "We'll see."

I took that as my cue to put the angarkha back on the shelf, even though it was the prettiest one I'd seen all day. We were halfway out the door when the shopkeeper ran after us. "Six!" he exclaimed.

Jhalkari turned. "Five, and we don't need the matching slippers."

The man gave a vastly exaggerated sigh. Two women shopping inside the store giggled. I suspected they had just been on the receiving end of his complaints. "Five, without the slippers."

The way he wrapped my purchase! You would have thought we'd asked him to wrap cow excrement with the amount of sighing and head shaking he did. When we reached the street, Jhalkari rolled her eyes.

"Such a performance! That angarkha is worth four rupees, and not a single *anna* more! That's an entire rupee of profit for him."

"How do you know?" I was thinking that perhaps we really had robbed him of a meal.

Jhalkari gave me a long look. "My grandfather worked for twenty years as a street sweeper so that he could save his money to open a sari shop. When he had finally saved enough, no one wanted to rent him a space because he was a Dalit. So he built a shop for himself and sold his clothes to other Dalits. By the time I was ten, I could tell you the price of a piece of silk coming from anywhere from here to China."

"He must have been an extraordinary man." Even today, you

might be surprised to know, the idea of a Dalit touching silk is practically unthinkable.

"He was. He died hoping Father would take over his business. But Father wanted to be in the army. They wouldn't take him because he wasn't a Kshatriya, so he became a sepoy for the British instead. Mother never gave him a son, so he trained me."

As we walked, two British women passed us, struggling with their skirts in the extreme July heat. Their skin had somehow turned red, making their blue eyes shine like aquamarines. I wondered at a race that could change its color like a chameleon.

"Did you see them?" I asked Jhalkari after a moment.

"Who? The British women?"

"They were *red*."

"That's what happens when you burn."

I shrieked. "Who burned them?"

"No one." Jhalkari laughed. "It's the heat. They're not built for the sun like we are."

"How horrifying." To turn a painful red every time you walked out the door. "So why do they wear such heavy gowns?"

Jhalkari turned up her palms. Who knew why the British did what they did? We had come to another shop, and I could see the rows of necklaces inside, hanging from silver hooks like waterfalls of brightly colored gems. "Did you know," Jhalkari said, hesitating on the first step, "that the rani's father had no sons, so he raised her like one. I've heard the British call her the real Raja of Jhansi. And do you know what they say about Raja Gangadhar?"

I looked behind us to make sure no one was listening to our conversation. "What?"

"They call him the rani." She waited to see my reaction.

"Who says that?" I whispered. If anyone heard us, I was fairly certain what would happen to our positions in the Durga Dal.

"The British soldiers. They've all been to his plays and seen him perform. We're going to see one in two days, so if you see another necklace you like, you should buy it. There'll be lots of plays to attend."

I dressed in my new angarkha when we returned, with purple bangles and a large amethyst necklace. Jhalkari pressed a silver bindi between my brows, and when I strapped my weapons onto my waist and looked in the mirror, instead of feeling pleased, I felt a growing uneasiness about how much I had changed since arriving in Jhansi.

The woman in the glass had spent more than her father earned in a month on her purple angarkha, and that was without taking into account what her new silk slippers and heavy necklace had cost. She was the same woman who had suddenly grown used to cool baths, soft sheets, and plush rugs after only three weeks in the palace. And now, when she thought about returning to Barwa Sagar, instead of feeling pride, she felt a deep irritation that, for seventeen years, she'd been confined to purdah without ever knowing that life could be any different.

At first, I'd thought it was the clothes themselves that were making me feel so uncomfortable. But that wasn't it. The changes you couldn't see in the mirror were just as great as the changes you could, and I was afraid that when I went home, no one would be able to recognize me. When I told this to Jhalkari, she laughed.

"You think there's a single Durgavasi who hasn't changed since coming here? The ones who were here before me say that even Kahini has grown more attractive."

But that afternoon, as the ladies' durbar progressed, I found it hard to believe that Kahini could ever have been less beautiful than she was now. The queen's room was crowded with petitioners, and while the rani was dressed in an exquisite sari of cinnamon-colored silk, it was Kahini whom most of the women were watching. Like the rani, she was dressed in Benares silk, but the eggshell blue of the fabric made her skin look luminous, and the rani's beauty paled in comparison. A diamond ring glinted from her nose, and thick clusters of diamonds glittered from her anklets. Even her bare feet were studded with gems, and each time they moved, her toe rings caught the light. I wondered how Kahini had come by such jewels. Perhaps they had been gifts from the rani.

Because the petitioners were entirely women, there was no need for discretion or mystery. The rani reclined on a pile of silk cushions, while we sat on velvet cushions of our own. A trio of female musicians made light music in the courtyard, and throughout the afternoon, each petitioner who approached the rani pressed her forehead to the ground in the deepest gesture of namaste, offering bowls of tilgul—little balls of sesame and molasses—in return for sugarcane and rice. After this exchange, their petition was read, and the rani discussed its detractions or merits.

Toward the end of the afternoon, a young girl stepped forward. She presented the rani with her gift in a simple terra-cotta bowl. The little round sweets looked like all of the others that had been presented; yet Kahini rose from her cushion, aghast. "This girl is from a *village*," she said. "Who knows what might be in that bowl?" She took the vessel and crossed the room to an open window. Then, with a single motion, she dumped the contents out, as if the girl had offered a gift of dung.

The young petitioner began to weep and hurried away. She had given the only gift she could afford, and it was discarded like trash.

Kahini resumed her seat next to the rani. The musicians were still playing, but now the remaining petitioners appeared frozen in their spots.

"Kahini," the rani said, "please return to the Durgavas."

"Your Highness," Sundari began, "I'm sure Kahini—"

"This is not a request." The rani's voice was sharp, although she never raised it above a whisper. "*Now.*"

Kahini did as she was told.

"Where is the girl from Rampura?" the rani asked. When no one stood up, the rani's voice softened. "Do you all see this woman?" she said, nodding toward me. "Sita comes from the village of Barwa Sagar. And do you think I care? Now, where is the girl who was standing here?"

There was no movement among the two hundred women before us. The rani was pregnant and eager to conclude the day's business. But she could not abide injustice.

"Sita, will you say something please?"

I stood; I had never spoken before a crowd. "What the rani has told you is true," I said. "I am from the village of Barwa Sagar, just as this woman here"—and I indicated Jhalkari—"is a Dalit from another village."

A murmur of surprise passed through the women.

"Do not be embarrassed. Some people are so impoverished all they have is gold. We, however, have pride."

The girl stood, and the rani motioned her forward. She had come with a request for land. Her father had died without any sons, and their farm was being given to the father's youngest brother, a drunk and a cheat. This girl had come all the way from Rampura, against the advice of her elders, to see what could be done.

"And what did your elders think would happen when you arrived here?" the rani asked.

The girl concentrated on her feet. "It was said I would meet with shame," she admitted, "for trying to change the way of things, and that no one would help me."

"Well, from this day, the farm belongs to you, and anyone who thinks to challenge this, challenges the law of Jhansi!"

"Well done!" said a male voice, and someone began to clap. Immediately, the women rushed to cover themselves with their dupattas, and many of them pressed their foreheads to the ground. "Resume your places!" the raja said.

The rani stood from her cushion, and she looked pleased to see him. "Your Highness."

"Like something out of one of Rumi's poems," he said. He crossed the room and recited: "'The lion is most handsome when looking for food.' You were born to do this, Manu."

The rani look embarrassed. "How long were you standing there?"

"Long enough to hear one of your Durgavasis say something very clever."

"Sita Bhosale." The rani turned to me, and I pressed my forehead to the ground.

"Sit," the raja said to me.

I waited for the rani to resume her seat and then returned to the cushion next to her.

"'Some people are so impoverished all they have is gold.' That was very creative. Did you make it up?"

"I suppose I did, Your Highness. Yes." I tried not to stare at the rouge he'd applied quite liberally to his lips.

"Well, Sita Bhosale, if your aim is half as good as your imagination, my wife can feel quite at peace in Jhansi."

With this, he gave the petitioners an elaborate wave, and was gone.

That evening, after everyone returned to the Durgavas from the temple, I discovered that someone had broken my image of Durga. Her beautiful wooden head was lying on my bed, as if the person had wanted to make sure I knew it had been broken intentionally. My eyes filled with tears, since Father had carved it from a hollowed out piece of mango wood. The lower half of her body had been cleverly separated from the upper half, and inside, my father carefully filled the hollow space with prayer beads. I showed the broken head to Jhalkari, who immediately said what I was already thinking.

"Kahini!"

Before I could stop her, she took the murti from my hands and walked across the room.

Kahini was sitting on her bed, brushing her hair and twisting it into braids. As soon as she saw Jhalkari, she put down her brush. "Don't come any closer. I don't care what the rani has to say about Dalits, I won't have one despoiling my bed."

"Did you do this?" Jhalkari said.

"What? Our little recruit couldn't come and ask me herself? Was she too afraid?"

"Answer the question!"

Kahini shrugged. "Yes. It was an accident."

"How do you break a murti by accident?"

Kahini stood and walked across the room toward me. "I apologize, Sita. I was practicing malkhamba."

"Inside the Durgavas?"

She ignored my question. "If you give me the murti, I'll have someone repair it."

I glanced at Jhalkari, suspicious of some trick. "How long will it take?"

"By the end of this week. It was an accident," she said, then, with uncharacteristic regret, "I really am sorry."

Jhalkari seemed to think this was fine. She handed me the broken murti, and I gave it to Kahini.

But I couldn't stop seeing the image of Durga, lying in two pieces, broken at the neck. I took out my diary and tried to write away my anger. "Of the very few things I own," I wrote, "Kahini chose the most precious one to break. Jhalkari believes it was an accident. I think Kahini's a snake who struck on purpose."

Chapter Ten

Although sometimes it felt very much as if we were ladies of the court and not guardswomen, Sundari never let us forget our primary purpose. "Vigilance is the difference between a tragedy and a comedy," she said to us on the evening I was to see my first performance at the raja's theater. "Tonight, you are present to watch the audience, not the stage. Who is near Her Highness? Are they carrying anything? Who is looking at her suspiciously? This pregnancy is a threat to every pretender to our raja's throne. And make no mistake, they exist."

I thought Sundari was done, but then she took a heavy breath and continued.

"All of you must be aware," she said, "that the British are acquiring vast territories in our country. Bengal, Orissa, Bihar . . . our raja came to the throne of Jhansi because the British approved his ascension. There are some who feel the British chose wrongly. These men are dangerous, and they are traitors. You are Durgavasi," Sundari said. "Remember that."

With this, we followed her into the rani's chamber. She

emerged from her changing room dressed in a simple red sari. A ruby and gold tikka began in the middle of her dark hair, then dipped between her brows, as red and brilliant as blood.

We helped her into the gilded palanquin she used for official occasions. Sundari called on the rani's male guardsmen to join us in surrounding her palanquin bearers. I was given a position in the front, with Moti and two men I'd never seen before. Then we walked to the baradari, the theater where all of the raja's productions were held.

The sky was clear enough to see the moon, which cast a silvery light over the mossy stones of the wet street. I had never been out so late after dark, and I felt a small thrill. But the sounds of the night were different from the sounds of the day, and the rustling of the trees suddenly seemed louder and more dangerous than they ever had before. Ahead of us, hundreds of small lights flickered like stars. As we drew closer to the open-air pavilion where the raja and his court were waiting, those small lights turned out to be oil lamps suspended from the ceiling of the baradari. Cushions of gold cloth were spread out on the ground, and I could see the raja laughing with a young man in a British uniform. There were probably two hundred guests within the baradari, both British and Indian.

From inside the palanquin, I hear the rani ask, "Who is he with?"

"Major Ellis," Sundari said.

The palanquin bearers lowered the rani to the ground, and as she emerged, the raja rose to greet her. "Your Highness, you are exquisite tonight."

"I left my jewels behind, as I suspected you would be wearing enough for both us," she teased.

"Even without jewels," Major Ellis said, "Her Highness shines as brightly as that star." He pointed to the North Star, and all of us smiled. He was tall and very well built, with eyes the color of turquoise and skin like rice powder. He, at least, hadn't been burned in the sun. I wondered if he kept indoors all day.

While the rani continued speaking English with the major, we were led to the best seats near the front of the stage. The rani's male guards took seats behind us. But from this position, it was impossible to watch any of the audience members. When I turned around to survey the crowd, I found myself looking at Arjun, the captain of the guards.

"Ever read Kalidasa?" he asked without greeting.

I really hoped he wasn't speaking to me, but I was the only Durgavasi who was doing as Sundari had instructed by checking to see who was around the rani. "No. Is he the one who wrote this play?"

"Yes. Her Highness has him in her library. You should make a request to read him."

"Why would she do that when we're about to see the play?" Jhalkari asked.

"Because some people enjoy reading even more than watching," Arjun said.

Jhalkari dismissed his suggestion with a wave. "Not me."

Just then, Kahini turned around. "What is this about Her Highness's library?" she said.

"I was suggesting that Sita might want to borrow one of the books in the royal library," Arjun said. "Her Highness has been very gracious to me in the past."

"And what makes you think she wants to be gracious to Sita?"

"Oh, I think the rani is gracious to everyone, even people who don't deserve it."

I'm sure Kahini would have replied to that, but suddenly, someone called for silence. I turned back to the stage to see a feminine-looking boy dressed as the goddess Indra. Today, women are allowed to perform on stage. But then, it was the same as it was in Shakespeare's day: women's roles were played entirely by men, the younger looking the better.

The room became quiet.

"Try not to look surprised," Jhalkari whispered. "And watch the Englishman's face," she said. "Major Ellis is terrible at hiding what he thinks."

I looked over at Major Ellis, who was seated in the place of honor to the rani's left. Whenever the rani said something to him, his pale skin flushed. I kept thinking of a Sarus crane—a white bird with a long body and bright red cheeks.

Music began to play, and then a beautiful woman appeared on stage. She raised her arms to the sky, and I was completely transfixed by the way her bangles made soft clinking sounds as they slid down her wrists. Suddenly, nothing else existed for me. Just the baradari and the stage and this beautiful woman. Then the woman began to speak and I realized that she was Raja Gangadhar.

I looked at Major Ellis: his jaw was hanging loose.

Truthfully, the raja resembled a woman so closely that if I had passed him in the street, I doubt I would have given him a second look.

I searched the crowd, and several men who were sitting together began whispering intently. Were they shocked like I was? Or was it something more?

The play went on, and as the music began for the final act, one of the men reached suspiciously beneath his kurta. I clenched the holster of the pistol at my side. Who would be faster? I was about to rise when suddenly the man met my gaze and froze. He whispered something to the other men. All three turned to look at me.

Sundari saw me tense.

"Did you see that?" I asked.

She nodded.

We watched them for the rest of the performance.

When the play was finished, everyone in the audience clapped. Since this seemed to be the thing to do, I clapped as well. I would have thought the raja would have taken off his sari and wig as soon as possible, but he remained in costume while servants brought tea and sweets on platters. Then he hurried over to where the rani was sitting.

"Well?" he said, like a little boy searching for his mother's approval.

"Kahini was right." The rani grinned. "It was your best performance."

The raja closed his eyes and let out a staggered breath. "Adesh!" he called, and the actor who had played his husband, King Dusyanta, came over. "Meet one of the finest actors the kingdom of Jhansi has ever known."

Adesh pressed his hands together and bowed in front of the rani.

"You were magnificent," the rani said. "Completely believable."

Although he'd been exceptionally appealing in the false beard and heavy makeup he'd worn on stage, now without all the trappings of the theater, Adesh was even more handsome. He was much larger than the raja, with such broad shoulders and heavily muscled arms that I immediately thought of a bull. In fact, the only man I'd ever seen with a wider chest than Adesh was Shivaji.

"Your Royal Highnesses are much too flattering." Adesh bowed again.

Then the raja put his hand—with painted nails and sea-foam bangles—on Adesh's arm. It felt strange to see the raja dressed as a woman, resting his hand so tenderly against another man. Then he recited the lines Adesh had performed earlier, "'Love torments you, slender girl, but he completely consumes me. Daylight spares the lotus pond while it destroys the moon.' I could absolutely feel his pain when he said that, the same as if someone was taking a knife to my chest."

The rani smiled briefly. "His Highness is tremendously passionate about his plays," she explained to me.

The raja exchanged a meaningful look with Adesh. Then he said, "Major Ellis was completely distracted during the second act."

"Perhaps there is a serious reason for that," the rani offered. "The major is concerned about the sepoys. Let's schedule an audience with him," she said. "With the right words, the British might be persuaded to substitute their cartridges and their leather caps and we can put all of this unhappiness to rest."

The raja gave an exaggerated sigh, as if he really didn't care one way or the other.

Back in our room, Jhalkari was still dressed in the expensive yellow silk she told me her husband had purchased for her, waiting for me to ask the question she knew I was burning to ask. And finally, I couldn't keep it inside myself any longer. I had to know. "Does the raja always take women's parts?"

Moti and Heera both looked at us and frowned. But no one could fault me for asking, or even Jhalkari for answering.

"No, not *always*." By which she meant, most of the time.

"I don't understand."

"Oh, why not tell her the truth?" Kahini said. She had a package in her hand, and I realized when she put it on my bed that it must be my murti. "On the night the rani's child was conceived," she said gleefully, "the rani went to my cousin dressed as a man."

"You shouldn't spread malicious rumors," Jhalkari said.

"There's nothing malicious! We were all there that night. She asked us to get her a man's uniform."

"Is that my murti?"

Already, Kahini was walking away. "Repaired as promised," she said over her shoulder.

No one said anything more about the play, but after unwrapping my murti and seeing that it had been properly fixed, I lay awake for several hours thinking about it. Outside, the rain was coming down in heavy sheets. Tomorrow, the maidan would be too wet for practice, and we would probably have to train inside the Panch Mahal instead. I found it curious that while the rani rarely missed our trainings, the raja was almost never to be seen watching his soldiers. There was talk that he enjoyed riding his elephants, but in the month since I had been in Jhansi, I hadn't seen him anywhere near the stables. Obviously, the theater was keeping him very busy.

Or perhaps someone in the theater.

Because try as I might, I couldn't stop thinking about the way the raja had touched Adesh's arm, and how Adesh had been happy to let him. There are some men for whom female company is not enough, so they seek out close friendships with men who have similar interests and tastes. This was what the raja was doing.

But even after I had puzzled out most of what Kahini had been referring to, instead of making me feel better, it only made me feel lonely. I was coming to know more about the royal family than I did about my own. Anu wrote letters back every week, but it wasn't enough. I had no idea whether she was happy or sad, since it was impossible to write the truth while Grandmother was in the house. It had been more than a month since I had last seen her, and Jhalkari said there wouldn't be an opportunity to see our families until we celebrated Durga Puja in October.

That was three months from now.

I thought of everything that had changed in just a month, and tried to imagine what would be different in three. I would have more money by then, possibly enough for Father to begin the search for a husband for Anu. And if I was careful, I might even be able to bring home a few sweets and some clothing. But what if life in Barwa Sagar had changed? What if Anu was different? I thought of all the times she had wanted to be in the courtyard with me while I trained, and how I'd told her to watch from the window. Why hadn't I simply risked Grandmother's anger and let her stay?

I opened the chest near my bed and searched for the latest letter Anu had sent me. Then I reread it, smiling over each of her words.

Sita, you won't believe what's happened. Avani convinced Father to adopt the little kitten that's been mewling outside my window at night. She told him how badly I wanted to keep it, and even though Grandmother said she'd rather adopt the demon Ravana, Avani convinced him, because the next day I woke up and he was sitting in my bedroom. A real kitten! With orange fur and a completely white nose. Avani thinks I should name him Mooli, like my wooden cat, but I think he looks more like a lion, so I'm going to name him Sher. Then we'll both have a Sher to take care of.

I grinned, imagining her joy and the tender way she'd take care of her little pet. But then I wondered who I would be in three months and whether Anu would even be able to recognize me.

Chapter Eleven

As the rani's belly grew larger and we made fewer trips outside the Panch Mahal, I had more time to socialize with the other Durgavasi. I spent as little time as possible with Kahini and Rajasi. And since Heera and Priyala were nearly ten years older than I was, I didn't have much in common with them. But Moti became a good friend, and Kashi and Mandar, who were always with each other, were entertaining as well. In fact, just to see Kashi and Mandar together could make me laugh, since Kashi was unbelievably petite, and Mandar could not have been larger unless she'd been born a man.

Their personalities were extremely different as well. All Kashi ever talked about were children, while the only thing Mandar appeared interested in was training. I have no idea how they came to be such close friends, but to see them, you would have thought they had known each other all of their lives.

"Be honest," Kashi said to me one day while the five of us were sitting in the courtyard—myself, Jhalkari, Moti, Kashi, and Mandar. "If you could marry and have children tomorrow, would you do it?"

I looked up at the clouds, which were threatening to rain at any minute, and shrugged. "I don't think about it," I said.

"But if you had to think about it," Kashi pressed. "Would you give up your freedom as a Durgavasi to marry?"

"Not me," Mandar said, and Kashi shushed her.

"I already know what you would do. Moti, what would you do?"

Moti put down the laddu that was about to make its way into her mouth. "*Me?*"

"Yes, if you can stop eating for long enough to answer."

She giggled. "I would marry, and spend all of my time in the kitchen."

Kashi rolled her eyes playfully. "I guess we don't have to ask Jhalkari."

"Yes, she's the only lucky one," Moti said.

But Kashi hesitated. "Still . . . no children."

The five of us settled into an uneasy silence.

"What if you could give up your life in the Durgavas?" Kashi asked.

"I'm like Sita," Jhalkari told her. "I never think about it."

"On purpose?"

"Of course on purpose," Jhalkari told her. "What's the point?"

Mandar nodded. "We're all allowed to go home to see our families. That's more than many of the raja's soldiers get."

"Only ten days now," Kashi said. "What are you going to do when you get home?"

"Eat my fill of kheer," Moti said.

"I want to see my niece," Kashi replied. "She'll be two years old the day I visit."

I pictured a miniature version of Kashi, with soft brown curls and big eyes.

"And what are you going to do?" Mandar asked me.

I pictured my house in Barwa Sagar and my eyes instantly welled with tears. "Wake up next to my sister," I said, "and hear about everything I've missed these four months. See Father's new carvings."

"He's a carpenter?" Mandar asked.

"And an artist. He carved the image of Durga that Kahini broke."

For the most part, none of us mentioned Kahini, for the same reason most of us tried not to think about what life would be like if we were somehow made wealthy and found ourselves free to quit the Durga Dal. Because really, what was the point?

"It's a shame she's so close to the rani," Mandar said. "I bet she's in the rani's chamber right now."

We hadn't seen either the rani or Kahini all afternoon after Sundari had told us to spend the remainder of the day in leisure.

"Well, in ten days," Kashi said, "we'll be with people who've never even heard of her."

But that wasn't how it happened.

The next day, just as we were leaving for our walk to Mahalakshmi Temple, Sundari took me aside. "Thank you for volunteering," she said. "I know how difficult it is to be away from your family, so I understand the sacrifice."

I didn't understand what she was thanking me for. "What?"

"Your offer to remain with the rani over Durga Puja. One Durgavasi has to stay behind and it was very kind of you to volunteer. And of course, the rani is grateful."

I could feel the blood rushing to my face. "No! But I—"

Sundari waited for me to finish. "You did offer, didn't you?" she asked.

Kahini had tripped me again. More than anything in the world,

I wanted to be with my family for Durga Puja. But if I said that now, I would disappoint the rani. I felt a crushing pressure in my chest as I made my choice. I said, "I am happy to do it."

For the next week I watched as all of the other Durgavasi prepared to go home. Everyone understood what Kahini had done, but it had been my own choice not to disappoint the rani by telling the truth. A part of me wished I had spoken out, and the night before everyone was going to leave, that feeling very nearly became a wave of emotion, threatening to overwhelm me.

The Durgavas was filled with packing chests. Jhalkari was laughing with Moti, warning her not to eat all of the laddus her mother baked, or she'd be sorry when she returned to the maidan. Kahini and Rajasi came in from the courtyard, trailed by two older women who had once been Durgavasi themselves. "I was very specific when I said I wanted my yellow sari cleaned for *today*," Kahini said. "Tell me, Rajasi, wasn't I specific?"

"I heard you tell them myself."

"So where is it?" Kahini demanded.

"I'm very sorry," the oldest woman said. "It's very delicate cloth—"

Kahini reached back and slapped the woman's face. "I didn't ask for excuses!"

I rose from my bed.

"It's not your business," Jhalkari whispered. "Sit down."

"I'm sorry," the woman wept. "I'll do it now." She left at once, and the other woman hurried out behind her. Kahini saw that I was watching and her face lit up. "Decided that your village wasn't worth going back to after all?" she asked.

"Your behavior in this Durgavas is shameful," I said.

The other women turned around. I knew it was foolish of me to speak, but what did it matter? She had already taken from me what I wanted the most—to visit my family.

"Really?" Kahini said, drawing out the word as if this was the most interesting piece of information she'd heard. "I'm sorry. Which one of us was raised on a farm, and which at court?"

"Leave her alone," Mandar said.

"You keep out of it! Sita here thinks that she knows more about palace life than I do. Well," she said as she walked toward me. Her slippers slapped against the floor. "I guess we'll find out over the next three days. A favor which you never even thanked me for."

She was standing so close to my bed that I could smell the jasmine perfume on her skin. I wanted to hit her hard enough to make her regret every petty thing she'd ever done to me. But then I would be dismissed. And Anu would have no future.

"You see, I thought you would enjoy not having to return to that hole you call a village. How much better is it to be here, with beds and toilets and running water?"

"Enough," Mandar said.

"And good luck with the raja. I'm sure that when he visits the rani you'll have all sorts of entertaining things to talk about."

Mandar rose threateningly from her bed, but Kahini only smiled and walked away.

The next morning, I watched from the courtyard as the women left, and my heart felt as if it were made of stone.

"Jhalkari told me what happened," Sundari said. She put her arm around me and steered me back to the queen's room. It was empty, the only sound coming from the trickling fountain. She took a seat on a long yellow cushion next to the door and indicated that I should do the same. I crossed my legs and waited for her to speak.

"Kahini will never care about what's fair," she said. "She will keep needling you. Small holes, until she finds the spot where the needle can make a great wound. The less you say around her, the better. We must always remember she's a great favorite of the raja's. However, Kahini thought she was punishing you, but what she's done instead is give you a push toward a better life. This is an opportunity."

"She's stolen my chance to see my family!"

"Don't think of it that way. For the next three days," Sundari advised, "prove your worth to the rani. You will have her undivided attention. Kahini has been so eager to see you suffer that she's overlooked something very important. I've heard you speaking with the rani, and I know you can be entertaining. You're very fortunate. Your father did you a great service by teaching you English."

I did not feel fortunate at that moment, and I said so.

"Use these days to your advantage," Sundari insisted. "It's the last thing Kahini will expect."

The rani summoned me at noon. I followed the servant she sent until we reached a pair of soldiers posted outside a pair of heavy wooden doors. One of them had gold earrings, and as we drew closer, I recognized him as Arjun. He smiled when he saw me, and for some reason, my heart beat faster in my chest.

The old woman pressed her hands together in namaste, but when Arjun made the gesture in return, it was me he was watching, his face full of concern. "I thought you would be going home to celebrate Durga Puja," he said.

I tried to keep the resentment from my voice. "Not this time."

He nodded, and something told me he had already heard the story about what Kahini had done. "The rani is waiting for you inside. She wants someone to read to her in English. It's certainly becoming a popular language. They say that we'll all be speaking English if things continue the way they are."

"And what way is that?"

"Well, I can tell you this—the British certainly aren't praying for the rani to deliver a son."

I frowned. "They have far more soldiers than we do. If they wanted Jhansi, they could easily take it."

Arjun gave a half smile. "That's not the British way," he explained. "In order to justify acts of aggression to their people, they need to look as if they have a good reason. And what better reason than a kingdom without an heir?"

The rani's servant shifted from foot to foot, but I ignored her. This time, I wanted to know the truth. I was tired of being an ignorant village girl.

"Is that why they haven't reissued new hats and new cartridges? Because they're hoping the sepoys will rebel?"

"Yes. And when they do, they can take over Jhansi under the guise of crushing a rebellion."

The guard next to Arjun shook his head sadly, and a chill went up my spine like cold fingers on warm skin. What would that mean for the rani? What would that mean for any of us? Then I realized why the guard was shaking his head. "The rani doesn't believe this, does she?"

"No. The British can be very . . . convincing. Particularly Major Ellis and another captain named Skene."

I glanced at the tightly sealed doors of the library and wondered what I should do.

"Are you ready?" The rani's servant sounded nervous. "Her Highness has been waiting. . . ."

"Yes. Take me inside."

Arjun and the second guard opened the door, and for a moment, I was too overwhelmed to move.

"It had the same effect on me the first time I saw it." Arjun grinned.

It was the most beautiful room in all of Jhansi. The doors swung shut behind me, stirring up the scents of leather and dust. From ceiling to floor, the entire chamber was filled with books, each of them bound in leather, brocade, and extraordinary silks. At the farthest end, beneath a high arched window, the rani was settled comfortably on a wide leather cushion.

"Sita," she said, as if she was welcoming a very old friend. "This is your first time inside the library, isn't it?"

I made the gesture of namaste with my palms, and bowed as I approached her. "Yes, Your Highness. And this—well, this is magnificent."

She followed my gaze up the high walls of the chamber to the carved wooden images of Saraswati at the top. The goddess of the arts was one of Father's favorite images to create. I thought of him now, celebrating Durga Puja without me, and blinked back tears.

"It always stirs my emotions as well," she said. "I'm sure that Sundari told you, but I appreciate your dedication. When Diwali comes next month, you must take the entire week to be with your family."

"Your Highness—"

She held up her hand before I could properly express my gratitude. "Come," she said, patting the cushion next to her. There were bowls of food around her—fruits, nuts, a platter of roasted corn. I maneuvered around the long silver trays and adjusted my sword so that I could sit.

"I've received another missive from Major Ellis." She handed me the letter, and after I'd read it in silence, she said, "Well?"

She was asking my opinion. Had she heard me speaking with Arjun outside the doors? I began by repeating the most relevant facts. "The British aren't replacing the greased cartridges."

"Yes."

"And they aren't exchanging the leather caps."

"What does this make you think?"

My heart beat quickly. "I'm sorry, Your Highness. Perhaps your advisers—"

"I know perfectly well what my advisers think. Or what they claim to think. Right now, I'm asking Sita Bhosale. A girl from a farming village. Why won't the British make these simple replacements?"

I looked down at my hands. "Because they hope for rebellion," I whispered, my heart pounding. Why couldn't I ever just listen without giving my opinion, even if it was asked for?

"But why would they hope for that?"

I had already spoken out; there was no sense in changing the tune now. "Because if Her Highness gives birth to a girl," I said, "and the sepoys are rebelling, Jhansi will be viewed as an unruly kingdom with no future."

"And then the British will come to save us all. That's exactly what I think as well now," she said. She folded the letter and placed it back inside its envelope. "So I will have a son," she said simply.

Just then, the doors of the library swung open and a giant man appeared. His eyes looked wild and excited, and I leaped to my feet reaching for my pistol.

"Sita—no!" The rani got to her feet as quickly as her swelling belly would allow. "This is my father, Moropant Tambe."

Immediately, I lowered the gun and apologized. But instead of being angry, Moropant laughed. "I will never worry for my daughter's safety while you're here." He turned his attention back to his daughter. "Manu!"

"Baba!"

The pair of them met in the center of the room, and even though I knew it was rude, I couldn't keep from staring. The rani's father was dressed in loose-fitting churidars and an open vest, the same outfit Arjun and the other male guards wore. A pair of golden hoops hung from his ears, and a dark beard shadowed his chin. I doubt anyone would have described Moropant Tambe as handsome, but there was a larger-than-life quality about him, as if he had stepped from the pages of *Robinson Crusoe*.

"So who is this?" he said, looking at me.

Immediately, I lowered my eyes to the ground.

"My youngest Durgavasi, Sita Bhosale." A silent conversation seemed to pass between them and the rani added, "She can be trusted."

Moropant strode across the room. I bowed in front of him.

"Stand up, Sita, so that I can get a better look at you."

I did as I was told, and the rani's father studied my face, which made me extremely uncomfortable.

"You're almost as pretty as Kahini. I'll bet two of you have become good friends, haven't you?"

"No, not exactly."

When Moropant laughed, the rani scowled.

"Enough," she said, but her father ignored her.

"Don't take it personally," Moropant said.

"Kahini was raised much like my Manu here, believing she was destined for titles and thrones. If she is bitter about her station in life, she has only herself to blame."

I glanced at the rani, and was surprised to see her nod. "She was engaged to a very wealthy man," she confided. "But she was carrying on a secret relationship with someone else, and when the letters were discovered—" The rani spread her hands, and in that empty space was everything that didn't need to be said. To be caught writing to another man while negotiations are being made for your marriage to someone else . . . Well, it will end your chances at marriage forever. "It was a young woman's mistake," the rani went on, "but we pay for those the same as we do those we make when we're older."

I tried my best to look sorrowful. "I had no idea."

"I never learned who she was writing to. Her father's servant found the letters, but two days later, that servant was found in the Ganges."

I gasped.

"She didn't kill him," the rani clarified. "She wouldn't do such a thing."

"But her father might have," Moropant remarked. "I knew him when he was young," he reminded his daughter.

"Her father has passed," the rani explained to me, "but he swore to me—to this entire family—that nothing more transpired than letter writing. If it had, she wouldn't be here."

"Sit." Moropant gestured toward the cushions, and he clearly meant me as well as the rani.

"Another letter from Ellis?" he said, seeing the envelope on the carpet. "The sepoys *will* rebel. You know this. And I hope those men drive the British from here to the sea."

"We cannot have rebellion," the rani warned. "It would be the end of Gangadhar's rule."

"Only if we lost. I could train them."

"And when the British discover the rani's father in league with rebels?"

"These men aren't rebels, Manu. They are citizens of the kingdom of Jhansi."

"Who have signed contracts with the British to fight for *them*," the rani reminded him.

"Their allegiance is to Jhansi, whatever contract they've signed. The British Empire reaches from Hong Kong to Ireland. If the sepoys make enough trouble for them, they might think twice about how much effort a tiny kingdom in the north of India is worth."

The rani was silent. Neither raised the point that the child she was carrying might be a girl.

"I could be ready to train them at your word," he said. "Talk it over with the raja."

"Gangadhar is . . . you know what he will say."

The rani's father glanced at me. "Manu—"

"I know. Something has to be done. I will ask Shri Rama what he thinks."

"Shri Rama is a guru, not a general."

"Lord Krishna was not a general, but I believe he counseled Arjuna well."

The rani was referring, of course, to the story of the *Bhagavad Gita* in which Lord Krishna came to Prince Arjuna to guide him during a very difficult time. Arjuna's family was at war, and although Arjuna didn't wish to enter the fray, Krishna's advice was to fight; however peaceful you may wish to be, we all have the responsibility to rise up against evil.

Moropant nodded, then gestured toward me. "Be sure you take this one with you. Any Durgavasi willing to shoot the father of the rani is dedicated indeed."

○ ○ ○

That evening at temple, after all of the food had been served to the poor, I met Shri Rama. Usually, Sundari was the only Durgavasi invited to sit with him alongside the rani, but this time, the rani said, "Sita, I want you to join us."

I followed them through a series of painted halls, and was careful not to walk too close to the oil lamps, which were suspended by long chains from the ceiling. Kahini had told stories about women who, due to inattention or some unlucky wind, had caught their dupattas in the flames and ended up vanishing in great blazes of fire. But the lamps were beautiful, and their flickering lights cast deep orange hues over the golden statues that watched us quietly from various niches.

The three of us made our way to the very back, and when we reached the last room in the temple, the servant stopped before a curtained door and called loudly, "Her Highness, Rani Lakshmibai." Then the servant parted the curtains and the three of us entered.

Inside, an old man was sitting cross-legged in the center of a room covered with jute mats. He was surrounded by all of the religious items you might expect—candles, incense, flowers, broken coconut shells. But these were all details I noticed later: as we entered all I saw was the extreme peacefulness in Shri Rama's face. If you've ever met someone completely at peace with his life, this is exactly how Shri Rama appeared. He couldn't have been younger than sixty, yet his skin was completely smooth, like a river stone that has had its roughest edges caressed by water. His eyes, too, were different. They gave the impression that whatever difficulties you placed in his lap, they would be quietly considered and calmly solved.

The rani approached him with a very reverent bow; from his position on the ground, Shri Rama did the same. Sundari and I made the same respectful gesture of bowing and placing our hands together, then we seated ourselves to the rani's left.

"You brought someone new," Shri Rama said, his voice as smooth and calm as his face.

"Sita Bhosale, my youngest Durgavasi."

He gazed at me for several moments, then nodded. "Welcome, Sita."

I wondered what sort of exotic ceremony a guru like Shri Rama would perform, but it turned out to be a puja like any other. It wasn't until after he'd given each of us a red tilak mark on our foreheads that he rocked back on the jute mats and said casually, "Well?"

"The sepoys are growing angrier and more agitated with the British. Father believes we should arm them for rebellion."

Shri Rama took in this information. "Have they perpetrated evil?"

"I believe they are guilty of thoughtlessness. I believe they may be inciting the unrest among the sepoys."

"Would killing British soldiers be perpetrating evil?"

"Yes. I believe in diplomacy. Diplomacy until the very end. But what is the end?"

"I suspect it's the destruction of Jhansi," Shri Rama said.

I could not believe my ears. I looked to Sundari but her face revealed nothing.

"And is that acceptable?" the rani asked.

"All kingdoms and empires come to an end. The question is what replaces them, and who commits the first act of aggression."

"So I wait?"

"That depends. What kind of ruler do you wish to be?"

The rani put her hand over her brow, and spent several moments in deep thought. "Father will not like this," she warned.

Shri Rama nodded, but said nothing.

"Thank you," the rani said.

Shri Rama turned to me. "Someone is making life difficult for you. Why are you allowing this?"

I was so shocked that I sat in stunned silence for several moments. "I . . . I don't know." But of course I knew. Kahini was the rani's favorite and a cousin to the raja.

"Well, if you don't know, I certainly can't tell you!"

I glanced at Sundari, who didn't look surprised, then at the rani herself, but she was lost in her own thoughts.

"Keep Durga close to you," he said to me, and immediately, the ten-armed goddess of war appeared in my mind. Each of the gods had contributed something divine to her creation. Shiva sculpted her perfect face, Indra endowed her with breasts like the moon, Vishnu gave her many arms, the god of fire formed her glittering eyes, and Yama spun her hair like black silk. Other gods armed her with invisible weapons and the Divine Craftsman clothed her in invincible armor. When the gods saw how perfect she was, they set about presenting her with various gifts. Bejeweled ornaments soon glittered from every part of her body, and she wore garlands made from flowers whose fragrances never faded. Finally, she was given a lion to ride on her quest to rid the world of violence and evil. That Shri Rama should tell me to keep Durga close was a curious thing, because I never imagined her being very far away.

After we left the temple, the rani said, "Your father is a woodcutter. You told me once he gave you a carving of Durga."

In that moment I realized that the rani's memory was like the mythological Akshayapatra, an inexhaustible vessel that could never be filled. She could reach into her mind and retrieve any detail she wanted, no matter how trivial.

"Perhaps Shri Rama meant you should never part with this carving," she said.

This had not even occurred to me.

"Let's take a stroll through the gardens," the rani suggested. But Sundari had to oversee the delivery of gunpowder to the magazine where it was to be stored in Star Fort, so the two of us carried on alone. When she was gone, the rani said, "Why don't you tell me your favorite piece of literature, and I'll tell you mine." When the rani saw me hesitate, she added, "There's no right answer, Sita. Just tell me what you like best."

"Shakespeare," I admitted.

I could see the rani was surprised.

"My father read his plays with me."

"Do you have a favorite?"

"*Hamlet*."

"That ends sadly, doesn't it?"

"Yes, but there are many profound moments. And yours, Your Highness?"

She grinned. "Anything at all in the *Puranas*. I love the old stories and the heroic deeds. But mostly, I like the sound of the words—the language."

I knew what she meant. My father had read the *Puranas* with me as well; they are some of the oldest texts written about our gods, and they are lyrical as well as interesting.

"What would you say if I told you that sometimes I dream of the episodes written in them?"

I smiled. "I dream of literature all the time."

"You do?"

"Yes, especially if it's a well-written tale."

The rani smiled. "I think you and I have more than it appears in common," she said. And this is how we spent the afternoon. Walking and speaking together like friends.

When we came to a beautiful bower on the edge of Mahalakshmi Lake, the rani sat down and admitted, "I wonder sometimes what it would be like to be the stonemason who carved this." She ran her fingers over the bench and indicated that the seat beside her was for me. "Tell me about your father. Does he carve all day? How many pieces? What is his workshop like?"

I answered her questions.

"Does he like it?"

I had to think about this. "Yes. But his dream was to be a soldier." I told her about Burma, and his accident, and Shakespeare.

"These British . . ." she said, but didn't finish her statement. "So you grew up with your father and sister. No brothers?"

"No. Just a grandmother," I said.

"How lucky. Mine was already gone by the time I was born."

I pressed my lips together, so I wouldn't say anything that would reflect badly on me.

"What is village life like?"

"I . . . can't say. Outside of Jhansi, all women are in purdah."

I could see the rani flush. "Of course. Then your whole childhood?"

"Yes."

"I'm sorry."

"I made a world out of my house. And reading."

"Yes. Even prisoners can escape if they have books." She smiled at me, and I felt deeply how wonderful it was to serve a rani who was so well educated. We had both been fortunate in our upbringings.

That evening, after we returned from the lake, the rani brought me into her chamber and asked me to choose from several saris. I picked a beautiful yellow silk that would go beautifully with Anu's complexion and eyes. Then she gifted me an entire basket of cosmetics and thanked me for a very lovely day.

"The pleasure was truly mine, Your Highness."

When I was dismissed, I found Gopal and told him to send the gifts to my sister.

"It'll be more expensive than a letter," he warned.

"How much more expensive?"

"Two *anna*."

I gritted my teeth. "Fine."

The gifts wouldn't be the same as having me, but at least Anu would understand that what I was doing, I was doing for her.

Chapter Twelve

When the other Durgavasi returned from visiting their families, my name was on the rani's lips wherever we went. She asked for me to read to her every night. Sometimes, I read from Shakespeare's *First Folio*, other times from Charles Dickens's latest work, and since we were the only ones who understood English, none of the other women joined us when we laughed or cried. It was just as Sundari had hoped. Kahini's plan to punish me had worked out in my favor. The rani and I were becoming true friends.

Kahini behaved as if nothing extraordinary was happening. Even when Rajasi made an ugly face in the courtyard after the rani asked me to accompany her to the stables, Kahini remained composed. I thought she had made peace with the changing of the currents. But it wasn't peace she was making: she was damming the river so that the waters would stop entirely.

"I see you've become quite close with the rani," Jhalkari remarked before bed one evening.

I glanced across the Durgavas to see who might be listening. Most of the other women were asleep.

"She's very compassionate, and I think sometimes she's in need of a friend."

"She's the rani. She has plenty of friends. But you're making enemies."

I sat at the edge of my bed and waited for her to explain.

"Sita, don't think the other women aren't jealous."

"Which other women?"

"All of them!"

"You?"

She didn't say anything.

"Are you upset that I've become closer to the rani?"

"It is petty of me, but it hurts. I thought we were close."

"Of course we are!"

She shrugged. "Well, my jealousy isn't dangerous to you. But Kahini's is."

Still, it didn't seem as if Kahini cared. Then, two days before Diwali, our largest, most joyful festival celebrating the return of Lord Rama after his triumph over the demon king Ravana, a physician arrived to check on the rani and her growing child. Since this was a weekly occurrence, there was no reason to suspect that anything out of the ordinary might happen. I was sitting in the queen's room with the other Durgavasi, when Sundari appeared looking terribly grave.

"There is news from the court physician," she said.

We were so silent I could hear Moti's heavy breathing from the other side of the room.

"Two messengers arrived from Bombay, carrying a pestilence. Both men were sick on their arrival, and they died immediately after entering Jhansi. The physician wishes to examine each of you today. If you are ill there will be signs in your throat."

"If it came from Bombay," Kahini said, "it must be Dalit's curse. So many Dalits live—"

"This is not the time," Sundari warned.

The room settled into tense silence. It was several minutes before the physician arrived. In that time, most of us tried not to breathe. If this new disease began in the throat, then it was obviously borne on the breath as well.

"Namaste, Doctor," Sundari said.

He was an old man, with hair as thick and white as spun wool. There was an image of Dhanvantari, the physician to the gods, around his neck. We all pressed our hands together in namaste, but the physician made no acknowledgment of our presence. Instead, he said matter-of-factly, "I'd like everyone in this room to stand in a line. When I come to you, open your mouth as widely as you can so I can see to the back."

Imagine the embarrassment we felt at being asked to do this! Bad enough to stand with your mouth gaping like a washed up fish, but to do it in front of a man . . .

"Fine," he kept saying as he went down the line. "Fine." Then, when he came to Jhalkari, he said, "Please stand to the left."

"Is the rani sick?" Kahini asked when it was her turn.

"No, and her child is well. But anyone with symptoms will be dismissed until they have recovered."

I had read an account of the black plague, which killed off a third of Europe's population. What if this was a kind of plague?

The physician came to Moti. "Fine," he said, and she released a staggered breath. But when he came to me, his forehead crinkled. "Stand to the left, with her."

My heart thundered in my chest. When the physician was finished, three of us had been separated from the others. Myself, Jhalkari, and Mandar.

"What have you found?" Sundari asked. Her feline eyes darted about the room.

"These three." The physician shook his head. "Dismiss them for a month—at least."

Mandar exclaimed, "This is nonsense! Two riders die and suddenly I'm ill? Have we met these men? Did they step foot in the palace?"

"I can't say."

"Well, I can!" Mandar shouted. "Where is your evidence that we are infected?"

Sundari held up her hand. "Mandar, let him speak."

"This is a very clever disease," he said. "It hides in the chest and manifests within weeks."

"Did you interview the dying men?" I asked boldly. "How do you know this?"

"Because I did exactly as you said. The messengers showed symptoms two weeks ago."

"I thought they died as soon as they arrived in Jhansi," Jhalkari challenged.

He spread his hands and said tensely, "With the rani in the condition she's in you must go."

Sundari asked everyone to return to the Durgavas, but asked the three of us to stay behind. I felt like a leper. What if I made my family sick as well?

As soon as the room was empty, Sundari said, "I do not believe that any of you are sick." She looked angry. "This is a foul-smelling dish cooked up by Kahini. I saw her with that physician this morning, whispering. I do not believe there are any dead messengers. None of you are sick." Sundari was adamant. "This is a trick to keep Sita away from the rani."

Mandar and Jhalkari both looked at me. If ever there was a time to band against me, this was it. "Kahini hasn't just banished us," Jhalkari asked. "She's robbed us as well. We will not be paid if we are absent."

"What if the rani is too afraid to let us back after a month?" Mandar said. "She must think we are lepers."

"That's how I feel," Jhalkari said. "A leper dressed in Benares silk."

"Perhaps we should tell her what Kahini did?" I suggested.

"Who would you believe?" Jhalkari said. "A physician or us?"

Sundari agreed. "The rani is heavily pregnant and much weighs upon the delivery of a healthy child. Do not test your friendship now, Sita. It is wiser to wait the month. In that time I will convince her that no pestilence threatens this palace."

Three men brought our horses; one of them was Arjun. He handed me the reins, but didn't look particularly fearful. "Is it true?" he asked. "Are you sick?"

"She's no more sick than you are," Mandar replied, looking at the several dozen soldiers that followed behind Arjun, ready to escort us to our homes. "Someone convinced the rani that there's a plague in Jhansi, and that the three of us are showing signs of infection."

Arjun looked incredulous. "Kahini?"

"She must have bribed the rani's physician," Jhalkari said.

"I'm sorry. The guards are asking about the sickness and no one knows what to believe." Arjun glanced at me. "I wish I could escort you to Barwa Sagar," he said quietly. "It's a long way to travel." He reached into his bag and pulled out the same red book I had seen him reading the first time we'd met. "For your trip," he said, handing it to me.

I ran my finger over the gilded lettering. *A Collection of Rumi's Poetry.*

"There's one poem in particular I thought you might enjoy. I marked the page for you."

My cheeks felt hot. "Thank you," I said.

"What?" Mandar joked. "Nothing for me?"

"Do you read poetry?"

She snorted. "Not unless I'm forced to."

The journey to Barwa Sagar took most of the day. I rode like a horse with blinders on, because the only image I saw was Arjun's face—his expressive eyes, his slender nose, his long hair pushed back from his pale forehead by his muretha. I felt slightly lightheaded imagining him standing so close to me. He was very handsome. He was also a captain, so why wasn't he married? A captain of the rani's guards should be married with a growing family. Perhaps there was something wrong with him.

As we entered my village, and boys ran to the sides of the road to steal a glimpse of our small procession, I was still distracted. It wasn't until we turned onto the narrow street where I had lived for more than seventeen years that I was suddenly in Barwa Sagar again.

I could see from a distance that the door to my house was thrown open, and the courtyard was filled with Father's guests. Children threw flowers at my feet, and distant cousins held up offerings of sweets. Was this how the rani felt every time she left the Panch Mahal? It was as if I had left the village a cat and returned a lion.

I saw myself in their eyes: my green silk angarkha was more beautiful and more expensive than anything anyone in my village had ever worn. My silver-handled pistol gleamed in the sun, as conspicuous as my kattari and my sword. A vain part of me hoped that Grandmother was watching and withering with envy.

"Sita," Father mouthed the word as soon as he saw me.

I dismounted as quickly as I could to touch his feet. Then suddenly everyone was there and talking. The soldiers who'd traveled with me were given food, and water was brought for the horses. A crowd of at least a hundred people swelled around me, encouraging me to see what was waiting inside the house. When I stepped into the kitchen, every dish imaginable had been prepared for my arrival. Avani must have worked all day for a week just to cook the sweets. Father squeezed my hand, and words were entirely unnecessary. That moment was possibly one of the happiest in my life. And when I looked for Grandmother, she wasn't there. I imagined she was pouting in the back of the house.

"Where is Anu?" I asked, searching for my sister. "Anu!" I shouted, but she didn't appear.

"Anu is hiding," Avani said. "She's in her room. There are too many people."

I found her huddled on her charpai, her knees drawn up to her chest. If it was possible, she seemed even smaller and younger than before. "What are you doing in here?" I seated myself next to her, taking her in my arms.

"I miss you so much," she cried into my chest. Then she looked up at me through her wet lashes. She was wearing the yellow sari I had sent her; someday she would be a very beautiful woman. "Everybody is happy about you," my sister said. "But I want you back."

"Oh, Anu," I said, and stroked her hair. "I wish I could live here, too."

I coaxed her out into the crowd of smiling faces from all across Barwa Sagar, and everyone wanted to know the same things. What was the rani like? Was the palace as beautiful as they said? Did the maharaja own twenty-three elephants? What about the food, and the beds, and the baths? Did all women wear angarkhas, like me, or did they wear saris as well? Could I show them my pistol? Had I killed anyone yet?

It was exhausting, and the last of the guests didn't leave until sunrise, long after Anu had gone to bed. When the house was finally empty, Father came into my room and seated himself at the edge of my charpai. His bald head reflected the rising sun, turning his skin first gold, then orange. We both looked over at Anu, who moved as if she were dreaming. I took his hand and wrote, "I brought more earnings for her dowry fortune."

He traced over my palm. "You have changed in five months."

My eyes met his, and there was such intensity in his gaze that I became worried. Did he think I—the girl from the palace mirror—had become unrecognizable?

"You've grown more confident," he wrote. "None of the women in Jhansi keep purdah, do they?"

"No." I was worried about what he might say next.

"Well, I don't believe you should keep purdah here either."

My eyes met his.

"Dadi-ji will be upset," he predicted. "But when Shivaji and I go out, I want you to come with us."

Of all the gifts he might have given me on my return, this was the greatest.

Chapter Thirteen

"I suppose you have something to say about the quality of your charpai now," Grandmother remarked over breakfast the next morning. "You will be demanding a fancier bed, I imagine."

As always, her hair was perfectly combed. It swept over her shapely head like a waterfall, cascading down her back in three silver braids. But her sharp cheekbones, which other women envied, revealed her nature. She was all angles and no softness.

I put down my bowl of yogurt and bananas. "Did you hear me complain?" I said.

Anu gasped, and Grandmother's eyes widened. I had never spoken to her with such disrespect.

"How dare you!" She rose from her chair and I rose as well. I was taller, younger, stronger. She was not going to intimidate me anymore.

"How dare I *what*, Dadi-ji? Answer you? Earn my sister's dowry fortune?"

"And what will you do? Go searching among the imbeciles who

beg outside the temples to find her husband? I assume she's told you how long it took for her to master making rotis?"

"Do not insult Anuja." I turned to my sister. "Anuja, has Grandmother been unkind to you?" Her letters had never said so.

Grandmother laughed. "Oh, it's not an insult. It's the truth."

"You will never speak about her that way again!" My voice rose, and my sister covered her ears with her hands. "If I learn that you've beaten or insulted her, or acted in any other despicable way, you will be sorry."

"And exactly how will I be sorry?"

"Someday, when your son is too old to work," I said, "I will be the only one bringing money into this house."

"And you think he would let you starve me?"

Her dismissal of my threat caused something inside of me to break. Suddenly, I was bamboo that not only bends, but snaps, creating edges that are sharp as knives. "I think no one knows which of us will die first," I said. "And Lord Shiva help you if it's your son."

I turned and walked away. Inside my room, I could hear Anu's small feet hurrying behind me. She collapsed onto my charpai. "Dadi-ji is going to kill you!"

"Anu, nothing could be further from the truth. And she is not going to treat you cruelly again. Here is something you must do differently: if she insults you, or threatens you in any way, you must write these words: 'Dadi-ji has been very kind this week.'"

Anu's eyes opened wide.

"Do you understand? She will still have someone read your letters, and you can never write the truth. But if I see that phrase, I will know, and I will come to help you."

Anu was speechless.

"Can you repeat the phrase to me?"

"Dadi-ji has been very kind."

"*This week.*"

"This week," she replied.

I had changed. But not in the way Grandmother thought: I didn't believe I was too good to sleep on a traditional charpai, and I certainly hadn't grown so accustomed to the rich fruits and curries of the palace that I couldn't enjoy Avani's cooking. But it was as if my mind was an hourglass and the thoughts inside my head were the tiny grains of sand, and by becoming a Durgavasi, the hourglass had been turned completely upside down.

For one thing, I understood more about cruelty. After living for five months with Kahini I understood that Grandmother's bitterness was something she nurtured, feeding it like a vine until it choked out all other feelings. Secondly, I now understood what suffering meant, and could truly see the difference between the very rich and very poor. I'd had no idea that we were poor until I saw the splendors of the Panch Mahal. Yet the time spent at Mahalakshmi Temple, serving curry and sweets to people who would have no other meal—it made my life in Barwa Sagar seem fortunate. It also made me think that with enough charity and dedication, the people who lived on carpets with silver bowls had the ability to make other people's lives better.

I won't pretend I was suddenly like Buddha, making keen observations about the world now that I was a part of it. But new ideas certainly occurred to me, and I found myself thinking about the rani's guru, Shri Rama, wondering what he would say about life in Barwa Sagar and the women who lived inside like caged parrots.

During a trip to the market with Father and Shivaji, I was the only woman walking in the streets. Men stared, and most of their gazes were hostile.

"Does it feel strange to break purdah here?" Shivaji asked.

"It did in the beginning. Now it feels like being a fish emptied from the bowl it's spent most of its life in back into the river where it was actually born."

By December, the air was bitterly cold and I had read Arjun's book of poetry twice. Our family was seated on thin cushions around the brazier while Avani fanned the coals, and I couldn't help but think of the warmth of the palace, where rugs covered the stone floors and there were always enough blankets. Father took out the book he carried with him and held his pen over the heat, warming the ink. When it was ready, he wrote, "What use is Rumi at court? Why aren't you practicing your English?"

"The rani values poetry as much as anything else."

"Who could be a finer poet than Shakespeare?"

I considered my answer. I didn't want to offend him, but I also didn't want to lie. "I believe Rumi may have been just as talented, Pita-ji."

Father frowned. He didn't like this new direction.

"At court," I went on, "English is useful, but it's also looked down upon."

"Why?"

"Because the English are not well liked in Jhansi. There are conflicts—"

"Is that why you haven't gone back?"

It was the first time Father had questioned why I was staying in

Barwa Sagar for so long. A vacation of a week, possibly even two, was believable. But Diwali had come and gone, and the rani's child was due. Why wasn't I at court to protect her?

"I will return in two weeks," I wrote.

He didn't press any further. But he glanced at my sister before writing, "I know someone well suited to her. And if their Janam Kundlis match, I would like to make the necessary arrangements."

Marriage would mean that Anu would go to her father-in-law's house. Father would be alone with Avani and Dadi-ji, neither of whom could write.

"Who?"

"Ishan."

Shivaji's son. I thought of his tenderness when he'd come to our courtyard to heal the broken wing of the tiny bulbul. He was only seven years older. And Anu would only be one house away. I wrote swiftly, "It's perfect. More than perfect." I found myself wondering who Father might have found for me if life had been different and I had been destined to marry. But I pushed these thoughts away, since they didn't serve any purpose. I was forever duty-bound now to the rani. Fortune's wheel had turned in a different direction for me.

Father reached out and patted my leg. "*Sab kuch bhagwan ke haath mein*," he wrote. And in Hindi, this means, *It's all in God's hands*.

Father spoke with Shivaji, and it was agreed that a priest should be called to read the Janam Kundlis of the prospective bride and groom. I have already spoken about the difficulties of being born manglik. But neither my sister nor Ishan were bad-luck children, and according to the priest, their Janam Kundlis matched.

When the priest was gone, Anu found me in the kitchen, placing bowls of water under the legs of the small table where we kept our vegetables so the insects couldn't climb into the vegetable bowls.

"Is it true?" she said. "Am I really going to marry Ishan?"

"Yes. Next year. And I don't think I need to tell you how fortunate you are that both of your charts matched."

Because Anu was a worrier, it took some days for her to become accustomed to the idea that her marriage had been arranged. Then, as I suspect most nine-year-olds do, she forgot about it entirely, opting instead to play with her dolls whenever she wasn't helping our grandmother in the kitchen. And once the excitement of Anu's marriage died down, there wasn't much for me to do. It was too cold to visit the markets, or to go with Father to deliver his carvings. So I sat by the brazier and read Rumi.

Be with those who help your being.
Don't sit with indifferent people,
whose breath comes cold out of their mouths.
Not these visible forms, your work is deeper.
A chunk of dirt thrown in the air breaks to pieces.
If you don't try to fly,
and so break yourself apart,
you will be broken open by death,
when it's too late for all you could become.
Leaves get yellow.
The tree puts out fresh roots and makes them green.
Why are you so content with a love that turns you yellow?

The last line confused me. *Why are you so content with a love that turns you yellow?* What love did I have that was mediocre?

∘ ∘ ∘

At last a courtier arrived with a retinue of seventeen soldiers to bring me back to Jhansi.

I had the strange feeling of wanting to be in two places at once, like a sailor who misses the sea as much as he misses dry land. I was sad to kiss Anu and Father good-bye, but at the same time, I felt duty-bound to the rani. And I missed the other Durgavasi.

I mounted Sher, who had been forced to take shelter in Shivaji's stable these past four weeks, and my sister reached up to hand me a small box of sweets.

"I made laddus," she said. "Your favorite."

"Thank you, Anu." I realized that the next time I returned, it would be for her wedding. "Be kind to Pita-ji," I told her. "And listen to Dadi-ji. You remember what I told you?"

She nodded.

"I'll see you soon," I promised.

Chapter Fourteen

I studied Jhalkari in the warm glow of the brazier. She'd grown thinner in the past month, and now, she looked less like the rani. There were other changes as well. While we'd been gone, carpets had been hung on the walls of the queen's room to keep out the cold, and there were thicker, plusher carpets on the ground. Servants had brought in a dozen braziers, and the other Durgavasi huddled around them in small groups. Jhalkari and I were in the farthest corner of the chamber, separated from the others by the fountain, which had been stopped for the winter.

"So where is Kahini?" I asked. A very foolish part of me hoped that the truth had been exposed and Kahini had been banished from the Durga Dal.

But Jhalkari had returned a day earlier, and she gave me a look. "In the rani's chamber, with Sundari-ji."

"So Sundari-ji never told the rani—"

"How could she? There would have to be proof. Without it, Sundari-ji could lose her position, which Kahini would love. She's already cost the rani's physician his job. When the rani asked a

British doctor—Dr. McEgan—about the status of the plague, he said he hadn't heard anything. Then the rani summoned her physician to her chambers and demanded to know where the two victims had been buried. But, of course, there were none. So when he couldn't tell her, she dismissed him as a liar."

It was amazing to me that there were people who went through life like a sickle, cutting down everything in their path, except for what was useful to them. Didn't the hard work of constant destruction ever tire Kahini? Didn't it become depressing? Even Lord Shiva, the Destroyer of Worlds, regretted his act of burning down Tripura after it was done.

"Anyway, the rani won't be leaving her chamber now until the baby comes due. We're only allowed inside if we're called."

"Does she know that we've returned?"

Jhalkari watched me for a moment. "You mean, does she know that *you've* returned? Because I don't think she has any reason to summon me."

I'm sure my cheeks turned the color of my angarkha. I changed the subject.

"Imagine if it's a girl," I said.

"*Shhh,*" Jhalkari cautioned severely. "No one should say that. It has to be a son."

Later that evening, the rani finally summoned me to her chamber. I hoped I might run into Arjun there, but two men I'd never seen were guarding the doors.

The sun had dipped below the horizon, and the chamber walls were burnished orange. I expected to see the rani tucked into her bed, buried in half a dozen covers this late in December. But instead, she was pacing near open windows, her long blue robe flowing behind her like a stream and opened to reveal her very round stomach. She had grown prettier in the time I was gone, softened by the extra weight of her child.

"Sita," she said as soon as she saw me, and from the way she spoke my name, I knew she regretted sending me from Jhansi. "Oh, Sita." She closed her robe and walked toward me.

I made the gesture of namaste and touched her feet. "It is an honor to return to your service, Your Highness."

There were tears in her eyes. I had not expected to see the rani in tears, and certainly not over me. She took my hands in hers and then guided me to her bed. She drew the covers over her chest and indicated the padded stool so that I could sit near her. "Tell me about your father and grandmother and little sister."

"Father, Grandmother, and Anuja are all very well, Your Highness."

Her face brightened. "Your sister must be preparing for her marriage."

"Yes. Because Your Highness was gracious enough to accept me as a Durgavasi, I'll be able to provide her with a dowry fortune. Father made a very suitable match while I was home, and the engagement ceremony will take place next month."

"I should never have sent you and the other women away. My physician was either incompetent or deluded. I suppose you heard there were never any messengers from Delhi?"

"Yes. Jhalkari told me what you discovered."

"Well, my doctor has been dismissed," she said, "and Dr. Bhagwat has taken his place. Kahini arranged it all. She interviewed new physicians—"

"And Your Highness thinks this is a wise decision?" I blurted.

The rani's expression changed. She looked disappointed with me. "Sita, Kahini grew up at court. Our childhoods were very similar. And no one"—she emphasized the words *no one*—"is better suited to understanding what a rani requires in a physician than she is."

I lowered my head in shame.

We sat in silence. Then the rani took a stack of letters from her bedside table. "Deliver these to Gopal," she said. "Make sure to convey them as soon as you leave this chamber."

"Yes, Your Highness."

"And Sita, be careful of assuming too much."

I was dismissed. Outside the rani's chamber, Arjun had replaced one of the guards. As soon as he saw me, he grinned.

"I heard you were back." He searched my face, and I knew I should say something about his book.

"It was a long time to be gone," I admitted, "but Rumi was a great help in passing the time."

"Then you read his poetry?"

"Yes."

"And what did you like best?"

I knew he would ask this of me, so I had already thought of my answer. "The last page. Someone wrote their favorite expressions in the back. Was it you?"

"No. I bought it that way."

One of the expressions written suddenly came to me, and now I quoted it for him. "'Yesterday I was clever, so I wanted to change the world. Today I am wise, so I am changing myself.'" I should never have been so forward with the rani. Now, perhaps she would never forgive me.

Arjun blinked slowly. "That's one of my favorite lines, too."

As we were speaking, I had moved closer to him. So close, in fact, that I could reach out and touch his smooth face. Immediately, I stepped back. "Can you direct me to Gopal-ji's chamber? I'm to deliver these to him." I held up the letters the rani had given me. "She wants me to do it at once."

"Up the stairs, at the farthest end of the hall."

As I left, Arjun called, "Can you be in the courtyard tonight? I have something I want to give you."

I hesitated. "I can't continue accepting gifts. How will it look—"

"These aren't gifts." Arjun laughed. "I expect to be repaid."

I'm sure my mouth was hanging open.

"I introduced you to Rumi. Now it's your turn to introduce me to a great writer," he said.

I flushed, since that wasn't what I'd assumed he meant. "But you don't read English—"

"How do you know?"

"Well, do you?"

"Enough to read a little poetry."

I was stunned. "Why didn't you say so?"

"You never asked."

Suddenly, I felt foolish. Why shouldn't Arjun know some English when it was spoken all around him?

When I reached Gopal's chamber, a servant opened the door and escorted me inside. The walls were paneled in rich mango wood, so that in the light of the oil lamps, the entire chamber gleamed like a woman's newly washed hair. Every few steps, there were heavy bronze lanterns on elaborate pedestals, and they were lit as well. Books were arranged on shelves that stretched from ceiling to floor, and at the far end of the chamber, Gopal sat hunched behind a desk. He looked up and I made a formal bow and the gesture of namaste, and then offered him the letters. "The rani asked that I deliver these to you at once."

"This is Kahini's job," he snapped. He looked over my shoulder, as if I was contriving to hide her somehow. "Will you be replacing Kahini now?" he demanded.

"I don't believe so. Perhaps Kahini is occupied," I guessed. "So I was asked."

"Occupied with what?"

Gopal continued staring at me, and finally I said, "I don't know, and I don't much care. I have delivered the letters to you as the rani requested. Is there anything I should deliver to her?"

Gopal glowered at me. "No."

I was not invited to the rani's chamber during her lying-in again.

When the news came a week later that the rani was in labor, Sundari took me aside and asked what had happened between us. "Why hasn't the rani asked to see you again since you've returned? What happened the last time you saw her?"

"I don't know what you mean," I said, although, of course, I knew exactly. But Sundari kept staring at me. I hesitated. "I may have said something that led the rani to believe that I was overstepping my bounds."

Sundari sighed. "Tell me."

Reluctantly, I repeated the conversation. Then I waited for her to make a pronouncement.

"You may be the quickest girl the Durga Dal has seen in quite some time, but you can't follow even the simplest warning. At court, there is no telling whom you can trust. Your closest adviser may be plotting your overthrow. How do you sort your friends from your enemies? By keeping family close, Sita. Kahini is related to the raja. Yet you think you can walk into the rani's chamber and criticize her family. Who are you? A girl fresh from the village, who's never visited a physician in her life."

If Sundari had reached out and slapped my face, I would have felt less pain. The truth of her words stung like a physical blow. "I won't say another word about Kahini," I swore. "Or anyone else."

"I hope you get that chance. She's about to give birth; if it's a son, she might be in a forgiving mood."

As it happened, the gods smiled on Jhansi. The rani did give birth to a son, and without so much as a whimper, according to the servants who were inside the birthing chamber.

The celebrations that followed were beyond anything I had ever seen.

It may have been the coldest part of December, but for an entire week the city was filled with rejoicing people. They gathered in the streets to congratulate one another, as if someone in their own family had just been delivered of a boy. Sweets were distributed in the temples, and bells rang from morning until night, so that even though the weather appeared brooding, the city was cheerful.

Inside the palace, the tables, columns, door lintels, and windows were all garlanded with bright bunches of winter flowers from the raja's gardens. Loose rose petals were strewn across the courtyards, and jasmine oil burned continuously. The perfume of the flowers mingled with the scents of rich curries and roasted meats coming from the kitchens, and everyone in the palace was served two heavy meals a day, with thick lassi for drinking, and sweets for dessert. There were so many sweets prepared daily—puran puri, shira, anarasa—that it was impossible to taste them all.

Per custom, the rani was confined to her bed for a month, wrapped up like a moth in the silk cocoon of her chamber, with the windows shut and no visitors permitted except her closest servants and Dr. Bhagwat. Even Kahini was forbidden from visiting. Sundari said she was following every child-birthing ritual: the walls of her chamber had been whitewashed, and she was wearing a sacred pavitram ring made of kusha grass for an auspicious recovery.

Because we knew the rani was happy, we all had great fun in her absence, and everyone placed bets on what the child would be named. Eleven days after the child was born, a priest arrived for the naming ceremony. His name was to be Damodar. Rao would be added to signify his nobility.

That afternoon, the raja organized a procession to celebrate Damodar Rao's arrival.

The Durgavasi weren't part of the parade, but we were allowed to watch as Raja Gangadhar mounted his favorite elephant, a towering animal he'd named Siddhabaksh, and we followed the procession as it wound its way through Jhansi's festooned streets. It was extraordinary to see Raja Gangadhar towering above us in his silver and velvet howdah as if he were a god. Mounted servants rode alongside him, holding up the three emblems of royalty: the umbrella, the *chauri*, and the silver rods. All three gleamed in the low winter sun. A retinue of soldiers on white horses followed, dressed in ceremonial uniforms. And behind them rolled a long procession of carriages carrying gifts for the prince of Jhansi: silks, tapestries, marble vases, wooden toys, and elaborate brass statues from Lalitpur.

The people prostrated themselves as the procession went past. Even the British officers, whose flaxen-haired wives were protecting themselves from the weak midday sun by brocade umbrellas, stopped to stare.

"There's going to be a play tonight," Sundari announced. "Something from the *Ramayana*."

The *Ramayana* is one of our holiest texts, and for the next three nights, parts of it were to be performed in celebration of Damodar's birth.

"Another *Ramayana* play. Oh joy," Kahini said.

But the truth of it was, she was probably glad to get out of the Panch Mahal. Since Damodar's birth, none of us had been to the maidan, and our daily routine of practicing, bathing, and going to the temple had stopped entirely.

We all dressed in our best angarkhas, wrapping ourselves in two layers of pashmina—gifts from the rani upon Damodar's birth. But in the courtyard, a thin layer of frost covered the ground, and Sundari decided that we should all go back inside and change shoes. The silk of our slippers would never survive the short walk to the raja's baradari.

As the other women made their way back inside, Arjun appeared from the shadows. He was dressed in a double-breasted coat and held a white bag. "Something to entertain you," he said.

The other Durgavasi raised their brows at what this might be, but inside, I knew there would be a book. When everyone was gone, I unwrapped his gift and held it up to the light of the flickering lanterns. It was a collection of poems by Hafiz.

"I haven't read him," I said truthfully.

"He was a fourteenth-century poet from Persia. People still make pilgrimages to his tomb."

"If you wait here, I have something for you," I said, and hurried inside with the other Durgavasi.

I changed shoes quickly. Then I took out a book I'd been keeping in a chest beneath my bed and wrapped it in an old dupatta. Jhalkari was watching me.

"He must have been waiting for you in the courtyard," she said. "It's a cold night to be waiting for someone."

"Yes. We exchange books sometimes."

"What do you think he wants?"

"I told you, we exchange books." I didn't wait for her reply. I hurried outside with my copy of William Wordsworth and gave it to him. "English," I said coyly, "as requested."

He studied the plain blue cover and the simple black lettering. "And which one is your favorite?"

"'The Tables Turned.'" It was simply the first poem that came to mind. But Arjun nodded, as if my answer held greater meaning than it did.

Chapter Fifteen

1852

Damodar's arrival changed life in the Panch Mahal. We were no longer permitted to speak any louder than a whisper outside the rani's chamber, and the gardeners who tended to the courtyards were instructed to do their work only when the little rajkumar wasn't sleeping. Even the cooks were forced to change their routine, since the rani didn't want the rajkumar breathing in the scent of the fire first thing in the morning. Instead, she placed rose petals by his head, and long strings of jasmine. Our training resumed again, but without the rani to oversee it, no one exerted herself.

The raja visited his wife every morning and twice in the afternoons. He was so in love with Damodar it was a wonder he didn't strap him on his back and take him each evening to the baradari. When the rani's confinement was finished, we thought she would want to resume all of the things she had been forbidden from for so long. But it was another several weeks before she came to see us in the queen's room. Even then, it was only a brief visit, and Damodar wasn't with her. I bowed very low when she arrived, but she paid no more attention to me than to any of the other Durgavasi. The only women being invited to her chamber now were Kahini and Kashi; Kashi, because she had raised seven younger siblings.

Then, on the last day of January, the Durgavasi were summoned to the rani's chamber to meet the rajkumar.

"I'll bet he has his father's nose," Moti said.

"And the rani's hair," Heera added.

We looked at Kashi. She had seen the rajkumar dozens of times. "You've never seen a more beautiful child," she told us. "Nine years in the making," she said wonderingly. "It was about time the gods blessed them."

Kahini made a noise in her throat. "You think it was by praying she got a child?"

"Kahini, the raja is your cousin," Heera said severely.

"And the truth is the truth," Kahini answered.

"Well, I don't care if she went to him dressed as an English general," Moti said. "Jhansi has an heir."

As we made our way to the rani's chamber, I asked Jhalkari in a whisper why she thought the rani had gone to the raja dressed as a man. She looked at me the way you might look at a person who wants to know why breathing is essential for life.

"Isn't it obvious, Sita? It's because he's passionate about *men*."

The idea was shocking, mostly because I didn't think this was even possible. Did everyone know this except me?

Then Sundari announced, "Her Highness is ready."

The rani had never looked more beautiful. She was dressed in a cream and gold angarkha, and her hair fell in long waves over both shoulders. Thick clusters of pearls gleamed from her neck—a gift, perhaps, from Gangadhar.

"My Durgavasi!" she exclaimed, delighted to see us.

We gathered in a circle around the red and gold bassinet. The rajkumar was tightly swaddled so that only his face was visible. But with his thick, dark hair and delicate nose, he was as beautiful as Kashi had said.

"Look, he's opening his eyes!" Heera pointed.

We all leaned forward to stare, and the rani said, "He can't see very far, but if you put your face close to his, he can make out your features."

"Not everyone at once!" Kashi warned. "You'll overwhelm him."

So we formed a line, and each of us took turns peering into his bassinet. Now, in Hinduism, we don't believe in fate so much as karma. But the moment I peered into his bassinet, Damodar Rao gave an enormous smile. You probably think this is an exaggeration, since babies don't even return their mothers' smiles until they're at least six weeks old, but this is exactly how it happened.

"Did you see that?" The rani looked at the other Durgavasi. "He *smiled* at Sita!"

"Perhaps he mistook her for a *bhand*?" Kahini offered. Meaning, a clown.

"Stop it," the rani said. Then she looked at me. "You're the first person whose smile he's returned." She watched me intently, as if she could puzzle out my secret.

But I was just as mystified. I had done nothing that the other Durgavasi hadn't done. Maybe I had simply done something extraordinary in my past life to account for such luck.

"Someday," she said to me, "I want Damodar to speak English. Will you come in the evenings and speak to him?" she asked.

I said quickly, "I would be honored, Your Highness."

"When the other Durgavasi leave today, why don't you stay?"

The other women remained in the rani's chamber for another

hour, cooing to the rajkumar and chatting with the rani, until Sundari announced that everyone should return to the queen's room, with the exception of me.

"I'm happy to stay as well, if you'd like," Kahini offered immediately.

"Oh, I don't think that will be necessary. I'm sure the raja will call for you soon. I hear he has another play he's putting on," the rani said.

"Yes, by Vishnudas Bhave. His *Sita Swayamvar* was performed for the Raja of Sangli. Gangadhar has hired him to write something new, set in Jhansi. He is paying double the salary the raja paid in Sangli. A writer like Vishnudas Bhave won't accept anything less."

I could see the irritation on the rani's face. "You may go," she said.

Kahini slipped out the door. For a few moments, the rani didn't say anything, and I remained standing above the rajkumar's bassinet. Then she indicated the cushion next to her bed and I sat.

"Sita, I've been very disappointed in you these last few weeks."

"Your Highness, I'm—"

She raised her hand, and I was silent.

"There are times when I simply need you to listen."

Shame burned my cheeks and I lowered my head. "I'm sorry."

"I know you are honest, sometimes to a fault. But you must understand that Kahini is family. She may be irritating and arrogant . . ."

And self-serving and malicious.

"But she has done me a great favor. You must understand by now that the raja doesn't visit me in my chamber."

I couldn't meet her gaze, so I mumbled my response into my lap. "Yes."

"Kahini was the one who suggested *I* go to him." She looked over at Damodar in his bassinet. His dark lashes rested softy against his fat cheeks, a perfect child. "To hold him in my arms at night, to rock him to sleep with a song, to feel the weight of him against my chest when I feed him . . . He's the greatest blessing in my life. Without Kahini, he wouldn't exist."

I felt the same way you might feel to learn that the man you were hoping to marry has been married off to someone else, someone with greater charms than you could ever hope to possess. Nothing I could ever do for the rani could compare to what Kahini had done.

"I want you to go to the theater tonight. The raja isn't telling me what he spends on these plays. I want you to discover exactly how much this Vishnudas Bhave is being paid and how long he will be here."

I stared at the rani, wondering how she thought I could accomplish this.

"My husband can't keep anything in his stomach," she said. In India, this means that a person can't keep their thoughts to themselves. "I need this information, Sita. If the treasury is being depleted, it will change our relationship with the British. We don't want to need them any more than we already do." She looked at Damodar. "He is everything to me. Someday, he will inherit this kingdom. But first there must be a kingdom to inherit."

I won't pretend I wasn't nervous when everyone began preparing for bed and I was expected to put on a fresh angarkha and make my way down to the raja's baradari. The rani had called for two of her men to escort me through the darkness, and I hoped that one of them would be Arjun, though if anyone had asked, I certainly would never have admitted to this. I waited for Kahini to leave, then changed into lavender churidars with a heavy purple cloak. When Jhalkari saw what I was doing, she raised her brows.

"By the rani or the raja's request?"

The other women looked over to see how I would answer. "Both," I said, since whichever answer I gave, Kahini would hear of it.

I doubted that Jhalkari believed me, but she didn't say anything more as I fastened my holster and crossed the Durgavas. Outside, two men were waiting in the dim light of the courtyard. Their breaths formed white clouds in the bitter night air. One of them was Arjun.

"So you're following in Kahini's footsteps," Arjun remarked curiously as we walked.

"I wouldn't say that."

"She's the only other Durgavasi who's invited to see the raja's rehearsals."

"Well, this isn't an invitation I sought out. The raja believes I'll have something of value to add to his performances. I'm afraid he's about to see that he's mistaken."

"I don't know. I think you have more to add to people's lives than you realize."

I looked up at Arjun, but even in the light of the full moon, his expression was unreadable. So I changed the subject. "Do you know which play he's rehearsing?"

"Yes. *Ratnavali*," the other guard said.

"A comedy?" I exclaimed.

"The raja believes he possesses comedic genius that's waiting to be uncovered," Arjun said. I couldn't tell whether he was being sarcastic. "Now that the rajkumar has been born, he wants happier plays."

"And the raja's part?"

"The princess Ratnavali. Of course."

We arrived at the baradari, and Arjun pushed aside the heavy curtains, which had been tied between the pillars of the open-air pavilion to keep in the warmth. The raja was on stage with Adesh. They both wore wigs, but only the raja's wig had long, silken tresses. The moment the raja saw me, he clapped his hands together.

"Sita!" he exclaimed, and a great fuss was made over my appearance. Wasn't it nice that I had dressed in peach nagra slippers? And look how the black trim of my cloak brought out the fairness of my skin. Everyone wanted to know what I used for my hair. "It even shines in the darkness," the raja remarked. I had to tell him I didn't use anything special, but Adesh was certain I was concealing some trick.

"I want the three of you to sit right here," the raja said, pointing to several cushions near the front of the stage. Kahini was occupying one of them, and when she saw that we were making our way over, she purposely got up and moved.

"Don't be so rude," the raja said.

"I'm not being rude," Kahini defended herself. "I just don't like anything around me when I'm watching a performance."

"You mean you don't like any other beautiful women around you." Adesh laughed.

"Well, if that was the case, I could go back to sitting over there," she said.

"Kahini," the raja reprimanded, but there was playfulness in his voice, and she grinned in response.

For my part, I simply ignored the banter. But if this was what it was going to be like every night, the rani would have to forget about my coming, because it would simply be intolerable.

"We're rehearsing *Ratnavali*," the raja said. "Are you familiar with the play, Sita?"

"Yes, it's a comedy."

"That's right. Now watch and let me know if you have any comments."

I glanced at Arjun, but he was at as much of a loss as I was. What did he expect from me? Comments about what? His performance? The writing? The play began, but as the night progressed, nothing came to mind. Midway through the performance, when Adesh was no longer needed on stage, he sat down next to me. He smelled heavily of perfume and something else. Wine?

"Have you heard anything about a playwright named Vishnudas Bhave?" he whispered.

Because I didn't know whether the rani would want me to lie, I told him the truth. "Yes."

"Is he really coming to Jhansi?"

"There's talk that the raja is inviting him—"

"It's absolutely unnecessary!" Adesh exclaimed. The raja looked down at us from the stage, and we both smiled quickly, so he wouldn't know we were talking about him. Immediately, Adesh lowered his voice. "Does the rani know how much a playwright like him will cost?"

"I can't say—"

"Well, there's no reason for it! I'm a playwright, but the raja won't even take a look at my plays."

This surprised me. I had thought Adesh was the raja's favorite. I was about to respond when Kahini rose from her cushion and came over to join us.

"And what are the two of you whispering about?"

"How beautiful your cousin looks tonight," Adesh said. "I can't think there's ever been a lovelier Ratnavali."

Kahini looked from Adesh to me, then back again. "I can keep a secret—"

"Honestly," I said, "we weren't—"

"I didn't ask *you*."

"What's happening here?" the raja demanded. He strode to the edge of the stage and put his hands on his hips, so that he looked exactly like a pouting woman in his long wig and sari.

"Sita here was discussing your performance with Adesh," Kahini said. "I was just asking her to share her comments with the rest of us."

I glanced at Arjun, hoping he might devise some way of saving me, but he remained silent.

"Well, what is it, Sita?"

I felt my breath catch in my throat. "I . . . it's nothing."

"You have nothing to say? That's disappointing. I brought you here because the rani said you were clever."

"Perhaps it's past her bedtime," Kahini said.

Several of the actors laughed.

"If you're tired and have nothing of value to add, you had might as well go. Next time, come rested."

When the raja resumed acting, I turned to Arjun. "You might have helped me."

"How? You were whispering with Adesh. Did you think the raja wasn't going to notice?"

Tears of shame burned in my eyes, but I willed them not to fall. It was unlikely the raja would call for me again after this. I had failed the rani.

When I returned that night, Jhalkari was still awake. She waited until I had changed into my kurta and slipped beneath my covers before she whispered, "It was the rani who wanted you to go, wasn't it?"

I didn't lie to Jhalkari. "Yes."

"Is she afraid of what the raja is spending?"

I pushed myself up on one elbow. "How did you—"

"It's an easy guess. I'll bet the British rub their hands together every time he throws a party for his actors or hires one from Sangli or Bombay."

"She wanted me to find out how much he's spending, but I can't see how that will change anything. He's the raja—"

"And he listens to her. Why do you think she presides over the Durbar Hall? He treats her like a mother. And no son wants to disappoint his mother."

"But she's fifteen years younger than him."

"That doesn't matter. I'm sure you've heard people say she's old beyond her years. Our rani was born to rule."

I wondered if, in the history of India, there had ever been such a raja as ours. "He was performing another woman's role tonight."

In the flickering light, I saw Jhalkari shrug. The other Durgavasi may have accepted that this was how things were in Jhansi, but I still had trouble understanding it. From the moment I'd left the baradari to the moment that the rani's guards had brought me back to the Panch Mahal, I couldn't stop thinking about the raja in his long, black wig, as convincing as any woman who might have been playing his role. I'm sure I should have let the matter go, but I couldn't stop wondering what might have happened if the rani hadn't gone to her husband's chamber dressed as a man.

"I just don't understand it," I whispered. "How can a raja not want any children?"

Jhalkari frowned. Now that the rani had lost the weight of her pregnancy, they once again looked like sisters, and it felt a little strange talking about the rani with someone who looked so similar to her. "Who said he doesn't want any children?"

"Well, if he has no desire to visit the rani's chamber—"

"Some men simply have no interest in women."

"But is this only in Jhansi?"

Jhalkari popped herself up on one elbow, and behind her, Moti stirred in her sleep, dreaming, probably of food. "Sita, don't tell me you think this is unique to Jhansi. This has existed since the beginning of time. The raja was born this way, the same way you were born with an interest in men. And one man, in particular."

I sat up a little.

"You should be careful," she said.

"Why?"

"Because the other Durgavasi are talking."

"There's nothing indecent about exchanging books!"

"It starts with books. But they know he requested to escort you tonight."

"How—"

"Kashi was with the rani when he volunteered. And it starts with this. Then suddenly he's escorting you to the shops, and next he's trying to touch your hand."

I could feel my face becoming hot. "He would never try that!"

"He's a man."

"He's the *captain* of the rani's guards."

"And that makes him any less of a man? I should think it makes him much more of one. Be careful of your reputation, Sita. He's not looking to marry a Durgavasi."

"How do you know?" Immediately, I felt embarrassed that my daydreams were so transparent.

"Because he was married once before and his wife died in childbirth with the child." Jhalkari looked very sad for me. "He obviously wanted a family, Sita, and I doubt that anything has changed."

When we left the Panch Mahal the next morning, Arjun was

sitting on the ledge of the fountain, dressed in his white vest and gold churidars. Jhalkari raised her brows at me.

"There he is. Probably looking for you," she remarked.

But he rose as soon as he saw Sundari, and the two of them began talking in hushed tones. I heard Sundari exclaim loudly, *"No!"* Then the pair of them hurried into the queen's room and disappeared down the hall to the rani's chamber.

"What was that about?" Kashi said.

I wanted to be concerned. The fleeting thought even crossed my mind that perhaps the rani was ill, but I dismissed it. After all, the rani could survive anything. She was like Father's bamboo, bending, but never breaking. Hadn't she found a way to conceive a child when the rani before her had failed? And didn't she rule over Jhansi even while the British were busy hoping for rebellion? But even if I had wanted to focus my thoughts on her, I honestly couldn't have. At that moment, I was preoccupied with Arjun. How long ago had he been married? What had his wife been like? Was it a son or a daughter who had died?

Then Kahini entered the queen's room, and her face was pale. "I think something has happened to the rajkumar," she said.

Chapter Sixteen

You can probably imagine the kind of panic that ensued in the Panch Mahal when word spread that Damodar was suddenly taken ill. At first, it was only that he couldn't keep anything in his tiny stomach. Then, he began having difficulty breathing. The rani tied a small black string around his wrist to keep away the evil eye, but still he was sick. The curious thing was, his troubles came and went. The doctors gave him an Ayurvedic tea made from raw honey and thyme. He got better, and would sleep and eat contentedly, then the next day he would seem paralyzed again. His feet would stop moving and the stillness would travel slowly up to his arms. Physician after physician was called and all sorts of herbs and teas were tried, but the symptoms persisted. Soon, everyone was banished from the rani's chamber except family.

Weeks passed like this and the strain was felt by everyone. We all waited and prayed; then in April, on Rama Navami, the start of our festival celebrating the birth of Lord Rama, Kahini returned from the queen's chamber and immediately we knew.

I thought Kashi would break she cried so hard.

For myself, I felt as if I'd swallowed stones.

On the day of the rajkumar's funeral, his small body was borne on a litter, and taken to the shores of the lake next to the Mahalakshmi Temple. Fiery orange trees we call Flames of the Forest rose to meet the blue sky and swayed in the wind as a priest worked to build the funeral pyre. When he was finished, he set the pyre alight, and I thought I would choke on my grief.

Hundreds, possibly thousands of people, stood on the banks of the lake while the rani leaned on Sundari for support. Without her, she would have collapsed under the weight of her sadness. As for the raja, he sank to his knees before the funeral pyre and wept into his hands. He remained like this for as long as it took for the flames to devour his son's tiny body.

No one should have to endure such misery.

It didn't seem fair to me on that day that people who have done no wrong in this life are punished for deeds they don't remember in their previous ones. I refused to believe that the rani had done something so terrible in a past life that her punishment was the death of her child. I wanted to ask Shri Rama about this, and vowed to do so.

For the next seven days, neither the rani nor the raja emerged from their chamber. I remained with the other Durgavasi in the queen's room, and three more days passed. The only glimpse we had of the rani was when she made her way to the raja's chamber, dressed entirely in white, from the pearls on her neck to the sandals on her feet. The rani stayed with the raja for four days, and on the fifth day, I wrote to Anu:

You can't imagine the change that's overcome the palace. Once, it was a place of light and joy. Now it has become a fortress of sorrow. The windows in the rani's rooms remain shuttered, as if she's afraid of seeing light. And maybe she is. When Mother died, I remember being angry that the world was carrying on with its business as if our world in Barwa Sagar hadn't stopped. But Nature goes on and on. The karmic wheel turns. And it makes me feel ill to think that I'll never visit the rani's chamber again and see the rajkumar's cheerful face. The rani's mourning is so deep that she doesn't even heed her advisers anymore. Shri Bhakti has warned her that if the Durbar Hall remains empty for too long, someone else will arrive to fill it. And there are many pretenders, Anu. They're there, waiting in the shadows, watching for the right time to step into the light. Sundari-ji thinks the rani might go to durbar this week. I am hopeful.

But it was another two weeks before the rani attended her first durbar, and when she did, she wasn't actually there. Not in spirit, anyway.

From her cushion behind the rani, Kahini muttered, "This mourning can't go on forever. There's a kingdom to run."

"What's the matter with you?" Kashi hissed. "The heir of Jhansi has died. Her *child*."

"You really don't have a heart, do you?" Moti asked.

"Oh, I have a heart," Kahini replied. "I also have eyes and ears."

The rani ate her meals alone in her chamber, and in the evenings she remained there. Not even Kahini was allowed inside. A month passed this way, and the bitter wind howling through the courtyard outside reflected our dark mood. When Gopal arrived to collect our letters, only Kahini had written anything. I wondered whom she wrote to every night: her parents were dead and she had no siblings.

"If you're ever in need of comfort—" Gopal began.

"The delivery of my letter," Kahini said sharply, "is all I need from you."

Immediately, Gopal lowered his voice, but not so low that I failed to hear, "I realize that Sadashiv is important. But—"

"Do not speak his name," Kahini said through clenched teeth.

The Master of the Letters stepped back in shock, and when Kahini turned around, she knew I had heard everything. "I can't imagine a life so boring," she said, "that I'd need to eavesdrop on other people's conversations."

Before I could respond, Sundari walked into the room. Her face was pale. "Sita." She motioned for me. "Go to the rani."

I was pleased. The rani had asked for me, not Kahini. But once I was before the rani's chamber, I hesitated. What could I say in the face of such loss? Unfamiliar guards opened the door for me, and I stepped inside. The chamber was dark, and the rani was lying on her bed. She didn't say anything. I waited for what felt like an eternity. Then finally, she said, "Write a letter for me. Address it to Major Ellis." The man I had seen at the raja's play. "Begin with all the regular English salutations."

I did as I was told. Meanwhile, the only sound in the room was my pen as it scratched across the paper. When she could hear that I had stopped, she continued.

"Tell him that there will be another heir."

I looked at her in shock, and realized that she was crying. "Your Highness—"

"It hurts so badly, Sita." Her shoulders began to shake, and she covered her eyes with one hand. "Durga help me," she whispered.

I was scared that I would say the wrong thing, but as she

continued to weep, I knew that whatever I did wouldn't matter. I reached out and squeezed her hand. "I'm sorry."

"I know there are children outside, laughing. Everywhere in Jhansi there are women with children, and Shiva forgive me, but why should they be blessed and not me?" She looked young and vulnerable. It was easy to forget that she would be twenty-five soon. "Isn't that terrible? I think of women begging and I feel jealous of the poor because they have living sons."

I held tighter to her hand, and she began to weep the way truly stricken people do, loud and deep.

"At night," she whispered, "I can hear him crying. And in the baths." Her tears came harder. She took a staggered breath before finishing her sentence. "I can hear him making little sounds. While the water is running, I can hear him."

She was making me cry, so I looked out the window. Below, the city of Jhansi sat gray and still, like an old man hunched over against the cold. "Do you think we did terrible things in our past lives?" I asked. "To come back as women . . . perhaps it's a punishment for some previous misdeed?"

The rani sucked in her breath. Then she exhaled it with great force. "Do you think Damodar did something terrible in his past life to have died in infancy?"

"Of course not."

"I must be the one being punished then."

I didn't have any answer for her.

"Shri Rama says we're all in a constant state of evolution, that pain moves us forward, changing us into something else, something we need to be."

We sat together in silence for some time. Finally I said, "Shall I finish the letter?"

The rani shook her head. "No."

° ° °

"So did you tell the rani we're waiting for her?" Kahini asked when I returned. "Did you suggest she join us tomorrow on the maidan?"

The other women in the Durgavas turned to follow our conversation.

"It was not the time," I said.

"Her mourning will stop," she warned me. "And when it does, she'll associate you with the darkest time of her life."

"That's a *vile* thing to say," Sundari said. "No wonder the rani doesn't call for you."

"And how many times has the *raja* called for Sita? He rules this kingdom. Not the rani, however powerful she may *think* she is."

I tried to ignore their bickering. There was already enough grief in the palace.

By the time Diwali arrived in October, I had enough not only to pay for Anu's dowry fortune, but to buy a year's worth of new kurtas for her trousseau. But planning for my sister's happy future and preparing her elaborate bridal chest felt like a betrayal to the rani's grief. So it was doubly astonishing when the rani called me to her chamber to give me a gift for Anu.

"Give my blessings to your sister," she said, and reached behind her braid to unfasten her necklace. "I'd like you to ask her to wear this on her wedding day."

"Your Highness—"

"She may keep it or sell as she wishes. But I'd like her to have it."

When the sun broke through the clouds the next morning, I made my way back to Barwa Sagar with a retinue of seventeen men.

Chapter Seventeen

My father's eyes filled with tears when he saw the gift the rani had given to me for Anu's wedding day. He took my palm and wrote swiftly, "How?"

The rani's gift would change my family's fortunes in Barwa Sagar. My place in the Durga Dal had already made my family famous. But now we would be considered wealthy as well, and Shivaji's family would be looked upon with even greater respect, since the rani's gift was ultimately destined for his house.

It may seem strange that a good friend like Shivaji would demand a dowry fortune from us, particularly since my father had saved his life in Burma. But in India, these things are not matters of friendship; they're matters of esteem: your family will only be held in high regard if they've managed to procure a good dowry fortune. Every neighbor who comes to your house, and all of their children, and even their children's children, will know what your son received with his bride. If she came with only a chest full of silk, no one is going to say, "Did you hear what so-and-so brought to her father-in-law's house?" Instead, they will let the conversation pass, since what is there to say about a bride who only arrives with clothes?

When my sister heard what she'd been gifted, she buried her face in her hands and wept. "Thank you," she kept saying.

"I haven't done anything. The rani gave it to you."

"But the rani doesn't even know me."

"Yes she does. I talk about you all the time."

She looked up, and her eyes were giant pools. "You do?"

It hurt me that her question was in earnest. I sat down on the bed next to her and said, "Anu, I never stop thinking about you. Just because I'm in Jhansi doesn't mean that my heart isn't here with you. And Pita-ji."

I could see she wasn't convinced. "And you'll be with me tomorrow, right?"

"At every step of your wedding," I promised.

"What about tomorrow night?" she worried. "I'm going to miss Pita-ji."

"I know. I miss Pita-ji, too. But what happens tomorrow is going to be very special, and it's something that both Pita-ji and I have been looking forward to for a long time. You'll see," I promised. "You're going to make a beautiful bride."

And she did.

There are many bridal rituals in India, and every village performs them differently. In Barwa Sagar, the rituals begin the night before, when girls throughout the village arrive to help the bride prepare. By six in the evening, our house was filled with giggling children and neighboring women. As soon as Aunt arrived, we all helped Anu into a bath of scented oils, washing her hair in coconut oil and then rubbing her skin with turmeric. Four henna artists were summoned to decorate her hands and feet.

They carefully applied the dark green paste, then instructed her not to move too much while she slept, or the dried paste would come off and ruin the elaborate designs underneath. As soon she woke the next morning, Anu scraped off the dried henna to see the final design.

"Look how dark!" one of our neighbors exclaimed. "You know what they say. The darker the bride's henna, the happier the marriage."

On my sister's pale skin, the henna had taken on a deep maroon color.

Little silver bowls of different pastes were brought, and sandalwood was applied to my sister's forehead, sindoor to the parting in her hair, and rouge to her lips. But despite her nervousness, it was impossible not to laugh. Weddings in India are joyous events, with singing, and eating, and dancing. We could hear the musicians playing in Shivaji's courtyard across the field. In a few hours, they would accompany the bridegroom to collect his bride.

When the bridal dress was unveiled, everyone gasped. It was a sari of red silk that I had bought in Jhansi, embroidered with gold thread and encrusted with tiny beads that shimmered whenever they caught the light. Half a dozen women helped Anu dress, and when they were finished, the final vision was breathtaking. In her ivory bangles and heavy pearl necklace, she could have been the rani's daughter.

"Am I pretty?" Anu asked.

"More than pretty," I told her while the other women stood back to admire her. "Ishan is going to be very proud."

Of course, he wouldn't take her to his bed until she became a woman, but already her beauty was arresting.

After that, there was no time for talk. A dozen rites had to be performed, starting with the arrival of six girls bearing terra-cotta jars painted with symbols that have been lucky for Hindus for thousands of years: the alpana, the swastik, the feet of Buddha. The girls had filled these jars with Ganges water, and now they held them and circled my sister three times. A seventh girl blew a conch shell as they danced. There were more rites, then eating, then more rites still, all culminating with the shraddha, which is a ritual done to honor a person's ancestors.

Then we heard the musicians coming closer and knew that the bridegroom must be on his way, surrounded by laughing, dancing relatives. When he arrived in our courtyard, I took Anu's hand in mine and whispered, "Are you ready?"

She nodded, and I drew her dupatta over her face so that she was completely veiled. After the ceremony, Ishan would be able to look into her face and see the woman who would someday bear his children. For many men, this is the very first time they see their brides. Of course, Ishan had seen Anu before, but their situation was quite unusual.

I led my sister into the courtyard where Ishan was waiting, surrounded by all of his relatives. He was dressed in rich Benares silk and his brothers had covered him in garlands. His eyes went very wide when he saw us, and I thought I saw the faint traces of a smile. Then everyone seated themselves on the cushions we'd provided. It was the start of a very long day: anyone who has attended a Hindu wedding can tell you, the rites last for more than twenty-four hours, and even the priest must rest before the event is considered complete.

By dawn, the priest was finished, and the relatives who had stayed awake joined the tired but happy procession from our courtyard to Shivaji's house. I told Anu to go inside and rest, since there would be more festivities come nightfall.

"Anu, tonight's also Diwali," I reminded her. She was married during the most auspicious time of the year. "I'll be back before dinner and we'll light diyas together."

When I saw her again in the evening, Anu was laughing. There was so much joy in Shivaji's house. She would have a very lucky life. I went outside with the men as they lit the diyas and placed them near the walls of the house. If you were a bird and could see our village from the sky during Diwali, you would look upon endless strings of glittering oil lamps.

Ishan had procured a chest full of fireworks, and that evening the bright explosions even made Grandmother smile. At the end of the night, it was strange, walking through the gate of Shivaji's home without Anu. But Shivaji's home was her home now. She'd never live with my father again.

When we reached our house, my father stopped in front of our door and took my palm. "I am going to remarry," he wrote.

I wasn't shocked. My father had waited years. It was time. "Who?"

"Avani."

This did shock me a little. Widows rarely remarry in India. Certainly, it happens, but it is as common as snowfall in the summer. Yet they were the perfect match—they had seen each other daily for many years. We no longer knew each other well, but it seemed likely that she felt great affection for him. He waited for my reaction.

"I don't know why I never thought of it," I said. Then something occurred to me, and I'd be lying if I said it didn't bring me a certain joy. "Have you told Dadi-ji?"

"Yes. She was upset."

I imagined the shouting, pacing, and throwing of things. But obviously Father felt passionate enough about Avani that he had risked Grandmother's wrath.

"And Anu?" I asked.

"She was the one who suggested it," he said.

I went to bed that night feeling like a vessel brimming over with sweet water.

Chapter Eighteen

I returned home from Anu's marriage to find the road leading to the Panch Mahal completely empty. There was no one in the street, not even a chai wallah selling tea. At the doors of the Panch Mahal, there was no one to take our horses back to the stables. One of my escorts left three soldiers in charge of our mounts while the rest of us went inside.

"I've never heard it so silent here," I said. The entire palace felt abandoned. On our way to the queen's room, we spotted a servant and stopped him in the hall.

"What's happening? Where is everyone?"

The old man peered closer at us. "Where have you been?"

"In Barwa Sagar! What's happening?"

The old servant stepped back, slightly offended. "The raja is ill. He collapsed in the baradari three nights ago." He cleared his throat and took some time before continuing. "The rani has called on a British physician."

Immediately, my heart plunged. "Where is he now?"

"In his chamber." The old man looked at me. "Are you Sita Bhosale?"

"Yes."

"The rani has asked that you join her in his chamber immediately."

I turned to the soldiers and pressed my hands together. "Thank you."

The old servant motioned for me to come, and I followed him down a magnificently painted hall to a pair of elaborately carved wooden doors. The servant pushed open the doors and disappeared, leaving me alone with several guards. When he returned he said, "You are not to go beyond the entrance chamber. The rani will meet you there."

I was about to enter the raja's personal chamber: few people were ever invited here.

The old man held the door open for me, and I entered.

The only way to describe the room would be to use the word *grandiose*. Nothing was tasteful. The walls were red, the color so glossy that I knew the painters had employed a trick women use in Barwa Sagar, rubbing hibiscus flower over them in order to make them shine. An ostentatious chandelier hung from a gold and yellow star-patterned ceiling. The furniture was silver. The padding on the couches and cushions was bright blue. It was an assault on the eyes.

The rani arrived as I entered, and her face looked stricken. I bowed and pressed my hands together. "Your Highness, I'm so—"

She waved away my pity. "He is with Dr. McEgan. He can be trusted," she said, before I even asked.

"What are his symptoms?"

Vomiting, lethargy, an unwillingness to eat. "Then last night, he couldn't feel his legs. It was as if he was paralyzed, like Damodar. His own physician suspected poison," she said, "but his taster is well."

I heard the raja's voice—as clear as if he was standing on stage—shout, "I will *not* have an Englishman tending to me. Get out! *Out!*"

The doors swung open again, and an Englishman emerged, looking completely unflustered. His voice was soft and kind when he said, "Summon Major Ellis. Begin making plans for yourself and for Jhansi. Your Highness, the raja is very ill."

The rani waited until the doctor left before covering her eyes with her hands.

"What will you do?" I asked her. The raja couldn't be that ill; he was still strong enough to shout.

"I don't know. The question is, how do the British define *heirs*?"

The child was taken from his mother on the fifteenth day of October. I remember this because that evening there was a hunter's moon, the only full moon that appears in October. It was as bright and red as a giant ruby. I was watching it from the courtyard outside the queen's room when I heard screams. The sound was so pitiful that I rushed inside to see what was happening.

The rani was surrounded by three of her advisers and was cradling a little boy in her lap. He was no more than three, and tears streamed down his tiny face, pooling on his pudgy cheeks. His lower lip turned down, and he was shouting repeatedly for his mother.

"I want you to meet Anand," the rani said.

The other women had also come running, and now we all stared at the little boy. The childless rani had made another woman childless.

Shri Bhakti stepped forward. "The official adoption will take place tomorrow."

At twenty minutes before noon, the rani appeared in a lavender sari with yellow jewels. She was carrying the boy, and he looked a little calmer.

We walked in a quiet procession to the Durbar Hall, where the raja was seated on his throne, propped up by several pillows and looking extremely ill. He had lost a significant amount of weight. Men stood on either side of him, ready to catch him if he should fall.

In the years since, I have heard some claim that this child's adoption took place in the raja's bedchamber. But I was there to witness the event, and I can tell you, it happened at noon in the Durbar Hall. A dozen or so British officials were in attendance, including Major Ellis, dressed in uniforms of bright scarlet serge.

It took several hours for the papers to be drawn up, but eventually a will was made, and Anand was declared to be the rightful heir to Jhansi's throne. In the case of the raja's death, the rani was to act as Anand's regent.

The papers were read aloud, and then the raja, the rani, and nearly all of the British officials in attendance signed them.

When this was finished, the raja requested that everyone leave the room with the exception of the rani. We filed out into the hall. The British officials left, but the rest of us remained standing near the open doors. We could hear the raja just the same as if we were standing next to him. His voice was hoarse and weak.

"Manu," he said. "If life had been fair, I would have been born a rani, and you would have been born a raja."

"Next time," she said.

"If I die, the other kingdoms will see Jhansi as weak. Remain friends with the British. They're strong enough to save us from our enemies."

I'm sure the rani was clenching her jaw, but we heard her agree.

There was silence after this. Perhaps he was weeping. Maybe they both were.

It was October fifteenth.

By the twenty-first of November, the raja was dead.

For thirteen days—the very minimum—the rani didn't leave the Panch Mahal. When she emerged, she only did so to break her bangles outside, as was the custom, leaving behind the pieces for poor women to sweep up and sell. She didn't shave her hair or change her colorful saris for widow's white. But as we made our way through the silent fortress to the lake near Mahalakshmi Temple, the sight of the raja's funeral pyre made me suddenly nervous.

I glanced at Sundari, who was standing near the rani as the raja's lifeless body was lifted from his gilded litter onto the neatly piled wood. But she was too distracted by the rani to notice me. I looked at the growing number of people: advisers, soldiers, farmers, and merchants—all of them crowded onto the lakeshore to bid the Raja of Jhansi farewell. Many of them stole secret glances at the rani, wondering if she was going to do as her ancestors and countless other women before her had done.

"She can't do it," I said.

"Committing sati is the greatest form of respect a wife can show her husband," Kahini replied.

How could Kahini be so callous? I felt sick. Without the rani, what would become of Jhansi? What would become of the Durga Dal? But Shri Bhakti's head was bowed, and the Dewan kept looking from his adviser Shri Lakshman to his adviser Shri Bhakti and back again. No one spoke, no one moved.

The priest stepped forward with a torch and intoned a few important words in Sanskrit. Then the pyre was lit and everyone turned. I could hear my heart beating in my ears.

The rani moved toward the pyre and the taste of metal was thick on my tongue. Everyone believed she was going to do it, and no one was willing to cry "stop!"

Not even me.

Then she stood in front of the flames and shouted, "What Jhansi needs now is a leader, not a martyr!"

The cheer that went up was deafening.

"There are people standing in front of me today who will condemn me for not entering the flames. But what woman has ever changed her husband's fate by joining him on his pyre? And what woman has ever built a stronger kingdom by disappearing from it? Our ancestors believed that committing sati was an act of courage. I say that with the exception of the goddess Sati, who after all, is immortal, it is an act of cowardice! Who will raise her children, or care for her parents, or tend her garden? No. If I die, it will be by the sword, not by the flame."

Shri Bhakti began to weep. Even the seemingly emotionless Dewan had tears in his eyes. Behind me, people began repeating the speech the rani had given, and word began to spread through the thousands of mourners that Jhansi was not going to lose its queen.

There was a feeling of triumph in the air, as if suddenly, we were attending a celebration, not a funeral. The rani stepped away from the burning pyre, and when her eyes met mine, I was grinning widely.

When the funeral was over, the rani made her way to the Durbar Hall. This time, she heard the petitioners not from behind the latticed screen, but from the throne. Hundreds of men had come, and as the last of the petitioners filed out the door, Arjun appeared from beyond the curtains to ask if the rani might give one last audience.

"Your Highness, I believe this is important."

There was something in the way he said it that made all of us sit up straighter on our cushions. The rani no longer kept purdah in the Durbar Hall, so when Major Ellis arrived, he could see that her face was thinner and that she no longer wore the red vermillion mark of a wife in the parting of her hair.

"Sita, will you take Anand for me?" the rani said.

She passed her son to me, and the rajkumar gave an enormous screech. He began kicking his little legs, afraid of being separated from yet another person he now loved. Next to him, Kashi held out her arms.

"Want me to take him?"

I passed the rajkumar to Kashi, who somehow knew how to hold him, because he settled against her chest just the same as he did for the rani.

The major looked particularly worried today. His hat was in his hands, and he kept twisting it around, too nervous to meet the rani's eyes.

"Major Ellis, we have been friends since I first arrived in Jhansi. You know I can handle whatever it is. If it's bad news, then simply give it to me."

"I'm sorry, Your Highness—"

"For what?"

"I—" His eyes filled with tears, and I realized at that moment how young he was. The rani's age, maybe twenty-five. "The British are talking among themselves. They wish . . ."

He couldn't bring himself to say it, and a cold feeling seized my spine, the same as if someone had put an icy hand beneath my angarkha. Next to me, Kashi felt it, too, because she froze, and Anand began to whimper.

"Major Ellis, I want you to say it. Whatever they wish, we are allies, and I'm sure it can be accommodated."

"Your Highness, they wish to annex Jhansi. I'm sorry."

This was not what she was expecting. She stood from her throne. "Have I been a poor ruler?"

"It isn't you."

"Have I disobeyed any of their commands? Ignored their requests?"

Major Ellis looked beside himself with grief.

"Why would they want to do this?" she cried in English. "We've done everything for them! Bent to all of their rules! They were here for my son's adoption. You saw it, you signed the papers."

"Yes." The major nodded. "I know. But now they're saying it isn't enough. That he isn't your actual son. When they set their minds on something—"

Everyone began speaking at once, and Kahini's voice was the loudest. "They will never take Jhansi!"

The rani looked down at the major. "What can we do?"

"Why are you asking *him*? He's one of them!"

The rani held up a hand to silence Kahini.

"We must begin the appeals process," he said.

She returned to her throne. "It's gone that far?"

"The letter will arrive in a few weeks. Your Highness, I don't know what you intend to do. Whether you wish to remarry—"

The Durgavasi began talking again, and the major looked from face to face, confused.

"Major Ellis, I am an Indian woman. I have been married, and we only marry once."

His face turned as red as the uniform he was wearing. "I didn't know. I'm sorry. I—" He stood. "Perhaps I should go."

"No! Please. We need your help. What can I do to stop this?"

"I don't know that it can be stopped."

"It *has* to be!" The rani sounded desperate. "Jhansi is my home. It's my *life*. It's the kingdom Anand was born to rule."

Ellis gave a pitying look at the baby in Kashi's lap, as if he were a poor substitute for a real heir.

"He is my son," the rani said. "And this is my kingdom. What right do the British have to rule in my place?"

"None," he admitted.

"Then help me, Major. Please."

"In December, we can appeal to the governor-general in Fort William."

"Yes. What's his name?"

"Lord Dalhousie."

"Will you help me write it?"

"Of course, Your Highness." His eyes met hers. "Anything you wish."

He left, and we all remained where we were. The horror of it was too great to comprehend. The British were our allies. On his deathbed, the raja's very last words had been about his treaty with them. He'd begged the rani to honor it at any cost, afraid that our neighboring kingdoms would arrive like vultures to pick at his dead carcass. And he'd been right. Except that neighboring kingdom was England.

When we reached the queen's room, I wrapped myself in my warmest shawl, then excused myself and went into the courtyard. Arjun found me beside the fountain.

"Did you hear?" I said. My breath fogged up the night air. It was going to be a cold December.

"Yes. But she must have known it was coming."

I sat back. "Why?"

"Didn't you hear the way the British spoke of the raja at his funeral?"

I thought back, but nothing stood out to me.

"You speak better English than I do," he said, "but even to me it was obvious. They were calling the raja a prince, not a king. And the painting that Captain Malcolm presented to the rani . . . Did you see it?"

"No. The rani refused to hang it."

"Because it shows the governor-general meeting with the raja, and they are both seated on Western chairs—at equal levels."

I gasped.

"When that letter arrives in a few weeks"—his voice grew low—"there is going to be rebellion. The sepoys won't stand for it," Arjun predicted, "and the rani is going to be in a very delicate position. If she supports the rebels, the British will kill her. If she supports the British, then the rebels will do it."

"What do you mean *kill*?"

"There is going to be war, Sita. The British are coming to take over our kingdom."

I felt as if someone had pushed the breath from my chest. "But what about the appeal?"

"Did an appeal work for the Mughal emperor or Baji Rao?"

Despite the cool air, my head began to feel dizzy. My entire life was the rani. What would happen to the Durga Dal? What would become of the cooks and gardeners and thousands of other people who depended on her throne? What would become of Jhansi?

"Our job is to protect the rani and rajkumar at all costs," Arjun said. "There may be dangerous times coming. I want you to be careful."

"They'll listen to an appeal. They have no reason to take Jhansi. We haven't violated any treaty," I reasoned.

But Arjun didn't look convinced.

Chapter Nineteen

1854

When the rani announced that we would be practicing yoga with Shri Rama every morning, the Durgavasi were upset. With so many problems threatening Jhansi, no one thought we should be spending our time doing salutations to the sun.

"The goal of yoga," the rani announced, "is to remind us that we are not oxen; we can put down the burden of our worries whenever we want."

Most of the Durgavasi laughed privately at this. Within weeks, however, my body felt more limber and my mind felt sharper.

I know that in the Western world, yog—or yoga as it has come to be called—is seen as exotic. It's something mystics practice with their hands resting, palms upward, while they close their eyes. All sorts of nonsense exist about this form of meditation, but I will tell you what yoga is and what it isn't. Yoga is not something a person practices with music or mirrors or any other distraction. Its purpose is less about *samyoga* than it is about *viyoga*, which is to say, it is more about disconnecting than it is about connecting, which many Westerners find strange, until they hear it explained. The reason a person practices every day is to disconnect from their deep connection to suffering.

The author of the ancient *Yogatattva Upanishad* believed that without the practice of yoga, it was entirely impossible to set the atman free. The atman, of course, is the soul. And just as the rani said, we are so burdened down by our daily worries that many of us have become no different from beasts. We walk around eating and drinking and caring very little about our purpose in this life. Some of us are not even very clever beasts. We are merely trudging through our work, yoked to some terrible master or job. The goal of yoga is to change all of this; to remind the human who has become like an ox that their yoke and harness can be taken off, even if it's only for a few minutes a day, and that through silencing the mind, we can silence greed, and hunger, and desire as well.

Of course, this all sounds very nice. But the theory of yoga and the practice of it are very different. One is easy to learn, the other takes much time and dedication.

Eventually, even Mandar, who had scoffed the loudest when the rani decided that we must embrace yoga, was noticeably calmer. But yoga can't change reality, and on the fifth of December, the letter arrived from Major Ellis: Jhansi was indeed to be annexed by the British East India Company. And as advised by the major, the rani appealed. A response arrived on the twenty-fourth of February. The rani's father delivered it to her in the library, where I was sitting with Kashi on a soft yellow cushion, reading with the rani and Anand. He joined her on her wide orange cushion and waited while she read.

I watched her face. It was bad news. "Kashi, will you take the boy to my chamber?" After they'd left, she said, "They're giving me three months to pack."

She saw the confusion on our faces, so she handed me the letter and asked me to read it aloud. As I did, I felt the world shift beneath my feet, as if the hand of Brahma was actually pushing the earth out from under me. The rani had three months to move from the Panch Mahal into a smaller palace at the bottom of the hill. The Company was euphemistically calling it the Rani Mahal, and they promised to give her a yearly pension large enough to run it with a "suitably sized household."

"And what will happen to our people?" the rani asked. There were tears in her eyes, but they lingered at the edge and refused to fall. She pressed her lips together, and I followed the direction of her gaze to the flag of Jhansi, a kettledrum and whisk on a field of red. "Tomorrow, it will be a British flag," she whispered. She stood. "I am going to appeal the governor-general of India himself." He was the man elected by Company officials to oversee the Company, and his election was subject to the British queen's approval.

I had never felt so angry or afraid. What gave these foreigners the right to destroy our kingdom? Our people lived here for five thousand years—now a company would be deciding our fate.

"We should encourage the sepoys to rebel," her father said. "It is time."

"Not if there is a chance that the British East India Company will listen to reason."

That night, I lay awake in my bed, thinking about how the Durgavas would belong to the British. The walls, the carpets, the beds where we slept, even the small tables where we made our pujas to Durga. I tried to imagine what the rani was feeling, lying in the room where she'd spent every night from the time she was fourteen, knowing that soon, a foreigner would make it his home.

All because she'd had the misfortune to lose her husband and son.

When the sun rose the next morning, I didn't wait to hear the soldiers blowing conch shells in the courtyard to rise. As soon as the sun pushed its way through the windows, I dressed myself in my warmest shawl.

"Where are you going?" Jhalkari said.

"I want to see it for myself." A few other women were dressing as well. Mandar, Heera, even Rajasi. Jhalkari sat up, and I took her folded angarkha from her chest. "Come," I said, handing it to her.

We went outside, and a small group of the queen's guardsmen followed us down the avenue. Arjun was among them. He was dressed in his usual outfit, only this morning, his long hair wasn't tied back by a muretha. The way it framed his face made him seem younger. We walked to where we could see the south tower, and there, snapping in the crisp morning breeze, was the Union Jack. Tears rolled down several of the men's faces.

Rajasi said, "There wasn't even a fight."

"Exactly how the British like it," one of the guardsmen said bitterly.

Thousands of people attempted to reach the Durbar Hall. They crowded the halls of the palace, and the soldiers had to keep order as soon as the British officers began to arrivc. Inside the hall, only the rani's advisers and Jhansi's most important officials had been given seats. We led the rani through the angry press of citizens, and when she took her throne, silence—as heavy and still as water—filled the room. We stood behind her, with our hands on our pistols in case there should be violence. Behind us, her guardsmen were ready as well.

"My people," she began formally. "*Main Jhansi nahin doongi!*"

A cheer rose up in the audience and the British officers exchanged nervous looks.

"I will never leave you!" the rani vowed. "But today, I humbly surrender the government of Jhansi to the British. Major Ellis"—she indicated who he was—"will be speaking on behalf of the British East India Company. Major Ellis, please relay for us the information you received from the governor-general of India, Lord Dalhousie."

Major Ellis rose from his chair. "Subjects of Jhansi," he began, and immediately, men began to shout. The rani held up her hand, and there was silence.

"Lord Dalhousie, under the command of the British East India Company, has declared the kingdom of Jhansi to be British territory." There was silence in the room. "The Rani of Jhansi shall take up residence in the Rani Mahal, where she will continue to be a source of inspiration for the people of Jhansi."

They were reducing our capable rani to a figurehead. The rani would keep the Durga Dal and her personal guards, but the army of Jhansi no longer existed.

"A pension will be provided to the rani on a yearly basis, and her adopted son shall receive an inheritance that is as yet to be determined." He lowered the paper.

"And when do the British plan to tell the rani what this *pension* will be?" the rani's adviser Shri Bhakti demanded.

Major Ellis flushed. "I'm sorry. That's all I know."

The rani's other advisers rushed to their feet, but it was General Singh who shouted the loudest. "What about the Panch Mahal? What happens to the palace?"

"British officers will be arriving next week to take up residence."

"In the palace my ancestors built?" someone cried.

"This is an outrage!" the Dewan said.

Someone else shouted threateningly, "This is the precursor to war!"

The rani stood. "We will conduct ourselves peacefully and with dignity. The move will begin tomorrow," she said.

And then it was over and our kingdom belonged to the British.

Many people have asked me what it was like to move from the glittering Panch Mahal into the Rani Mahal. They imagine terrible scenes, but as anyone knows who has experienced an unpleasant change in their life, so long as it happens gradually, there is rarely drama. I suspect this was why the British gave the rani three months to change actual residences.

At first, the British didn't want the rani to take any belongings with her. The carpets, the furniture, even the elaborate peacock throne—these were all things the British had hopes of keeping. But the rani wrote appeal after appeal, and finally, the governor-general himself weighed in with the following announcement: "It is beyond the power of the Government to dispose of the property of the late raja, which by law will belong to the boy he adopted. The adoption was good for the conveyance of private rights, but not for the transfer of the principality."

"Do they understand the irony?" asked the rani, almost amused, instead of growing angry as her father did while he read the announcement aloud. "The adoption *is* legal when it comes to property rights, but *is not* legal when it comes to inheriting a throne."

"They're making up laws as they go along!" her father shouted.

But we were all so in shock that no one had any time for rage.

° ° °

Thousands of people lined the roads to watch our procession to our new home, and they were utterly silent. For the British who were watching, it must have seemed eerie. The only sounds in the streets were the birds in the trees and our horses' hooves.

The Rani Mahal was one of the raja's old palaces. It was a two-storied building, nestled like an exotic yellow bird in the midst of a bazaar. When we arrived, the heavy iron gates were thrown open. Then we entered, single file. The flat-roofed building was sixty years old, with a quadrangular courtyard in the center and two small fountains trickling in the sun. Everyone dismounted, and four stable boys took our horses to a building outside the Rani Mahal, since there was no stable.

Inside, there were six corridors leading to six grand halls and a few smaller rooms. Nearly all of the rooms were painted red, and someone with a passion for flowers had decorated the walls with them. The arches were adorned with images of peacocks and rosettes, and stone sculptures from the Gupta period stared down at us from brightly painted niches. Both the queen's chamber and the Durbar Hall were on the second floor. Both had wood-paneled ceilings and windows overlooking the streets below.

"There isn't room up here for a Durgavas," Sundari remarked.

"Take one of the rooms downstairs and turn it into a Durgavas," the rani said. "Arjun, the same goes for my guard—put them next door."

I glanced at Arjun. Only a wall would be separating us at night, and I felt the heat rise in my cheeks. If anyone noticed they didn't say anything.

It took all afternoon to organize the palace. We sat on cushions in the Durbar Hall and took turns entertaining Anand while servants attempted to bring order to the chaos. Some time before the sun set, Gopal arrived to deliver our mail.

"That's it? One letter?" Kahini complained.

"I'm sorry." Gopal looked flustered. After all, he'd lost his privileged place in the Panch Mahal as well. "That's all there was for you."

"You're certain?"

"Yes."

Gopal delivered two letters to me, and immediately, I realized his mistake. A better person would have spoken up immediately, but I took the letter that was addressed to Kahini and slipped it into my angarkha. For the next two hours I wondered if I had the nerve to read it. But as soon as the time was right, I went downstairs and sat on a small marble bench in the courtyard. There were so many people entering and leaving the palace that no one paid any attention to me. I unfolded the letter as quickly as I could, before I could change my mind about it. I'm not sure what I expected to find, but it certainly wasn't this:

> *My love, I'm sorry to hear that life has been so difficult for you. There is talk that the sepoys are growing angrier. Is there any sign of revolt? Should I come? Are you in any danger?*
>
> *—S*

I folded the letter and hurried off to find Jhalkari. She was in the new Durgavas, a small chamber barely large enough to fit ten beds. She was speaking with Mandar, and I summoned both of them to a corner of the room.

"You have to see this."

Both women read the letter and shook their heads.

"It doesn't make sense. Gopal reads everything. Why would he continue flirting with Kahini if he knows she has a lover?" Mandar took the letter and read it again. Then she said, "Return it to Gopal. See what he does."

Jhalkari's eyes brightened. "He'll be beside himself."

Mandar agreed. "He won't even tell her you opened it."

"Or maybe he won't give it to her at all," Jhalkari said. "Look, there he is." Outside the window, the Master of the Letters was searching his kurta, patting every possible fold. "He knows he's lost it. Go," Jhalkari suggested. "We'll watch."

I approached Gopal with the letter, and his eyes darted madly from my hands to my face.

"You have it," he said accusingly. He reached out and tried to snatch it. "Give it to me!" he shouted, so that several servants stopped what they were doing to see what was happening.

"You gave me an extra letter," I said evenly.

"Did you read it?"

"Yes." I watched his face. A twitch formed under his left eye.

"You can never tell Kahini!"

"What are you covering up for her?" I asked, and let him take the letter from my hand. "She isn't in love with you; another man is writing to her. She's in love with someone else."

"You have no idea—"

I shook my head and started to walk away.

"Wait!" he called after me. "You won't say anything?"

I didn't respond.

After our move to the Rani Mahal, nothing seemed to make sense anymore, especially to Anand, who had already lost one home, and then had to lose another. For three nights he screamed, and there was nothing the rani could do to calm his terrors. "He's only voicing what all of us feel," Kashi whispered from her bed next to mine. Jhalkari was on the other side of me. There wasn't even any room for our own puja tables. Now, we all shared one altar near the door.

I'm sure there are a great many people who believe that when the rani lost her kingdom, she immediately began plotting all of the ways in which she could fight to win it back. But since I was there with her from the very first day she held a durbar in the Rani Mahal, I can tell you that nothing was further from the truth. The very last thing the rani wanted was war. She believed, the very same way you or I believe that the sun will rise tomorrow, that the Company would someday grant one of her appeals. If I could tell you the number of appeals she wrote, arguing in her best English each of the most logical points you would have argued if you had been in her place, then the rest of my memoirs would be spent doing so. It was like Arjun said to me the first night we spent in the new palace. "I don't know what's more depressing. Watching the rani believe that British law will triumph, or listening to her father explain there is no alternative to war."

But then, just as the rani and her son seemed to be making their peace with the sudden change, even worse news came. A servant announced the arrival of Major Ellis outside the Durbar Hall.

"Your Highness, the honorable Major Ellis is here."

The servants still called the rani, "Your Highness," and she still held a durbar, even though there was no longer a kingdom to administer.

"He may enter."

The major stepped into the hall and blinked several times as he took in his surroundings. Just as she had in the Panch Mahal, the rani was sitting on her gold and emerald throne, which the governor-general had finally agreed she could take. She was surrounded by a half circle made up of her Durgavasi. Each of us sat on large red cushions that matched both the walls and ceiling of the chamber. To the rani's left, on thickly padded chairs, sat all of her important advisers, just as they always had when she had been the Rani of Jhansi. Her father was there, along with the generals Gul Mohammed and Raghunath Singh. She wasn't presiding over the Panch Mahal, but in her blue silk sari and silver bangles, she still appeared regal.

The major bowed very, very low, and addressed her as a queen. "Your Highness, I come with news."

"You always come with news, Major Ellis, and it never seems to be to my liking. What is it today?"

"The Queen of England and her Parliament are interested in this land as well."

The rani looked at her father, but neither seemed to understand what this could mean.

The major explained. "Parliament has become very interested in the British East India Company's holdings here."

The rani shook her head and her small silver earrings caught the light, reminding me of a pair of fish dangling from two hooks. "Explain clearly what you mean," she said bluntly.

"I mean the governor-general may no longer have the power to hear your appeals. You may need to appeal directly to the Queen of England and her Parliament." He paused. "Also, the governor-general has transferred me to the state of Panna, effective June first."

"That's in seven days!" Moropant said.

"Yes. The man who's coming to replace me is Major Erskine. I have already spoken with him. He understands your situation. He is coming tomorrow."

"To my kingdom? Without my knowledge?" But it wasn't her kingdom anymore.

"Your Highness, I'm sorry. If I could change it, I hope you know that I would."

The rani began to smooth her sari. "Tell me what I should do."

"When Major Erskine comes, don't let one of the sepoys take him on a tour of Jhansi; assign the job to one of your guards. Let him see the kingdom through your people's eyes."

The rani assigned Arjun the task of showing Major Erskine the city of Jhansi. She could have done it herself, but imagine the heartache of that. Here is the library where I read my books, here is the temple where my late son was blessed, and there is the lake where I erected a necropolis in honor of my husband. . . .

So Arjun introduced Major Erskine to Jhansi, and when they returned that evening to the Durbar Hall, the chamber was lit with heavy bronze lamps and the rani was dressed in her most beautiful sari. Blue silk fell in waves around her feet, and the pearls around her neck were luminous.

"Well?" she said in English when the major arrived.

He bowed very low, and made the gesture of namaste first to her, then to her father, who was next to her on a thick red cushion.

"Jhansi is truly the jewel of India, Your Highness."

The rani sat back against her throne, and I could see she was satisfied with his answer.

"And what did you like best in Jhansi?" she asked.

He thought, and while he did, I studied his features. He was not at all like Major Ellis. His eyes and hair were dark. His face was also long and thin, like the sharp faces you see carved out above church doors. "I would say that of all the sights in Jhansi,

Your Highness, I was most impressed when I visited your temples. I asked Captain Arjun about your elephant-headed god, and he explained to me that you believe there is only one god."

The rani raised her brows.

"Hindus represent god using many faces to remind worshipers that there is divinity in all things: rivers, trees, elephants, monkeys." The major smiled. "Inspiring."

"Will it inspire the Queen of England to restore my kingdom?"

Erskine's smile vanished. He quickly recovered himself. "I don't know, Your Highness."

She sat forward. "The governor-general claims that my son will only inherit my husband's property when he 'comes of age.' I want this property. And I want to be relieved of Jhansi's debts. The governor-general says I owe thirty-six thousand rupees to him for debts this kingdom had when he took over. That is *grossly* unfair. What should I do?"

"Send a lawyer to England," he said immediately.

"To England?" I could see that this wasn't the answer she'd expected.

"Yes. Send a lawyer to the queen herself, and appeal this annexation."

"Send Umesh Chandra," Kahini suggested. "He's Bengali."

Bengalis are known for being worldly and well educated. If anyone could make an impression on the queen, it would be a Bengali. The rani agreed.

But sixty thousand rupees and two months later, word came from across the seas that Umesh Chandra had failed. Everyone was gathered in the Durbar Hall, from the rani's advisers to her father, Moropant, and as the rani read the letter aloud, her father's face changed from hopeful to enraged.

I have done everything I can, Your Highness, but the Queen of England has not agreed to give me an audience. I'm afraid this trip has been for naught. We are beneath her consideration.

"*Beneath* her consideration?" Moropant shouted. "*Beneath her consideration?*"

"Your Highness," Major Erskine said. "The queen rarely acknowledges a first attempt."

The rani nodded for him to continue.

"I am a foreigner to this country, but it seems that the women of your Durga Dal are highly educated and extremely independent. Send two of them to England. The queen won't refuse to see such an unusual delegation."

The rani's advisers began talking all at once. It is one thing to establish an army of women in your own kingdom, but to send them across the seas to a foreign land—well, that is something else. Men who traveled outside of India were rarely welcomed back to their villages, often because they returned with radical ideas. They were considered tainted by their travels, as no one knew what sort of evils they'd be bringing back with them. So what Major Erskine was proposing was not just radical, it was very possibly dangerous.

I could see this conflict on the rani's face. "You say the queen would absolutely grant an audience to my women?"

"If they had traveled across the ocean from Jhansi? Yes," Erskine said.

"I would go myself. But there are pretenders to my throne who would not hesitate to claim the rights to my property if I did." She looked at her father.

"It's forty-five days to England by boat," he said. "A thousand things could change by the time anyone reached her shores."

"Have you forgotten what the raja said to me before he died?"

"Within *reason*," her father said. "Is this reasonable?"

"I will send Sita and Jhalkari. If they agree to go."

Everyone in the Durbar Hall looked to us, and a knot formed in my stomach that was so tight I was sure that if I pressed on it, I would actually feel it. It's one thing to read about foreign lands, and another thing to go there. I thought about my father and Anu, who would be sick with worry imagining me on a voyage. I wondered how the rest of Barwa Sagar would feel. Would I ever be welcomed back home? It would depend almost entirely on the British queen's response.

Jhalkari's response was immediate. "I will go."

Everyone turned to me, and I responded, "I will go as well."

"They'd need escorts," Moropant said. "At least a dozen men."

"I will send Arjun," the rani said. "Arjun attended an English boarding school. He understands English."

"They can leave as soon as passage is arranged," Major Erskine said eagerly. "Of course, they will all need training in British customs. But Dr. McEgan and his wife could see to that."

Dr. McEgan was the British doctor who had confirmed for the rani that there had never been a plague in Jhansi. He was also the doctor the raja had angrily dismissed before his death.

There was new hope in the rani's face. "What do you say?" she asked her father. "What about their reputations when they return?"

Suddenly, even Moropant seemed inspired. "If they can succeed where Umesh Chandra failed, I don't see that it should matter if they'd traveled to the moon!"

Everyone laughed. There was no reason that this shouldn't work. The ruler of England was a woman. So was the ruler of Jhansi. And now she was sending two female guards across the seas to plead her case.

"The lessons will begin at once," the rani said.

◦ ◦ ◦

The three weeks Jhalkari and I spent with Mrs. McEgan were extraordinary.

The rani arranged for our first meeting to take place after yoga. Even though I knew I should have been clearing my mind, I lay on my jute mat and couldn't stop thinking of England. What would it be like to walk the streets of London? I tried to imagine the food and the sights, and couldn't. The London of Shakespeare's day was more than two hundred years in the past, so not even Shakespeare could prepare me for what we were about to see.

"And that's why I'm here," Mrs. McEgan said when she arrived at the Rani Mahal. She was dressed in the most extraordinary gown, with her stomach completely covered and her bosoms practically hanging out. Her waist appeared unusually small, and her entire dress was green, like the hat on her head and the trim on her boots. She peeled off her white gloves as soon as she entered the first-floor room the rani had prepared for us. And when she seated herself on one of the thirteen chairs that had been arranged in a circle for her arrival, she lowered herself with a slow and pretty grace I was sure I'd never possess. Like Jhalkari, I was wearing a red angarkha, with a pistol on my right and my sword on my left.

"So this is all of you?" She smiled, and I glanced at Arjun, to see what he made of this woman with her water-blue eyes and pale-as-butter skin. But like the nine other guards who would be traveling with us, he was averting his gaze, on account of Mrs. McEgan's inappropriate dress. "Well, don't sit there staring at the floor. Look at me!"

If the men had looked, they would have seen a young woman with honey-colored hair arranged in thick curls around her head. A smile took up most of her pretty face. But no one obeyed. Not even Arjun, who spoke English. She looked at Jhalkari and me.

"The men are embarrassed," I explained. "They won't look at a woman whose chest . . ." I indicated her bosoms with my eyes. Her face turned red, the same way Major Ellis's used to. She reached for a shawl and covered herself. One by one, the men looked up.

"I had no idea. The women in Jhansi all show off their waists."

"Perhaps the glimpse of a woman's waist for you is the same as the glimpse of a woman's breasts is to us."

"There's going to be a good deal to learn," she said, "isn't there?"

We began with dress, and we discovered a great many things about the British we had never imagined. For one, it was extremely baffling to learn what they considered appropriate versus horribly inappropriate. Burping in public, perfectly fine in Jhansi, was considered uncouth by the British; something only drunks or small children did. Yet not bathing before going to a place of worship was perfectly fine, and in fact, some of the British didn't bathe for weeks. Their food consisted of dead animals, which they speared with metal items called forks and knives. And almost nothing was eaten by hand. As for the women, according to Mrs. McEgan, they ate in front of whomever they pleased, laughed like she did, with their mouths wide open, and didn't think twice about allowing a man to kiss their hands.

But the most extraordinary lessons of all featured court etiquette, and what should and should not be done before the queen. A woman's neck and shoulders were to be bare at all times, even if there was rain or snow. Her gown's train must be exactly three yards in length, so the queen could see it spread by the lords-in-waiting in the room. Dinner at six meant dinner at six fifteen, not a minute before and not a minute after. If we should be so fortunate as to be invited to a meal, ten courses would be served, with all of the accompanying, confusing silverware. No noise in the dining room. No singing in the halls. And children were not to laugh or speak unless spoken to.

By the end of our first lesson, the queen's court sounded like a prison, not a palace.

"You'll feel differently as soon as you see it," Mrs. McEgan promised. "There's nothing like London anywhere in the world. 'This blessed plot, this earth, this realm, this England.'"

I recognized Shakespeare's *Richard II* and grinned.

Chapter Twenty

The setting sun gilded the walls of the palace and reflected from Arjun's golden earrings. He looked the way I imagined Lord Krishna had when he was alive and enchanting the pretty *gopis*.

"I will meet your family someday. Maybe not soon, but I will. I want to see what sort of man produced a daughter like you," he said.

The rani was allowing us a week to visit our families before we left for England. I was excited, but also sad that Arjun wouldn't be coming with me. I had thought the rani might allow him to escort me home.

"Yes. My father would enjoy your passion for literature," I told him. "You two have much in common."

"Be safe," he said with unusual tenderness.

We were standing outside of the Rani Mahal. It was September, and the monsoon had turned the courtyard to mud. In one of the rain pools, I could see our reflection, the ripples pushing our images together.

"I will."

° ° °

At home, my father was overjoyed to see his little peacock. But the house wasn't the same with Anu living in her husband's home next door. I took my father's pen and wrote, "Do you see her often?"

"Nearly every week. She couldn't be happier. But what about you?"

I wanted to answer him honestly, but didn't know how. Was I excited for my journey? Afraid? Nervous? I struggled to choose a single emotion. Finally, I wrote, "It's been very difficult to see the British flag in Jhansi."

"The British have better weapons and superior training," my father replied, and I could see from his handwriting how angry he was. "What is the rani planning to do?"

"She is sending a delegation to England to petition the queen." I met my father's gaze, and suddenly, he understood.

"You're going."

"Yes. With another Durgavasi and ten of the rani's guards, including her captain. It will take two months to travel there. We'll be there for a month, and then it will take another two months to return. I want to tell Anu and say good-bye. I'll be back in the new year."

My father reached out and covered my hand with his. Tears welled in his eyes.

We stood at the doorstep of Shivaji's house and my father knocked, although most people usually just called through the open window.

Shivaji answered the door. I bent to touch his feet, and when I came up, he was wearing a great smile.

"Sita!" he exclaimed. "Amisha," he called to his wife, "it's Sita! What are you doing here? Did you just arrive? Come inside!"

Shivaji's house was much finer than ours. His wife had brought with her a large dowry fortune, and many of the items had been hers from childhood. We walked through a hall painted with images of Lord Krishna as a baby, and I wondered if one of Shivaji's other sons was an artist. Then I heard a familiar voice call my name, and as we entered the common room, a pair of arms wrapped themselves around me.

"Anu!" I pulled back and was shocked by the change I saw in my sister. She was a woman, with a woman's features and a woman's body. She bent to touch my feet, and when she stood I saw that new curves filled out the blue and yellow sari I had sent to her. She wore gold around her wrists like my mother had and their resemblance was so strong that for several moments, I was too startled to say anything. "You're a woman."

She giggled. "How long are you staying?"

"A day. The rani needs me to travel. I came to say good-bye."

Her smile vanished. "Where are you going?"

"To England, to petition the queen. The rani is sending me and another Durgavasi. She sent a lawyer several months back, but the queen refused to hear his petition."

My father and Shivaji seated themselves on a pair of low cushions across from my sister and I did the same. It was only later that I realized I had chosen to sit with the men versus the married women.

"I've never been farther than Burma," Shivaji said as he folded his legs. "But if I was offered the opportunity to go to England . . . It's almost two months at sea, is that right?"

"Yes. We will arrive in the middle of December and experience their largest festival. Christmas." I told them the story Mrs. McEgan told us, of Lord Jesus and his virgin mother. "The rani has told us to honor everything they do in this festival, so long as it pleases Lord Brahma."

I looked over at my sister, who was staring at me the way you might stare at a stranger. Perhaps I really was a stranger to her now. The thought made me sad.

"Tell me about life as Ishan's wife," I said.

Anu blushed, and I knew she was in love. "He is at the animal hospital right now. Sometimes, he brings home wounded birds. We've raised three, and watched them fly away."

"He's a good man," I said. "It must be his father's influence." I smiled at Shivaji, who returned the gesture, then asked me what life was like as the rani's Durgavasi. "Different now that the British have Jhansi."

"It's unthinkable," Shivaji said. "Queen Victoria and her Parliament are just as greedy as the Company, wanting more land, more valuable goods, more trading routes. You will need a very persuasive argument when you go. What will it be?"

"That the young queen is a woman the same as the rani, and understands a woman's struggle to rule. Why would one queen wish to rob another, when so few of them remain?"

Shivaji stared at me. "Is that it? You are traveling such a distance to remind the British queen that she is a woman?"

My face felt hot. It did seem ridiculous hearing his words. "No. We are going to appeal to her humanity." Because what other peaceful option was there?

Shivaji didn't look persuaded.

"They say she's wise," I said, feigning confidence. "She'll understand that diplomacy is the best solution."

° ° °

The day after we returned from visiting our families, we departed for England. The rani and the other Durgavasi surrounded our horses to bid us farewell. The rani gave a short speech describing her pride in our mission, and she was full of praise for what Jhalkari and I were about to do. No other women in all of India had undertaken the journey Jhalkari and I were about to take—none that we knew of. So you can imagine our feelings as we made our way by horse, then cart, then horse again, to the port where our ship would sail for another country.

"I've never seen anything like it," Jhalkari kept saying, in every city we passed. And everything was new not only to us, but to everyone in our group. In one city, the women wore what looked to us to be long black shrouds. Even their faces were covered in black. In another, the men were dressed entirely in white. The buildings, the food, even the animals we encountered as we made our way from Jhansi to Madras, were completely unfamiliar. We might as well have been traveling across different continents.

When we reached Madras, Arjun looked over at me, and we both stared at the expanse of water before us. Neither of us had seen the ocean before, and the brightly colored sails of the small fishing boats framed against the blue sky were beautiful. "I wish my father could see this," I said to Arjun.

We dismounted and stood on the shore, watching as boats bobbed and swayed on the sea. The wind tasted like salt instead of earth, and Major Wilkes, the British officer who would be escorting us to England, put his nose in the air and smiled. He was a little older than the rani, twenty-nine or thirty. He was making this trip to England to bring his fiancée back with him to India. "Home." He sighed.

He helped us unpack the horses, then several of his men appeared to escort us onto a towering white steamer. None of us had been on a boat, and as soon as we stepped onto the wooden plank, the steamer gave a giant lurch to the side and we were all forced to grab on to the rails.

"We're going to sail to England in *this*?" Jhalkari cried.

Although I'm sure Major Wilkes didn't speak a word of Marathi, he understood what she said, because he laughed. "No. We'll be sailing to Suez in this. Then we'll be traveling overland to Alexandria and taking another steamer to England. You'll go on to London by carriage."

We boarded the steamer and stood in the largest hall of the passenger ship and stared. From ceiling to floor, the walls were paneled in richly carved wood. Plush carpeting covered the floors, and in one corner, a heavy silver mirror reflected the light of a gilded candelabrum. Upholstered couches were arranged around small inlaid tables, where several English men sat puffing on long cigars. I watched the smoke curl up over their heads and make its way out of the shuttered windows. The shutters were made of teak, and the trays on each of the tables were pure silver. The rani had spent a fortune sending us to England. She saw it as an investment.

Arjun stepped toward one of the windows to get a better view, and Major Wilkes cleared his throat. "I'm sorry," he said. "This room isn't for you."

We all turned.

Major Wilkes glanced at the other men sitting in the room, since they were all watching us now. "This room is only for the British," he explained. Then he apologized, "I didn't make the rules."

"But you will enforce them," I said.

"There's nothing I can do."

Arjun looked at me, and we explained to the others what the major said. Several of the men protested. "If we're not allowed with the British," Jhalkari said, "where are we staying?"

Major Wilkes led us through a series of halls to the very back of the ship. Four rooms were to be ours: two for the men, one for Jhalkari and myself, and a fourth one for eating and talking together. They were the most beautiful chambers our group had seen outside of the Panch Mahal. The major let us choose which rooms were to be which, and then we began to unpack.

When Jhalkari shut the door, I said, "It doesn't seem real. An entire room just for us!"

"I feel like the rani," she admitted.

We explored everything, from the silver door handles, to the small tidy beds, to the wooden night tables with their mahogany bookends. The beds were on opposite sides of the room, and I chose the one closest to the window. I lay back on the mattress and looked out at the vast expanse of sea. I began to wonder if traveling such a long distance was actually safe. I was about to turn twenty-one years old, and the only thing I knew about ships was that they had a habit of finding themselves in uncharted waters—in English fiction anyway. I glanced at Jhalkari, who was still standing, arms crossed, looking out over the water.

"Do you think travel by boat is safe?" I asked.

"The rani wouldn't have invested so much money if it wasn't."

But what if a great storm swelled up and we were in its midst? Might we be cast on the shores of some unknown land, like Viola in *Twelfth Night*? Or worse, on some uninhabited island like Miranda in *The Tempest*? There was a knock on the door, and Arjun appeared with two other guards.

"Would you like to tour the ship?"

We went from bow to stern, and Arjun described the construction of the steamer drawing only on what he had read in the rani's vast library. When we reached the stern, the five of us watched as the shore faded into the distance. When it was nothing more than a smudge on the horizon, Arjun said, "'No one knows for certain whether the vessel will sink or reach the harbor. Cautious people say, "I'll do nothing until I can be sure." Merchants know better. If you do nothing, you lose. Don't be one of those merchants who won't risk the ocean.'"

Jhalkari wrinkled her nose. "What are you saying?"

"Rumi," I told her. "We are the merchants now."

That evening, the twelve of us were told to gather in the common room. We sat around a long wooden table wondering what was going to happen, and when half a dozen waiters appeared with silver trays, Jhalkari and I looked at each other in horror.

"They think we're going to eat together!" I exclaimed. I rose from my seat to try to find Major Wilkes just as he was coming in the door.

"They think we're going to eat together," I told him.

He stared at me and I stared at him, then I realized he didn't understand. "Women don't eat in front of men," I said. "It isn't done."

"Ma'am," he said very politely. "There will be many occasions in England when you'll be expected to eat together. It's a custom in England. You could take your food back to your room now," he suggested. "But I'm afraid there will be times in London when you will either eat with everyone or go hungry."

"So come and eat," Arjun said lightly.

But I just couldn't imagine doing this. Imagine farting on a stage for everyone to hear; it felt that shocking. Now imagine you're told you'll have to do it all the time!

Jhalkari and I returned to the table, slowly, as I translated what Major Wilkes had said.

"So what are they serving you?" the major asked. He'd said before that he couldn't imagine how vegetarians survived without lamb, or cow, or pig for eating.

The waiters removed the silver lids from the trays and steaming piles of strange foods were revealed.

"Ah! Quiche," he said, pointing to the tray of yellow and green cakes. "And there's something you know. Broccoli and carrots. I'm not sure what that is"—he was looking at a soup—"but bon appétit," he said, which didn't sound like English.

With that, he left.

There was no bread to eat with, no lentils or chickpeas or anything with protein. We looked at each other and laughed.

"This is what they eat?" one of the men said.

"No, they have meat mostly. They don't understand vegetarians," Arjun explained. He started making a plate, then handed it to me.

I flushed.

"Eat," he said. "No one here cares."

As everyone was trying out the tiny cakes, Jhalkari whispered to me, "I understand now."

I looked around the room, but the men were engaged in conversations about ships, as if they had all dined with women and taken multiple sea journeys throughout their lives. "You understand what?"

"Arjun. He's in love with you."

I glanced at Arjun and felt suddenly light-headed, though not from the motion of the ship.

"Imagine what the rani will do for us if Queen Victoria restores her to the throne of Jhansi? She might retire us from the Durga Dal. You would have the freedom to marry."

"I don't know. . . ." To find love at court and marry at twenty-one? It was an unbelievable dream.

"Sita, if it can happen for me, it can happen for you."

"I don't dare to hope for it," I said.

"Why not?"

"Because I was never the one who was meant to marry. My sister—"

"Has been married and her dowry fortune paid. Sita, what if this is *your* chance?"

I felt a lightness inside of me that almost made me dizzy. And though I knew I shouldn't hope for it, secretly I did.

In the mornings Arjun and I started practicing yoga. We sat on our blankets and watched as the sun rose over the ocean, sparkling over the cresting waves. In the afternoons, we read poetry together, and in the evenings, we gathered with the others to read the *Puranas*, our most holy Sanskrit texts. Suddenly, the impossible seemed less so.

It was an enchanted time.

Then, a day before we were set to reach England, Jhalkari came to me with shattering news. I could see from her face that something was wrong. I thought it might be the rocking of the boat, since it made us all sick at least once a day. But she requested that I sit with her in one of the small wooden chairs in our room, and then asked me when I had last spoken with Arjun.

"This morning," I said. "We practiced yoga." I couldn't imagine why her face was making so many contortions, or why it was taking her so long to speak. So finally I said, "Jhalkari, what is it?"

She folded her hands in her lap. "We were just on the deck having a conversation about our futures—what he wanted for his life, what I wanted, what we would do if the queen granted our petition."

Already a knot was forming in my stomach.

"When I asked him what he saw ahead of him, he said marriage."

I exhaled. That wasn't bad news. If the queen granted our petition, the rani would certainly give us her permission to marry.

But Jhalkari's face was solemn. "Sita, I'm sorry, but when I asked him what sort of girl he might choose, he said one from the city."

I didn't understand. "What city?"

"Jhansi. He said, 'I have my eye on someone from Jhansi.'"

It felt as if the breath had been ripped out of me. "He said *from* Jhansi? Jhalkari, are you sure?"

She lowered her head. "I'm sorry."

I didn't sleep at all that night.

The next morning, a sailor shouted, "Land ho!" the way they do in books, and everyone rushed up to the decks to see England for the first time. A heavy fog hung like loose gauze over the shore, but beyond it, rising into the mist, were the tallest cliffs I had ever seen. They were covered in green, trees so tall and thick that they looked like fistfuls of jagged emeralds. We were all silent, trying to imagine what sort of world we would find beyond them.

Arjun came and stood at my side, but I stiffened. "Beautiful," he said.

When I turned, he was looking me. I lowered my gaze in shame. How could he stare at me like that and want another woman as his wife? It was no one's fault but my own. I had allowed it, encouraged it even. I held my chin high, but the pain in my chest felt as if it would crush me. "Yes," I said and walked away.

I joined Major Wilkes on the other side of the ship, and tried to look as if it were wind, not tears, in my eyes.

"December in England," he said as I joined him. Just as he had in the port of Madras, he inhaled. England had a particular smell for him, the same as Barwa Sagar had for me. I believe this is how it is for all men who serve abroad. Their lives are full of waiting to go home, and after ten, twenty, even thirty years in a foreign country, they never truly feel at peace in their souls. "I have no idea what we're doing in Jhansi," he said to me, opening his eyes. "Or why any Englishman would even want to live there. No one wants you to convince our queen to leave India more than I do. Though I'd deny it if anyone said as much."

I studied the major's face, and he seemed to be in earnest.

He inhaled again as the ship docked, and I did the same, trying to smell what he did. But my thoughts returned to Arjun. How could he share books with me and practice yoga and then say he hoped to find a bride? I gulped the air, trying to clear my head. The cold wind was heavy with the scents of brine and the sea. It carried with it the sounds of the dock, crowded with merchants, sailors, and travelers disembarking from other ships. It was impossible to know what to look at first. All the carriages with their passengers in pretty bonnets and top hats, or the sailors who hurried to arrange the gangplank?

We stepped off the pier onto solid ground and I kept close to Jhalkari. It wasn't fair to let Arjun see how much I hurt. He'd never made any declarations of love to me; never once mentioned marriage or how things might have been different. I let the new sights and sounds overwhelm me, and the twelve of us huddled together on the busy pier until Major Wilkes joined us by announcing, "We'll be taking four carriages to London. It's going to be a long journey."

We wrapped ourselves in the fur cloaks the rani had gifted us, then sat four to a carriage. Jhalkari seated herself next to me, and with the soft ermine fur brushing her cheeks, she looked like the rani. We would probably never own such luxury again even if we lived another hundred lives. Across from us, Arjun and Wilkes took their seats. They pressed their backs against the soft velvet of the carriage, and I wondered if all Englishmen traveled this way. Then I thought of Arjun with a young wife from the city and my stomach felt tight again. It was a feeling I would have to learn to live with. He had never made any promises to me. I was the one who had been foolish.

"You're going to be quite amazed when we reach London," the major said.

But as the carriages lurched forward, we were already amazed.

The hills of England rolled on forever, dotted by churches and pretty stone villages. The major had closed the windows, but I could still smell the rich scent of burning wood as we traveled along. We passed through several crowded cities, and the noise reminded me of Jhansi. Women walked as freely as men, some even commanding carriages. They rode horses wearing skirts and sitting sideways; they laughed with their mouths open, showing their teeth like hyenas. But most outrageous: they wore dresses that displayed more than half of their bosoms.

"Did Mrs. McEgan explain to you about the queen's court?" the major asked as we rode.

"Yes." Unlike the rani, the queen only allowed certain members of society to be presented. Military men, religious men, physicians, lawyers, and any of their wives, were all acceptable. But businessmen, merchants, and their families—however wealthy—were not welcome. Did the Queen of England know that Jhalkari and I had been born in a village, and that Jhalkari was a Dalit, no less?

"Then I assume you know that once we arrive, the queen will decide when to receive you. It may be today, it may be another day. Until then, enjoy the sights."

How can I explain to you the excitement of seeing London for the first time? Everywhere we looked, there were women—barefaced, laughing, drinking cups of tea. Even with the bitter wind, their hats towered above them, all lace trim and feathers, like birds wanting to be seen. We passed Hyde Park where handsome couples walked children and tiny dogs. In Jhansi, such a park would be in daily use for weddings. Here, there was not a single wedding celebration to be seen.

"There goes Park Lane," the major said as we rode. "Those are the most fashionable houses in London."

A dozen families in Barwa Sagar could live in a house meant for a single family.

"And there is Fortnum and Mason, the grocer to the queen."

The major had a comment about everything.

Then Arjun's eyes grew wide and he took in his breath. I saw it at the same time: Buckingham Palace. It sprawled across our entire field of view, a majestic palace surrounded by sweeping gardens.

"I thought you might like to see this before we reached the hotel," Major Wilkes said.

Everything I'd seen in Jhansi seemed small by comparison. We slowed briefly in front of the gates, and then the coaches took off toward Albemarle Street, where we stopped in front of a towering building with a sign that read BROWN'S HOTEL.

"*This* is where we're staying?"

Wilkes smiled at me. "This is it."

It was like a palace itself. A dozen men in black coats and white lapels appeared to take away our luggage. Outside, the air was crisp and smelled of trees. Wilkes said it was the evergreens used to decorate the outside of the hotel.

"Then these garlands aren't normal?"

"No. They're for Christmas. Like those holly berries over there."

Inside, the evergreens gave the reception room a delightful smell. Everything was bright and cheerful. We were shown to our rooms, seven chambers on the same hall, and told that dinner would be served downstairs in the dining room. Everything felt new and large and strange. The British wore shoes indoors, even though our rooms—like all the other rooms—were carpeted, and even the bathroom had a working gas lamp. I desperately wished that Anu and my father could see all of this. They wouldn't have believed it.

That evening, at a long table trimmed with fresh evergreens and flickering candles, Wilkes told us not to expect any word from the queen for several days. "Think of all the petitioners who want to see her."

"But we've come from Jhansi. Who else has come all that way?" I said.

Still, there was nothing to do except wait. So over the next few days, we passed the time walking the wet streets of London, admiring the beautifully decorated shops and large Christmas wreaths on wooden doors of houses. One day we walked to the famous Hyde Park. The next day we made our way to Regent Street. We attracted attention wherever we went. Beneath our cloaks, it was impossible to tell we weren't dressed like Englishmen, but the color of our skin stood out, and also our jewelry. Jhalkari and I were still wearing our nose rings. Arjun still had on his pair of gold hoops.

By the third day, we had all grown very anxious. What if the queen called on us in two months? Or if she didn't care that we had come at all? But as we sat down to dinner in the common dining room alongside Major Wilkes and several hotel guests, a very well-dressed messenger arrived.

"From Buckingham Palace," he announced to the room, and everyone held their breath. Then he unfolded the letter he was carrying and read it aloud.

We were being summoned to court the next day and were to be there at twelve o'clock!

We all let out a cheer. Even the other hotel guests smiled. By six the next morning we were already awake and starting to prepare. Major Wilkes had warned us to adopt Western dress. "The men must put on black suits and white ties, and the women need to dress as proper ladies." When I had questioned what he meant by "proper ladies," his cheeks had turned red. "I'm sorry, ma'am, but your waist—I'm afraid that no one has ever seen that body part in the queen's chambers."

That might have been true, but we ignored his advice and dressed as we had always intended—in silk saris and kurtas. Jhalkari braided my hair, then I did the same for her, and we both decorated our braids with golden choti, a series of long flowers wrought in twenty-four-karat gold and embellished with rubies and emeralds. When we were finished, we stood in front of the mirror and admired ourselves.

"I don't even recognize us," Jhalkari whispered.

It was true. We were a vision of gold and silk, Jhalkari in a sari of red and gold, myself in patterned yellow and purple. Strings of pearls glittered from our necks, and ruby earrings matched our ruby nose rings and thick ruby bracelets. Gold and ruby bells tinkled musically from our ankles. It was a measure of the rani's trust that she had lent such jewels to us. Truthfully, none of it seemed real. Not our clothes, or our jewels, or the ornately carved mirror hanging from the paneled wall of our hotel.

Outside, waiting in the hall for Major Wilkes, Arjun and the other guards were all dressed as magnificently as maharajas, in gilded kurtas, heavy gold earrings, and elaborate pagris. If you have never seen a pagri, it is a turban adorned with a heavily jeweled sarpech, meant to resemble Krishna's peacock feather. I gasped when I saw him. He was what Jane Austen would have imagined as "dashing." None of us were dressed in our heavy cloaks, as apparently, this was not done when meeting the queen. We would have to brave the cold in our thin kurtas and silks.

"You look stunning," Arjun said to Jhalkari and me.

"As do you," Jhalkari complimented him.

I gave him a brief smile, but I still couldn't forget what he'd told Jhalkari on the ship. It had hurt more than I imagined it could, and there was no reason for it. He had never made me any promises of love. We shared books. That was all. I was the one who had daydreamed about something more, something lasting.

When Major Wilkes appeared, he frowned at our attire but held his tongue, and we were taken to the carriages. Our second view of Buckingham Palace was no less impressive than the first. We rolled up to the gates, and I tried to quiet my nerves as the major spoke with the guards. Their accents were difficult to understand, but they all seemed to be laughing, which seemed to be a good sign. Then the gates were thrown open to us and suddenly, we were inside.

Servants opened our carriage doors, and faces pressed against the tall windows of the palace, their owners straining to get a better view. And as we entered the plush halls of the queen's residence, everyone stopped to stare. The servants and the courtiers watched us as we went. We were all too busy looking at the furnishings to take much notice. We passed beneath endless chandeliers into an empty drawing room where a servant instructed us to have seats on the plush velvet chairs. Everywhere we looked were rich carpets, carved banisters, and gilded wall hangings.

"We wait here until we're formally summoned into Her Majesty's Presence Chamber," Major Wilkes said.

We'd arrived more than an hour early. Finally, at twelve in the afternoon, a very tall man who looked tremendously grave announced to the room, "Her Majesty, The Queen invites you to meet with her in Her Majesty's Presence Chamber."

All of us rose, feeling as nervous as convicts about to be summoned before a judge. I squeezed Jhalkari's hand and she squeezed back. I made a small prayer to Ganesh, the remover of obstacles. "Please just let this go smoothly," I begged him.

Chapter Twenty-One

We approached the throne just as we would approach the rani's in Jhansi, and when we reached the dais, we bowed our heads and folded our hands in respectful gestures of namaste. We were standing in pairs, Jhalkari and I first, followed by Arjun and a guard named Manoj, then the rest of the guards. And I can only imagine how we looked to Queen Victoria at that moment: barefooted and dressed in elaborate silks in the dead of winter, wearing nose rings and adorned with peacock feathers.

"I have never seen the like," Queen Victoria said as she rose from her throne, descending three velvet steps to stand before us. She was a small woman, with round cheeks and a very plump figure. Her husband remained seated.

"You are one of the queen's female warriors?" she asked me.

"Yes, Your Majesty."

She was staring at me, as if she found this hard to believe. "You are able to protect her as well as these men standing behind you?"

"I believe so."

"How?"

"By using my weapons. And if necessary, my words. Today, my words are all that I have, and I am here to ask that you protect the rani's kingdom."

The queen turned to her husband, then back to me. "You speak English quite well."

"I learned from my father, who was a soldier in Burma with the Company."

She looked at Jhalkari, then back at the men who stood behind us. I knew they were averting their gazes, on account of her very low dress. "I want to speak with you and this other woman alone," she said.

"I'm afraid she does not speak English, Your Majesty. The man behind me is the captain of the rani's guards, and he speaks English as well as I do."

"Everyone else, then, is dismissed," she announced.

I explained her command to Jhalkari, who led the guards back out the way they'd come.

The queen called for two chairs, and Arjun and I waited side by side while they were fetched. He looked at me, and there was a deep respect in his eyes. When the chairs arrived, we were seated beneath Their Majesties. They both took several moments to look us over. Then the queen shook her head again and said, "Extraordinary. Do all the women in India dress as you are?"

"Yes. But with fewer jewels," I said.

"And the men?" Prince Albert wanted to know. His voice was thickly accented; I knew his first language was German.

"I am wearing a traditional kurta," Arjun said. "This is what we wear on great occasions."

"You are also well spoken. I'm exceptionally pleased that the rani has sent you. How did you like the journey to London?"

I glanced at Arjun to see which one of us should speak first. He nodded toward me, and I said, "Your Majesty has a beautiful country, particularly the churches."

"And what did you like best?" she asked Arjun.

"The rolling hills spotted with sheep."

The queen smiled. "And now you have come to see me."

"Yes. We have come on behalf of Rani Lakshmibai," I said, "who is looking to have the throne of Jhansi restored."

The queen nodded heavily. "Tell me about her. What does she look like? How many children does she have?"

I found it difficult to believe that the Queen of all of England didn't know these things, since we had learned nearly all there was to learn about her, from her birthday in May to her third child's name.

But Arjun began, "The rani is extremely beautiful. She had one child, who died before his first birthday, and has adopted another."

This interested the queen. "Why? Was her husband incapable of more children?"

I glanced at Arjun, and we were both struck dumb.

"I've heard rumors he dressed in women's clothes."

So she *had* heard about Jhansi. "Yes," I admitted.

She gave a triumphant look to the prince.

"The people of Jhansi fear living under Company rule," I said, guiding the conversation back to the rani. "They wish to keep their customs and way of life. If Her Majesty would agree to help another queen in need, it would mean a great deal to our people."

The queen said, "Come to dinner tonight. All of you. And after, you will have an answer."

We bowed and prepared ourselves to leave, when suddenly she said, "Wait! I have something I want to show you." She was smiling like a child. Next to her, the prince frowned. "Bout," she said.

Then he smiled, too, and a servant was summoned and instructed to bring Bout.

Arjun and I exchanged a quick glance. Was it a type of food? But when the man returned, he was leading a massive canine by a leash.

"Bout!" the prince called, and the enormous dog went bounding toward him. The queen laughed as the canine made its way up the dais. I believed this was a very good sign.

"A Tibetan mastiff. A gift from Lord Harding, my governor-general of India," the queen said. "Are all dogs this giant in India?" she asked. "Lord Harding tells me tales that are difficult to believe; that everything in India is abundant—the spices, the palaces, the gods."

"I'm afraid he is exaggerating, Your Majesty."

Prince Albert buried his face in the dog's coat and patted its back.

"Well then, we look forward to seeing you tonight," the queen said, and it was clear we were dismissed. She was cooing the mastiff's name as we left.

We left the Presence Chamber and each hall we passed through was more lavish than the last. Great stone fireplaces burned rich cedar wood that perfumed the halls, but no smoke was filling the rooms, as would have happened back home. Somehow, it was sucked up into the air. The mirrors we passed were hung with garlands of fresh evergreen, and everywhere, there were bright sprigs of holly, part of their Christmas traditions.

At last we rejoined the others in a large hall. Yet another great fire was burning and everyone was warming themselves next to the smokeless flames. "What happened?" Jhalkari asked.

"She said we must all come for dinner and that an answer would be given afterward."

"Is this good or bad news?"

"I don't know." What would be expected of us at dinner? Only two of us spoke English, and most of the guardsmen had yet to master the use of a knife and fork.

A man in a handsome black suit arrived to announce that our rooms were ready.

"We have no rooms here," Arjun explained. "We are staying at Brown's Hotel."

"That may be, but the queen is allowing you to stay the afternoon, and expects you will want to change for dinner."

"We haven't brought any changes of clothes," Arjun said. "They're all at the hotel."

The man looked down his long nose at us and sighed. "Your trunks will be fetched, then brought back to the hotel when you're finished with them."

"Do the cooks understand that Indians never eat meat?" Arjun asked.

"They have been appraised of all possible situations," the black-suit answered. "Including the possibility that our guests have never dined at a table on chairs."

I passed an angry look at Arjun, who said in Marathi, "Not now. We're so close."

We followed black-suit through another series of halls into a wing of the palace reserved for guests. We passed a large window and saw white flakes falling from the sky. Jhalkari was the first to rush to the window, then the rest of us followed.

"What is it?" Jhalkari exclaimed.

Black-suit gave a second heavy sigh, as if this day was turning out to be the most trying of his career. "Snow. It's what happens when it's very, very cold."

I translated, and we all stood and watched the snow for a while, until black-suit cleared his throat and said, "You may behold the wonder of snow from your rooms, if it pleases you, for the next two hours."

The rooms were as grand as the palace itself, with vast windows overlooking a garden, and mahogany furniture pressed up against blue and gold walls. Although there were rooms for each of us, the men all sat with Arjun in his chamber, and Jhalkari stayed with me. We sat in a pair of blue velvet chairs and watched the snow falling, like thin wisps of lace, from the gray and black sky.

After some time, Jhalkari leaned forward and asked, "What was she like?" She had lowered her voice, even though she had spoken in Marathi.

"Polite. Reserved. Intelligent, like the rani."

"She's the largest woman I've ever seen. Her chin: there are two of them!"

"Jhalkari!" I scolded her, then giggled.

"I wish we could take the snow home, so everyone could see."

We looked out over the strange, unfamiliar landscape. "I have a positive feeling about this," I said. "Why would the queen ask us to dinner unless it was to relay good news?"

Despite the opulence I'd seen all day, it was nothing compared to the lavishness of that evening in Buckingham Palace.

More black-suited men with white lapels had arrived to deliver our trunks, and we dressed in fresh clothes. Jhalkari chose a sari trimmed in gold and stitched with golden leaves. She wore the same rubies on her neck and wrists, but changed her ruby tikka, which trailed from the center of her hair down the middle of her forehead, to one of emerald and gold. For myself, I decided on a sari of rich purple bordered by elaborate silver paisleys. The rani had given me a set of rare violet sapphires to match.

I believe we all have images of ourselves in our heads, but they're rarely the images other people have of us. Whenever I imagine myself, for example, I am twelve years old, dressed in the rough cotton angarkha that my father sold two of his carvings to obtain. But in this moment, when I saw myself in the glass, it was as if I were seeing myself for the very first time. I placed the sapphire tikka in the center of my hair. The jewels dipped onto my forehead and a large violet sapphire hung between my brows. The sapphire nose ring completed the picture.

"You're as beautiful as the rani," Jhalkari said. "And definitely more beautiful than Queen Victoria."

I laughed, but Jhalkari was serious.

"It's a shame you became a Durgavasi. I don't mean that as an insult," she said quickly. "Sometimes, I think it's a shame I became one as well."

"You married," I reminded her.

"But there will never be any children," she said quietly.

I looked at myself in the mirror, with gold gleaming from my neck and across my fingers. "We came here with a purpose," I reminded her. "If we succeed, imagine how life in Jhansi will change. The rani might reward us and our families in ways we can't imagine."

"Perhaps," Jhalkari said. She sat on the edge of the bed and stared out the window. "Do you really think this queen is going to restore the throne of Jhansi to the rani?"

"Of course. Don't you?" I had to believe it to be true.

"No. I believe what my husband does: if she had wanted to do it, she would have already done so."

The same black-suited man who'd brought us to our rooms arrived to escort us to the dining hall. Jhalkari and I waited in the hall while he knocked, without success, on several doors. We knew all the men were in Arjun's room, but we kept this to ourselves, so we could watch him heave heavy sigh after sigh. Finally he knocked on the very last door, and Arjun emerged with the other guards. He was dressed in a kurta of silver and white, with silver churidars and silver juti. When his eyes found mine, they traveled first to my neck, then to the folds of my sari, and finally to my eyes. He said softly, "Sita."

"This way," the black-suit said before I could respond.

We followed him down a series of gaslit halls to the dining room, where another black-suited man announced our arrival. Inside, three cut-glass chandeliers presided over a long mahogany table the length of the rani's audience chamber in the Panch Mahal. Perhaps it was the light reflecting in the mirrors, or maybe it was the special ornamentation for Christmas, but nothing had ever looked so beautiful to me. Everything was red, and silver, and gold. A handsome damask linen spread across the table, which was filled nearly to bursting with glittering crystal and china. Next to every plate were multiples of silver cutlery: two spoons, four forks, two knives. And the glasses were so wide that a person could place a fist inside of them. The room was already half-filled with guests, and I noticed that there were as many women as men.

We were expected to stand in front of our chairs and wait until another black-suit pushed them forward after we seated ourselves. My place was near Arjun, and across from us were the empty chairs for the queen and her husband, Prince Albert. As I reached forward to take the cream-colored napkin from the table, as Mrs.

McEgan had instructed us back home, another man arrived. He was unbelievably handsome—Indian, but dressed in an Englishman's clothes. His suit had two tails following behind him like a pair of ducks. I had never seen an Indian man in formal British clothing before.

A black-suit led him across the room, and all of the women paid attention as he walked. When he arrived at the seat next to me, he pressed his hands together in namaste and made a polite bow.

"I heard that the Rani of Jhansi was sending ambassadors to England," he said, "but I had no idea they would be so beautiful."

He looked from me to Jhalkari, who was seated on the other side of Arjun, and I'm sure I turned several shades of pink. Then this Indian man took my hand and kissed the top of it. I had never been treated with such disrespect. Arjun rose from his seat, and several of the guards around the table did the same.

"It's an English tradition," the man assured them with an amused look.

There was deep alarm on the British guests' faces; they had no idea what was happening.

"Molesting a woman is not a tradition in *any* country," Arjun said in Marathi. "You will apologize."

The man bowed very, very deeply. "I am sorry."

Everyone resumed their seats.

"I was only practicing British courtesy," the man explained to Arjun. "Forgive me. My name is Azimullah Khan." When Arjun didn't respond, Azimullah continued, "My patron knows your rani. In fact, they grew up together."

"What is his name?"

"Nana Saheb."

Well, this got everyone's attention. Although I've already mentioned this story, it probably bears retelling, on account of the fact that it played such a significant role in the rani's life. When she was young, the rani was known as Manikarnika, or Manu for short. She was raised at the court of Baji Rao II, and her father treated her like the son he'd wanted. He allowed her to dress like a boy and play like one, too, even though this might have diminished her chances for a successful marriage. Of all the children at court, the rani's closest friends were Tatya Tope and Nana Saheb. The first boy was the son of Pandurang Rao Tope, an important nobleman at the Peshwa's court. And of course, everyone has heard of Nana Saheb, the adopted son of Peshwa Baji Rao.

Many people thought the rani would marry Saheb, but it didn't turn out this way. In 1817, Saheb's adopted father was defeated by the British. His treasury, lands, estates, even his furniture, which had been passed down from generation to generation, was confiscated. In return, he was told that he and his heirs would receive an annual pension of nearly eighty thousand British pounds. But when the Peshwa died in 1851, they refused to give Saheb his father's pension.

I don't know how the heirs of other defeated rajas reacted, but Saheb responded the same way the rani did. By petitioning the Company to restore his kingdom, and on failing that, at least his father's pension. We'd all heard the stories of Saheb's appeals, and this was partly why the rani's father was so suspicious of any attempt to negotiate with England. Saheb told him what sort of fruit such appeals would bear. But the rani, like Saheb, was utterly persistent, and now here we were, representing two separate cases of British injustice and hoping the queen could solve them both.

"So of all the men in Bithur," Arjun said, "Saheb chose you."

Azimullah grinned. He was truly an extraordinary-looking man, with lightly tanned skin, black hair that fell in waves, and light green eyes. "You may insult me as you wish, but I am very popular here."

"Is that why you haven't returned for two years?"

Azimullah looked a little surprised by this.

"I've heard the rani talk about you," Arjun said.

"Your rani may say whatever she wishes, but this is hard work."

I leaned forward. "What? Attending dinner with the queen?"

"Convincing her that Indians are capable of ruling."

"And it's taken two years to do this?" Arjun said.

"No. She was convinced of this the moment she met me. Now she needs to be convinced to act. And *that* takes time." When Arjun glanced at me, Azimullah laughed. "You didn't think you were going to come here and receive an immediate answer, did you?"

I glanced around the table, but everyone was chatting happily in English. We might as well have been a group of the queen's servants for all the attention they were paying to us. "We were told there would be an answer tonight."

"Ma'am," he said, and although he was using a polite form of address, I knew he was doing so in a belittling way, "that's not how things work in England. An answer may come tomorrow, or the next day, or not at all, but when it does, the queen will send it by letter." I'm sure he could read the shock on my face, because he added, "You didn't think she was going to make an announcement here? In front of all these guests?"

"I did. That is what she told us she would do."

"Ma'am, I was raised by these British at the Kanpur Free School. Nothing they say is to be believed. A squat woman wearing a crown—"

I gasped, and Arjun turned red.

"None of them can understand us. Do you think she can wave

her fat hand and make this better? She doesn't have that kind of power. Parliament is making the decisions."

"She's the queen," Jhalkari protested.

"And everything she does must go through Parliament. Trust me," he said. "I have lived with these people. I know their habits. They wear shoes in their houses and bathe once a week. They may look clean, but they are dirty on the inside, both morally and physically."

"Are they blind as well?" I demanded. "Or can't they see how you despise them?"

Azimullah smiled. You would have thought for all the world that we were talking about civil things, like the weather. "Oh, yes. They're blind as well. That's why, when I return, I will give Saheb my carefully considered opinion."

Arjun didn't bother hiding his disgust. "And what will that be?"

"That British men are weak and can easily be defeated. He simply needs to rise up."

We didn't speak again that evening. After all, Azimullah Khan didn't know everything. Our circumstances were different, and the queen had liked us. But when the queen arrived at the banquet with Prince Albert on her arm and dinner was served, I began to wonder if she was really going to address the rani's plight that evening. There were boiled potatoes, a green vegetable I'd never seen, steamed carrots in rich sauce, and great heaps of meat. And everyone seemed far more interested in eating than in why we'd come. The conversation turned from the weather, to food, to riding in Hyde Park. Then suddenly, the queen stood and everyone rose. A servant announced, "Her Majesty, The Queen will be retiring for the night."

Arjun and I looked at each other. We rose from our seats and before we could utter a word in protest, the queen was gone. The other guards looked in our direction.

"Where is she going?" Jhalkari said. "What about Jhansi?"

Azimullah looked extremely satisfied with himself. "Jhansi is probably the furthest thing from her mind right now."

"What do you mean?"

"Tomorrow is their Christmas Eve festival. There are parties to attend."

Days passed. Then weeks. Finally, we left England in January. We had been given an audience with Queen Victoria, we had dined at her table, and a week after the Christmas holiday, we had been invited back to court to meet important members of her Parliament. But ultimately, Saheb's ambassador was right. She had allowed us to travel all the way from Jhansi and then back again to India without any verdict. There would be no triumphant return. No great reward.

Jhansi was still lost. The British queen was more interested in India's dogs than her people.

Chapter Twenty-Two

1855

In the short time that we'd been gone, everything had changed.

We rode through Jhansi in stunned silence. The Temple of Mahalakshmi, where we always fed the poor, was closed, its colorful windows boarded and covered with signs in English that read, THIS TEMPLE IS SHUT. And next to it, on a vast stretch of land enclosed by a crude wooden fence, the British had set up a butchery. These days, when I talk to Westerners, there is only one thing they know about India, and it is that we hold the cow sacred. Some have the misconception that we believe our ancestors come back as cows. This is absurd and couldn't be further from the truth. We simply never slaughter any animal that gives milk, and the cow is especially sacred to us since babies will drink their milk if their mothers no longer have any to give. So of all the offensive things the British could do, this butchery was by far the worst. The slaughtering of cows was terrible, but to see it happening next to the most sacred place in Jhansi—it would have been more acceptable if the British had destroyed the temple completely.

The bookstore whose blue and gold sign once enthralled me

with its promise of "Books: Hindi, Marathi, English," now read simply "Books: English." And everywhere we looked, the red and black Union Jack snapped in the cool breeze. It was as if the British had made a game of seeing how many places they could mount a flag. It flew from the tops of stores, from the balconies of houses, even from the well where women drew water each morning.

When we reached the Rani Mahal, it looked as if someone had taken the palace and draped its bright walls in a heavy gray sheath. Part of it was the weather: the sun appeared only through breaks in the clouds. But it was the garden as well. Everything was bare, as if Lord Vayu, our god of the winds, had focused all of his strength on my home. The trees, the shrubs, the flowers, even the bushes, were entirely devoid of leaves. Home, I thought, realizing that for the first time, I was calling a place home that wasn't Barwa Sagar.

There was no one to greet our return. We had sent a letter ahead, detailing what had happened in London. Perhaps it hadn't arrived.

Or perhaps it had been met with too much disappointment.

I felt embarrassed in my fur-lined cape, gifted to me under far different circumstances, and when I dismounted, I took it off and carried it in my arms. Jhalkari and the soldiers did the same. A guard bowed very low before letting us inside, but the halls were silent.

We climbed the stairs. And there, in the rani's Durbar Hall, was Azimullah Khan. No person on Earth could have been more unexpected—or less welcome to us. Next to him was another man who I assumed was Saheb. The rani was dressed in a soft blue angarkha of pattern chiffon with white rabbit's fur trim at the wrists and neck. She looked regal on her silver cushion in front of them. As soon as she saw us, she rose and asked, "Why didn't anyone tell me that you'd returned?"

I looked around the room and saw the other Durgavasi starting to rise. Azimullah turned to see us, and I wished I could wipe the smug look from his face.

Our group approached the rani, and we all took turns touching her feet, then pressing our hands together in namaste. Then everyone was talking at once and more cushions were being arranged around the room. Arjun, Jhalkari, and I were asked to sit to the left of Saheb, and the rani asked whether the queen had changed her mind about restoring the kingdom of Jhansi to her control.

Our letter had not arrived.

"Queen Victoria has many interests," I said, "but giving prompt answers is not one of them."

"Yes," the rani said quietly. "My friend Saheb has been here for several days, and although my father isn't here at the moment, he agrees with Saheb." We all waited to hear what it was her father agreed with. Finally she said, "The British have no interest in returning Jhansi. But there are forty-four Indian soldiers for every one British soldier here."

"That's *two million* Indian soldiers compared to a mere forty-five thousand British men," Saheb said. "When word gets out of this Circular Memorandum—and it will—there is going to be a revolt. The pot has been boiling for long enough."

"It's time to boil over," Azimullah said quietly.

"What is the Circular Memorandum?" I asked.

"A document issued by the East India Company giving orders to commanding officers that Indian women are to be taken from every village and set up in special houses for the use of British men," the rani answered darkly. "And any girl seen speaking with a man may be denounced as a prostitute and sent to such a house." Her voice was steady, but I could hear the rage underneath, like a fire beneath smoldering coals.

"How can this be?" Jhalkari exclaimed.

No one else in the room was incensed. Clearly, this had already been discussed. I thought of Queen Victoria, who was probably dining at her glittering table as we spoke, and I wished I had known this before. "Have any girls been denounced?" I asked.

"Yes."

"Without a trial?" Arjun pressed. "Without any intervention?"

"They are simply taken away," the rani confirmed. "And now that the Kutwal know they have this power, they're going from house to house, demanding bribes."

"The Kutwal have always been corrupt," Arjun said. The Kutwal are police. And it is true, they have always been tainted by corruption. No good family will give a son willingly to the Kutwal.

"This is happening in every village?" I said. I immediately thought of Anu in Shivaji's house. Had the local Kutwal visited them yet? Had they been able to pay the bribe?

"Yes. And the girls who are sent to these houses are being used and then discarded if they become diseased. Their families don't want them back, and now, I have no means to help them," the rani said. "No power and no money."

"The sepoys are going to rise at last," Azimullah predicted, "and we will all be prepared."

"People are talking about this memorandum," the rani told him. "But for those who haven't lost a wife or a daughter yet, for those who won't believe it until they see it, Azimullah has brought us a gift from France."

We all followed her gaze to a very large item beneath a blanket in the corner of the room. Saheb stood and unveiled his ambassador's gift. It was a large metal machine.

"A printing press," Saheb said. "We will print this despicable memorandum in every language in India. And we'll distribute it to every village. I am going to march on Delhi. Ten thousand men strong."

"With what aim?" Arjun asked.

"To restore the Mughal emperor to power. Under his rule, India will return to a land of kingships, just as it was before the British came."

Imagine the Mughal emperor as the pope and all of the kingdoms in India as Catholic countries under his rule. Saheb was proposing to restore the defeated emperor to power, and in return, the emperor would see to it that all of the kingdoms the British had conquered would return to Indian rule.

"The ten thousand are Saheb's men," Arjun said. "What other kingdoms will join you?"

"Any who don't wish to live under British rule," Azimullah replied. "Because you're either with us or against us." He boldly turned to face the rani, but I could see the conflict on the rani's face.

"As I've told you, if I give aid to the sepoys and the British succeed in defeating them, what will the British do to me? Or, more important, to Jhansi? My situation is difficult. I have to remain neutral."

"And your conscience lets you do this, even after this memorandum?" he raged. "Suppose you do not aid the sepoys? They will believe you supported the British," he warned. "What will happen to Jhansi then?"

As soon as the rani dismissed us, I hurried down the stairs to the Durgavas to write Anu a letter. She had to be warned about the memorandum and what the Kutwals were doing. She had to hide if they came to Shivaji's home. The moment I was finished, I went to Gopal and instructed him to post it for me. Then, as I was returning to the Durbar Hall, I met Arjun on the landing. In the light of the softly swaying oil lamps, his face looked as if it had been carved from stone.

"So what do you think of Azimullah's *with us or against us* threat?" I asked.

Arjun looked around. Mandar was standing near us; Moti was talking with Kashi a few steps away. I doubted they were paying us any attention. "The British must be stopped," he said. "And I have always believed the sepoys might revolt. But I worry about letting Azimullah lead any sort of revolution."

"Yes. But I understand now why Azimullah is so bitter," I said.

"Sita, I've been wanting to ask you something."

We stood together in the flickering light, letting other guardsmen pass us by.

"That last day on the ship . . . why did you walk away from me when I said you were beautiful?"

I couldn't believe he would even ask such a thing. "After you told Jhalkari you wanted to marry someone else?"

He stared at me, and I could see he was shocked.

"You told her you wanted to marry someone from Jhansi."

"Yes," he replied. "*You.*"

"But I'm not from Jhansi."

His eyes were wide. "Sita, *in* . . . *from* . . . those are just words. Of course I meant you."

I placed my hand against the wall to keep myself steady. Why would he admit such a thing to me now? We had failed in London; I was never going to be released from the rani. How could he even mention such a wonderful possibility when he knew it was beyond hope? "I'm a Durgavasi, Arjun. I'm twenty-one years old with a father to support. Let's not ruin the friendship we have with daydreams now."

I know I sounded bitter. And I know I saw regret in his eyes. But he bowed to indicate he understood, then escorted me into the Durbar Hall.

Inside, I choked down the feelings that threatened to overwhelm me. I would survive this. I'd survived worse things. After all, I was bamboo, and bamboo bends. It doesn't break.

Chapter Twenty-Three

There are only a handful of times in my life when I can tell you exactly where I was when such and such event occurred. When my mother died, for example. I can still smell the turmeric and cardamom that was in the air, and tell you exactly how the rain sounded as it dripped from the corner of our house into a clay pot outside. When I was told that I had been made a Durgavasi, when I learned of young Damodar's death, when the rani discovered that Jhansi would no longer be hers . . . These are all times I can recapture in my mind with a photograph's precision. And when the rebellion arrived in Jhansi? This is a moment forever etched in my memory.

We were eating peanuts in the Durbar Hall. The rani was reading a letter from Captain Skene, regarding the sepoys in the nearby cantonment of Meerut. They were refusing to obey British orders. Then, like a wind, word started to spread that sepoys were disobeying orders in Jhansi, too. That morning, a hundred men had been sent to the whipping post for refusing to do as the British commanded. I looked across the hall at the male guards. They had been joining us for evening tea ever since we had moved into the Rani Mahal; the palace was too small to live separate lives the way we once did. Our eyes met and we knew.

The rani cleared her throat and continued reading Captain Skene's letter. She never said how she'd come by the stolen copy, but the rani had spies all across Jhansi.

> *The troops here, I am glad to say, continue staunch and express their inbounded abhorrence of the atrocities committed at Meerut and Delhi. I am going on the principle of showing perfect confidence, and I am quite sure I am right. . . . All will settle down here in Jhansi.*

We were still marveling at the naiveté of his words when a messenger arrived, escorted by four of the rani's guards. As soon as we saw him, we rose, and the rani did the same. He bowed deeply, but the rani waved off such formalities. "What's happening?" she demanded.

"Your Highness. The sepoys have burned two of the barracks inside the Fortress of Jhansi, and now a third one is burning!"

There is an expression you have in English: *The color drained from her face.* Well, this is exactly what happened when the rani heard this news. She turned so white that the messenger stepped forward, thinking she might faint.

"Your Highness!" Sundari said.

The rani held on to Sundari's shoulder for support.

For two days you could feel the tension in the city; it was as if Jhansi was an instrument improperly strung and so taut its strings threatened to snap. We all attended to our duties the same as before, but we were waiting to see what would happen next.

When it happened, we were practicing in the front of the Rani Mahal before the sun came up. Shots rang out and all of us froze.

Kahini was the first to sling her bow over her shoulder and run. We followed behind her as more shots rang out and people began running from the crowded marketplace. A short man in a sepoy's uniform made his way toward the gates and asked to see the rani. We took his pistol and his sword and let him through. The rani was in the courtyard: when he saw her, he rushed to touch her feet and bowed.

"The sepoys of Jhansi are rebelling against the British, Your Highness! A man named Havildar Gurbaksh is leading the seventh company of the twelfth regiment, and they have taken over Star Fort."

There were three forts within the city of Jhansi. The one that had once been the rani's home, Star Fort, and Town Fort. Only the magazine in Star Fort held supplies and ammunition.

"What else?" the rani said. I could see that she was doing her very best to look neutral. Because if she openly supported the rebels and the British subdued them, they would kill her.

The short sepoy shifted from foot to foot. "Two officers have been killed, and the rest of the British are fleeing for their lives. Captain Skene is trying to persuade his people to take refuge in Town Fort."

I thought of Dr. McEgan and Mrs. McEgan, who had helped us prepare for our journey to London. I also thought of Major Wilkes, and hoped he hadn't returned from England with his fiancée.

"Who sent you?" the rani asked.

The sepoy looked at his sandals. "No one, Your Highness. I came on my own."

So the other sepoys didn't trust her.

The rani sent her Durgavasi and her personal guards to assemble inside the Durbar Hall. As we did, the two hundred soldiers the British had allowed her to hire made a protective ring around the Rani Mahal. She remained downstairs with Arjun and Sundari.

"What are we doing?" Kahini demanded on our way up the stairs. "Why aren't we helping the rebels at Star Fort?"

"That's assuming the rani wishes to help them," Mandar said.

Inside the Durbar Hall, there was barely room to stand, let alone sit. The room had been built for fifty people, but with all of the mahal's servants crowded inside, there were nearly two hundred. I stood near one of the windows, and Jhalkari and I tried to make out what was happening below. Smoke filled the marketplace, and people were running and closing up their stalls, but there was no sign of any flames.

"The British can last quite some time in Town Fort," Jhalkari said. "It was designed to withstand a siege. There's a well, and at least a week's worth of food."

Finally, the rani appeared with Arjun, Sundari, and her father. After speaking briefly with Kahini, they asked Jhalkari and me to follow them into her personal chamber. When we were seated, it was her father who spoke.

"There are sixty-six Europeans in Town Fort," he said. "More than half of them are women and children."

"So the question is now, what do we do for them?" the rani said. "There must be something we can do."

In contrast to Queen Victoria, I thought, who hides behind her Parliament and does nothing.

We all looked at one another. None of us wanted to be the first to respond.

"Think rationally, Manu," said her father. "You only have two hundred men—all of them are needed to guard this palace. You know what happens during times of rebellion. Pretenders to the throne crawl out of the earth like worms drawn by flood."

I thought this was a very clever analogy, but I wondered if it would happen now. Weren't we all fighting for the same cause? To rid India of the British?

"I could talk with the sepoys," the rani said.

"Why should they trust you when you're taking a British pension?" Moropant asked.

I could see the hurt on her face. "Then at the very least, we should tell them to flee. Get out of Jhansi, and take shelter in Sagar or Datia."

"And you think they don't know that?" Kahini said rudely.

"I think their plan is to wait it out," Sundari countered. "Let's send your Dewan to warn them," she suggested. "As a gesture of goodwill, we can send some of your personal guards."

And this was what the rani did. Forty men accompanied the Dewan to Town Fort.

We waited all day for word. By nightfall only the Dewan had returned. The rani's guards had joined the rebellion.

The Dewan shook as he recounted the scene. "It was chaos, Your Highness. The women were in a panic and the children couldn't be calmed. Captain Skene is not going to flee from Town Fort. After seeing your men joining forces with the rebels, he believes you're setting a trap."

No one slept more than a few hours that night. The Durgavasi stood guard in the rani's chamber, and as soon as the sun rose, there was a commotion beyond the gates. We hurried to the window just in time to see two men walk past the guards and shout the rani's name from the courtyard below.

"Rani Lakshmibai!" one of them cried.

The other one shouted, "Rani of Jhansi!"

Neither of them was carrying weapons, but they still looked threatening. The rani hurried to the window, and when the men caught sight of her face, they gestured wildly.

"Your Highness, you should probably step back," I said.

"No, let them speak. What is it that you want?" she shouted down.

"We want to know which side you're on! Do you stand with the British, or do you stand with us?"

Her response was very clever. "I stand with justice—for my people, for my son, and for my kingdom."

The men exchanged looks. Then they decided she meant she stood with the rebels, and one of them raised his arm in the air, and shouted, "Har Har Mahadev!" In English, this would be like saying, *By the Grace of God!*

The other one took up the shout, and the pair left as quickly as they'd come. But their intrusion served as a warning to us: we now knew the rani could count on the guards outside the mahal the same way she could count on the British. Her only real defense was her Durgavasi and her remaining personal guards.

Nothing of any consequence happened the rest of that day, though we kept waiting for the sound of gunfire, or the din of voices to tell us that a mob was growing outside. But the marketplace was eerily silent. I wondered how the British were surviving in Town Fort. Did they think the prolonged silence meant they were safe? Had Captain Skene realized that the rebels had all the time in the world and it was the British for whom time was running out?

The next morning the rani requested breakfast to be served in her chamber while she discussed private matters with Sundari. There was no sign of the rebels who had forced their way inside the courtyard the day before. I sat with Moti in the Durbar Hall, hoping that it was going to be another quiet day, when raised voices echoed near the gates, followed by the sound of heavy boots on wooden stairs. Immediately, I reached for my bow, and Moti was on her feet, wielding her knife. I yelled for the rani to stay inside her chamber just as her father burst through the door.

"Are you determined to kill me?" he asked.

Immediately, I lowered my weapon. "I'm sorry, Shri Moropant."

He pushed aside my apology with a wave. "Two British soldiers have been killed. One a captain, the other an ensign. They were delivering letters to the fortress when it happened."

"It was sepoys who killed them?" I confirmed.

"Yes."

The rani heard her father's voice and emerged from her chamber. He told her the same thing he had just told us, then boots once again thumped their way up the stairs. I reached for an arrow, but it was Arjun. "I have a messenger from the fort, Your Highness. May I send him inside?"

"Of course."

An Englishman appeared, dressed in the most ridiculous fashion I had ever seen. He was trying to imitate Indian dress, but his cotton churidars were too small, his juti too formal, and his pale skin contrasted starkly against the black fabric of his kurta. His face showed extreme fatigue, and something else I had never seen on a British soldier before—fear.

"Your Highness," he began, then he collapsed at the rani's feet. "My three companions have been killed!"

The rani looked at Arjun, who couldn't confirm or deny the story.

"Stand," she said.

The man rose. His knees were shaking. "Captain Skene sent us for help. We need you, Your Highness. The rebels are going to kill us all. The women, the children . . ." His voice was rising to an hysterical pitch.

The rani put her hand on his shoulder. "What would you have me do?"

"Stop the rebels!"

"I'm no longer the Rani of Jhansi."

The soldier was trembling. "Can't you speak with them?"

"I can. But I gave your captain advice and it wasn't heeded. I told him to flee."

"He'll listen now! Whatever you ask him to do, he'll listen!"

"*I'll* speak with the rebels," Moropant said.

The soldier's face seemed to transform itself. "Will you tell them to grant us safe passage? That's all we want," he swore. "Then we'll all be on the first ship home. None of us asked to be here," he said. "None of us want to be here at all!"

But I thought of the Circular Memorandum and I felt very little sympathy for this man.

"I will press whatever advantage I have," Moropant promised. "For the sake of the women and children," he clarified. "But you should return to the fort."

"They'll kill me!"

"No. I'll be your guard."

The rani exchanged a look with her father. He led the man out the door, and the room was silent. I fanned myself with my hand. The windows had been thrown open to try to catch a breeze on such a sweltering day. At the Panch Mahal, long kusha grass shades would have blocked out the sun, but there was nothing like that here. Just painted wooden shutters.

"Is there anything you'd like me to do?" Arjun asked. "Shall I go into the marketplace and see what I can learn?"

The rani nodded.

An hour later, Arjun returned. "Your father escorted Johnson back to Town Fort. That was his name. The other three—Purcell, Andrews, and Scott—were killed, just as he said. The assault is planned for tomorrow."

"And?" the rani asked. "What will happen to the English?"

"Safe passage," Arjun said. "There are women and children inside. Safe passage will be granted."

"You heard them say this?"

"I heard General Khan make the promise to your father."

I thought this would ease the rani's concerns, but she still looked troubled.

The next morning, the rebels surrounded Town Fort, as promised. The English were marched to Jokhan Bagh, a large garden just beyond Jhansi's city walls. There, all sixty-six of them were killed, including Captain Skene, Dr. McEgan, Mrs. McEgan, and all the tiny children we used to watch running through the fortress. A celebratory group of rebels made their way to the Rani Mahal and demanded to be let in through the gates. When the guards didn't put up a fight, we secured the doors and listened through the heavy metal and wood as they shouted in the courtyard, demanding to see the Rani of Jhansi at once.

"She isn't going to risk appearing, is she?" I worried.

"I don't know," Jhalkari said. "She's not afraid of many things."

Arjun and the other male guards were with us, weapons poised, in case any of the rebels should get the idea to force open the doors. I drew back an arrow, the bowstring tight and ready.

"Send out the Rani of Jhansi!" someone shouted, and then one of the men began a chant. "Rani! Rani!" They shouted it over and over until a sudden break in the noise told me that above us, the rani had appeared. A sudden cheer went up, as deliriously happy as it had been angry just moments earlier.

"Come down!" someone shouted, and this time, the men cheered and sounded ecstatic.

There were footsteps on the wooden stairs behind us, then the rani appeared in a white Chanderi sari with a red crescent moon painted on her forehead. On her waist, she carried a sword, and behind her, a shield. She was dressed like a soldier. After all, her father had trained her as one.

"Open the doors," she said.

Arjun and the other men hesitated, but she repeated her command.

"How many men shall escort you?" Arjun asked.

"None. I want three Durgavasi behind me. Sundari, Kahini, and Sita."

Arjun knew better than to question this. Sundari was armed with her weapon of choice—a pistol—while I carried my bow and Kahini her knives. We fell into position behind the rani. Then the doors opened, and the shocked rebels stepped back. I could hear their sharp intake of breath, as the realization hit them that this woman in soldier's dress had once been their queen.

"What would you like of me?" she demanded.

At first, no one said anything. Then one by one the rebels fell to their knees. At last, one stood and addressed her personally. "Your Highness!" He raised his fist in the air, and I could see that his arm was covered with blood. I stepped closer to get a better look, and it appeared that his hair and heavy beard were matted with blood as well. "The rebellion has begun with the lives of sixty-six Englishmen! General Khan gave orders to kill them all, and we obeyed, beginning with Captain Skene."

"Did you spare the women and children?" the rani asked. I could hear her strain to hide her disgust.

"No one was spared." He said this with pride assuming she'd agree with General Khan's decision. "Captain's Browne's sister was screaming," he said. "Begging for her life, throwing herself into the arms of a sepoy so they would have to kill him as well as her. But he detached himself and threw her to the hungry knives. One of them called your name," he said. "A pretty doctor's wife. She pleaded for us to spare her husband, and when we killed him, she cast her body on top of his."

"Then she's—"

"Killed with the rest of them."

I thought of Mrs. McEgan, with her pretty blond curls and sea-blue eyes, and then I imagined her covered in blood and felt sick.

"What will be done with the bodies?" the rani said. Her voice was dead, as if she'd removed herself from this reality the same way you might separate yourself from unpleasant company by going into a different room.

The man shrugged. "Let them rot. This country belongs to us!" he shouted.

The other men took up the cry.

"We are marching to Delhi," the rebel said. "We will restore the emperor to power and strike these Englishmen where they least expect it!"

"Then Durga protect you," the rani replied, but she might have been saying to watch out for rain for all the emotion that was in her words. The rani returned to the mahal, and we remained at the doors, trying to shut them before the mob grew violent and wanted more.

"Stand back!" Kahini snapped as the men pressed forward. "Or the rani will tell you what she truly thinks of your rebellion."

"And what is that?" one of the men asked.

"That you are a bunch of dogs versus lions," she accused as Arjun yanked the doors shut and lowered the bar.

"Why would you say that?" he shouted.

Kahini looked him in the eyes, and if you have ever come face-to-face with a feral animal, then you have already met her gaze.

The damage was done. Word would spread like disease through the rebel camps. And now they would believe a lie. The rani's position was precarious. Unless she remained neutral, her life and that of her son's would be in danger.

We didn't tell the rani what happened, but Arjun and I kept a careful watch over Kahini after this. When evening came, I quietly followed her to Gopal's chamber and stood outside the door while they spoke in hushed tones. "I want you to give this to my parents," she said. "Tell them I am well, and there is nothing to worry about."

Kahini didn't have any parents. Her mother had died in childbirth with her, and her father had died several years later. Gopal said sternly, "I don't see why I should give this to him."

"*Them!*" she hissed. "Give them this sapphire ring. And remember our deal."

Obviously, the ring in question wasn't destined for her parents. But who?

"I missed you last night," Gopal said. There was longing in his voice.

"I miss a great many things, including the Panch Mahal." Then Kahini's voice softened. It was like listening to another person altogether. "There are bigger things to worry over right now," she said. "Give it time."

"That's what you always say."

I heard a smacking sound, like lips on flesh, and my stomach turned.

The rani's father believed a letter should be written to the British at once, explaining that the rani had no role whatsoever in the massacre; that, in fact, she had tried to prevent it by telling Captain

Skene to leave the fortress. But most of her advisers were of the opinion that all of the letters in the world weren't going to persuade the British that the rani hadn't been an accomplice. And if the British were going to condemn her as a rebel, she might as well publicly join them.

It was decided she would write the letter.

She dictated what she wanted me to write, and then I translated it to English and read it back to her. When she was satisfied she had covered all of the details, she sealed it and called for Gopal.

Then there was banging at the door, and Arjun's voice. "Your Highness, there is an army approaching!"

My fingers went at once to my bow as he burst into the room.

"The guards are saying they're from Unao. About five *kos* from here. A man named Sadashiv Narayan is leading them, and says he's come to lay claim to the throne."

I saw the color drain from the rani's face. "A Newalkar relative," she said.

"There are between two and three thousand men. Their plan is to install this Sadashiv Narayan on your throne and then make their way to Delhi."

The rani was already out the door. I followed her and Arjun to the Durbar Hall, where a call was raised for everyone to prepare. "We will not give this palace to rebels," she said. "Sundari, take the Durgavasi to the first floor. Kashi, guard Anand in my chamber. Arjun, take your guards to the courtyard. These men believe they're going to put someone on the throne who opposes the British more than I do. The British will kill him before the harvest is finished."

There was a flurry of activity in the mahal, and I took up a position next to Jhalkari on the first floor. I had my arrow aimed out the window at the gates, so that the first rebel to pass through would be shot through the heart. I could not keep three thousand men at bay, but many would die before making their way into the courtyard.

We stood in silence as the sound of the approaching army grew nearer. I could hear men's voices carried on the wind, along with the odd burst of gunfire. If you have ever waited for something terrifying, then you know that expectation can be worse than the actual thing.

"I'm going out to meet them," the rani said.

"No!" Kahini lowered her bow and stood in front of the rani. "They'll kill you!"

"Come with me then. If that's what they've come to do, none of us are going to stop them for very long," the rani said.

Kahini was actually trembling. I'd never seen her express such concern for the rani. Her face was pale, but she led the way out the door, then to the gates. You could see Arjun's surprise, but he nodded slowly and said something I couldn't hear. Then he joined the women, and the three of them left the courtyard and the soldiers closed the gates behind them.

I kept my arrow ready as the rebels appeared, thousands upon thousands of them dressed in no particular fashion. These were men who had come from both cities and villages, probably joining the march as it went. It was impossible not to hear their raised voices now, some of them shouting for the rani's death. But as the sun began to set, igniting the sky in a blaze of oranges and reds, their voices grew more muted. Then there was silence. Finally, the gates swung open and the rani appeared again with Kahini and Arjun walking quickly behind her.

Kahini said, "They're leaving." Her face was expressionless.

"Arjun convinced them that the men in this city are loyal to me and me alone," the rani explained. "They will continue to Delhi.

They're also asking for a bag of jewels," she continued. "Someone will need to bring it to them."

"I'll do it," Kahini said swiftly.

"Someone should go with her," Sundari said.

"It isn't necessary," Kahini replied.

"Two women should go," the rani decided, and I found myself volunteering.

We waited for the rani to bring down a pouch filled with loose emeralds and rubies. Then I followed Kahini through the courtyard. Arjun didn't approve, but he instructed his men to open the gates, and we stepped into a mass of reeking bodies and ill-dressed men. They had been marching all day in the heat, without a bath or food or likely much water. Kahini raised her voice and asked to see the one they called Sadashiv Narayan. When he stepped up, I saw that he was a good-looking man, tall, with hair to his shoulders and a well-groomed mustache. I thought he was probably twenty-five or thirty. He held out his hand, and I was shocked to see Kahini brush his fingers as she handed over the bag.

"Thank you," he said. He emptied the contents into his hand, then I thought I saw him slip something into the bag; something blue and gold, possibly a ring with a sapphire. "I don't need this," he said, giving her back the velvet pouch.

"I'll take it back to the rani then," she said.

Their eyes never met.

I said nothing, but later, when the others were eating, I hurried to our chambers on the first floor and searched through Kahini's chest. There, wrapped in several layers of blue silk, was a sapphire ring. Why would Gopal send this to Sadashiv Narayan, a pretender to the rani's throne? Should I go to Sundari? Or maybe the rani herself? There was the sound of footsteps behind me. I held my breath, preparing to hear somebody shriek.

"What are you doing?"

I exhaled. It was only Jhalkari. I slipped the ring in my pocket without thinking. "I had a hunch," I said.

"About Kahini's belongings?"

"Yes." The other women were coming in. "I'll tell you later."

Chapter Twenty-Four

In reporting on this event to Parliament, Earl Stanley has called what's happening throughout India a mutiny, and the British newspapers are stating this as well," the messenger said.

"It can only be a mutiny if we're British citizens!" the rani's father exclaimed.

The messenger glanced nervously in Moropant's direction, but the rani waved her hand for him to continue. "Please."

"As . . . as a leader of this mutiny," the man said, "a warrant has been issued for your arrest. It calls for Your Highness to be hanged in Fort William. I'm sorry," he whispered. There were tears in the man's eyes, and his hands shook as he offered her the letter.

Moropant removed himself from the chamber. In light of such news, it hardly even mattered what the second messenger had to say. But he stepped forward, and pressed his hands together in namaste.

"Yes?" the rani said quietly.

"I'm afraid I've come with more bad news, Your Highness."

"Go on."

"Sadashiv Narayan has taken over the nearby Fortress of Karhera and held an enthronement ceremony for himself. He's appointing his own officials, and has sent out an official announcement about taxes."

If it hadn't come on the heels of such bad news from England, it might have been comical. But the part about taxes was more than the rani could bear. I could see her resolve beginning to crumble when the doors of the hall suddenly opened and her father returned.

"For the Rani of Jhansi!" Moropant said, waving a document.

We all stared at him, wondering what could possibly account for his sudden change in mood. Then he produced a kharita and handed it to me.

"It's from Major Erskine," I said. I read as fast as I could. "And they're requesting that you take charge of the kingdom of Jhansi on behalf of the British government."

Everyone in the room was overcome with joy. Some of the Durgavasi even began to weep. But I suspected the British and their motives. They simply needed someone to keep the peace until they could return to power here.

"So what will your first act be?" Moropant said.

"To go to Karhera and arrest this pretender."

It took exactly two hours for the rebels to give up Sadashiv Narayan. We returned to the Panch Mahal shortly after. Armed guards escorted the prisoner to the Durbar Hall, where the rani handed him a sentence of death. At this, Kahini grew hysterical.

"Please," she begged. "Send him to prison. Don't take his life!"

"Kahini," the rani hissed. "What's the matter with you? Do you know this man?"

"Yes. We grew up together in the same court in Unao."

I thought immediately of the letter Gopal accidentally handed to me. It had been signed "S." For *Sadashiv.* So this was Kahini's lover. I looked at the tall, handsome man in the open vest who had been raised at court with Kahini. How had she deceived Gopal into delivering her letters to him?

Across the hall, Arjun frowned at me. I shook my head. I had no idea. Was Kahini a traitor? Had she been preparing Sadashiv to march on Jhansi, then sent her ring as proof that the right time had come?

The rani and Kahini stepped outside to speak privately. When they returned, Kahini looked composed, and a tense knot formed in my stomach. She had gotten her way because I'd kept the contents of the letter and the suspicious ring a secret from the rani.

I watched the rani take her throne. She said, "Sadashiv, you are a foolish but lucky man."

He glanced at Kahini, but his gaze didn't linger. His dark eyes turned to the rani, and I wondered how many women he'd seduced with those eyes.

"Your sentence will be life in prison. I do not believe you understood what you were aiming for when you came to Jhansi looking to take my throne. You should have remained in Unao." She nodded, and a pair of guards led him away.

He was strangely composed, bowing and thanking the rani for her mercy. He didn't look at Kahini, and Kahini didn't make any further scene. It was as if her hysterics had never taken place. How had Kahini convinced the rani to spare a traitor's life? But if Sadashiv was a traitor, so was Kahini. I possessed the ring to prove it. Only how could I be sure? And how could I ever go to the rani unless I was certain?

The rani rehired the thousands of soldiers she'd been forced to dismiss, and their first order of business was to arrest every Kutwal who had helped enforce the British's Circular Memorandum. The Temple of Mahalakshmi was to be reopened; the butchery next to it shut down. Most significantly, the Union Jack was to be removed from the south tower and the rani's red flag, with the whisk and kettledrum, was to be restored. As soon as the rani was finished in the Durbar Hall, we made our way to the Durgavas to change from our formal angarkhas to simpler ones. The other women threw questioning glances at Kahini, but even Rajasi kept her silence.

I waited until the other women had left for the queen's room before confronting Kahini.

"I know you have my ring," she said as she slipped her pink angarkha to the floor. She was even more beautiful naked than she was dressed. Was this how she had persuaded Gopal to deliver her letters? "I'd like it back."

"I saw you give it to Gopal."

Her shoulders tensed. She bent and picked up a soft cotton angarkha to replace the one she was wearing, then she held it out in front of her, as if to examine whether she liked it or not. Finally, she put it on. "Is that all?"

"No. I was there when Sadashiv gave it back to you. And I saw the letter he wrote asking if you were in any danger and whether he should come."

"You've been stealing my letters?" I had finally surprised her. "Rajasi!" she called, and I reached for the dagger on my thigh.

"Oh, don't worry. Your precious life is safe."

Rajasi came in from the queen's room.

"Sita believes I'm *conspiring* with Sadashiv to overthrow the rani." She made the idea sound as if it were silliest, most inconsequential thing. But even Rajasi had her doubts now.

"Why did you ask to save his life?"

Kahini became livid. "Are you implying that I'm a traitor as well?" When Rajasi didn't say anything, she crossed the room to my father's statue of Durga. "Well then, maybe we should take a look at the secrets our little *ganwaar* has been hiding." She nodded at me. "Show us what's in the compartment."

I'm sure I looked just as confused as Rajasi.

Kahini went ahead and twisted the head off my murti. Inside, where my father's prayer beads should have been, were dried green leaves and white flowers. I stepped forward to have a better look, and Kahini thrust them at me. "Hemlock!" she accused. "I know a murderess when I see one."

Rajasi looked at me. Then she said, "You had this murti fixed, Kahini. I don't know what game you're playing, but these are dangerous times."

Kahini's voice grew unnaturally low. "Maybe I should question what you're hiding as well, Rajasi. Because this is poison."

I grabbed the murti from her hands and shook the contents out the window. "And now it's gone," I said, "just as mysteriously as it arrived."

Rajasi and I left Kahini in the Durgavas, but I was scared. Kahini had placed hemlock in my murti. I thought of Kahini profaning my image of Durga in this way and a hot rage rose up inside of me. I wanted to expose her for the traitor I thought she was. Then I remembered the rani's reaction the only time I had ever criticized Kahini to her. I'd been afraid of what kind of doctor Kahini had chosen for the rani. At the time, my fears had been misplaced. How could I be certain they weren't misplaced now?

When I finally found a moment alone with Jhalkari that evening, I asked her what the symptoms of hemlock might be.

"I don't know. Moti could probably tell you," she said. "So what do you think about Kahini?"

"I think she can't be trusted." I didn't explain any further. I immediately went to Moti and asked her what she could tell me about hemlock. Next to her, a musician was lazily strumming the veena. Over the sound of her voice, no one could hear us.

"It's a strong poison," Moti said. "A person could use it to kill someone over time and no one would ever suspect it. There'd be a great deal of vomiting. A strange heartbeat. Finally, there'd be paralysis and then death."

I thought of the way little Damodar had died, and then it occurred to me that the raja's death hadn't been much different. What if it was possible that Kahini was more than just a traitor?

That evening, Jhalkari made several attempts to persuade me to talk, but I told her, "Not now. There's too many people."

Finally she said, "Come under my covers. No one will hear us."

I crawled into her bed and she put the blanket over our heads. If Kahini wasn't asleep, then she would guess what we were talking about.

"I think Kahini's a murderess," I whispered. Then I told her everything, from Gopal to the ring to the hemlock Kahini had discovered in my murti.

I could feel Jhalkari go very still. "Have you told this to anyone else? To Arjun?"

"Of course not. What if I'm wrong?"

"You aren't. Arjun has guard duty tonight outside the rani's chamber. Go now."

I dressed myself and in the light of the full moon I could see that Kahini's bed was empty. Where had she gone? Was she with the rani, trying to poison her before I could give her away? The sound of my sandals slapping against the marble woke several guards, who were supposed to be on duty. But in front of the rani's chamber, Arjun was awake.

"What is it?" he asked immediately.

"Kahini? Is she inside?"

"Not tonight. Why? Is something the matter?"

I paused to catch my breath, then led him away from the rani's door to a niche with a statue of our god Shiva dancing in an aureole of gold flames. I told him what I had told Jhalkari, adding that now Kahini was missing. "Do you think I could be wrong? Before her marriage, a servant discovered her with a letter to a lover. That's why she became a Durgavasi. Two days after the servant exposed Kahini, he was found floating in the Ganges. . . ." Had she been a murderess even then?

"It doesn't take much to imagine Kahini plotting out a life for herself as the rani and Sadashiv as the raja," Arjun said. "Or perhaps she plans to poison Sadashiv as well, once he's on the throne. A widowed rani who doesn't commit sati has a great deal of freedom."

Kahini had killed Damodar. She had killed the raja, her own cousin. An image of my grandmother taking me to the Temple of Annapurna to sell me as a devadasi entered my mind. "When do you stop trusting family?" I said.

"When the proof is irrefutable. If Kahini is wise, she'll realize that people are watching her now. She was foolish to expose hemlock in your murti and think Rajasi would accept that it was yours."

I was sharing a chamber with a woman who killed the Raja of Jhansi and his child—Damodar had only been a few months old. The most innocent creature on earth . . . how different life would be if not for Kahini! Instead of Damodar's ashes being scattered into the Ganges, he would be alive, delighting his mother. And the little boy who was now living in his place? He would be safe with his real mother, snuggling at her breast. I thought of all the lives Kahini had ruined. Why hadn't she tried to poison me as well?

Two men on the stairs interrupted my thoughts. One was a guard, the other a messenger. Arjun and I stepped away from each other, and I hated to think how we looked to them.

"News from Kanpur," the guard said. His face was grim, as if someone had taken the edges of his lips and pulled them down with tiny weights.

"The rani is sleeping," Arjun told him.

"Wake her. What this man has to say is important."

Arjun knocked until Sundari answered. It was obvious she'd been sleeping as well.

"A messenger from Kanpur," Arjun said. "Tell the rani it's urgent."

"Letters from Kanpur," the messenger said. "From Saheb."

A few moments later the rani appeared.

The messenger stepped forward to touch the rani's feet with his right hand, then straightened and handed two envelopes to her. In the flickering light of the oil lamps, she unfolded the first one and frowned. "I don't understand why he is in Kanpur," the rani said. "He was going to march to Delhi to return the former emperor, Bahadur Shah, to his throne."

The rani continued to read. Saheb had stopped on his march to Delhi. He had decided to retake the city of Kanpur from the British. The siege of Kanpur had taken three weeks.

The rani stopped reading, unable to go further, and handed the letter to Arjun, who read: "There was a massacre and three hundred British men, women, and children were killed."

Saheb claimed he had arranged for the safe passage of British citizens to the city of Allahabad, in the north, and that what ultimately happened was the fault of Azimullah Khan.

Saheb sent the British to the banks of the Ganges, which was in full flow. Forty boats awaited, but they had trouble launching in waters so rough. Azimullah Khan became impatient and shouted that if the British didn't leave at once they would all be killed. Panic ensued, and in the chaos that followed, shots were fired. Saheb's general, Tatya Tope, ordered all the British men killed; the one hundred and twenty women and children were taken as prisoners.

They were taken to a villa called Bibighar, meaning House of the Ladies, a house for prostitutes. The British women would be used as prostitutes. And why not the children? Weren't there soldiers who would enjoy a British boy? Or generals who might like a young British girl?

Azimullah Khan disagreed: he wanted all of the prisoners killed. When the men refused, he threatened them with death.

"The only thing I heard clearly above the gunfire," Saheb wrote, "were shouts of 'mummy,' but the mothers couldn't protect their children. *I* couldn't protect them. Allah forgive me, Manu. I hope you will forgive me as well. Azimullah and Tatya Tope wish to drive the British from our land by whatever means necessary. You must know I would never have condoned this. But I'm afraid we'll all suffer for their actions."

I imagined the terror the children felt as they looked to their mothers, searching their eyes for signs of reassurance that never came.

The letter seemed to have no end of horror. Saheb reported that some of the women and children survived the shooting. But they were not allowed to live. A prostitute favored by Azimullah Khan gathered several butchers, who carved up the survivors, removing their genitals and breasts.

None of us spoke when Arjun finished reading. Was it possible we lived in a world where such things could happen?

"Your Highness," the messenger said, "I ask that you read the second letter as well."

With trembling hands, the rani opened the envelope.

In it, Saheb detailed the British retaliation. When the Company's soldiers reached the site of the massacre, they discovered that none of the British dead had been buried. Their mutilated bodies had been dragged into a well and the stench was unbearable. The hair of the victims had lodged itself in the trees, caught on shrubs, and still blew about in the wind. Several witnesses attested to the fact that three of the women and children had survived the massacre and the butchering by hiding beneath dead bodies. The next morning they were thrown into the well alive, alongside the corpses of their friends.

When the British commander, General Neill, heard of this, something in him must have broken. He began arresting every man he could, even men who had never been to the House of the Ladies. They were forced to clean the blood from the floors with their tongues. The Muslims who were arrested were sewn into pigskins and hung. The Hindus were executed by Dalits. The remaining prisoners were tied across the mouth of cannons that were then fired. This, we learned, was how Azimullah Khan's soldiers had killed the men they had taken hostage. A nearby village protested the deaths of the innocent civilians at Kanpur as inhumane and was set on fire. Anyone who tried to flee was shot and killed.

"They've taken up a new cry," the rani read. "'Remember Kanpur!' The British newspapers cover nothing else, Manu. They're calling you the Rebel Queen, since it was under your rule that the sepoys rebelled. Be ready for anything. Azimullah Khan and his general have given the British every excuse they need to wage war on India."

The rani looked ill. "Is that it?"

The messenger looked tremendously sorry for himself. "No. The rebellion in Delhi has failed. Yesterday, Delhi was retaken by the British."

Chapter Twenty-Five

1858

Be it known to all people belonging to, or residing in the Government District of Jhansi, that owing to the bad conduct of the sepoys in Kanpur, valuable lives have been lost, and property destroyed. But the strong and powerful British Government is sending thousands of European Soldiers to places that have been disturbed, and arrangements will be made to restore order in Jhansi.

Until our soldiers can reach Jhansi, the Rani will continue to rule in the name of the British Government and according to the customs of the British Government. I therefore call on all great and small to obey the Rani and to pay their taxes to her, for which they will receive credit.

The British Army has retaken the city of Delhi and has killed thousands of rebels. We will hang or shoot all rebels wherever they may be found.

The British government was sending soldiers. The rani's advisers believed that this was the English government's way of saying that the Company had been wrong to remove her, that the rani would now rule again, only this time with the British government's blessing.

"Nowhere does it say that," Moropant corrected them. "*Until our soldiers can reach Jhansi*," he read. "*Until* then."

Men's voices rose in the Durbar Hall. The rani drowned them all out by saying, "I will write and ask them to clarify my position. In one breath, they're calling me the Rebel Queen. In another, I'm administering justice with their approval. So let them tell me where I stand."

A man arrived in the Durbar Hall claiming he was a messenger from the rani's secret admirer. He said these last words in English, leading me to believe the man whose message he was carrying had to be British. At this, the rani's cheeks turned very pink.

"Hand my Durgavasi the letter," she said, and the old man gave me a thick note sealed in a large blue envelope. I sliced the paper open with my finger. The first line read, "For the Rani of Jhansi, from Major Ellis." I handed her the letter, and she read the contents and passed it to her father, who said, "It's settled then."

"The British have no intention of keeping me on the throne of Jhansi," the rani said, and I could hear the pain in her voice. "The warrant for my arrest still stands." She lowered her head as if something heavy was pressing it down. "They have no intention of coming peacefully. Major Ellis warns us to look at Lucknow as an example of what's to happen here."

Lucknow was burned to the ground; its women raped, its men and children slaughtered. The rani covered her eyes with her hand. This treachery by the British was too much. Then I glanced at

Kahini and wondered what the rani would think if she knew how deep the treachery spread.

It took several moments for her to recover, but when her voice was steady she went on. "We will issue our own proclamation now. Let it read that men and rajas of all faiths must come together to rebel. The British are not coming peaceably."

Calls were made for volunteers, and in Jhansi alone fourteen thousand men came forward to be trained as soldiers. And if you have ever poured water into an anthill and watched the ants scurry to save themselves, this is how our city looked over the next few weeks. Both day and night, you could hear the rumbling of carts as they passed through the streets. People were moving families, guns, food, anything you could think of. Temples and treasuries were emptied, and the money used to buy weapons. I was there when two hundred pounds of gunpowder arrived from Gwalior, a neighboring kingdom that was too cowardly to stand against the British, but too greedy to resist selling us their ammunitions and arms. A magazine was constructed down the road from the palace in order to house so much gunpowder and ammunition. Meanwhile, guns, swords, arrows, and knives began filling up the armory. Six new cannons appeared, along with eight gunners from Kalpi, a neighboring city where the British had chosen one girl from every house to be used as a comfort woman. The men brought with them the knowledge of manufacturing brass balls, and the production went on all day and all night.

The rani also reached out to farmers, telling them to burn their fields, poison their wells, and chop down any tree that grew on their land. There would be nothing for the British when they arrived, not even water. The farmers themselves would have to survive on whatever they could stockpile or hide.

As a carryover from our days in the Rani Mahal, Arjun and his guards spent their evenings with us in the queen's room, and no one protested.

"I heard the British left their wounded soldiers to die while they plundered the temples in Nagpur," Mandar said. She moved closer to the brazier. It was the first night we'd needed a fire. "Nagpur is only a three-day ride south." Meaning it wouldn't be long before they were doing the same in Jhansi. I thought of Barwa Sagar and what might happen there, but Barwa Sagar was a tiny village. Surely the British had no business in such a place.

"These British soldiers have no allegiance to anything but money," Moropant swore.

"The governor-general, Lord Caning, has condemned their behavior," the rani said, looking into the burning coals. "The British papers are saying that Queen Victoria is critical as well."

"Are you hoping for a change of heart? Because this fire began when the Company first came to India. It's just taken two hundred and fifty years for the flames to start spreading."

But I didn't want to hear any more talk of flames. I rose from my cushion and went outside. Frost covered the ground, gleaming under the cold moonlight. I shivered, and behind me Arjun asked, "Do you ever wonder how many more nights we have to look up at the moon like this?"

"Yes."

"I wanted to marry you, Sita."

I turned to stare at him in the moonlight. Although it was pointless to cry, tears blurred my vision. "A woman lives and dies a Durgavasi."

"You don't think the rani might have made an exception for you and me?"

That was exactly what the rani might have done. And now it was too late. The reality was so unbearable that I couldn't look it in the face or I'd be crushed under its weight. I allowed Arjun to wrap his arms around me, and inhaled his scent of charcoal and cedar. He whispered, "If we live through this, I want you to marry me."

"But—"

He put a finger to my lips. "You are going to survive. When the British come, we are both going to live to see the end."

In February, dismal news came from neighboring kingdoms—stories of looting, destruction, and rape. And in the midst of all of this, there were the kingdoms of Scindia and Orchha, both providing soldiers to help the British.

When Holi came, the streets of Jhansi should have been filled with children throwing colors in celebration, but the skies were overcast and the city was silent. We were all sitting in the queen's room eating roasted nuts. Anand held one up and said, "My real mommy used to make these for me."

The look on the rani's face would have pierced your heart. These nine words were crushing to her, and my first thought, of course, was that Kahini had done this. If not for her, the rajkumar might have lived and the kingdom of Jhansi might never have been annexed. There would have been no march to Delhi, no massacre at Kanpur, no retaliation by the British. I looked across the room and our eyes met. She didn't flinch. She wasn't even the first one to look away. And I thought again about telling the rani everything I knew. But who would she believe? Me, or her favorite cousin, the woman who had helped her keep the raja happy when he was alive?

General Hugh Rose and his army appeared outside of Jhansi on the twenty-first of March. The weather was crisp and every alarm in Jhansi was sounding. A messenger arrived from the general with an offer of peace. Moropant took one look and rejected the offer. "Their peace includes the surrender and death of every male over the age of thirteen."

Two days later, on the evening of the twenty-third, the British invaded the city of Jhansi and discovered that the wells were either poisoned or dry, and not a single crop remained to feed their army. Still, they made their way through the shuttered neighborhoods toward our fortress, toward the palace and temples and barracks inside. Seen from afar, the Fortress of Jhansi is simply a granite building on a low-lying hill. But in reality—with the sole exception of the southern face—it is impregnable. A sheer mountain wall rises to the west, and to the south, and the walls are protected by towers, one of which is capable of housing five cannons. No one remembers when the ramparts were built, but they extend from all eight gates around the city. Yet the British opened fire.

Although it may sound strange, we grew used to the sound of gunfire.

In the morning during yoga, at the temple when we prayed, even on the maidan, it became so common that you simply stopped hearing it. It was frightening, and children huddled closer to their parents or asked to be carried when they walked through the streets. But otherwise, nothing in the city changed: the bookseller was open, the vegetable carts still lined the streets, even the man who made roadside puris was there, hot oil popping from his metal pan and greasing his shirt.

On the fourth day of the assault, Sundari woke us an hour earlier than usual. When we arrived on the maidan, the rani was already there. A blue muretha was tied around her head. It matched her white and blue angarkha and blue churidars. As soon as we were all assembled on the grass, she rose from her cushion. Her speech was very brief.

"Many of you have been with me for almost a decade. Some, like Sundari and Heera, even longer. No one has ever said that the life of a Durgavasi is easy. But no Durgavasi has been required to give up her life for a rani. The British cannons will arrive soon, and the real war will begin. So now you must decide whether you wish to ride into battle with me, or go home. I will not pass judgment on anyone who chooses to leave the Durga Dal today."

The maidan was so silent that I could hear the horses whinnying in the nearby stables.

"If there is anyone who would like to leave, please do so now."

We looked at one another and waited for the first person to rise. I thought perhaps Kahini might leave, or Moti, who was so sweet and so small, but they both remained seated.

"Do not make this choice lightly. I don't know what I would choose if I was in your position. Particularly if I had a husband." She looked at Jhalkari.

"We are staying with you," Jhalkari said.

We raised our fists, and the rani briskly wiped the tears from her eyes.

It was decided that if the British broke through the fortress walls, Kashi's only job would be to protect Anand. The rest of us were to protect the rani; her personal guards were to protect the women and children inside the Panch Mahal. I tried to imagine a scenario in which our fortress was breached, but I could not. The granite masonry was built to withstand any siege. We had six thousand soldiers; our spies told us the British had fifteen hundred. Our seven wells and food supplies were large enough to last us for two months. They had no access to fresh water.

The massive cannon we'd named Ghanagaraj, meaning Mightiest of Mighties, was positioned in the southern tower overlooking a hill named Kapu Tikri, and eight other cannons were wheeled into position on the ramparts. Then the British rolled their own cannons into view.

Many people have described the sound of cannon fire as it tears through walls, and the agonizing cries of the wounded whose limbs are torn off or mangled. Fire, rubble, chaos, death. I will tell you that I have never read an account that accurately describes the horror.

From my position near Arjun and Moti on the ramparts, I witnessed the destruction of the southern tower. I had joined Arjun and Mandar in an overhead assault. With each arrow, I thought, am I killing someone's father? Who will be mourning the loss of her son? Then a sudden blast shook the foundations of the fortress and our chief gunner was dead and no one was launching cannonballs from Ghanagaraj.

"Keep shooting!" Arjun shouted, "Keep firing!"

"What's she doing?" Mandar suddenly cried out.

We watched as Moti scrambled up the broken steps of the tower. Small, fast Moti. I saw her ignite a single cannonball before gunfire tore open her chest and a blast knocked me on the ground. Then everything was gunfire and screams. I rushed to my feet and together, Mandar, Arjun, and I ran through the burning rubble toward the Panch Mahal.

"Where is the rani?" I shouted, but no one knew. People were running, and children were screaming, and then Arjun pointed to the shattered courtyard where the pretty tiles lay cracked and the fountain was blackened by ash. Advisers and military men surrounded the rani, and her forehead was smeared with soot.

"The English will stop firing as soon as it's too dark to see," she said when she saw Arjun. "But at first light . . ."

The unsaid words hung in the air.

"What do you want us to do?" he asked.

The rani stared into the distance, where smoke was billowing from a mortar hit. "Make a protective ring around the palace to guard the women and children in the Panch Mahal."

Inside, the halls were crowded with people. Anyone who either couldn't or wouldn't flee ahead of the British army was taking shelter here. But we knew the British were capable of setting fire to buildings and burning everyone inside, and then shooting anyone who tried to escape.

That night, we slept in the hall outside the rani's chamber. Arjun took first watch and I dreamed of Moti running up the tower calling, "Sita! Sita! Wake up! I had a dream!"

I opened my eyes and saw the face of the rani. "I had a dream," she repeated.

The rani had never spoken of her dreams. "I had a vision of an angel," she confided.

In Hinduism, we do not have angels. But there are angels in Islam and Christianity.

"She was all in red, and the gems on her dress were brighter than this light." She gestured to the oil lamp hanging next to her. "Then she was holding a ball of flame. Her hands were starting to burn and she said this was the fortress's fate. Jhansi is destined to be destroyed by fire."

"But why an angel?" I began to shiver. "Why not Durga or even Kali?"

"I don't know. But she was as real as you are to me."

"Have you told anyone else?" I didn't think she should.

"No. But, Sita, it was more than a nightmare. It was a vision."

We were quiet for several moments. Then I said, "In a few hours, the sun is going to rise and the British will be here."

"Yes." But I could see her trying to shake the vision from her mind. "We must prepare."

We began rousing the surviving Durgavasi and the palace guards. She woke Kahini first. By five in the morning, everyone was waiting.

We stood around the breach in the wall, weapons readied, listening to the sound of birds calling to one another. It didn't matter to them whether we slaughtered one another, or even who won. Tomorrow, they would be singing even if all of us were floating in the Ganges. The rani was peering over the ramparts, and I saw it at the same time she did: a wall of fire burning the grass along the northern banks of the Betwa River. And in the light of the flames, it was possible to see an army so vast that you couldn't perceive its end.

Chapter Twenty-Six

Shouts of joy went up as we recognized the rebels' red and white uniforms in the breaking light of day. Saheb's general, Tatya Tope, had come with more than twenty thousand men. The King of Banpur was with him. The King of Shahgarh was with him. The Nawab of Banda, the sepoys of Kanpur, the sepoys of Assam. The numbers were so far in our favor it was a wonder the British didn't turn around and run.

We watched from the ramparts as elephants materialized in the gray light of dawn, hauling cannons and weapons and carrying men. Our own elephants were for show, not war, but to see the giant beasts lumbering toward the plains beyond the fortress made everyone's heart light. The rani gathered her guards around her. Heera and Rajasi were to join the soldiers outside the magazine, where all of Jhansi's gunpowder was kept. The remaining Durgavasi and twenty-two men still left from the rani's personal guards were to remain in the Durbar Hall until further notice.

Inside the palace, the feeling was celebratory. Twenty thousand men had appeared in the mist like a celestial army sent by the gods. This was our land. These were our people. The gods were on our side. We seated ourselves on the stage while the rani took her throne and we waited for victory.

Then, the unthinkable occurred. Word came that General Rose had split his forces and was defeating the rebels at the river. As the day progressed, more bad news came, and Arjun couldn't understand why Tatya Tope had exposed his outer flanks in that way.

"It doesn't make any sense," he kept saying over the din of crying infants and nervous women inside the palace.

A few moments later, everything changed. Two British mortars hit the magazine where our gunpowder was kept. The explosion could be felt by every person in the fortress. The women inside the hall shrieked, terrified. It was as if the granite walls were about to crumble. Then the crowds inside the Durbar Hall grew silent as we waited for a second hit. It came, followed by a third.

"What's happening?" Mandar exclaimed.

A soldier rushed in to report to the rani. "They've destroyed the entire magazine!" he cried. "All of the—"

The rani covered her mouth with her hands. Her first thought wasn't that all of our gunpowder was gone. "Heera and Rajasi . . ." she whispered.

Mandar closed her eyes.

"Come," the soldier said, leading the rani away. "You must see this."

We waited an hour for the rani to return, listening to the rising panic in the hall. Heera and Rajasi were gone. I couldn't believe it. They were dead.

When the rani returned, she summoned three of us into her chamber. "Arjun, Sita, Sundari," she said. We followed her down the stairs into her room. Inside, she told Arjun to lock the door. Then she held out what looked like an official letter from the palace. "From Tatya Tope." Her hands were shaking. "He discovered it on one of the British soldiers."

I took it and read it aloud. It was a letter in English from Gopal, detailing where the powder magazine could be found inside the fortress, and how a pair of ten-inch mortars could destroy the whole thing and cripple Jhansi's army.

"We've been betrayed," Sundari whispered.

"And not just by Gopal," Arjun said. "Has he already been arrested?"

"Yes. And I have men questioning him."

I felt sick. My entire body was like a heavy stone, dragging me toward the earth. If only I had told the rani before. Arjun looked at me, and it was all I could do to whisper, "There's something I know."

I could see from the rani's expression that she was afraid I was going to confess to being a traitor. Instead, I told her what I'd seen. How Kahini and Gopal had sent someone a ring, how that same ring had appeared with Sadashiv when he arrived, her insistence that Sadashiv's life be spared, and finally, how Kahini had discovered hemlock in my murti.

The rani walked to her bed and sat down. She didn't look at me. She didn't look at anyone.

"I'm sorry," I said, and felt the inadequacy of the words even as I said them, the way you feel when offering a starving woman a cup full of rice. "I didn't know if you would have believed me."

She was quiet for several moments. Then she admitted, "I wouldn't have. The raja once said that was my greatest fault as rani. I trusted too many people. And so did he . . ." Her voice slipped away, and we were silent while she spent some time with her thoughts. "I want to hear Gopal confess. I'll tell the men to spare his life if he'll expose Kahini. The British will kill him anyway."

Of course they would. If a man was willing to expose his own country's secrets, what made them think he wouldn't expose theirs?

"Go back to the hall and keep a watch over Kahini. Make sure she doesn't leave. If she does, restrain her."

We returned to the Durbar Hall. Inside, infants were still screaming while their siblings did their best to pacify them. Their mothers looked shocked. Some rocked back and forth on their knees, praying. Others stared blankly at the wall in front of them. Were the husbands of all these women still alive? Would they ever see them again?

Kahini was sitting in the queen's room on her favorite cushion. Perhaps it was animal instinct: she rose the moment she saw us and fled into the courtyard, navigating the broken tiles.

The three of us gave chase.

"Stop!" Sundari shouted, and to my surprise, Kahini did as she was told. But when she turned around, she leveled the pistol at Sundari's chest and fired.

I launched an arrow, striking Kahini in the arm. She stumbled backward, and in the time it took to regain her balance, Arjun was on top of her, taking her weapons. He shouted and several guards came to help while I went to Sundari.

The captain of the Durga Dal clutched her chest. After so many years of devoted service, the enemy had come from within, not without.

"You're going to be fine," I swore. I thought of the first day we'd met, when she had reminded me of a cat. There is a saying in English that cats possess nine lives. But Sundari only had one. Her breathing became ragged and she squeezed my hand. A thin trickle of blood escaped her lips. "Sundari!"

Kahini's face was a perfect mask.

"You killed her!" I screamed. Kahini's arm was bleeding heavily, but she didn't look down at it. "You poisoned the rajkumar," I said, moving toward her. "You poisoned the raja. The rani was next, but you were hoping the British would do your work for you!"

"And what did you do about it?" She wore a satisfied smile.

"Take her to the prison," Arjun said. "Guards!"

But I reminded everyone that this was where her lover, Sadashiv, was waiting.

"Why don't we just give her to the British?" one of the men suggested.

For the first time, Kahini's face registered fear. "I'll kill myself first!" She struggled violently, but there were four of them around her. We could hear her screaming all the way down the hill. Soldiers carried away Sundari's body and we returned to the rani's chamber. From the redness in the rani's eyes, I assumed she had heard everything that had happened.

"I'm so sorry," I said, glancing at Kashi, who was holding Anand. "They've taken Kahini to the British to do with her . . . as they will."

The rani was confused. "I don't understand."

I glanced at Arjun. "I thought Your Highness was upset because you'd heard about Sundari."

"That I'd heard what about Sundari?"

I whispered, "Kahini shot and killed her."

The rani buried her head in her hands and Kashi sobbed aloud. Then the rani looked up and gestured to a pile of opened letters. "Some of them are for you," she said. "Gopal was hiding them."

I started digging madly through the pile. One, two, three letters from Ishan, my sister's husband. One from Shivaji. Three from my father. All of them dated within the past four months. I unfolded a letter from my father first.

You are needed in Barwa Sagar, Sita. Please come at once, and bring soldiers with you from the rani's court. The British are arresting the most beautiful women in the village and they have taken your sister. . . .

I could barely breathe.

Shivaji:

Sita, they've taken Anu to a house of prostitution and are refusing to let her go. The gods only know what they're doing to her and we're hoping force or money will persuade them. Sita, please . . .

I pressed my hand to my forehead to make the words stop moving. Arjun read them as I put them down. Note after note imploring me to come. To bring money or men or both.

My son says he will still accept her as his wife, but what will he be accepting back if we don't rescue her now? Imagine what they are doing? I can't think you are getting these letters or you would have been here by now.

I pushed the rest of the letters away. Whatever fate lay ahead of Kahini, I felt strongly that it would not be terrible enough.

"As soon as we can, I'll send money and men," the rani swore.

But who knew when that would be? If I died in Jhansi, my sister would remain enslaved in a British brothel. The thought was enough to make me understand what had driven Azimullah Khan. I could understand the rage. Now, I really could.

"What about Gopal?" Arjun asked.

"He admitted that what Sita suspected was true." The rani's

voice was empty. "She promised to make him her lover if he would help put her and Sadashiv on the throne."

Arjun swore, "Sita, when this is over, we'll ride straight to Barwa Sagar." Then he turned to the rani. "Our men are still fighting."

The rani stood. "Let's drive the British from Jhansi," she vowed, "and from this entire continent."

She summoned Mandar, Priyala, and Jhalkari. Then the five of us made for the ramparts. As we reached the walls, General Raghunath Singh descended the stairs to give us a report.

"The fort's water supply has been sabotaged," he said. "It will only last two more days."

The gunfire was ceaseless, and we had to shout over the noise.

"Tatya Tope?" the rani asked. "Is he fighting effectively?"

"There is news he has fled to Charkhari, Your Highness. The rebel forces are without a leader. The British have moved a twenty-four pound Howitzer into place. When it fires, the walls of Jhansi will crumble."

The six of us stood in a circle. A soft breeze brushed against my neck. It was April. Somewhere in India, a woman was braiding her long hair with jasmine blossoms.

"The rebels are regrouping in Kalpi," General Singh continued. "My advice is to find a way to escape Jhansi. Take your son and head to Kalpi so that you may save yourself and fight again."

We made our way back to the Panch Mahal, listening to the shrieks of women in the streets who were pleading with the rani to save them. Inside the palace, the chaos was even greater. People were running through the halls, screaming. As soon as we reached the rani's bedchamber, Jhalkari asked to speak with the rani alone. So we waited in the hall. Every few moments, a woman with a child came up, begging us to help her escape. "I know the rani will leave with the rajkumar, and you will go with her. Take my son," one woman pleaded hysterically. *"Please."*

"Shrimati-ji, we can't," Priyala said gently. "We don't have any way of leaving the city."

"Then what hope is there for me? Or him?" She held up her son. He looked to be six months old, with big eyes and dimpled cheeks. "He won't be any trouble. He's a happy child."

"Shrimati-ji," Priyala whispered, "I'm sorry. We'll pray for you."

"Please!" the woman begged. "He doesn't need much milk. He eats food—"

Priyala began weeping openly, and Arjun looked away. I knew he felt as useless as I did.

When the rani opened the door, she and Jhalkari both had red eyes. "Arjun, Sita. I wish to see the two of you alone," the rani said.

Jhalkari smiled sadly at me as we passed.

For several moments the rani didn't speak. When she did, her voice was rough, as if she'd been talking very loudly for many hours. "We are leaving Jhansi tonight through the Bhandir Gate. My father and four hundred of his men will be with me. Anand, Kashi, Mandar, and Priyala will be with me as well. And all of Arjun's guards. We're going to wait until the British have entered Jhansi and chaos reigns. Then we'll dress as soldiers from Orchha," she said.

It was a very clever ruse, since the kingdom of Orchha had sent soldiers to help the British, and they would look exactly like any of the rani's men.

The rani gave a blue velvet satchel to Arjun. "I want you to take this," she said. "It will be enough to free Sita's sister from the British. Neither of you are coming with me to Kalpi."

We both raised our voices to protest, but the rani cut us off with a firm shake of her head.

"Choose ten men to take with you, and when she's free, find me if you can. If not, use whatever remains in this bag and flee. Find a city far away from here and marry. Have children. And never let the British find you."

She waved us away before we could say anything, and for the next hour, she called on the people who were most important to her, so that she could make her good-byes.

Arjun and I sat in the hall with Jhalkari and waited to be called on. No one said anything. When I tried to make conversation with Jhalkari, to ask her what sort of diversion she planned and how she would still make it to Kalpi, she rebuffed my attempts. I didn't understand why she was being so stubborn. Did she not trust me anymore? I kept stealing glances in her direction, hoping she'd change her mind, but her face remained a locked box. She was planning something and didn't want me to be a part of it.

By midnight, we had all dressed ourselves as soldiers from Orchha, putting on loose churidars and dirty kurtas. From the look and smell of our garments, I guessed they came from the bodies of dead men. The rani carried a long cloth and all of her weapons, but nothing else. If she had jewels hidden under her kurta, I didn't see them. Outside, our horses waited, with none of their usual tack. The queen's mare, Sarangi, had been stripped of her finery. An old cloth had replaced her saddle. Kashi brought Anand, and the rani tied him tightly behind her, then covered him with her woolen cloak. He didn't speak a word, either to complain or cry, and I wondered what he would be like as an adult if he survived this.

I patted Sher's flank. The constant sound of gunfire made him skittish. He pawed at the ground, eager to be gone. Kashi, Mandar, and Priyala fell into formation behind the rani. Then Jhalkari appeared. As soon as I saw her, I understood what she meant to do.

"Jhalkari, you have a husband!" I cried. "What are you doing?"

She was dressed in a blue angarkha, with pearls around her neck and a ruby ring in her nose. Only someone who truly knew Lakshmibai would be able to say it wasn't her. She was going to create a distraction at another gate and pretend to be the rani. But as soon as they discovered the ruse, the British would have her executed.

I started weeping. Jhalkari wrapped her arms around me, and I cried into her chest. "Why are you doing this?"

"So the rani can fight again at Kalpi. Can you think of another way?"

But in my heart, I couldn't. I separated myself from Jhalkari and had to look away.

Arjun mounted his horse and I mounted Sher. Then we rode toward Bhandir Gate. My heart ached. At the gate soldiers stopped us. "We're the troops from Orchha," General Singh said. He used a Bundelkhandi accent.

An Englishman looked directly at the rani, and saw only an exhausted soldier. "Move on then!"

We rode out of Jhansi as quickly as we could.

When I looked back, the entire city was on fire.

We hadn't ridden for long when word that we were being pursued made it to the front of our procession. We stopped on the side of a farmer's field. "We must split up," Arjun persuaded the rani. "Our group is too slow. You ride ahead; take only my guards and the Durgavasi. You'll make it to Kalpi faster."

"The soldiers know she is in military clothes. We must change," I said. "We could pass as peasants."

We could hear the sound of distant gunfire; Arjun looked skeptical.

"In Homer's *The Odyssey*, Odysseus returned home after an absence of twenty years and wasn't sure whom he could trust. So he successfully disguised himself as a beggar," I insisted.

The rani ordered Mandar and Priyala to buy clothes from the farmer who owned the field. When they returned, the rani and I headed to a small hut to change. We removed our clothes in silence, and when we emerged, the queen looked for all the world like a peasant. Before we remounted and rode on, she took my hand.

"Thank you." She didn't say what for, but I squeezed her hand and hoped she knew how much she meant to me. "Let's ride."

At a fork in the road, Arjun and I headed to Barwa Sagar. To the north, the rani and her group rode hard toward Kalpi.

Chapter Twenty-Seven

It was eight hours before we reached Barwa Sagar. We stopped only to rest the horses and give them water. Most of the villages we passed were peaceful; they had offered no resistance. Their women were taken to British whorehouses, their crops would be taken as a form of taxation.

As dawn quickened, casting a rosy glow across the village, no one came out to see us as we rode through. There were no boys tending to buffalo in the fields; all windows remained shuttered. Did they think we were part of the British army?

When we reached my family's house, the plants in the courtyard had withered and there was no smoke coming from the kitchen. "Pita-ji?" I called, and nobody answered. We dismounted and entered the house; it was dark. We checked the rooms, and memories came rushing back to me: my sister curling up next to me on my charpai. The wooden chest where I had kept my favorite things, like the wooden block my father had carved into a bear for me. But nobody had been inside for some time.

"Maybe they fled," Arjun said.

But that was impossible. Fled where? With whom?

I hurried back through the courtyard, and while the other guards waited, Arjun followed me to Shivaji's house. There were voices. I could hear them, as low and faint as a slow trickle of water, coming from inside.

"Shivaji!" I pounded on the door. "Shivaji!"

Ishan answered. "My father isn't here."

Then his brothers appeared.

"Sita," the eldest said. I remembered meeting him once with his father. His name was Deepan. "You should come into the kitchen." Deepan led us inside and asked, "What do you know?"

"My father sent a letter saying that Anu was taken." My voice was shaking. "He told us to bring money and help. We have both."

"With the rani's blessing," Arjun added.

"That was in February," Deepan said. He lowered his gaze to his lap. "Sita . . ."

"Just say it!" I cried.

"Your father is dead. The local Kutwal arrived and said he had orders to find the most beautiful women in Barwa Sagar. Someone had told him about Anu, and when they saw her, they arrested her at once. They had guns. It happened so fast. When she was gone, your father asked Shivaji to help him."

I felt as if someone had robbed me of my breath.

"Their plan was to buy her back, Sita, but when they reached the *chakla* the British wouldn't hear why they had come. So your father and Shivaji returned with more men. They shot them both," Deepan said. "Your father died immediately. My father lingered for three days."

Father. My father was dead. Shivaji was gone.

"We can take you to the *chakla*, Sita, but they won't release her."

"What about Avani?" I whispered. "And Dadi-ji?"

"Your father's wife committed sati," Deepan explained. "No one could stop her."

I covered my mouth with my hands. Avani had not been able to envision a life in which she had been made a widow twice. Was she afraid that no one would take care of her? Had she asked someone to write to me and gotten no response?

"Your grandmother fell ill and died within the month."

Regret, as hot and searing as fire, burned through my body. When I had first arrived at Jhansi, Jhalkari had warned me not to send my letters through Gopal. But I had wanted to save money. My act of thrift had cost me everything.

If someone had told me that my acceptance in the Durga Dal would come at the cost of my family, I can say with certainty I would never have continued. Whatever my fate might have been, I would not have risked my father's life, or the lives of Anu or Avani, to save myself from the Temple of Annapurna.

"We are bringing my sister back," I said.

But Deepan glanced behind him. "Sita, she has been gone for four months."

I knew what he meant. Ishan didn't want her anymore. "Is it true?" I turned to him. I wanted to hear it from his lips. "Are you casting her off?"

He looked away.

"Say it!" I screamed.

He began to cry.

Arjun took my arm. "Sita, let's find her. Lead us to the *chakla*," he said. "How many soldiers are there?"

The second brother guessed, "Maybe fifty. The British posted them in any village large enough to cause trouble."

"And how many women do fifty men need?" I wanted to know.

Deepan flinched. I'm sure my bluntness offended him. The women in his house didn't stand in the company of men, wearing pistols on their hips and quivers of arrows on their backs. They were quiet and demure. Two months ago, my sister had been one of these women.

"Ten," he said quietly. "They took ten girls."

"I can't just save Anu," I said to Arjun.

He nodded. "I know."

Deepan led the way while the rest of us rode. The sun was up, but the village was silent. It was harvest time. The fields should have been teeming with people harvesting barley, wheat, peas, and mustard. But unlike the burned fields surrounding Jhansi, these fields had been abandoned.

"When we reach the *chakla*," Arjun told his guards, "no one fires. If British soldiers are killed, the entire village will pay. I will buy the women out of servitude. Then we'll return them to their homes."

"And if their families don't want them?" one of the guards asked.

"Then we will use what the rani so generously gave to us to buy them a home where they can live together."

The *chakla* turned out to be a small house built next to the Temple of Durga.

"Stay here," Arjun said to me when we arrived. "We're supposed to be men from this village. If they recognize you as a woman, they're going to wonder where we have come from."

I remained with the others while Arjun dismounted and walked with Deepan to the wooden door. An officer answered and they were taken inside. A hundred terrible scenarios passed through my mind. What if the British killed them? What if they refused to let Anu go?

But in the end, gold was more tempting than flesh.

Deepan came out first. He was followed by nine girls, and finally Arjun. It took me a long moment to recognize her. She was thinner, with dark hollows under her eyes. But it was the roundness of her belly that made my breath catch in my throat. I dismounted as swiftly as I could and ran toward her. I didn't care that there were officers watching us from the windows.

"Anu!" I said. "Anu, it's Sita!"

"I know who you are."

It wasn't her voice. It was the voice of someone distant and hard.

Arjun said, "Go with Deepan and take her to your house. I'll meet you there once we've delivered the rest of these women to their homes."

"No. I'm not going back there," Anu said, and I could hear the torment of the past four months in her voice. Then she shrieked, "I want Ishan!"

I glanced at Deepan. She was pregnant with another man's child. A *British* child. Not even the most understanding husband would take back a wife in such condition.

"Take me back!" she screamed. "Take me back to my home!"

She was like someone possessed. But none of the other women appeared surprised. I looked at Deepan, since it was his decision.

"Yes. Let's go to our house right now," he said.

I put her in front of me on the horse, but she sat as far forward as she could. She didn't want to feel my touch. When we reached Shivaji's home, the knot in my stomach had grown so tight that I'm sure I could have pressed my hand there and felt it.

I helped her down, and Deepan slowly opened the door. The

other women rushed forward, but as soon as they saw my sister, they drew back. One of them covered her face with her hands and began to weep. But it was Ishan's reaction that broke her.

"That isn't my wife."

"Sita, you should take her," Deepan began, but my sister pushed her way inside the house. "Ishan," she begged.

"You aren't my wife."

"Ishan!" She clung to his legs, forcing him to push her away. "Ishan!" She sounded like a wounded animal.

I stepped forward to take Anu in my arms but she resisted. "You're not my sister! You're not my family. This is my family!"

The other women were crying. The men had tears in their eyes.

"Ishan!" my sister shrieked. "Please! Just look at me."

But his face was averted. "Go away!" he cried.

Then the fight went out of her. She went limp in my arms, repeating his name over and over like a mantra. I carried her back to our empty house, and she threatened to kill both the child and herself. I told her about Gopal and the letters. But it wasn't enough.

"You chose the rani over me," she screamed, her entire body trembling, and I feared for the child she was carrying. "And then the British wanted me because I was pretty! It was for all those silks and juti you sent me!" Then a familiar sound appeared in her voice. "You didn't save me," she hissed. I realized it was Grandmother I was hearing. "You should have left me there to die with my bastard," she said. "Leave me."

I did as she wanted and wandered outside to our peepal tree. Feelings of guilt and sorrow crashed over me in waves. Father had been killed by a British soldier; possibly the son of someone who had fought alongside him in Burma. I tried to imagine Avani's despair when she heard that my father had been killed, and how the flames had felt searing her body as she climbed onto Father's funeral pyre, and then the only thing I could focus on was my rage.

I went back into the house, and Arjun could see my fury. He was sitting with several guards around our kitchen. "Shall we go outside?" he asked.

"I just came from outside."

"Then let's sit in your father's workshop."

I didn't want to go. But I followed Arjun there and the woodsy scent of teak immediately made me cry. Arjun took me in his arms and shut the door. We sat together on the jute mats and he held me while I wept. When I'd drained myself of every possible tear, he tenderly wiped my face with his hand.

"What they've done to my family—"

"It's finished, Sita. It's over," he said. "The walls have crumbled and you're asking why instead of trying to rebuild. Your sister is in the next room. She's what's left, and that's no small thing. She's carrying a child."

"Yes. A British—"

"Baby," he said before I could finish. "An innocent child. That's the future."

I won't pretend that his speech changed the way I felt about the British, but it comforted me over the next few weeks. And it clarified in my mind what I needed to do now. We could not rejoin the rani; I had to heal my sister. So we stayed in Barwa Sagar, and when I was too overwhelmed by sorrow to get out of bed or get dressed, Arjun would encourage me to go on.

On a warm evening in May, after we'd been in Barwa Sagar for more than six weeks, Arjun took me into the courtyard and said quietly, "One of the guards met someone in the marketplace who has news of Jhansi. His name is Balaji and he was a silk merchant in Jhansi."

"Can I meet him?"

Arjun returned with a well-dressed man in his fifties. He had white hair and a mustache, and I imagined he'd been very handsome in his youth. We stood outside in the courtyard, near the old peepal tree, and waited for him to say something. As a child, I had thought all trees grew this big. I put my hand on its solid trunk. Finally the man from Jhansi said, "I have heard that the British pursued the rani to Banda. She killed two British soldiers and shot a lieutenant. One of her soldiers was killed. But the rest of her party reached Kalpi."

"And the city of Jhansi?"

"Burned."

"And the people?" Arjun asked.

"Killed."

"But there were thousands of people!" I protested. Five thousand by the rani's count.

"Yes. The British lost one hundred men."

These are the actions demons take. Humans didn't do this to one another. But Balaji's gaze was unwavering, and I knew it was true. The British had taken five thousand lives in retaliation for an action a dozen men had perpetrated. I thought of the woman who had been desperate for us to take her child, the round face of the baby she'd been carrying, his dimpled cheeks and large, bright eyes. I buried my head in my hands.

"The rani's father was captured after the fall," Balaji continued.

We were all shocked. Arjun especially. "He didn't make it to Kalpi?"

"No. He reached Datia, but the people there turned him over—they didn't have a choice. The British were hanging villagers from the trees for housing criminals. Even the suspicion of doing so was enough. They hanged him in Jokhan Bagh."

The next revelation was equally shocking: in Kalpi, Saheb's brother, Rao Saheb, wrested control of the soldiers from the rani, leaving only two hundred and fifty horsemen to defend the borders of Kalpi. Rao Saheb went west with the rest of the men. Witnesses said they saw the rani in a fit of rage, cursing Rao's cowardice. In the hundred-and-eighteen-degree heat, water was scarce and the supplies at Fort Kalpi dwindled. The fort was captured, but the rani and her people escaped and found Rao Saheb. The rani was reported to have said, "When people remember this war they will remember you, Rao Saheb, and when they do, they will think to themselves: *coward*."

The rani suggested the soldiers, eleven thousand men in all, should take nearby Gwalior Fort, which is the largest and most significant fortress in central India. The British did not yet occupy the fortress. Its twenty-three-year-old ruler, Maharaja Scindia, was still on his throne. He was, however, supporting the English with weapons and food.

I imagined exactly how the rani had laid it out: as soon as they arrived, the soldiers could persuade the maharaja to house them for just a few days. Then, once they were safely inside, they could give him the chance to join the rebels in the fight against the British or flee. I could hear the rani's voice in my head, pronouncing Maharaja Scindia a traitor.

"So have they gone to Gwalior?" Arjun asked with a note of hope in his voice. "With Gwalior as a base, victory is possible."

Balaji actually smiled. "Last night. And now I am making my way to Delhi to start over. I have family here in Barwa Sagar. As soon as we pack their belongings, we are leaving."

The rani was a full day's journey north of us, preparing to storm the Fortress of Gwalior. I had sworn an oath of loyalty to her and Arjun had done the same. "I don't know what to do," I admitted. "I can't think clearly anymore." I sat on the grass and drew my knees up to my chest. The guards were watching us from the porch. I'm sure they knew what we were talking about: a decision had to be madc. We either needed to ride for Gwalior or commit to remaining in Barwa Sagar for the rest of the war. It would be so simple to just stay put. I tried to listen to the voice inside of me, but there were so many other voices drowning it out. I closed my eyes. "The rani has three Durgavasi and your men, who else can she trust?"

Arjun didn't say anything. He just listened.

"But if I leave, what do I do with Anu? We could come back for her. . . ." I rose. "We're going to Gwalior." It was what my father would have wanted me to do. And what Shivaji had trained me for. "If we don't go, we'll spend the rest of our lives on our knees. I'd rather die on my feet."

He gripped my hand.

The guards began packing as soon as we told them. Anu didn't say anything. "I'll leave you enough money so that you'll always be provided for," I assured her.

"My life is finished."

"You're carrying life," I said. I looked down at her stomach, its gentle curve the same as the vessel we used to bring water from the well. "Nothing is finished unless you want it to be."

I didn't wait for her response. I went to my room and began to pack. But by the next time Balaji appeared, a week had passed, and none of us expected the news he brought this time.

Instead of joining or fleeing, the Maharaja of Gwalior had chosen to make war against the rebels. He planned to capture the rani and make a gift of her to the British, so they would shower him with gifts and his crown would be secure. Yet when his eight thousand soldiers heard the rani's troops shouting, "Har Har Mahadev!" they responded by raising their arms and echoing their cry. They marched peacefully to join the rani. They all sat down to have a meal together on the banks of the Morar River.

We were all incredulous.

Gwalior belonged to the rani. She had taken it peacefully, and it was the heart of India.

Chapter Twenty-Eight

When I said farewell to my sister, I was bidding a stranger good-bye. I understood what I hadn't before: love can be like the seasons, turning a green leaf into something frail and yellow. Anu didn't come out to see us leave, and by dawn, Barwa Sagar was behind us. I'd only return there once more in my life, to collect my sister and bring her to a place where no one knew her story. I had become a Durgavasi not only to save myself from prostitution, but to save Anu from that fate. And although life had nevertheless delivered her into the hands of the British to be used as a common *veshya*, I felt I could still save her. Nothing mattered to me more than this. But first the people who had done this to her had to be driven from India.

We met no resistance on the way to Gwalior. Around noon, we stopped outside a village to roast chapatis over a small brushwood fire. Then we dusted off our clothes and took to the roads again. When the fortress finally reared into view, all twelve of us reined in our horses and stopped. The sun was setting, casting the turreted fortifications in a rich amber light, and nothing had ever looked more magnificent to me, not even the Fortress of Jhansi.

Built on a plateau at least a hundred meters high, the fortress was so beautiful that it was hard to believe we weren't staring at a painting. The tile work was blazing in the setting sun with such magnificence the entire fortress was blue and gold. We rode our horses up to the gates. The guards stumbled outside to inspect us, and it was obvious that all four had been drinking.

"What do we have here?" one of the guards asked.

Arjun introduced us but he was forced to repeat himself several times before they understood that we were there to rejoin the rani.

"The Rebel Queen!" one said at last, and all of them laughed, as if this was funny. "Why didn't you say so?"

"Disgraceful," Arjun muttered under his breath.

They opened the gates, and the guard who appeared the drunkest led us across the gardens toward the entrance. I could hear music and laughter inside, and I exchanged a look with Arjun. "Are they celebrating?"

The man turned, shocked by my voice. "Are you a man or a woman?"

"I'm one of the rani's Durgavasi," I said.

He used one side of his face to smile, as if he was a puppet and his master was too lazy to raise both sides. "*Really?*"

"Yes. She fought with the rani in Jhansi and has come to fight alongside her again," Arjun said.

For a very brief moment the guard sobered. "Well, there's no fighting here. Haven't you heard? They've opened the treasury. We are all rich! There's been a ceremony," he continued. "Saheb has been crowned Peshwa, and Rao Saheb has been made his viceroy."

They held a ceremony declaring Saheb Peshwa when all of

India was falling apart? When General Rose and his army would arrive any day?

The guard began whistling a merry tune, and we fell into line silently behind him.

People were feasting and dancing in the halls, congratulating one another as if they were part of a wedding baraat. It took our guard twenty minutes to find the rani. No one knew where she was. Several people suggested the Durbar Hall on the first floor. When she wasn't there, I was told to go upstairs and look through the women's rooms. I checked each chamber. I even went to the roof terraces. Then someone said the rani was on a fourth-floor balcony.

"The fourth floor is the rajanivesana," the guard said, looking doubtful because the raja's apartments were there.

But I knew the rani. "That's where she is," I said. She'd be with Mandar, Kashi, and Anand.

We trudged the four flights up to the apartments, and we heard her before we saw her, shouting about waste and something else I couldn't make out over the music and singing.

The guard stopped at the door leading to the raja's apartments. "Is this all you need me for?" he said. I imagined he was eager to get back to his drinking.

"That's it." Arjun's voice was clipped.

As soon as she saw us, the rani was overwhelmed with joy. I hugged Mandar and Kashi. Even Anand wanted a warm embrace. Then I saw the Nawab of Banda, sitting cross-legged on the floor. He pressed his hands together in namaste, and we joined him at the rani's invitation. As soon as we were seated she wanted to know everything, what had happened in Barwa Sagar, if we had heard about Jhansi, how we had reached Gwalior without being seen. She was very sorry to hear about my losses. She didn't say anything about her own father, and I certainly didn't ask.

Fireworks began exploding in the warm night air.

"I've warned them that General Rose is coming," she said. "But Rao Saheb wants the celebrations to last two weeks."

"These men ignored the rani's advice in Kalpi," the Nawab of Banda said. "If they haven't learned from her by now, I doubt they ever will."

There was a knock on the door. Kashi answered and a well-dressed man appeared. It was Saheb. A feather sprang jauntily from one side of his bejeweled turban, making him look as if he were about to grow wings, and thick clusters of pearls hung around his neck.

"Look at yourself, Saheb!" said the rani. "Dressed for a baraat when this is a war! Look at your entire court!"

"At least I have one!" He stomped back out without telling us why he'd come, slamming the door behind him.

"He's like a child," the nawab said wonderingly.

The celebrations went on for another nine days.

Then, on the twelfth of June, just before midnight, there was an urgent knock on the rani's door. A messenger was there: General Rose had reached Amin, one day's journey to the south. The rani gave Kashi a blue velvet satchel similar to the one she'd given Arjun. "Tomorrow morning," she said, "I want you to take Anand away from here."

Kashi looked stricken as the rani told her where to go and what to do if they should be discovered. Then she turned to me, and to my surprise, took my hands in hers. They felt cold, despite the summer's heat.

"I'm not leaving you," I said, in case this was going to be her request.

"I know. You're too stubborn and foolish, like the man who wants to marry you. But if something should happen to me on the battlefield, Sita, I don't want you to stay in Gwalior."

"Please don't talk like this," I whispered.

"We all die. Some of us are fortunate enough to die fighting for justice."

"And I can't think of a more just reason than this," Mandar said quietly. "They are taking over India kingdom by kingdom."

Below, word was spreading about the British advance, and with the exception of a few pockets of drunken men, the singing had stopped.

"Sita, promise me you'll flee. With Arjun if he's alive, by yourself if he isn't," the rani said. "I can't prepare for this battle unless I have your promise."

I gave it to her. She exchanged a glance with Mandar; they seemed to have made a quiet pact between them that made me remember Jhalkari, and my heart ached deeply. *I hope you have reached Svarga,* I thought.

On the seventeenth of June, scouts spotted General Rose's army in the distance. We rode out to nearby Kotah-ki-Serai. There were fifty-eight cannons at the rani's disposal; if Tatya Tope took charge of the front line at Kampu, Gul Mohammad took Kotah, and the Nawab of Banda took Katighati . . . the British would have nowhere to go.

I won't describe for you the bloodshed and cruelty I saw that day. I don't wish to remember it, and I don't like to accept that I am capable of the acts I committed. I will only say that nothing in Jhansi prepared me for what I saw in Gwalior. We fought for hours in the brutal heat, and by the time the sun set there were patches of earth so slick with blood that our horses had trouble keeping upright.

At the hottest part of the day the tide began to turn against us. General Rose overcame the gunners in Phoolbagh, seized their cannons, and there was chaos as our own cannons were used against us. Our soldiers attempted to flee, crossing the Sonerekha River and heading for Morar, but there were too many of them and so they became easy targets.

"Don't go by river!" Arjun yelled. But Mandar and the rani were already halfway across.

Even today, I can't accept what happened. Before Mandar's horse could gain the banks, a bullet pierced her chest. I drew my bow, and my arrow found the man who shot her, but Mandar was already face down in the muddy waters of the Sonerekha when I reached her. The rani herself made it to the far side of the water when a British soldier raised his arm to slash her with his sword. And there was a moment—a brief but eternal moment—when anything was possible. I thought of weapons that didn't exist with which I might have saved her. I thought of Lord Hanuman, our winged god, flying in to take her in his arms. I thought of pushing back time, forcing it to reverse, so that she never crossed the river in the first place. The pain of it was—and still is—that his blow struck her neck and cleaved our way of life: one moment the queen of Jhansi was healthy and alive. An instant later she was gone. One second, *one*, is all that separates life from death.

Her hand went immediately to her neck, and before the British soldier could slash at her again, Arjun's arrow pierced his heart.

Even in the chaos of fleeing soldiers we were at her side at once. For a few brief moments, she opened her eyes. Then she slid from her saddle into Arjun's arms. I pointed to a house in the distance, and he lifted her onto his horse. By the time we reached it, her face had gone pale.

"She's bleeding heavily," I said.

We laid her down on the cracked earth, then stripped her of her armor so we could see the wound.

"It's deep," Arjun confirmed.

"Rani!" I wept, but her body was rigid. In the golden light of sunset, she might have been sleeping. "Rani," I kept repeating, "rani!" I laid her head in my lap, but she was already with her father and son.

Epilogue

1919

My hands are trembling now. I put down my diary, and suddenly, it doesn't matter that sixty-one years have passed. I can still taste the dirt of the battlefield in my mouth; hear the screams of the men and horses in my ears. There was a time I used to read these words over and over, as if reliving my trauma could change it somehow. Shri Rama was the one who instructed me to put my diaries away. I was becoming a tree rooted in the soil of tragedy, he said, and with every fresh reading I was watering the roots, sinking deeper, allowing my pain to grow stronger. "Plant your roots in fresh soil," he told me. And so my words were shut away. Until now, when Miss Pennywell and all of her readers will find them.

When the war was finished and the British flag was hoisted over every fortress, Arjun and I were married by Shri Rama, who not only survived the war, but made a new life for himself in the city of Bombay. Since Arjun and I were both rebels, it was impossible to remain near Jhansi. So we moved to the bustling city of Mumbai. It was a city that had been renamed Bombay by the

British, reminding us every day that we had lost; that the kingdom of Jhansi was gone. Now, we were part of an empire. We asked my sister and her son to live with us, but she refused. She held me accountable for the fate she had suffered. She believed that my loyalty had never been to my family, but to a queen who had given me both a marriage and jewels. Still, we offered to buy her a house nearby overlooking the Arabian Sea and arranged for her to live a comfortable life as a widow. This she accepted.

It pained me to think of Anu alone in a strange city. We visited her many times, but she would never open her door. We would watch her son playing in the nearby fields—a light-skinned child with eyes the color of the sea. Did she love him, or did she punish him for what he had cost her? I never knew. Arjun counseled me to wait until the boy was older, and establish a relationship with him then. But during his tenth year, he died. Two years later, my sister was dead, too. In her house, I found the diary I had given her as a child, with all of the memories of my mother inside. It had been wrapped in an old muretha. I held it to my nose and inhaled. It still smelled of Barwa Sagar.

I often felt guilty for the happiness Arjun and I found in Bombay. With the rani's generosity, we bought a house on Malabar Hill, and we had three children—two boys, and a little girl named Raashi. They are all still living in Bombay, married and with numerous children of their own. I don't know why this didn't happen for Anu, why her fate was so different from what I had planned. Shri Rama said something very interesting at my wedding, and Arjun would remind me of it constantly: we can help pave the roads of those around us, but we can't choose their direction. Even trying is against the laws of samsara.

Sill, sometimes I sit on my bed and think of all the faces that have come and gone—the rani, Moti, Jhalkari, Mandar, Sundari, my father, Shivaji. The war stole so many people from us, and still it's not over. Sometimes, when Raashi is taking me on the train, I'll catch a glimpse of a young man struggling against the guards who are trying to remove him from the first-class cabin, where only the British are allowed to sit, and that's how I know the war isn't finished. The goddess Durga is still here, whispering to her children, "I'll only be happy when I am free."

Historical Note

On June 20, 1858, just two days after the rani's death, the "rebels" across India surrendered. Nearly five months later, the British East India Company was abolished, and Queen Victoria was declared the Empress of India. When you consider the life of Rani Lakshmi and the unbelievable lives of the women in her Durga Dal, it's not difficult to see why she's the most famous woman in India's history. There was almost nothing about her life or the lives of her Durgavasi I needed to embellish. If anything, so many legends have sprung up around her that I needed to be careful to separate what was fact from fiction. For instance, her famous jump from the fortress walls while mounted on her horse and carrying her son certainly never happened. But her Durga Dal, her decision to practice with the Durgavasi (unprecedented for a Hindu queen), her presence in the Durbar Hall while her husband took to the stage, and her subsequent role in the rebellion, are all part of the historical record.

After her death, General Hugh Rose returned in triumph to

Gwalior. The Raja of Scindia joined him, and the pair of them entered the city accompanied by fireworks and celebratory parades. Despite his victory, Rose remained so disturbed by the rani's escape that he ordered Bhandir Gate to be sealed. It remained this way for the next seventy-five years. On his return to England, Queen Victoria made Rose Lord Strathnairn of Jhansi. India's annexation was complete. The British population was told its conquest was necessary, and they were fed stories of misrule and human rights abuses.

Most of the rani's Durgavasi were killed in their fight against the British. However, Kashi did escape with Anand, and eventually, the British granted the boy a small pension.

What became of the traitors Gopal and Sadashiv is uncertain, but both men probably met quick ends, like Tatya Tope, who was captured by the British and executed. As for Nana Saheb, who spent days celebrating his own coronation instead of preparing for the advancing British army—it's likely he escaped British detection by living with one of his wives in Nepal. Unlike Azimullah Khan, who died of an unknown illness before the British could capture him, he probably led a long life.

Some of the more surprising elements of the book really did occur. Shakespeare was extremely popular among Indians learning English. And the play, *Śakuntalā*, which once impressed the raja, eventually served as an inspiration for Goethe's *Faust*. However, even though I tried my best to remain faithful to history, a few dates were altered. Azimullah Khan's arrival in England happened in 1853 and not 1855 as it does in this book. And the despicable Circular Memorandum was actually created in 1886. An Englishman who was in India to observe the British had the following to say about what came to be known as the Infamous Memorandum:

> The orders specified were faithfully carried out, under the supervision of commanding officers, and were to this effect . . . The regimental Kutwal was [an under-official, native] to take two policemen (without uniform), and go into the villages and take from the homes of these poor people their daughters from fourteen years and upwards, about twelve or fifteen girls at a time. They were to select the best looking. Next morning, these were all put in front of the Colonel and Quartermaster. The former made his selection of the number required. They were then presented with a pass or license, and then made over to the old woman in charge of this house of vice under the Government. The women already there, who were examined by the doctor, and found diseased, had their passes taken away from them, and were then removed by the police out of the Cantonment, and these fresh, innocent girls put in their places.

As Josephine Butler wrote in *The Revival and Extension of the Abolitionist Cause* in 1887, "What can a poor Army slave-woman do when thus turned out? Her caste is broken, because she has lived with foreigners, and her friends will seldom receive her back; she has been compelled to follow the soldiers on the march; and when dismissed may be hundreds of miles away from any human being who ever saw her face before." The likely end for these women was ignominious death.

Further changes were made in instances where the history was unclear, and I had to make my best guess as to what the truth might be. It is unknown, for example, whether Rao Saheb (sometimes spelled Sahib) was Saheb's brother or his nephew. Similarly, the birth of Rani Lakshmi is contested, with her memorial plaque in Gwalior reading November 19, 1835, yet biographers often claiming a date of either 1827 or 1828. These earlier dates seem most probable, and November 19, 1828, is ultimately what I went with.

The life of Rani Lakshmi was extraordinary in the truest sense of the word. In Jhansi, women enjoyed an unprecedented amount of freedom, and it was in this environment that the queen flourished. On a memorial in front of Phoolbagh palace, she is remembered as:

> The nurturer of the city of Jhansi who dressed like a man, who could ride the tallest of horses, who held a raised sword in her hand, who was thrilled by the frenzy of war like the Goddess Kali, who many times challenged the English generals such a Hugh Rose in battle—that Lakshmi (the goddess of fortune), was killed here as if by an unfortunate turn of destiny and went [back] to heaven!

On August 15, 1947, eighty-nine years after Rani Lakshmi's death, India achieved its independence.

Glossary

angarkha: a long dress that reaches either the knees or the ankles and is worn with pants

bagh: garden

Bhagavad Gita: the sixth book of the *Mahabharata* in which the god Krishna speaks to his disciple Arjuna. The principle ideas in the *Bhagavad Gita* are mishkama karma (working without seeking any reward) and bhakti (devotion to god)

bhand: clown

Brahma: creator god

Brahmin: the priestly caste, considered the highest caste by Hindus

charpai: a wooden bed with a mattress made of rope

choti: a covering, usually made of gold, for a woman's braid

Dadi: grandmother

dhoti: a long cloth worn by a man from waist to foot

Didi: elder sister, often used to address girls who are elder, even if there is no relationship

dupatta: a cloth worn around the neck, similar to a scarf. It can also be used to cover the hair.

durbar: meeting

Durbar Hall: a meeting hall

Durga: the Mother Goddess

Durga Dal: an elite group of female guards trained to protect the rani

Durga Puja: an important Hindu festival celebrating the Mother Goddess

Durgavasi: a member of the Durga Dal

ganwaar: a person who is considered uncouth and possibly illiterate because they come from a village

guru: a religious teacher and spiritual guide

Har Har Mahadev: Mightiest of Mighties

Holi: an ancient Hindu spring festival called the Festival of Colors

ji: a term of respect

Krishna: the eighth avatar of Vishnu

Kshatriya: the second-highest Hindu caste. Traditionally, members of this caste were involved in the military or some aspect of governing.

Mahabharata: one of two great Sanskrit epics. It is supposed to have been written by the wise man Vyasa and tells the story of the contest between the Pandavas and the Kurus.

mahal: palace

maharaja: great king

maidan: a large open field

mandir: a temple

Mughals: Muslim rulers of India from the sixteenth to eighteenth centuries

namaste: a form of greeting made with the palms pressed together, fingers pointed upward

nawab: a provincial governor of the Mughal Empire. Also used in reference to a man of great wealth

Pita-ji: father

puja: a prayer

purdah: the seclusion of women from public viewing

raja: ruler

rajkumar: son of a king

Rama: the god and hero of the Sanskrit epic the *Ramayana*

Ramayana: one of two great Sanskrit epics. It tells the story of the god Rama, his wife Sita, and his brother Lakshmana.

rani: queen

rupee: unit of currency used throughout India and its former kingdoms

sari: a garment of Hindu women that consists of yards of cloth draped so that one end forms a skirt and the other covers the top of the body

shaadi: marriage

Shiva: the god who destroys so that progress may ensue

Shri: a polite word used to address an elder male

swastik(a): a very ancient and sacred Hindu symbol with four arms bent at ninety degrees, symbolizing auspiciousness and well-being. Later, it was rotated to the right and used to symbolize the Nazi party.

tikka: a decoration worn between the parting in a woman's hair and ending between her brows

veshya: prostitute

Vishnu: the preserver god whose ten avatars include both Rama and Krishna

Acknowledgments

This book could never have been written without the help and support of my amazing husband, Amit Kushwaha. Without him, I doubt I would ever have stumbled across the life story of Rani Lakshmibai. I also owe a debt of gratitude to Heather Lazare, who originally acquired this book for Touchstone, and to my wonderful agent, Dan Lazar, who made it all happen. To the editor who worked with me on this novel, Sally Kim, you are absolutely amazing. What a lucky day when I landed with you. To the Kushwaha family who guided me throughout India and took me not only to Jhansi, but to Gwalior and other places where the rani both lived and fought, I am incredibly grateful. And to my fantastic team at Touchstone, including Cherlynne Li, Jane Liddle, Melissa Vipperman-Cohen, Susan Moldow, David Falk, Laura Flavin, Brian Belfiglio, Maria Whelan, Carla Benton, and Etinosa Agbonlahor, I owe you all a tremendous thanks. To my family and friends who have always supported my writing career: the Morans, the Kushwahas, the Ballingers, the Porters, the Carpenters, the Indigs, and the Avildsens. And to Chantelle Doss, who helped with the research of this book. Lastly, a very heartfelt thanks goes out to Allison McCabe, who edited the first version of this work and whose sharp mind and even sharper sense of humor is always refreshing.

Also by Michelle Moran

Nefertiti

When the Crown Prince of Egypt needs a wife,
the beautiful, ambitious and connected Nefertiti
is the royal court's first choice.

Before long, Nefertiti is as powerful as the Pharaoh
himself. But when her husband breaks with a thousand years
of tradition, it will take all Nefertiti's wiles to keep
the nation from being torn apart.

Quercus

ALSO BY MICHELLE MORAN

The Heretic Queen

When Nefertari's entire family is killed in a fire, she's left to grow up alone, a spare princess in the palace of the new Pharaoh. Her life is overshadowed by the past – the name of her infamous aunt, Nefertiti, still strikes terror into the hearts of all Egyptians.

When she finds herself falling in love with the young Pharaoh Ramesses she knows it's not going to be easy. Could Egypt's rulers – and more importantly her people – ever allow the niece of a heretic to rule as Queen?

Quercus

Also by Michelle Moran

Cleopatra's Daughter

Selene's parents are gone and she has been brought to Rome in chains, with only her brother Alexander to remind her of all she once had in Egypt. Invited to live among the ruling family, the siblings are taught how to be Roman.

But all is not well in the city and before long the Roman army is called to war. Selene and Alexander – the children of Rome's greatest rival – find their lives in grave danger.

Quercus